TIME-RYDER:
POWERSTONE
Book one

DON GALLOWAY

First Published in 2014
Second Edition

Copyright © Don Galloway 2014
The moral right of the author has been asserted

ISBN 978-1-291-83794-0

Cover by Don Galloway, copyright © Perragrim 2019

No part of this publication may be produced, stored in a retrieval system, or transmitted, in any form or by any means, without prior permission in writing of the publisher, nor be otherwise circulated in any form of binding or the cover other than that in which it is published and without a similar condition including this condition being imposed on the subsequent purchaser.

All characters and events in this publication, other than those clearly in the public domain, are fictitious and any resemblance to real persons, living or dead, is purely coincidental

"For Mum"
My guide, my encouragement
and the best friend I could
ever ask for.
And to all those who
shaped my life
and imagination
in ways that you will never know.

Time-Ryder: Powerstone Book One

THE FALL OF BALERAN

The sound of musket-fire erupted across the spanning fields and wastelands surrounding Baleran castle. Standing in the shelter of craggy peaked Eran Mountain, Baleran castle was the ancestral home of the Clan MacEran, all of whom lived in a small community on the edge of a vast estate.

The Castle had withstood the rigours of all its years, yet it remained a constant beacon of hope and security to all who lived in its shadow.

Built in the fifteenth century and surrounding the family tomb; it was a strategic part of the rebellion, a place where the heads of all clans could come together and a vital placement for any arms, should another uprising occur. Three hundred years had passed since the construction of the castle and with the country in turmoil; the Jacobites were being persecuted for their attempts to restore the true monarch to the throne. The loyal subjects were scattered all over Scotland, keeping their identities to the cause secret until the time was right to reveal them.

It was 1716 and had been less than six months since the last attempt, and those loyal to the Stuarts always held up hope that the pretender would take his rightful place, yet there were always those waiting in the wings to unmask them and bring them to their knees.

Battle was raging in the dead of night and it was somewhat one-sided. The watchmen all along the castle ramparts were being picked off so easily by the English Redcoats amassing around the heavily fortified structure that they barely had time to defend themselves or return fire.

Leaping over a shattered section of the outer wall, three figures in full-kilted battle regalia slashed through the sea of red troops and made their way into the outer courtyard until a stray shot brought down one of them.

The ragged clothed Scot bringing up the rear dropped where he stood and the others hesitated, looking back upon his fallen form before the taller of the two pulled the smaller one on, quickly avoiding more oncoming musket-fire.

Rushing through the smoke and the roaring sounds of cannonballs exploding, the two remaining highlanders fled from the darkness outside and stormed inside the inner courtyard, bracing themselves against the immense oak doors that dominated the entrance.

They were being pursued by a few errant Redcoats that had tracked them from the scenes of desecration at the village to the tall cathedral like building before them.

The impact of the field cannons on the exterior walls tore apart the beautifully crafted stonemason work, destroying the ramparts and fine ornamentation of the main castle walls, but the wise architects of Baleran Castle had prophesised such events and had taken steps in preparation for such atrocities.

The erection of a secondary courtyard wall twenty feet from the exterior wall served as a shield, giving those inside breathing space to prepare for the assault on the inner courtyard wall, but that too would only be a matter of time before it was breached. The cease-fire of cannonballs overhead showed them that the arrogance of the assailing English hoards had assumed that it was all over, even though they still implemented an unconventional variation of weapons in order to ensure that they took the Castle completely. They were focussed on taking the Castle, whatever the cost, even if it meant that their losses would equal that of the Scots.

Gasping for breath, both men braced themselves against the door before pulling a heavy wooden beam down from the solid oak frame. Extending the full length of the barrier over the door, they relaxed against it, despite the few pursuers constantly ramming it from the other side.

They tried their hardest to break down the doors before the impending arrival of the remainder of the garrison outside the main walls broke in and stole all of their glory.

James, the elder brother of the two highlanders was taller and broad shouldered, a typical rough and brutish man.

He held himself with confidence; whereas his younger sibling Alexander's shoulders slumped, and he fumbled forward like a nervous child. The fresh-faced young man looked up to his brother, ruffling his mop of dirty brown hair as James forked his nose into the air.

Already the signs of disaster were coming their way.

He could smell the smoke from the village wafting closer as they made their way across the stone flagged courtyard and into the main entrance hall.

Their faces were filthy, blackened by the smoke that was clouding outside the castle walls, yet Alexander's tears made streaks upon his face as if he had coated it with war paint.

"Ewan's dead!" he sniffed.

James patted his brother's arm.

"I know, but don't say a word of it to father, it'll only make him worse. Understand?"

The younger man nodded as he sniffed and wiped his nose.

James poked his head out of the arch in the hallway, hearing the desecration and thunderous sounds of cannon-fire beginning to soar overhead again as the English were determined to obliterate the walls. The sky flickered with a fiery red tinge and he saw it was coming from the crofts that were ablaze in the distance.

He looked on with disappointment, his eyes almost welling up with the thought that the imposing redcoats had slaughtered his brother and his friends, but he stood back, held out a hand and

Time-Ryder: Powerstone Book One

restrained Alexander from entry for a moment as he stopped to regain his composure.

"What are ye waiting for James? We have to tell father, it willnae take them long tae break down the main doors" said the fresh-faced young man.

His impatience showed clearly, yet his brother still refused him entry to the main hall.

"I dinnae think the sound of cannons will have escaped him!" he said, his rough voice burning from the extent of the smoke outside.

His words were lost on the impatient young man; who forced his way through the wood panelled corridor and into the main hall which was the centre of the house of MacEran.

The room was practically empty, decrepit and cobwebbed, save for an elongated ancient table that dominated the centre of the room, high backed chairs enclosed all around it.

The only occupant sat at the head of the table, a wrinkled hand stretched out ahead of him, clasping hold of a large claymore that rested on the table and the other reaching down to his side where an old shaggy haired Irish Wolfhound curled at his feet, lifting its head at the arrival of the young men and ignoring them just as quickly.

He lifted his wizened, bearded old face to the two young men and waited, but Ranald was tired of waiting.

He knew that whatever was happening outside the Castle was the culmination of centuries of waiting.

"They've burned the crofts and slaughtered the livestock Father," stuttered Alexander,

"Everyone is dead and the English are preparing to break into the courtyard!"

"I did hear the sounds of battle Alexander," said the old man in a raspy tone, "did it not occur to you to check the crypt?"

His abruptness was apparent, as was his fear.

Time-Ryder: Powerstone Book One

Ranald was just as frightened of the events about to unfold as his two sons were and even though he tried to conceal it, James could see that his father was worried.

"Need I not remind you of the prophecy?" barked the old man again.

"No father," they both replied in unison.

"Then remind me!" he growled, his deep voice full of conviction. James wanted to roll his eyes, but the sign of disrespect would enrage his father even more, even though he knew the old man was treating them both like children.

They'd been told the prophecy since they were boys and could recite it as fluidly as the Lord's Prayer; even though they thought it was just another old wives tale or another of Maggie's stories passed down through the ages.

Although they knew of the existence of the crypt and what it contained, neither one of them had actually seen it and it excited and frightened them that after all these years that they would finally find out what was the source of doom and foreboding that had gripped their family for centuries.

The inner courtyard served as protection to the watchtower and the concealed crypt that dwelled beneath it or more importantly what was contained within the crypt.

Ranald cleared his voice in a throaty cough and waited, his stare showing his impatience.

"No man shall touch the sphere," Alexander started off with James joining with a mumbled excuse of a recital.

"For its power shall be awakened and the beast will arise to ravage the world!"

James capped his mouth and leaned over sideways to his brother. "I wonder what they were drinking when they prophesised that?" he whispered softly. Normally Alexander would have laughed, but his thoughts were sidetracked, a constant reminder that their brother Ewan was dead.

Time-Ryder: Powerstone Book One

Ranald resigned himself with the smallest of smiles that his boys remembered their lessons, regardless if they took them seriously or not.

"Our family has protected the Sphere of Ancients for over three hundred years, I will not see the prophecy come true during my lifetime!" hissed the old man and he noted the absence of his eldest son, "Where's Ewan?"

Ranald was cut short as a lull in the sound of battle ensued, to which a voice carried forth, issuing a statement, clearly intended for the Laird himself.

"This is a message for Laird Ranald of Baleran Castle from my Lord Somersby" said a soft, yet clear and loud voice.

"This Castle and surrounding lands are now the property of Lord Somersby for substantial debts incurred to the Marquis of Ravayne. My Lord does not wish bloodshed, but he may be forced if passage into this property is not permitted. You have to the count of five to surrender all entrances and allow passage or those remaining will be interred to the tollbooth, by order of Lord Somersby."

The statement finished and both young highlanders looked to Ranald for an explanation.

"Father?" Alexander asked and his face flushed.

"That fool Ravayne!" spat the old man, "I took a measly sum from him to see us over the last season when our crops failed, he took security of the Castle if I failed to pay on time. Now it seems he has sold the debt to this Somersby."

Ranald's face was even more grimacing than usual, his dislike of Somersby was clear, yet he had only met the man once.

"If he was so concerned with shedding no blood, why didn't he send a messenger before he opened fire on the Castle walls?" growled the old man, "I've never hated anyone so much in my life"

James agreed.

Time-Ryder: Powerstone Book One

"There are a few stories about him father, but it's clear where his loyalties lie!"
"He has no loyalties, except to his own agenda. And all this because he suspects me of being a Jacobite!" snarled Ranald.
He restrained the dog at his side, becoming restless at the sound of his master's irate voice. Ranald ruffled its head and the beast sunk back to the stone floor unconcerned.
"But you are a Jacobite Father" Alexander stuttered nervously.
"I know that boy, but there can be no other reason for Somersby to want the Castle, there's nothing of value left here. All the tapestries are gone; all I have are the bare remnants of clothing on my back."
James stood forward, leaning on the edge of the table to which the dog started to growl again, and Ranald swayed the dog's anger, putting a reassuring hand down to pat the creature's head.
"Ewan has put men on the battlements, but they won't hold against all of their forces for long" lied Alexander.
"Their forces have the Castle surrounded father, there's just too many of them" resigned James.
He'd been dreading the thought of telling his father as the old man was frail and any shock might finish him off, which was one of the reasons he didn't want Alexander to declare Ewan's fate, but Ranald was made of sterner stuff, he'd fought many battles before and this was no different.
"What are we going tae dae father?" hissed Alexander, equally as worried as his father.
"Go to the crypt and check the Sphere. Deal with anyone who tries to enter" he paused as the young man broke off quickly to the door behind him.
"I'll send a messenger to Ravayne. Maybe we can stop all of this before it goes too far," said the old man worriedly.
He looked to the two young men preparing to leave and levelled his gaze at James.

Time-Ryder: Powerstone Book One

"You must protect the Sphere with your life's blood," he said in a gruff response.

"What about you?" James looked worried, a look that frightened Alexander even more so. Usually nothing seemed to bother his brother, yet this seemed to chill him to the bone.

Ranald grasped his hand around the claymore handle.

"I can handle this Somersby if need be. Now go."

With a look to his father as though it may be his last, Alexander fumbled towards the door as the old man rose from his perch, grasping his sword tightly. A tear welled in the corner of Alexander's eye, but he dare not let James see, he needed to be strong, especially since the loss of Ewan.

Turning his back upon Ranald, Alexander shot through the door as James received a nod of approval from his father and returned the look with a gentle smile.

He followed his brother through the door and knew that was the last he'd see of his father. Any messenger would take too long to get to the Marquis, but James knew it had been said for Alexander's benefit. Ranald had held his stance for long enough. Showing the pretence of strength in front of his sons was taking its toll and he sank quickly into the chair once again, exhausted. The dog brought its front paws up on top of the old man, sensing his distress.

He ruffled the dog's head and exhaled deeply.

"It's all right boy. It'll all be over soon!" he drawled and winced in pain again as he knew deep down that it was all coming to an end for him.

High up on the hillside, overlooking the scene of battle, a tall thin and gaunt looking man sat on horseback, looking down his long beak as the cannons started up again and began to bring the front facing of the main Castle wall to the ground.

Time-Ryder: Powerstone Book One

Shot after shot volleyed off the ramparts, killing all in the vicinity, those who fell prey to the cannons, crashing to the ground in a cacophony of tormented screams, their twisted corpses victim to the battle-hungry soldiers who were eager for blood.

He pulled back on the reins on his dark steed and cantered down slowly, joining one of the rifle-wielding Redcoats, still distancing his presence from the area of battle.

He masked his great nose from the smell of death with a frilly handkerchief that matched the cuffs of his flamboyant shirt.

"What news is there?" he said in a haughty tone and pulled his white wig down slightly over his shoulders.

"They have very few men left my Lord. Once we breach the main walls we shall have access to the inner courtyard and then the main hall. That would be the safest place for anything valuable and the hardest place to get into," replied the redcoat, bringing his horse closer to his master.

The wiry man spoke, his deep voice gruff; yet quiet in all but a hiss.

"Then take the Castle by storm. I want this place torn from existence," he said with a sneer, "Have you implemented the specifications that I requested?"

"Yes my Lord, I have engaged a group of archers, highly skilled for such a task!" he replied, although thought it strange that Somersby would ask for such an unorthodox and outdated weapon to be used.

"Prepare them with flame arrows; let them burn this place to the ground. By the time we are finished, no one will remember the name MacEran!"

The redcoat bowed graciously and pulled the reins tighter.

"Understood my Lord!"

Time-Ryder: Powerstone Book One

He moved off silently and prepared to return to the battle, ready to issue his new orders when Somersby beckoned him back again.

"Yes my Lord?"

The tall man leaned forward on his horse, his face rigid with contempt.

"Don't harm the old man, I want him alive!"

Somersby pulled back on the reins again and cantered off, returning his horse to his original viewpoint, overlooking the Baleran Castle again as the redcoat sauntered off to rejoin the troops.

The gaunt Somersby looked down his nose at the Castle.

"I've waited three hundred years, No filthy savage will stand in the way of my prize," he hissed arrogantly.

And the barrage continued; cannons ripping apart the main entrance to the courtyard to the jubilant cheers of the successful Redcoats. They took advantage of the shattered aperture in the main wall and thundered in, swords aloft.

Somersby grinned, patting the mane of the horse as he watched closely.

Edging out of the main hall of the Castle and back into the inner ring of the courtyard, James and Alexander made their way towards the crypt, slipping through one of the many gates that led from the main hall to the inner courtyard.

The crypt was an unusual structure in the centre, a set of stone steps leading underground, but more unusual was the circular building that loomed over it, almost like a watchtower.

It was centuries old, predating the main hall itself and was part of the building beneath it, holding the long dead kin of the MacEran clan, all at some point having watched over the crypt just as the two young men were charged with doing so now.

Time-Ryder: Powerstone Book One

It was almost as if the Castle and surrounding buildings had been built around the crypt, purposely preparing and anticipating the events of what had once been prophesised centuries ago.
As they moved past the large windows, Alexander took a glance into the main hall; where he could see his father raising his sword, prepared for anyone who entered.
He could see the main door smashing open and a group of redcoats taking the room by storm and freeing the old man of his weapon.
"Father!" cried out Alexander in panic as James pulled him down into hiding.
But his cries had alarmed the searching band of redcoats that breached the inner courtyard and they began to move towards their position.
"Do you want us both tae get killed?" snarled James, keeping his attention focussed.
"You cannae help him now, it'll only gie us away!"
"But he's…" began Alexander, but James cut him off abruptly.
"Father knew what he was doing and he knew the dangers if they get to the sphere"
Alexander wiped back his tears and sniffed as his brother beckoned him to the steps, leading to the darkened door.
They hid behind a hay-cart, moving around it silently as the Redcoats passed them by and disappeared to the rear wall of the courtyard, continuing their search.
Flaming arrows soared overhead, reaching their target of the roof of the main hall, which quickly caught fire; spreading to the annexes and turning the darkened night sky alight with the dancing blaze.
A stray arrow landed close to their position and ignited the hay-cart to which James dragged Alexander down the passage leading to the crypt.

Time-Ryder: Powerstone Book One

The passageway was dark, dank and foreboding. Blackened creepers split through the cracks in the wall, spreading upward and covering the stairs and the walls leading downward. The creepers were withered and twisted, yet each one offering protection with jagged barbs on every stem.

Alexander stopped carefully watching his step as he descended and joined James at the door.

James fumbled with a large circlet of keys and shoved the largest, rustiest one into the keyhole, turning it promptly and screwing his eyes up as the door gave the strained creak of the stress on its hinges.

The smell of damp overwhelmed him and he took a step backward to compose himself before he entered the small chamber.

Alexander followed closely at his heels, yet paused in the doorway, terrified to enter as the look upon his face clearly showed.

"What are ye waiting for?" hissed James.

"This place is cursed James, can ye no feel it? It reeks of evil!"

"You've been listening tae old Maggie's ghost stories for too long" spat James, "that's all they are, stories, meant to make you afraid of this place and keep you away."

He turned back to the door and prepared to enter, a grin spreading over his face as his brother continued to object.

"Aye, well it's working. I'm no coming in James; this is a place of death…" Alexander's self-declaration of fear was cut off as he gargled and was silenced from behind, the slender length of a long silver blade protruded from his gut, tainted in blood.

"You're right about that!" rasped an imposing Redcoat behind him, pulling free his blade and letting the young man slip to the ground.

He snarled and made an advance towards James, but the Highlander was too fast for him and wheeled quickly, pulling a pistol from his belt and flooring the Englishman with one clear shot. James took a forlorn glance to his dead brother for a moment and turned back to the door.

He had to hide. The shot would bring more redcoats to his position and his main objective was to protect the sphere.

Easing the door open slowly and trying to calm the creak of its hinges, he cringed as the damp smell hit him almost immediately and he recoiled, stepping backward from the waft again.

It took him a moment until he stepped into the chamber, looking at the smooth walls until he saw the flickering flames of burning lanterns that rested high up on the walls on either side of the door. The hanging lanterns made him realise that the crypt had been maintained and very recently, although the candles inside were almost down to their lowest.

He was grateful for the illumination, for he wouldn't have been able to protect the sphere if he couldn't find it, let alone see it. James looked around the chamber, spying the indented slots carved into the walls with stone caskets of the dead neatly resting in each nook.

The faint beginnings of the spreading creepers outside the door emerged through a crack in the wall, reaching out to the caskets, but he could see some effort had been made to keep the vegetation back from them.

The sound of cannon-fire continued overhead and the crypt shook as he craned his head to the ceiling and saw the faint trails of dust release from above and shimmer down like stars in the night sky.

He blinked, realising that he was becoming too mesmerized with what the crypt contained rather than his task at hand. Now that Ewan and Alexander were both dead, it was up to him to protect the Sphere or at least stopping others from getting to it. His eyes scanned the dank room in search, slowly moving to a raised stone sarcophagus that strangely seemed to dominate the centre of the crypt.

Crossing to the central sarcophagus, he stepped over an upturned coffin that had been tipped out in the blast from above. The skeletal remains of one of his dead ancestors lay upon the floor, the smell even more apparent to him, yet he disregarded it in his search for the sphere.

James lifted his eyes up to the sarcophagus again, or more importantly the crest that what was resting on the surface.

The stone tablet was intricately carved with images of fire and abomination, but James took no heed of what could be interpreted as a warning and he gritted his teeth.

The sound of a swishing blade behind James alerted him and he ducked, the sword in the intruding Englishman's hand narrowly missing his head by inches and striking the stone tablet with a clang.

The sound of his pistol despatching the Redcoat that had killed Alexander had clearly alerted another errant Englishman that was eager to claim the life of that last of the Laird's sons, but James wasn't going to let him accomplish it so easy.

The Redcoat advanced and James circled around the small confines, avoiding the path of the blade, but the Englishman moved so fast that he didn't have time to draw his own sword. James wheeled around as the blade tore past him again and he brought his fist up into his opponent's gut.

The Redcoat backhanded him and threw him to the floor as he readied to bring the sword down with both hands. James rushed him and forced him back against the sarcophagus, hearing the scrape of the stone lid moving and he forced the Englishman over the top. The lid was open barely, yet a sliver of light bled from the interior, bright, yet pulsing as if it were alive.

Flailing on the stone floor, the Englishman struggled to get up.

Time-Ryder: Powerstone Book One

Snarling, as he curled his hand around the sword. He slashed out at James, stopping him from unsheathing his sword yet again. James' arm wept, the blood spilling out and he placed his hand over the gash as the Englishman laughed and advanced upon him.

He saw no other option left to him and seized one of the flaming lanterns from its fixing by the door, swinging it around like a mace and smashing into the Redcoat's skull with severity.

The lantern shattered, flame dripping from the glow inside and setting alight to the Englishman's pristine tunic.

He screamed in torment as his whole frame lit up rapidly and he thrashed around in the small enclosure.

James took the opportunity and unsheathed his sword, disposing of the Redcoat, before his unearthly wails attracted any more unwanted attention.

The Englishman dropped to the ground and James quickly put out the fire with his plaid, patting the flame frantically.

He sank to the floor with an exasperated wheeze and then recalled the sound that their scuffle had made upon the sarcophagus lid.

James could see the faint glimmer of light enticing him closer and he quickly fumbled over to the stone tablet. He strained to force open the casket and the stone tablet fell aside with a deafening crash. James swept aside the uprising dust and looked inside, unprepared for what he was about to see.

He blinked at the pulsing beam of light, confused at what he was looking upon.

Instead of the withered bones of some battle-torn ancestor, the sarcophagus revealed a set of stone steps that led down into an even mustier chamber further below ground.

Snatching the remaining lantern from its fixings, James crept closer to the raised stone coffin and threw his legs over the edge.

Time-Ryder: Powerstone Book One

The flame flickered as he widened his eyes, not knowing what to expect in the bowels below.

He started his descent into the crypt, his fingers touching the slimy water soaked walls of the damp passage and cringing as he wiped them on his equally dirty shirt.

He'd never seen the sphere or known of the passage beneath the crypt, but his eyes were about to be amazed by the sight in front of him.

Stepping into the vast chamber, his eyes were alerted immediately to the centre of the room. Although the glare had enticed him downward, it had dimmed ever so slightly and the room seemed gloomy and just as foreboding as the upper crypt had been when he'd first entered.

A small raised wooden plinth sat in the centre of the room, housing a box with the same markings and inscriptions that had adorned the sarcophagus tablet.

Although the box was closed, the light shone through the slit, spreading out and encapsulating his vision.

James crept closer, prising open the lid with his sword and stepping back from the glare that he was clearly unprepared for. The blast almost blinded him and he squeezed his eyes tight into a slit-like gaze as he looked on, adjusting his vision as he opened his eyes slowly.

Inside the box was a gleaming ball, perfect in its construction. Even James knew that someone as skilled as the village blacksmith was at turning metal could not have fashioned an object as perfect as this.

First impressions were very deceiving. At first glance the ball looked metal, but the closer he got and became more aware of its construction, James realised that it was a perfect glass sphere, so beautiful, yet it's reflection showed the rigors of battle.

James saw his own face in the reflection, blackened, dirty and weathered, his hair matted and his beard ragged.

His clothes torn and battered and if situations were different, he would have been derided by his father for being dressed in such appalling attire.

His appearance meant nothing to him after the losses in the past few hours.

Friends had perished; his brothers and his father dead or so he assumed, or he wouldn't be far from death by the time the English forces were finished with him.

Shaking aside the despair, James looked at the hand-sized ball resting within the box. Bathed in crimson fabric, the white glare of the sphere began to turn colour, sensing his approach until it was a dim red glow, replacing the piercing white light.

James was intrigued and came closer as it ensnared his vision and the red glow started to bleed from within the sphere.

He could see that the colour was not a reflection from the fabric that lined the case, but was coming from inside the actual sphere itself.

Something seemed to shine from within, yet it began to grow so bright that it soon engulfed his vision and almost blinded him again. The tall highlander immediately lost all thought of his family or the chance that another Redcoat might have heard the screams from the burning Englishman; instead all of his attention seemed to be hypnotically linked to this shining ball that attracted him so.

Despite all of the warnings and old wives tales that swayed and swam in his mind, James lifted the sphere from the box, holding it in his hands as a smile gleamed across his bearded face.

He felt a sense of warmth and contentment as he held the shining orb and it continued to glow brighter, now turning a full blood red as his touch solidified the colour change.

The red eddy spanned out, spreading throughout the small chamber and upward to the crypt.

Time-Ryder: Powerstone Book One

The fiery glow continued to expand, splitting through the cracks in the exterior door, the gaps in the stonework and any uncovered orifice that lay in its path.

As the glow bled through the cracks and crept up to the sky, it aroused the curiosity of yet another Redcoat, quietly ambling around the side of the courtyard to where the flames of the burning hay-cart were dwindling.

Almost stumbling down the steps, he saw the twisted form of one of his fellow Redcoats and the slain Alexander and he drew his sword in caution, preparing to enter the door before him.

The door to the crypt was ajar, the bright red light filtering through, calling to him with its hypnotic pulsating rhythm.

He couldn't ignore it, especially if one of the other soldiers had perished and he could see that the dead soldier had fallen victim to a pistol shot, squarely in the heart by a crack shot.

With a sharp intake of breath and a look of determination, the Redcoat held his sword aloft and descended the few steps to the crypt door below.

The noise of battle carried on as he looked on cautiously, following the constant flickering light that led him to the door.

The ground shook again, shaking the castle and causing pieces of masonry to fall from the overlooking tower to which the Redcoat worriedly looked aloft.

Stripped of all his weapons, a bloodied and bruised Ranald was forced back into his chair by two brutish Redcoats, overly large for their seemingly small fitting uniforms.

Streams of blood poured from his mouth; his white beard matted, his forehead badly cut, yet he held all of his conviction and stubbornness with his angry gaze.

Time-Ryder: Powerstone Book One

The flanking redcoats at the main door parted and the flamboyant figure of Lord Somersby strode arrogantly into the room, leaning on his long black cane.

"I must say Ranald, I'm rather disappointed by your lack of vigour. I thought an old fool such as you would know when to surrender!" he said with a smile and dropped into the chair opposite the old man, banging his large black cane on the stone floor.

"I save the cowardice for fools such as you" the old man sneered, wiping blood from his straggly white beard. His hand restrained the dog; that snarled and fought at his side, staring down the redcoats ahead.

"You'd save my men a lot of time if you just tell us where the sphere is" smiled Somersby, "I might even let you live!"

Ranald gritted his teeth and leaned forward.

"Do you know what will happen if it falls into the wrong hands, or any hands?"

He could see that Somersby wasn't frightened, but was instead amused.

"Its touch will release a demon that will ravage the world!" Somersby sneered.

"Spare me your backward prophecies!"

The two guards either side of the door exchanged strange looks at Somersby's words, but turned their attention back to the table as the shaggy dog growled again.

"I've had enough of your little Roark's drift prequel Ranald. If you don't tell me what I need to know, by the time we're finished your clan will be nothing more than a memory, a very distant memory"

"History will decide what is remembered. You can't threaten me Somersby. I'm dead whatever happens here, even I know that!"

Somersby smiled.

"We'll just have to speed things up then, shan't we?"

Time-Ryder: Powerstone Book One

He nodded to one of the redcoats and he motioned forward with his sword drawn.

But Ranald anticipated the move and he let go of the dog as he outstretched his right hand to the handle of the claymore laid out before him.

The dog leapt onto the table and took Somersby by surprise, lunging for his throat and drawing blood with the snap of its mighty jaws.

The Redcoat behind Somersby, full of rage motioned forward upon the ravenous dog with his sword and it fell with a whimpered squeal. The Laird's mouth gaped as the limp frame of the beast toppled beside him and gave a last wheeze before falling silent at his feet.

Somersby fell back into the chair, his hand reaching upward to stem the blood, yet he seemed unconcerned by the extent of the wound.

"You know Red is just not my colour!" he said, clearly amused; yet his fawn waistcoat was steeped in the crimson stain.

"Last chance MacEran!" hissed Somersby.

Ranald held his ground and rested back in the chair, resigned to his fate, yet his face was flooded with conviction.

"Do you think that we weren't ready for this day?" he said gruffly, his face grinning wildly.

"We've had three hundred years to prepare and my boys will not let me down!"

Somersby snapped his fingers.

"Search the courtyard for the brothers!"

Ranald laughed.

"They'll be long gone by now!" he bluffed, "You'll never find it!"

And with the statement of contentment, he relaxed back in his chair exhausted. Rising from the chair and making for the exit, Somersby signalled to the two Redcoats flanking the door and they moved in on Ranald.

Somersby grinned wildly as the drawn out screams of the old man in his fight for life were cut short and he slumped down on the oak table, the blood oozing from his throat.
The first redcoat saw the extent of the gash on Somersby's neck.
"Do you need help with that my Lord?"
Somersby dabbed at the wound again and drew away his frilly handkerchief, revealing no sign of the dog's bite.
The redcoat looked on curiously and then lowered his eyes to the ground as Somersby turned on heel.
"I'm a fast healer!" he hissed and made for the exit again, "tell your men to sweep the grounds, they won't get far"
Revolving to see the old man's body, Somersby turned up his nose at the use of violence.
"And burn this place to the ground, leave no trace of him"
Somersby banged his cane on the floor twice and disappeared into the dark hallway.
The two Redcoats looked at each other again, yet said nothing and they proceeded to drop the wall hanging lanterns to the floor and let the flames do the rest.

The only thing preying upon James' mind was to protect the sphere at all costs, his brothers had paid the ultimate price and he wasn't going to let the invading Englishmen achieve what centuries of his kinsmen had sworn to protect.
Whatever this sphere was, it was dangerous. Maybe there was something in the prophecies after all. Maggie may have been a cackling old crone, but there was more to her than the ridicule and disdain that she seemed to carry with her.
Stepping out of the lower crypt chamber, James stumbled up the steps, sphere in hand as he led the way with the red intensity of the orb providing his light.

He emerged from the stone sarcophagus entrance and swayed his body over the edge, his bare knees scraping upon the stone floor. The burning intensity from the sphere was beginning to feel uncomfortable on his hand, so James tried to lay it down on the ground but the sphere had locked onto his palm so tightly that it seemed to burrow beneath his skin, attach itself and draw upon his very essence.

Something was different now and James had no idea of what was going on. His gaze directed at the fine light coming from within the sphere and then it started to react.

The area all around him had begun to look hazy, a white cloud like vapour swirling so fast that the crypt had turned into a blur, shimmering and frightening him as he feared Alexander had suspected on their approach.

The soaring winds began to rip higher as elemental forces were released from within the small sphere and circled, expanding between the rocks, spreading and cracking the walls and weakening the structure of all that surrounded him.

A purple current of electrical energy bled out farther, rippling up the tower wall and gliding over the masonry, hitting the stress points and loosening the stone blocks from each other.

The red glow seemed to blink as the ground swayed and with one almighty release of power the earth shook with a thunderous roar and for one moment James thought his touch had released the prophesised demon that was coming to ravage the world.

Outside the crypt, the curious Redcoat crept down to the bottom of the steps, his left hand caressing the cracked surface of the door as the ground beneath him vibrated. Things were quiet above, the bombardment of cannons had stopped and it seemed all opposition had been defeated as the jubilant cheers of the Redcoat troops bustled into the inner courtyard. But he thought it best to investigate the crypt, unsure of what he saw before him.

Time-Ryder: Powerstone Book One

There was a white glare and it looked as if there was someone at the centre of it. It was an impossible sight as he narrowed his vision to peer closer.

The door of the crypt creaked open for the last time and the Redcoat stood in the threshold, his mouth gaping at the sight before him, but it was the last thing he would see.

The ground shook so much that the dead form of Alexander rolled down the remaining steps and fell inside the crypt door, just before an out-rush of wind swept from the storm that surrounded the highlander inside and pushed him backward out of the door as it slammed shut, barring his entry.

The ground rocked the whole doorframe, knocking him over fully as the force of tremors shifted the ground below his feet and the stone steps continued to shake, tremors lifting the earth and opening up the ground.

The ground level had moved so much that the area around the doorway sunk into the ground and the frame keeled over until it was almost horizontal. The redcoat panicked, seeing the red embers of light through the cracks in the door below him and causing the blast of unearthly forces that swirled around the highlander within.

He creased his eyes tighter and could see the man was holding something, but the swirling light made it impossible for him to identify it.

His determination and curiosity was going to ensure that he discovered what it was and he peered through a small gap in the door. The winds still circled around the man, a shining ball of deathly colour in his grasp and he wondered if this was what Somersby was after.

The purple irregularity of lightning expanded still, floating over the tower, releasing a section from the wall to which the redcoat sidestepped, letting the stone block narrowly miss him.

Time-Ryder: Powerstone Book One

It was too much for him to bear alone; maybe a squad of riflemen could take out these defences of this light, if that's what they were. The redcoat began to step backwards, avoiding the barbed creepers when the lightning field sparked upward to the watchtower, violently freeing a section of rock from the outer facing.

He looked up and the horrifying contorted image of a greyed stone gargoyle swept down upon him and flattened him in no more than the blink of an eye.

The redcoat floundered to the floor, blood splattering all around the area of the doorway and yet the structure of the crypt still held its position even though half of it had collapsed in on itself. It seemed as if the prophecy was a little premature as the doorway to the crypt was then bombarded with loose rocks tumbling onto the stone steps and barring any entry and sealing the crypt for the time being.

Inside the crypt, James was catatonic, gazing in his permanent trance coupled with his glazed expression of contentment and beaming wildly at the swirling eddy all around him.

The sphere blinked again and a succession of flashes came forth as if the energy it had so eagerly drawn from the young Scot was waning.

James sank to his knees, his skin becoming pallow and discoloured; his lips a wispy blue and his cheeks sullen and gaunt. The flashes increased in speed as if it were desperately trying to absorb as much energy as possible while it had the chance.

The skin on James' face began to blacken and crack and was now leathery, shrinking back onto his face and his once gazing eyes pulling back into their sockets before drying up and evaporating altogether.

Time-Ryder: Powerstone Book One

As the sphere drew every piece of life from him, all that was left were the ragged clothes on the frame of a limp skeleton. Collapsing into a heap of bones, James' bony hand fell aside and the sphere was released, rolling out of his grasp and sitting barely inches from the long bony fingers that had once held it so tightly.

Amid the shaking grounds and soaring winds that grew from the small crypt, Lord Somersby held his ground high up on the hill, looking through slit like eyes with contempt and disappointment. Things were taking a turn for the worse. If situations did not change the prize might be lost to him forever and all the work that brought him to this point would be wasted.

The roof of the main hall was ablaze, the smoke wafting upward and more visible than the faint flicker of flame that could be seen from what remained of the crofts below in the valley.

He pulled back on the reigns of his steed and watched over the dregs of soldiers clearing up the few Scotsmen that remained. Somersby watched as the Redcoats began to flee from the site of battle and he sneered with annoyance as the weight of the outer castle wall shifted and finally gave way.

He could see beyond the wall into the courtyard where the remaining section of the tower tumbled down and covered what was once the entrance to the crypt, until it was buried completely under rubble.

Wheezing and out of breath, a scruffy young boy stood before Somersby, gasping for air.

"News from the village my Lord," puffed the ragged clothed urchin.

"The Marquis is heading this way with a garrison of soldiers in his company sir."

Time-Ryder: Powerstone Book One

Somersby gritted his teeth as the Captain of the guard came closer and looked upward for instruction.

"What are your orders my Lord?"

Somersby looked down the bridge of his long nose and pulled out a gleaming fob watch, flipping it open and listening to the ghostly tune as he looked at the watch face.

"Disperse the men and have their uniforms burnt, I want no trace of them here. Let them assume it has been an internal dispute between the clans" he sneered again.

"But Sir. What of your Prize?"

With an air of displeasure, Somersby began to retreat his horse from the Captain.

"It can wait!" he replied in an exhaled hiss, "It isn't going anywhere!"

With that last declaration, he cantered off before Ravayne and his men approached the scene of desolation. He'd waited this long, he could wait a while longer.

The dim red hue in the entombed crypt started to recede as the sphere lay in the centre of the upper chamber.

Finally the ceiling had stabilised and was enclosed, shut off from the rest of the world. The red glow was still apparent on the top lens of the ball, even though it was slowly fading.

The sphere had lost one chance of completing its destiny, but there would be another.

Just like Somersby, all it had to do was wait…

Time-Ryder: Powerstone Book One

CHAPTER ONE

The Castle as it had been was no longer.
Standing where it had once graced the hillside with centuries of grandeur, dominating over all the lands on the vast Baleran estate was now nothing more than a ruin.
Its once magnificent facings and carved ramparts were withered, decayed and crumbling to dust, until now.
Almost Three hundred years after the events that heralded the beginning of the end of the Castle as a bolthole for Stuart sympathisers, a group of young people were crowded around a large gaping hole in the ground, in the shadow of what was left of the grand watchtower.
It was September 2013 and after a particularly dismal winter, spring had come and gone so quickly that the young people were making good of the weather presented before them.
Late summer was rearing its head, with one of the last few days of sunshine immersing the students, although a faint chill was apparent by the slight oncoming wind that drifted over them.
They were all dressed in shorts and t-shirt for the beautiful day that graced them, like many others that this particular summer had surprisingly revealed so many of.
But the weather was the last thing on their minds, they waited in anticipation for anything that might bring some badly needed excitement to the day and relieve them of the boredom that they'd been experiencing since first light.
Varying sections of the grounds were pegged off with small coloured flags detailing each section of an extensive archaeological dig, the colours denoting one team to a specific section of the site.
But the team of yellow section were becoming restless, hovering impatiently over the recently unearthed hole.

Time-Ryder: Powerstone Book One

They'd been forced to halt their efforts in the nearby section of ground by an injunction that strangely wanted all the attempts of restoration of the once magnificent building halted.

All they could do was look on and watch as one of the few sections that had been given the go ahead was being plundered by one student in particular.

A long gangly arm protruded from the hole, the fingers flexing into the air as a voice carried forth from the bottom of the dark pit.

"Here, gimme' a fibre brush!" announced the young voice with a rough Scottish burr.

A young woman shuffled forward excitedly through the group and handed a broad brush into the welcoming hand that quickly snapped back inside the hole again.

After a few brief moments of analysis the owner of the hand stood upright. He was youthful, in his early twenties, a shock of untidy dark hair sticking upright, faint smudges of dirt adorning his cheeky yet round and inquisitive face.

Nova Mitchell cleared his throat and knelt back down again, rolling up the sleeves of his dark blue shirt, although like his face it too was marred with dirt.

He pulled a pair of small rounded glasses from his pocket and perched them on the very edge of his stubby nose as he dragged the end of the brush over the upturned rock that he had been examining closely.

The hole was dark, the smell of freshly upturned earth clearly pleasing him as he smiled and started to clear the excess from the edges of the stone that had clearly grabbed his attention so.

It showed no signs of deterioration like the weathered stones on the wall above, but he kept at it with the brush, carefully exposing something beneath it.

From what he could see, the pit was slanted and he had begun to uncover the flat surfaces of a set of stone steps that led down to his current position. It was more progress than any of the other students had done in a week, yet he had accomplished the task in just a few short hours.

Nova raised his brow with surprise and dragged the brush over the side of the lone rock where it touched the ground, revealing a tiny white fragment barely visible in the soil.

Putting the brush into his top pocket, he picked up the smallest of the fragments, hard, yet smooth and put it in his mouth, ejecting it just as quickly.

"Dirty pig!" grunted a girl's voice from within the group, but one that Nova recognised; he even smiled at the comment.

He gave a wry grin and stood tall, glancing up at the overlooking bunch that seemed to part and reveal his accuser.

"You think so?" he grated, "That was a valid scientific test!"

Nova was older than all of them and appeared to be the senior member of the team.

With a little more knowledge and experience than the rest of them put together, he gave the unintentional impression that he was the leader of the scraggy bunch, even though he was still a student himself.

"And how do you work that one out?" chirped the girl's squeaky voice again.

"Common sense!" he hissed with a sigh, "Everything you learn doesn't always come from a classroom or a book you know. Practical experience will do you wonders!" he looked over his glasses at the small sneering redhead that emerged through the crowd, taking an imposing and arrogant stance at the front of the group.

"I had to find out if it was what I thought it was, and it's just as well, cause it isn't!" he continued, confusing them all.

"Are you saying that we should just put anything in our gob?" retorted the girl, her voice oscillating in disbelief.

Time-Ryder: Powerstone Book One

"From what I hear Brenda, you're not all that fussy!" he said with the smallest of smiles.

A frenzied series of loud guffaws came forth and Brenda's face was almost the same colour as her rich red hair.

And within seconds she became quiet and disappeared quickly, swallowed up into the middle of the crowd once again.

Nova hadn't even realised the connotations of his jibe and crouched back down into the hole, quickly getting back to the matter at hand.

He began carefully sweeping over the surface of the rock that he'd discovered, or more importantly what appeared to be under the rock. It confused him, but problems and questions were all part of the fun on a dig, or at least that's what he told himself.

He pulled a small vial from his top pocket and scraped a few of the white traces into it, thumbing on the rubber stopper once he'd finished.

Nova held it up to his gaze.

"Definitely not chalk," he mumbled softly with a smile, "the texture is too hard!"

"Yeah, but what is it?" came another voice.

A young blonde haired man tumbled to the edge of the pit, placing himself precariously close to Nova, and almost falling in. His clothes were much the same as the others, yet slightly dishevelled and buttoned up wrongly, making his shirt uneven.

"Not so much of what Brian, more of who?" whispered Nova, "You see the markings underneath? Well I can't be sure until I get some lifting gear, but I think it might be the upper part of a skeleton. These fragments are too shattered to be positive. I won't know till the area is fully exposed!"

Nova looked at his friend's distressed clothing.

"Which is more than I can say for you!"

Brian blushed and saw his unevenly buttoned shirt and he started to correct quickly, amid embarrassment.

Time-Ryder: Powerstone Book One

"And your flies are open!" whispered Nova, "What is it with you. You're like one of those wee dogs that keep humping someone's leg."

Brian asserted himself.

"Time's ticking, you know me, just not enough of me to go around!" he smiled.

Brian cleared his throat and tugged at his wave of blonde surfer dude locks.

"You've really found something, that's interesting," he said loudly for all to hear and changing the subject at the same time, but not sounding too convincing.

"No seriously, it's about time we found something," he drawled, "us lot are getting so bored we're thinking of bunking off to the King's Rest this afternoon to get shit-faced!"

Nova looked over his glasses at Brian.

"That's hardly going to keep your grades up though is it?"

"I'm bored man, I need something to do, I'm a man of action, take no prisoners!" Brian did a very feeble impersonation of a karate chop, which resulted in him losing his balance and toppling headlong into the pit beside Nova.

The crowd laughed again as he wiped the muck from his face and almost sprang to his feet like a jack in the box.

"I know you're keen and everything Brian, but I hardly needed a volunteer. What I need is a shifting rig!" Nova objected.

"You don't need a rig, I'll give you a hand!" he smiled cheerily.

"You'll give yourself a hernia more like!" snorted Nova.

"Rubbish, it doesn't look that heavy!" Brian retorted and knelt on the opposite side of him, edging his fingers around the surface of the greyed rock.

The raised voices of laughter and commotion caused the crowd to part as one of the senior members of the archaeological team made his way through like Moses parting the red sea.

Time-Ryder: Powerstone Book One

Professor Henry Carlson was in his early Seventies, a pair of small brown rimmed glasses perched on the edge of his elegant beak of a nose. His full white beard neatly trimmed and a mane of white hair swept away like a lion's ruff.

Today was something unusual for him, for he was dressed in his finest brown checked suit, at least it was what he assumed was his finest. A checked white shirt and maroon bow tie with a matching waistcoat, finished off with a pair of brown leather brogues that were polished to the max.

He seemed very out of place on a mucky archaeological site, compared to his usual attire of a ragged green woollen jumper, brown corduroy trousers, dark green Wellington boots, a worn green wax jacket and tweed fishing hat that was usually perched upon an uncombed head.

He crept to the edge and peered over, trying to see into the deep pit where the two young men were poised at either side of the rock.

"What seems to be all the commotion?"

The old man's shadow cast into the hole and obscured the light, forcing Nova to turn around and look upward with a smile.

"Professor!" he said with delight.

"When did you arrive?" asked the old man, excited and surprised at the same time, his accent was slightly upper class English with a faint Scottish lilt.

"Late last night, didn't want to wake you!" clipped Nova.

"You look well" smiled the old man.

"Ahem!" coughed Brian, "I thought we were going to move this thing?"

The Professor's face became slightly grumpy as he frowned and looked down on the blonde haired young man.

"Good morning Mr Wilde, I trust you've recovered from your little excursion last night?"

Time-Ryder: Powerstone Book One

"Yes Professor" Brian lowered his head as he blushed and tried to change the subject again.

"Look Nova can we get a move on with this?" he said trying to sway the conversation back to the rock.

"I'd better help him with this Professor!" Nova rolled his eyes.

"Anything interesting?"

"I'm not sure," returned Nova, "but it's down past the fourth marker. So it's been here, two maybe three hundred years?"

"Minimum!" said the old man gruffly, "is there any sign of disturbance?"

Nova shook his head.

"No. Should there be?"

"It's nothing, just Mr Jenkins the Groundskeeper said the main gate was broken into last night!"

Brian gave a strange look to Nova and then back to the Professor.

"Was there anything taken?" Brian looked concerned.

The old man looked down squarely.

"Nothing Mr Wilde, everything is accounted for. You didn't see anything out of the ordinary last night?"

"Well there was this...." Brian smiled.

Nova cut him off before he could finish.

"He means relevant to the break in, you twit!"

"No Professor!" the young man shook his head

Professor Carlson bit his lip, his mind clearly working overtime.

"Why would someone break into the site and leave everything in place? If it had been youths with a spray paint can, the evidence of their actions would have been apparent," he said; his face sullen and confused.

Snapping out of his brief daze, he looked down in confusion as to what Brian was doing in the pit.

"Brian's come to lend a hand, it'll save us erecting a shifting rig" announced Nova.

The Professor raised a brow.

Time-Ryder: Powerstone Book One

"Very well, just don't give yourself a hernia, unless your exertions last night have already done so!" he said sternly to which Nova stifled a laugh and looked right back at Brian.
"It could be something valuable next to the skeleton, if it is a skeleton" replied the blonde haired young man excitedly.
The old man gave a wry grin.
"Remember what happened with the two groat coins you thought had Sidney James' face on!"
"Well how was I supposed to know it was Henry the something?" Brian's expression dropped.
Nova couldn't help but see the funny side as the old man started to question his friend's motives.
"Mr Wilde, how you scraped by in my class last term is beyond me, but nevertheless I'm glad you're here to assist Mr Mitchell!"
"Thanks Professor!" he welcomed the old man and almost blushed, unsure if it was a compliment or not.
He had an idea that the Professor knew he was only in his history class to impress the girls on campus. But his purpose in attending the archaeology class was his only option on the curriculum that would keep his father off his back.
"Ready?" said Nova impatiently, he raised his brow to the blonde haired youth and Brian immediately squatted, flinging his hands under the bottom edge of the exposed rock.
Both of them gripped it and turned it over, almost frightening Brian half to death by what he saw.
He fell back into the dirt as Nova stood up and wiped his hands on his trousers, whilst grinning inanely at his friend.
"What the hell is that?" Brian shrieked.
"That would be a skeleton Mr Wilde!" retorted the Professor, just as amused as Nova was.
"No. Not that. That!" he pointed at the overturned rock that had a particular horrific shape to it.
"It's only a gargoyle!" snorted Nova in amusement.

Time-Ryder: Powerstone Book One

"A what?"
"A gargoyle. Ugly looking things that they used to put on the exteriors of old buildings!" announced Nova.
"To ward off evil!" added the Professor, "amongst other things."
"Oh you mean they look like Mrs Jenkins the groundskeeper's wife" Brian scoffed, turning away from the sculptural monstrosity.
But Nova was already somewhere else, this time looking at the network of bones that were embedded in the ground.
"Any Ideas?" asked the Professor.
Nova raised a brow, but he was stumped to the actual detail.
"Well it's a man" he thrust his hands into his pockets and looked up to the old man, "maybe five foot eight, maybe nine!" he said and looked back down to the framework again.
As the sun reflected off something, it caught Nova's eye and he bent to take a closer look.
"Then there's this!" he carefully dragged his small brush over the reflection and exposed more shining metal.
"What is it?" Brian seemed interested for the first time in god knows how long, but Nova ignored him, concentrating upon the find. Putting the brush away, he started scraping away the mounds of dirt with his hands and revealed a long shaft and hilt belonging to a sword. Nova smiled and pulled the ancient weapon from the ground, holding it aloft and cleaning off the excess dirt from the edges.
"Woah!" gasped Brian, looking at the sword in his friend's hand, "let me see that!"
The Professor resisted the temptation of sarcasm on Brian's behalf; a simple stern stare did it all.
Nova held it back from him, knowing exactly what he'd do with it.
"I'm not giving it to you Brian. I know you'll just go Thundercats Ho!" he sniggered.

Time-Ryder: Powerstone Book One

The crowd erupted in laughter again and a squeaking laugh from Brenda rose above all of the others.

"And you'll know a lot about being a Ho, eh Brenda?" Brian smiled.

"You weren't saying that last night were you Wild thing?" she retorted with a laugh that seemed to shut him up this time.

"Have you found anything else?" the Professor said loudly, silencing the surrounding group.

Nova passed up the weapon in his hands.

"Nothing yet, but I've been marking out a pattern and it looks like a set of steps leading downward into what I have no idea. These stone blocks have been bugging me since in got here and there's only one explanation as to why they're here!"

"I don't follow you!" said the old man teetering on the edge of the pit, looking at the rocks himself and trying to find clues in what they young man was referring to.

Nova looked from the gargoyle rock up to where the tower had once stretched to, putting his hand in front of his eyes to mask out the sunlight.

"I think it's safe to assume that these blocks were part of the tower weren't they?" he asked, trying to put the Professor on the same footing as he was.

"How can we?" interrupted Brian.

Nova pointed from the gargoyle up to what remained of the decayed tower.

"I'm thinking it must have fallen from there and killed this poor bugger right out!"

The old man frowned at his use of words.

"Sorry!" Nova hissed back, like a child that had just been told off.

"And it couldn't have fallen on its own accord?" the Professor asked.

"Nah, these babies were built to last, well except for a battle or two, but there's no record of a battle ever being fought here!"

Time-Ryder: Powerstone Book One

"Not to my knowledge. Not much is known about the area in fact!" returned the Professor, "But we have found a few cannonballs close by the north wall, strangely enough!"
"Then it's highly probable that whatever caused it to fall, supposedly caused the rest of the wall to follow on, isn't it?"
Nova pursed his lips, gulped and looked skyward again
The Professor gave a smile and nodded, very proud of the young man's deduction.
"Your theory is most probable!"
Nova took a step sideways and felt the ground slightly uneasy under his feet. He shifted his position again and yet it felt the same until he reached a point where he was comfortable to remove the smaller rocks from the mound by his side.
He'd already fashioned out most of the excess dirt to reveal the steps, but had come to a stalling point at the bottom where another few stone blocks barred his way to wherever the steps were leading.
"Brian, gimme a hand with this!" he called out, crawling forward on all fours.
The blonde haired Brian followed his example and began shoving aside rocks from the mound.
"What are you expecting to find?"
Nova shook his head.
"I dunno. But there's something not right about all of this. It's giving me a really weird feeling!"
"I get that!" said Brian without looking up, "but with me it's usually gas!"
Nova rolled his eyes and tried not to laugh.
As he moved position again, he looked curiously up at Brian and then to the looming Professor. Smoothing his hands out, he began to clear away the dirt on the ground as the spectators looked on in excitement.

"It's weird. It sounds like its hollow!" Nova patted the ground again and looked up to the Professor.

"Hollow?" narrowed the old man.

But before Nova had a chance to reply, the deafening sound of splitting wood opened up the ground beneath his feet and he vanished through the ensuing dust-cloud that was caused by the disturbance.

The creaking of age-old timber was followed by the dull thump of falling wood to which the panicking Professor craned his neck over the edge, trying to waft aside the debris and see what had become of Nova.

When the surrounding dust cleared and began to settle he saw that Nova was gone.

All that remained was a large gaping hole at the foot of what was supposed to be the bottom of the pit.

Time-Ryder: Powerstone Book One

CHAPTER TWO

"Mr Mitchell, are you alright down there?"
Professor Carlson teetered on the edge of the hole, his eyes wide with panic and his voice elevating in concern.
"Can you see anything Mr Wilde? Is he all right down there?" croaked the old man. Brian had edged away from the orifice; unable to help Nova who'd disappeared so fast. All he could do was look on with his mouth gaping, yet all he could smell was a disgusting stench that stung his eyes as it wafted forth from the dark opening.
The chamber was dark, only the fuzziness of the rising dust swimming around his head came into view and Nova sat up dazedly, wafting aside the air from the only source of light in the gloom that he had found himself in.
Nova had thundered onto the cold stone floor of the crypt beneath the gaping orifice, his head landing on his outstretched arms and saving himself an injury, not that he would have concerned himself, he was more interested in what he had fallen into, even if it could do with a life supply of air fresheners..
The first sense to react was his smell. The appalling odour hit him like a slap in the face and he immediately capped his mouth and nose with a handkerchief, masking the smell as he strained to breathe in the stuffy confines of the enclosure.
He looked around, eyes slowly adjusting to the dark and yet there were no distinguishing features in the small area.

Adjusting his eyes to the darkness, Nova looked around, making out only the barest of objects surrounding him, but the odour was foremost on his mind and it had to be coming from somewhere. He was becoming used to the stench, but still needed his hankie in case he was overwhelmed again and he

took a retreating step backward as his head began to clear and he became aware of the concerned voices above.
Nova scrambled through the dark to where the shaft of light broke through the hole into the gloom.

"Mr Mitchell, Are you alright down there?" repeated the Professor, his voice echoing to the chamber below.
The imminent silence was broken only by a few strained gasps was ended by a cacophony of staggered coughs and sneezes that finally let the Professor know he was fine.
Nova clambered up the few steps inside the crypt and poked his head through the shattered hole; his handkerchief still covering his face.
"I'm fine Professor; I just need to check something. Can you pass me a torch down?" he coughed again.
With the click of his fingers, a long handed torch was quickly passed through the crowd and the old man dropped it gently into Nova's welcoming hand.
"Thanks!" he said and disappeared quickly into the crypt again.
Flipping on the beam, he carried the circlet of light around the walls, taking note of the indented coffins and etchings around the surfaces.
The dark stonework was centuries old, yet had a polished look, unlike the weathered features of the castle exterior.
But he proposed that if the crypt had been protected by the ravages of time, then so had everything else inside, perfectly preserved until now. Nova moved around and fell to the floor once more, careering headlong over a body, or what appeared to be left of one. He took a dazed look to the remains and pushed himself up on his elbows, turning over onto his side where another ghastly sight lay before him.

"So you're the smelly one!" he remarked to the network of bones and knelt down to examine it, "how long have you been down here eh?"

Nova glided the circlet of light around the walls and came to rest on the area close to where he fell.

On the steps leading out of where he proposed the door had once been was yet another body. The layers of frayed garments and leather belt straps strewn across skeletal remains, half propped against the wall, the jawbone of the skull gaping wide and it appeared to be looking down upon the corpse at the Archaeologist's side.

Easing up slowly and rubbing his pained wrist, Nova shone the beam down with ease until it focussed on the rag-tag remains of drab clothing surrounding the floored skeleton. The patterned cloth looked like a kilt remnant, but not one that the young man was familiar with.

He knelt and carefully examined the item and part of it came away in his hand.

Fearing it would disintegrate further; Nova took a small plastic sleeve from his pocket and slipped the kilt fragment inside, returning it to his pocket and snatching up the torch from the floor once again.

He shone the torch-beam upon the propped up skeleton, noting all the same paraphernalia as the previous one, the dirty sackcloth shirt and kilt of a highlander adorning its withered frame.

Nova looked closely, picking up the small dirk and pistol from its belt.

In all his years of studying and following the Professor to both ends of the country, Nova had never become so excited and scared at the same time. His heart raced and with every slow breath as he moved forward cautiously to the raised sarcophagus in the centre of the crypt.

Time-Ryder: Powerstone Book One

Casting the beam around, Nova saw what was left of another body, half buried beneath the stone blocks that had barred his way into the small tomb. How he had missed it on impact he had no idea, but he could see the uniform of a redcoat, a large sword held in its skeletal grasp.

Nova's brow drooped curiously, but he disregarded them and moved back to the opening, completely ignoring the sarcophagus as he stepped into the beam of light that penetrated the crypt from above.

Extending his hand out of the darkness, a sullen and gaunt looking Brian quickly hoisted Nova from the crypt and from the look on his face Nova realised that his friend had just been sick. Pulled from the ragged hole to safety, Nova dusted himself down and stepped away from the broken aperture, finally removing his handkerchief and breathing more easily.

"What did you find down there?" began the old man who quickly remembered his manners, "Sorry are you alright?"

"Nothing a swift half wouldn't cure," joked the young Scot politely.

"There's another three down there, fully clothed and we can even take the opportunity to get this carbon dated!" replied Nova, he slipped the small plastic sleeve to the Professor and stretched his back.

"And here!" he smiled and passed up the small dirk he'd retrieved from the skeleton's belt.

The Professor took them with delight.

"Quite a day's work it seems?"

But Nova's attention was elsewhere; his vision strayed to Brian's feet, or more importantly next to his friend's grubby sick covered shoes.

He stooped down close to the embedded skeleton and quickly took a pair of tweezers from his top pocket. Gently reaching

Time-Ryder: Powerstone Book One

down, he prised another section of cloth, blackened by dirt but very well preserved between the rock and the stone steps.
Nova narrowed curiously and prised it free and quickly put it into another plastic container.
"What've you got there?" asked Brian, still capping his mouth.
"Looks like another piece of the puzzle!" he replied and looked up at the row of on-looking faces.
He gave the Professor a curious gaze to which the old man stood tall, looking around.
"This might be the opportune time finish for the day" he announced and almost like lightning, the crowd dispersed to the makeshift food hall in a far off tent.
Nova narrowed at the old man.
"But it's only two o clock, we've still got a good few hours of daylight left!"
"Come on, out of there you two," he said forcefully.
The Professor reached down and helped up first Brian and then Nova.
"What did you find in there?" asked the old man as he fumbled with the dirk in his hands.
Brian looked all around him, lingering and for the first time it seemed he was interested in what was going on, but the Professor wanted a discreet word with Nova and the young archaeologist could see it from the look upon the old man's face.
"I'll catch you up," said Nova cheerily to Brian, urging him on to the food hall so he could be alone with the Professor.
"Oh, right. I'll save you a space!" he replied and ambled off quickly amongst the other students before all the food was gone.
With the crowd dispersed, the Professor pulled Nova aside and the young man knew that he wanted to tell him something, the look was all he needed to gain some privacy.
"Don't you think you should tell me what's going on here?" said Nova sharply, raising his brows.

Time-Ryder: Powerstone Book One

The Professor gave him a blank look. Nova took a short breath and pointed back to the hole.

The old man smiled, his concerned face trying in effort to contain his excitement at the find, but Nova knew him too well.

Carlson sat on the edge of one of the tables and faced the young man, folding his arms.

"Are you ok?"

Nova looked at him blankly.

"It's been almost three months Mr Mitchell, You haven't attended any classes, there's been no communication except a brief message to Mrs Brendon and then you suddenly turn up here" breathed out the old man in one gasp.

"I would like to know where you've been!" said the old man softly.

"I wish you wouldn't call me that. My name's Nova, No-va!" he objected in return, trying to avoid explanations.

The Professor shook his head

"Why your mother persisted in calling you that ridiculous pet name I'll never know, you do have a perfectly good Christian name!"

"And before you attempt to use it, you'll see that I've got a gun in my hand!" smiled the young man and he handed over the weapon he took from the corpse in the crypt.

The old man put it aside, thinking it was yet another attempt to avoid answering the questions.

"Anyway, ridiculous is my middle name!" he smiled.

The Professor wasn't going to be distracted from the conversation, as he knew the young man was often able to do and laid the pistol on the bench behind him.

He'd become so used to the name, preferring it to his own that seemed so distant that he'd almost forgotten it, until the Professor would often remind him, usually by some form of embarrassment.

Time-Ryder: Powerstone Book One

"Look I'll stop calling you Unc if you promise never call me by my real name!"
The Professor gave a sigh, a smile and conceded.
"Agreed, now please go on!" he urged.
Nova pursed his lips, folded his arms and stared back.
"She died Professor!" he mumbled softly.
The old man was taken aback, his mouth slightly open in shock.
"I've been keeping myself out of everyone's way, just moving from place to place. I couldn't come back just yet!"
The young man rested back on the opposite bench, feeling relieved to finally get it off his chest and was glad that it was the Professor he could confide in.
His head was a massive jumble, full of emotions and it felt great to finally get back to some work to take his mind off it.
"There was an accident when I went to Canterbury. I'm not really ready to talk about it" said Nova, trying to fight back the tears that were verging on the corners of his eyes.
"You should have come home, we were getting really worried about you!" the old man held him tight and felt him shudder, still fighting back the tears.
"I had a run in with Barbara's mum and had to take off for a bit!"
The Professor straightened back and held onto the young man by the shoulders as he looked into his eyes.
"She blames you?"
Nova wiped his eyes and sniffed.
"She had quite a bit to say about it, took her a bottle of Brandy to get up the Dutch for it though!"
The Professor gave him a look and knew that he was still holding back. He nodded in sympathy and knew how it felt.
Losing someone he was so close to could send anyone over the edge, but he was glad to see the young man safe and in one piece.

Time-Ryder: Powerstone Book One

"That's a burial chamber down there, practically unheard of in this area, we've got a section of kilt that I've never seen before and then there's this!" he thundered.

He pulled out the two pieces of fabric and showed them to the old man.

"That's a crimson tailpiece from a redcoat, I know that because there's one in Edinburgh museum and there's another down there, but what's it doing in a burial chamber where there shouldn't be one?" he said accusingly, "There's no record of redcoats in this area!"

"Quite full of questions this afternoon aren't we!" the Professor grinned wildly.

"You know more than you're telling this lot don't you?" broke off the youngster, "Course you do. And while I'm on the subject, who's that creepy guy I keep seeing hanging around the main gates?"

It wasn't like the Professor to keep anything from him, but in light of the fact that he didn't know Nova was back, he'd let it slide for now.

The Professor raised his hands and patted the air in front of Nova.

"I'll answer all of your questions in good time, but first come with me!"

Nova shuffled his feet in the dirt behind the Professor, his hands buried in his pockets, yet feeling like a naughty schoolboy led away to the headmaster's office.

Professor Carlson entered the erected white tent, all those inside looking on immediately.

"Can I have the room please?" he cleared his throat.

The surrounding team began to put down their working materials and vacated the tent leaving the old man alone with Nova.

Time-Ryder: Powerstone Book One

A brief silence ensued as both men sized each other up, it was clear that there was some form of tension between them, but which one was going to speak first.

Professor Carlson scratched his beard and took off his glasses, cleaning them as he nodded.

"I did try to call, but I knew that you'd come back once you got whatever it was out of your system!"

"Not sure that I ever will!" sniffed the young man, wiping his eyes as he took in a deep breath and falsely smiled at the old man, trying to give him the impression that he was fine.

Trying his best to change the conversation, Nova turned his head back to the tent flaps and cleared his throat.

"I only came back sooner because your message said you needed me!"

The old man's brows met in confusion and he looked up at the youngster with confusion.

"What message?"

Nova pursed his lips.

"Don't give me that, you sent me a text message, telling me you needed me here ASAP. I thought it was something urgent so I dropped my stuff off at the house and came straight here. That's why I didn't get in till last night. What's up?"

The Professor was still confused.

"I didn't send any message!" he replied as Nova shrugged.

"Doesn't matter anyway, I'm here now" he smiled and leaned back on the table, "who was that creepy guy outside the gates?"

Professor Carlson straightened and gave a cough, still confused by the message.

"That would be the prospective Laird, at least if his claims can be verified. He petitioned the council to stop the dig and gained a partial order to stop us unearthing the remains of the great hall, but we're able to continue the work elsewhere until our appeal is finalised" the Professor took a breath.

"He practically rolled up out of nowhere with the title deeds for the estate, which is all a bit confusing"
"Do you think he's got something to hide?" said Nova bluntly.
The Professor shrugged.
"There may be a little more to it than that. He seems to be unwilling to let anyone have access to the great hall, even though The Trust is footing the bill for the restoration!"
Nova shook his head as it sounded a bit odd to him.
"Do you think he might be hiding something in there?"
"If he is, then it's well hidden, we scouted the remains and removed all of the debris. There's nothing in there!"
"Well if he isn't hiding something there, why didn't he ask for an order to stop the full restoration?" Nova shrugged.
"Yes I'm a little confused by that too and the title deeds he produced for the estate show no signs of age or deterioration strangely enough" replied the old man.
He saw Nova's confused expression turn from a frown to a small smile.
"And why the suit, did you lose a bet?" smiled Nova.
The Professor looked over the rim of his glasses at the young man and put down the specimens beside him.
"I'll ignore that remark Mr Mitchell. You didn't think I'd put on my best suit to go clambering in a hole now did you?"
"Best suit? I can see a few holes and…" Nova clapped his hands together jokily, "Is that a moth?"
"Very funny!" smiled the old man, "This was the height of fashion once!"
"Nineteen fifty five was a long time ago Professor!" Nova joked, "Wait a minute…" his face lit up with excitement.
"You've got a date!"
The glow of embarrassment coming from the Professor's face was enough to melt polar ice caps. Nova could almost warm his hands from it.

Time-Ryder: Powerstone Book One

The Professor winked.
"C'mon then, who is it?"
"It's not so much of a date, more of a meeting with the Trust. Miss Raynor wants me to extend my contract by another three months with an option to oversee the overall restoration of the castle," said the old man softly, "I just need to weigh it up with my tenure at the University!"
"When you say Trust, will there be more than one member there and is it a meeting in a restaurant?" Nova gave a smile, trying to get him to tell him more.
He could tell that the old man was keeping it on the down low and saved his questions from embarrassing him further.
"Well good for you!" Nova was pleased for him, "I don't think Aunt Rose would want you to bum about the house forever!"
The old man smiled slightly in remembrance at the mention of his wife. It had been less than two years since Rose had died. She'd taken a tumble at home and suffered brain damage and as a result it affected her memory.
There were periods where she was quite lucid, but they were few and far between. She battled her last few months in a hospice and put on a brave face, but despite the treatment she slipped away quietly in the night.
Nova thought it would be weird to see the Professor with someone other than her, but she wouldn't want him to be alone even at his time of life. As far as Nova was concerned Rose and Henry were his parents.
A freak accident had claimed the lives of his parents and he was brought up by his Aunt and Uncle. He couldn't have wished for a better life and was the nearest they ever had to their own child. He spent endless summers following the Professor around the digs and sitting at the back of the class during the history lessons, soaking up knowledge and eventually following his Uncle into the same line of work.

"I found something else down there that you might want to take a look at!" Nova announced and pulled out the long slender blade of the sword behind him and handed it over.
The Professor's mouth gaped in awe.
"Where did you find this?"
"It was on the floor of the burial chamber. It is a claymore? Isn't it?"
"And remarkably well preserved!" the old man was still in shock from seeing the sword, "I'd better get this logged in."
"Can't it wait a minute, there's something I need to talk to you about!" began Nova.
But the old man was elsewhere; Nova could see that the Professor was distracted by the sword so he slipped out of the tent quietly.
"I'll speak to you later then" he said softly, clearly perturbed by something.
"What? Oh yes. Yes!" smiled the old man again, smitten by the sight of the gleaming sword.
Leaving him with the sword, Nova stepped out into the sun, closing his eyes from the glare and smiling as he could feel the warmth of the sun on his skin.
He took in a deep breath, trying not to dwell on the smell from the crypt that had clearly begun to cling to his clothes.
And when he least expected it, a soft pair of hands capped his eyes from behind him.
The long smooth fingers touched upon his eyelids and he knew that it was a woman, but only because he could smell the familiarity of the perfume that accompanied it.
Nova wheeled immediately and beamed.
"Jess!" he squeaked in excitement, "How'd you know I was here?"
A tall, slim brunette; no older than himself stood just in front of him, her hair a mass of brown curls and her eyes a strange misty

Time-Ryder: Powerstone Book One

shade of green. Yet her eyes had a certain sadness about them, but Nova just thought that it made her more mysterious.
He picked her up and whirled her around excitedly.
She was his oldest friend, but he was a little puzzled by her sudden appearance here.
"I thought I'd pay you a visit, seeing you're slumming it with the students again!" she replied.
He threw his arms around her and she gripped him tight, her face alive with delight, just as his.
"What are you doing here? I thought you were still at Uni!"
"I pulled a sicky when Mrs Brendon phoned to say you were back, didn't take long to figure that you'd come to see Uncle Henry first!"
"How're you doing?" she ruffled her long locks and looked at him squarely.
"I just want to forget about the whole thing Jess!" said Nova sadly.
"Barbara is a little hard to forget!" smiled Jess, "as I remember!"
"Aye, well that's not what her mum thinks and hey, maybe she's right. Maybe I should just try to move on and forget her" he replied.
"It sounds like you're trying to convince yourself that!"
Nova felt his eyes welling up.
"What can I say Jess? It hurts like hell. Even when I try not thinking about her, I think about her!"
"Don't you think it's just as hard for her, she's lost her only daughter?" Jess put an arm around his shoulder.
"I know. I'm just trying not to think about it." he said gruffly.
"The accident wasn't your fault, the sooner you realise that you'll start to feel better, Barbara's mum is just hurting right now!" spat Jess.
"Maybe she was right," thought Nova, in some respects Jess put it plain language so that he could understand it clearer.

"Everything changes every day Nova. Nothing is meant to be forever, doesn't matter how much we'd like it to be!" said Jess softly, but it didn't console him.

Emerging from the tent, the Professor beamed upon seeing Jess and she came closer, hugging him tightly.

"Uncle Henry!" she said with a squeal of delight.

Even though they weren't technically related, she was treated as part of their family.

She'd been brought up with Nova and was the closest thing to a sister as he was ever likely to have; spending most of her childhood at his house in Riverdale, those endless summers hanging out of trees and hiding in the cornfields with him.

Jess had been very much the Tomboy, but you wouldn't know it to look at her now, as glamorous and polished as she could be.

"Nice threads!" she said approvingly, "got a hot date?"

"I might!" the old man grinned with amusement.

"So there's no hope for me then?" she joked.

"Jessica, you'll always be my best girl" he replied with a beaming grin.

"Very sharp" she said approvingly, "I like the tie!"

Nova looked at the old man with a mischievous smile.

"Listen Professor, bow ties are not cool, no matter who tells you otherwise, unless you're James Bond!"

"I think he looks quite fetching!" declared Jess with a wide gleaming smile. With that comment Nova moved away, grinning at them both as he sauntered off.

"I'll leave you two to catch up then, I'm going for a walk!" he declared and quickly moved through the main gates and down the dirt-path into the village.

Professor Carlson looked nervous, staring after the young man as he disappeared from view.

"I'll go after him!" hissed Jess.

But the Professor held her back.

Time-Ryder: Powerstone Book One

"Let him go, he looks like he's got a lot to think about."
He took off his glasses and began to clean them.
"What did he say to you?"
"He's taking it pretty bad, he's blaming himself for what happened to Barbara!" she replied.
"Did he tell you that?"
Jess looked on, watching Nova disappear down the track.
"He didn't need to!"
From high up on the hillside overlooking the ruined estate, a lone figure watched the young man trail off from the site towards the cliff-top overlooking the sea.
The tall thin presence hovered, watching hawk-like as the Professor and Jess left the antiquities tent to the mess hall, deeply embroiled in laughter and conversation.
His predatory stance had unfaltered as he observed the ruins, scanning the layout of the castle as if looking for something, occasionally tilting his head as if calculating his next move.
He was dressed in a drab fawn suit, neatly pressed and maintained, his long fingers reached down into his waistcoat pocket and pulled out a battered old pocket watch, flipping it open and studying the hands precariously as a haunting chime sounded off from within the watch.
Snapping it shut, Somersby turned upon heel and made off quickly into the distance...

Time-Ryder: Powerstone Book One

Time-Ryder: Powerstone Book One

CHAPTER THREE

Nova sat on the edge of the cliff-top overlooking the sea. The lapping waves thrashing violently off the shore gave a calming effect and he felt relaxed. It reminded him of Emerson Falls in his hometown of Riverdale. Whenever he needed time by himself, he'd crawl up the winding path to Emerson Glen, through the twisted vines that covered the cracked masonry leading to the ruined Estate house and through the overgrown gardens of Pinehouse Mill. Once there he'd relax and watch the beautiful sight of the waterfall by the disused pump house. It seemed to soothe him every time and this was no exception. He was glad to be back at work, away from the troubled memories that made him think of nothing more than Barbara, but there were other troubles on his mind and some that he'd rather push aside for the moment and bury his head in the sand. Here on the coast was the closest he was going to get to that home feeling.

Nova picked up a stray pebble and tossed it over the edge, watching it vanish beneath the sea along with all of his sad thoughts.

His thoughts were of Barbara and he wished they would disappear along with those errant stones, but he knew it wasn't going to be that easy.

"Like some company?" a soft voice echoed behind him.

His grimace slowly curled into a smile as he heard Jess' warm tones.

"And if I said no. What would you do?" he smiled.

"Shove you off. Simple as that" she said with a grin, "You really shouldn't sit so close to the edge, anything can happen!"

He took a deep breath.

"You don't know how many times I've thought about that. Not jumping off I mean, that's just daft" he hissed softly,

Time-Ryder: Powerstone Book One

"I mean choices in general, decisions and choices that are taken away from you!"

"Careful Nova you're getting a bit philosophical for a Thursday" replied Jess. She sat beside him, her long legs draping over the cliff edge and she peered all of the way down, almost giddy from the view.

"I know what you mean, the ledge could crumble, a gust of wind could sweep you off, I could push you off," she joked again.

"It's all part of life. You can't control everything you know!"

"Wish I could" he murmured, "am I just being paranoid thinking that the accident and everything is like it was designed to keep me and Barbara apart, you know how crazy we were about each other!"

"Yes, you are sounding paranoid," Jess felt the heat and pulled off her short leather jacket revealing a dark-blue vest top that clearly showed off her attributes.

Nova noticed the upper part of her right arm had a mark upon it and he narrowed his vision. It looked as if Jess had been branded, two triangles, the points meeting each other like the vision of an hourglass, bound together by a circle and a twisted barb like vine surrounding it.

"What's that? I haven't seen that before."

Jessica's face flushed.

"That's because I like to keep it covered up. I got burned leaning against a door at some incinerator plant and got left with this damned thing"

"Oh!" mouthed Nova, "looks like it stings."

Jess shook her head.

"It only itches every now and then," she took a deep breath and stared out to sea.

"It looks really relaxing out here" she smiled at him and nudged his shoulder with hers.

"It reminds me of that time near Foley's barn" she grinned so wildly that it set off his smile and he almost burst out with laughter.
"When you tried to sunbathe topless and his dog ran away with your bikini top" he shook his head, still disbelieving that day even happened.
"Didn't help that I put some of his treats in your top when you weren't looking!" he laughed and prepared himself for the biggest slap of all time.
Instead, her smile beamed and she grabbed a hold of his neck from behind, pretending to throttle him.
"You're terrible," she smiled, "I never did get that top back!"
But Jess' plan had worked; she'd cheered him up for the meantime, giving her time to work on him a little more.
"Are you really going to tell me what's wrong with you?"
Nova looked at her and she knew instantly that he couldn't keep it in any longer. His eyes started to well up and he wiped away the first tear, trying not to look at Jess.
"I dunno Jess; it's just all getting to me. First Aunt Rose then Barbara's and now…" he trailed off and fell silent once more, but Jess wasn't going to push it any further even though she could see that something was tearing him apart.
She put a reassuring hand on his shoulder and gave him a squeeze.
"You know that I'm always here for you" she said looking at him squarely, "and you know you can tell me anything in your own time!"
Nova took a breath again and exhaled really slowly, preparing himself.
"It's just so unfair Jess!" he moaned, "I thought I'd get back early, so I went home to Riverdale and drop my stuff off, you know see Mrs Brendon and all that," he said excitedly.

Time-Ryder: Powerstone Book One

"I actually managed to track down an Album the Professor has been looking for and thought it would be a surprise for him, but I was a wee bit surprised myself…" he sniffed and wiped his nose on his sleeve.

Jess rolled her eyes, smiled and offered her handkerchief, which he took and blew noisily into it.

"What do you mean?" she narrowed.

"I went to put it in his study, but I found a letter on his desk that threw me sideways."

He paused and wiped his nose again.

"He's been diagnosed with Cancer, it says he's gone into second stage, not sure what kind it is, but the letter said he'd been missing appointments!"

"Are you sure?"

"Can't forget a letter like that. It's just like losing Aunt Rose all over again. I feel like someone's just kicked me right in the nuts!"

"And I take it that he doesn't know that you know about it?" queried Jess.

"How do I break it to him? Oh by the way I found the album to complete your Sinatra collection and I put it right next to your test results letter, that'll fill him with joy!"

"Maybe it'd be better if you waited till he told you himself!" she said putting her arm around his shoulder and gave him her grubby handkerchief.

He dried the corner of his eye and she closed his hand over, letting him hold onto it for now.

"Sorry I'm not very good company" he said and looked back out to sea.

"You've still got me!" she pulled him tighter.

Nova stood up and moved closer to the edge, stepping down to the path below them. He felt better for being around Jess and he looked up to her beautiful smiling face.

"You promise?" he said softly.

"Forever and ever!" she replied with a broad smile, and looked down upon him as he moved down the winding path to the beach.
Jess continued to watch him disappear down the track towards the thrashing waves.
"More than you'll ever know!" she whispered.

Wandering through the open gates of the Archaeology dig, Lord Somersby walked calm and collected. His clothes were different, but his manner and haughty arrogance were very much the same.
He had barely aged a day since the assault upon the Castle all those centuries earlier and had decided that hanging around the exterior of the compound was getting him nowhere, and he headed straight towards the main hall.
It was partially cordoned off,
Half erected scaffolding spanning the main wall and already the rotted beams and dangerously loose sections of the wall had been removed for safety.
He took a look through what was left of the windows of the great hall and sneered down his almighty nose before turning around to face one of the senior team.
"You really shouldn't be here sir, not until the final passes are made over your credentials!" said an impish and balding Archaeologist approaching him.
"These are my lands and I am entitled to inspect them whenever I please, am I not?" hissed Somersby.
"Not until the checks are done sir, now I'm going to have to ask you to leave, this is a very sensitive area."
"What is your name?" Somersby sneered.

Time-Ryder: Powerstone Book One

"Patterson sir, but that doesn't have anything to do with your trespassing here!" said the bald man in a gruff retort, "if you please sir!" Patterson held a hand out to usher him away.
"I'll remember you Patterson, you'll be the first escorted off the property when the checks are finalised"
But Patterson was having none of the threats, certainly not from some effete snob with delusions of grandeur.
"Then you won't mind if I escort you off the property now sir" he clipped and held out a hand, gesturing Somersby forward.
He watched as the gaunt man strode slowly through the main gates and one of the others came out of the nearest tent.
"What was that all about?"
"Lord Snot trying to throw his weight about, don't worry, I've dealt with his type before, all mouth and no trousers" Patterson chuckled.
The other man laughed.
"Yeah, but don't you just get the impression he'll be back?"
Patterson grinned.
"Don't matter. Guess who's on call tonight?"
Patterson kept his inane grin.
"The Professor!"
The other man began to feel sorry for Somersby if he ever came back later. Professor Carlson had a reputation for dealing with bullies in the most colourful and unique way. He shook his head as Patterson kept his smile.
"Then if he comes back, he's really up shit creek!"

The darkness of night was on the horizon and after a few hours of deliberation and walking down every street in the small village, Nova decided that the reduced light was the opportune time to make a very reluctant return to the Lodge hotel.

Time-Ryder: Powerstone Book One

He'd walked around the coastline, making his way back up through the village, past the pub and through the olive grove until he reached the hotel where the students had been billeted. Nova had watched a few too many spy movies, and stealthily moved up the drive to the Lodge hotel.

His feet crunched on the white pearl gravel and he looked in the front window, past the mulling crowd in the reception, but there in the distance, behind the large walnut desk he could see the tall, thin blonde image of the one he was trying desperately to avoid - Mrs Norman, the landlady.

He eased his hand around the large brass doorknob and slipped inside the front door, darting behind the hat-stand over-brimming with the dinner guests' coats.

Nova slipped off his boots and as soon as she ducked down behind the desk, he made his move, darting up the stairway before she could see him.

Quickly slamming his room door behind him, Nova put his back to it closed his eyes, sighing with relief.

"Good I've missed her!" he grinned wildly to which a rap at the door almost made his heart jump.

"Yes?" he shrieked in a squeaky high-pitched voice and then cleared his throat.

"Yes?" he said, his voice overcompensating and growing deeper than usual.

"It's me you idiot, let me in" said Brian's voice through the door, chuckling as usual.

Nova turned the key and eased the door open.

"It's alright; she's down in the bar!"

"You think that'll stop her?" Nova eyed him through the crack before letting him in.

"She's still got the master key. I've only survived because I propped up the backrest of the chair against the door. I've only been here one night and I think I've worn it out already!"

Brian smiled widely and shook his head.
"I don't get you Mitch, she's practically handing it to you on a plate!"
He threw himself onto the bed and stretched his hands out behind his head, relaxing, but feeling slightly smug about it all.
"Some of us have got our standards," Nova smiled and folded his jacket as he started undressing.
"Not you, you'll hump anything with a pulse!"
"I have my limits as well you know!" Brian scowled.
"And what about Brenda, eh? You kept that one a bit quiet. Wild-thing!" Nova sniggered and sang to the blushing young man.
"Wild thing, you make my heart sing, you make everything groovy..."
He was stopped by a flying boot, one of his own and he realised he had hit a nerve.
"I'm not that surprised really, she's been round the block a bit. Like a female version of you," scoffed Nova, his tongue in cheek.
"That's different. Brenda and I are on more of an intellectual level"
"You mean you're both as sexually depraved as each other!" Nova replied and slipped on a fresh shirt.
"I'd rather be sexually depraved than deprived. Why don't you come to the other pub with us? It's less than half a mile away and you don't have Mrs Norman to worry about!"
"It's us now?" Nova grinned and raised a brow.
"Yeah well I said Brenda could come with us. They've got a pool table!" Brian said, trying to tempt his friend even further.
"You really like her don't you?"
"What's not to like? She scrubs up not bad, she's got really amazing knockers and she looks like that Doctor from Star Trek," Brian was about to go in to detail when Nova held out his hands in protest.
"I don't want to know, you'll put me off that show for life!"

Time-Ryder: Powerstone Book One

"You could do with getting a little yourself. What about that Jess? She's a cracking bit of stuff," said Brian, slightly envious and everyone seemed to notice that Brian had been eyeing her beautiful figure avidly.

"Jess? Are you serious? She's like my best friend, we've know each other since we were twelve and I have just lost my girlfriend" shrieked Nova.

"Ex girlfriend Mitch, remember, she did dump your ass. I don't know why you chased after her? She always walked around like she had a stick up her ass and looked down her nose like she was better than everyone!"

"Of course you're saying this because she knocked you back!" scoffed Nova, "She did tell me you know!"

"What about that Jess, eh? She doesn't look at you like a friend!" Nova didn't know if his friend was serious or just winding him up and decided to change the subject.

"Are you going somewhere with all these ramblings Brian?"

"Of course; all the ramblings from my depraved mind always do," he paused for a minute, still trying to get Nova to agree. "There's a cracking barmaid with Ursula Undress looks," Brian smiled.

"It's Andress and don't play to my Bond fetish, you know I'm an Octopussy man!" drawled Nova.

"There you go thinking about something else again!" snorted Brian.

Nova threw a pillow at him and grinned inanely.

"Alright I'll come!" he finally gave in.

"Good!" Brian shot up from the bed and moved to the mirror, swishing aside his wave of blonde hair, "And we're leaving at Ten, so be down in the lobby sharp-ish"

"Eh, no thanks. I'll meet you at the bottom of the drive," objected Nova, "I just need to find out a way of slipping past Mrs Norman again. God I feel like I'm twelve years old, trying to sneak out of the bloody house!" he shrieked.

"You do that" smiled Brian, "and I'll see you later" he slipped quietly out of the door and Nova rolled his eyes.

"Why do I let him talk me into these things?" he whispered to himself and smiled inwardly.

Maybe a bit of rest was what he needed, a chance to think about something other than Barbara for a change and with Jess here, he wasn't going to be short of conversation.

A couple of taps on the door startled Nova again and he jumped out of his daze.

A croaky high-pitched voice called out from behind the door.

"Mr Mitchell. Are you in there?"

Nova's eyes went wide and he froze as the doorknob rattled and the door creaked open slowly.

"Remember to lock your door at night" croaked the voice again and Brian poked his head around the corner, grinning like an idiot.

Nova threw one of his muddy boots to the door and Brian retracted his head as the boot narrowly missed him.

"Ha bloody ha!" said Nova; his face full of thunder and then he saw the funny side and smiled.

He closed the door, took no second chances, slid the bolt over again and propped a chair securely under the doorknob.

Time-Ryder: Powerstone Book One

CHAPTER FOUR

Stumbling through the darkness to the gates leading up to the dig, a slightly unkempt figure bent over, fumbling nervously with a large circle of keys. A double-barrelled shotgun was bent over his arm as he turned over the keys, looking for the correct one to the lock.

With a gruff grunt of annoyance, he pulled out a torch from his long green coat and flipped the beam on, concentrating upon the lock. The sun was almost down and the deep red sky was burning with orange, the clouds in the distance forming a pattern of rays that meant the following day would most likely be better than today.

"Damned keys!" he retorted, "Why is it I can never find the right key on a cold night?" he said and rubbed his hands for warmth. He stopped again and produced a small hip flask to which he swigged with a disgusting slurp and put the flask away again. When he finally located the correct key, the lock opened and he pushed the large rusty iron gates inward.

"Bloody kids!" he murmured in a thick raspy voice, only happy when he was complaining.

"Little shits, you'll get both barrels if I catch you this time!" he gave warning, but it fell upon deaf ears.

The dig was silent, with the exception of the flapping tarpaulin caught by the wind and drawing his attention to the foot of the tower remains.

"Vandals, that's what you are. Bloody vandals!" he ranted into the air.

He pursed his lips and moved closer to the edge of the pit, but could see no damage from within the dark hole.

Then something caught his eye, a glimmering speck in the bottom of the pit. It was nothing solid, just the occasional flicker of colour bleeding in and out of existence.

"Wouldn't be so bad if they stole something" he grumbled and started to lower his body into the pit via the makeshift ladder that the students had already procured.

His curiosity was his downfall and he followed the glimmer down the uncovered steps, through the ragged wooden aperture until he landed safely upon the stone-flagged floor of the crypt. He knew that he shouldn't be in there, but he was intrigued by the light.

The light kept its constant flicker, beckoning him closer like an errant flame in the wind as Jenkins brought the torch-beam around and settled upon the carved stone sarcophagus dominating the centre of the room.

He saw that it was open and crept closer, his eyes following the flicker onward.

There was an icy chill making the hairs on the back of his neck stand erect, and a thin seam of sweat coursed down his back that made him shiver ever so slightly.

He approached the sarcophagus with caution, ever ready to use his trusty shotgun, should he be forced to, and he peered inside. Looking down into the darkness, his heart almost leapt from his chest as two white beams shone back and started moving slowly towards him.

Suddenly the beams took form and became clearer as they came into the light. A large bat flew from within the stone coffin, almost frightening him half to death to which he stumbled.

Tripping backwards, Jenkins crashed to the floor and the shotgun in his hand sounded off, hitting the ceiling and frightening the bat just as much as he was.

He had to laugh at himself as he rose from the floor and shook the centuries of cobwebs from his coat.

Eager to view within the realms of the sarcophagus again, he eased slowly to his feet and pointed the torch downward into the dark recess. He saw a set of stone steps and let his curiosity

enthral him once again, but caution told him to be weary and he stepped back from the Sarcophagus, leaving well alone.
Jenkins lumbered back up the steps to the cracked aperture and took a brief intake of air, before scanning the upper crypt with his torch again. Quickly reloading his shotgun as he gazed around the vast stone chamber; his vision finally settled upon the source of the flickering light.
Sitting squarely on the floor was the glass sphere, faint light ebbing from within, yet just enough to catch his eye.
But what was it?
More disturbing was the sight of a few dead rats surrounding it, rigid and almost statuesque.
"I thought they stowed all these valuables away at night?" he hissed in brief annoyance.
"Better put them safely in the porta-cabin," he murmured again.
"Archaeologists!" he spat, "just as bad as those kids, bloody students!"
He reached over and picked up the gleaming sphere, looking at it curiously as he straightened his back and turned back toward the stone steps.
Jenkins felt a slight tingle coming from the ball, but quickly forgot it as he ambled back up the steps to the fresh air outside.
Stepping out into the night air again, Jenkins pulled up the collar of his green coat, unfurling it to warm his neck from the chill.
He felt the tingle again, like a quick flash of electricity, but the surge was more powerful and intense this time.
Retracting his hand, he tried to drop the ball, but instead, he found that it was stuck to his palm. The sphere pulsed, making him wretch as he stumbled back towards the set of ladders.
His fingers reached out and he dropped the shotgun, making it go off again as it skidded down the stone steps below.
Jenkins was in pain, he felt a twinge of tightness and his free hand clawed up to his chest, his breathing becoming sparse as he

finally dropped to his knees and keeled over face first into the mud.

Jenkins was dead; his lifeless body devout of all warmth and energy, yet the sphere was once again filled with the richness of life. The blood-red illumination had returned to the sphere, although it was dimming fast.

After a few moments the glass ball released itself from his grip and lay close to his prone form, sinking into the muddy steps. The sphere had still not completed its task, but it had collected what energy it could from the dead groundskeeper, and it still wasn't enough.

But the night was still young and now that it was exposed to the world, there would soon be another curious victim close at hand. The pulsing of the sphere dimmed until it powered down and conserved what little it had taken from Jenkins broken body as he lay in the mud, his dead eyes staring out.

Looking over his brown-rimmed spectacles, Professor Carlson was investigating title deeds for the Baleran lands.

He had all manner of documents spread over the desk in his hotel room and he was determined to discover where this seemingly pristine document had come from.

Somersby's documents were his only claim to the estate; if it could be proved that they were genuine, and it was a task that the Professor was only too happy to invalidate.

Moving his magnifying-glass over the area of text, Henry muttered to himself and pulled out other documents, bearing the signature of the then Marquis of Ravayne.

He narrowed his eyes and looked at it curiously, finally flinging himself back into his chair with delight.

Time-Ryder: Powerstone Book One

"It's a forgery!" he exclaimed, "a very clever one though I'll grant you, they've got the correct parchment and ink, but Ravayne's signature doesn't match" he smiled again.
"I wonder what this Mr Somersby is up to?"
He lifted the phone receiver and started dialling, waiting for it to ring.
"Yes, put me through to Miss Raynor, its Henry Carlson; tell her I have some rather startling news."
He sat back in the chair again, a beaming smile spreading across his bearded face, to which he opened the desk drawer and plonked a bottle of Whisky upon the top.
"We'll show him what he can do with his injunction," he grinned.

Crossing to the bedside table, Nova collected up his phone, keys and other assortments before sliding on his shiny black pilot jacket.
He smoothed it down and smiled, taking pride in his appearance, which was more than he could say about Brian.
Rushing to the door, he opened it and ran straight into the bulky form of Professor Carlson, who knocked the impatient young man to the floor.
"Off out?"
Nova dusted down his clothes and reached up to the Professor's outstretched hand.
"I've got a date with a pool table and a pint. You?"
"I'm not entirely sure," said the old man oddly, "I'm supposed to check in on Mr Jenkins at Ten o' clock but he doesn't appear to be answering the site phone!"
"Maybe he's doing his rounds with the hound of the Baskervilles!" Nova joked.

Time-Ryder: Powerstone Book One

"No, the dogs gone to the vet" replied the Professor and then he shook his head.

"Maybe I'm just getting worried over nothing!"

"Well if it reassures you, I'll come with you if you want to check the dig" offered Nova. but the arrival of Jess at the top of the stairs told the old man that they'd already made arrangements and not one that he'd want to barge in on, especially if Jess could get to the bottom of all Nova's problems.

"You could join us if you like?" asked Jess, smiling sombrely at the old man.

Somehow Nova couldn't imagine his rotund frame balancing precariously over the pool table.

The Professor smiled back.

"No, I'll be fine. You two go and enjoy yourselves!" he smiled, trying to put a brave face upon the situation.

"Well if you change your mind, we'll be in the King's Rest down the road" Jess smiled and linked her arm through Nova's and ruffled her hair.

"Just a minute!" hissed Nova, cautiously poking his head out at the top of the staircase.

He could see the bustle of activity in the hallway and the distraction was the ideal opportunity for him to slip out quietly and avoid the unwanted attention of Mrs Norman.

He eased down the stairs cautiously, much to the amusement of Jess and the Professor.

"Nova, what are you doing?" Jess shrieked.

"Ssshhh! Not so loud!" he whispered, but the volume of Jess` voice was enough to distract Mrs Norman behind the front desk.

"Aww shit, she's seen us!" Nova closed his eyes.

She moved like lightning from behind the reception and approached them.

"What was that?" croaked Mrs Norman's voice.

74

Time-Ryder: Powerstone Book One

"I said that's a Venus" Nova turned to the statue at the bottom of the staircase, pointing out the lack of limbs on the Venus De Milo reproduction.

The Professor moved past him and accompanied the nosy landlady back to reception.

"Mrs Norman, I'll be back in a short while, just thought I'd turn in my room key for safekeeping" he smiled warmly.

Mrs Norman warmed to the old man, her thick white make up almost daring to crack as she tried to smile back at him.

She was tall, her blonde hair held up in a bun with a long trail hanging down her front, like a bad wig from the Madonna video with the cone-shaped boobs.

Her face was what Nova would call handsome, not an image of beauty like Jess, but not one that was totally repellent, her perfume did that for her.

She wore a tight fitting white jacket with high shoulder pads that looked as if it had been swiped off the set of Dynasty twenty years previously.

It seemed to Nova that she had hijacked a trowel from the local builder to apply the polyfilla thick foundation that was applied to her face, yet didn't hide all of which she wished.

"And you Mr Mitchell, anything I can do for you tonight?" her eyes were inviting and alight with desire, but Nova declined.

His face looked like a rabbit caught in the headlights of an oncoming vehicle.

"Fraid not Mrs Bates, I mean Mrs Norman" he stammered, "We're off to the King's Rest. You know, the one with the pool table!"

"Very good then" she said politely; albeit very disappointedly, "I'll see you when you return"

There was that disturbing twinkle in her eye again.

"Not if I see you first" he hissed, but the Professor heard him this time and capped his mouth to avoid a stray chuckle.

Time-Ryder: Powerstone Book One

"What was that?" clipped Mrs Norman.
"I said I'm dying of thirst. C'mon Professor let's go!"
Jess stepped out from behind Nova, her arm still linked through his. She smiled over at Mrs Norman who grimaced and threw daggers back in the direction of the young woman, but her eyes started to blink continuously as Jess narrowed her vision and stared back at the woman.
It was almost like a staring contest and Jess never faltered. After a few moments Mrs Norman lowered her head away from Jess' intimidating glare.
With a quick intake of breath, Jess turned her attention back to Nova and gave him a hearty smile.
"Come on Darling. We're going to be late," Jess teased, giving Nova a stray peck on the cheek before pulling him out of the main door.

As they left, a fuming Mrs Norman stepped into the small office behind the reception desk and looked to the small bald-headed man perched behind it, firmly holding his 2b pencil.
"See I told you we should have got a pool table!" she thundered and slapped his shoulder hard.
"Yes Dear" he looked to the floor, clearly giving in, and not for the first time.
Not one for giving up so easily, she returned to the reception desk with a grimace, eagerly awaiting young Mr Mitchell's return and drew out a long kitchen knife she'd concealed beneath her jacket.
Stowing it under the ledger beneath the counter; her face stiffened and she stared ahead to the main doors of the Lodge.

Time-Ryder: Powerstone Book One

Nova gasped and leaned back on the heavy green door of the hotel.
Jess laughed as she stood beside the Professor; who stopped in mid-stride, a cherubic smile creeping over his bearded face.
"Do you mind telling me what all that was about?"
Nova felt slightly embarrassed and he gulped. Having the audience of the Professor was bad enough, but with Jess to boot made him even more uncomfortable.
"When I arrived last night, I went for a shower and came back to find her curled up in my bed with not a stitch on!"
The Professor's grin turned into a gasp of disbelief.
"And then what happened? No forget that, I don't want to know!"
Jess grinned.
"What do you think happened? I swapped rooms with Derek, but that hasn't stopped her from trying," Nova felt a weight off his mind telling someone.
Jess laughed and she growled jokingly at him, clawing her nails into the air.
"You animal!"
"That's not funny, I nearly was her dinner last night, and afters" he spat.
The Professor smiled and thrust his hands deeply into the pockets of his tweed coat.
"Oh the joys of impetuous youth" he smiled and started off up the hill.
"Don't get me wrong, she's not a bad looking woman" shrieked Nova, "I just don't fancy signing up with the wrinkly brigade. No offence!"
"None taken!" said the old man softly, still clearly amused by the young man's predicament.
As they walked up the hill to the fork in the road they parted company with the Professor.

Jess walked arm in arm with Nova, totally relaxed for the first time in what seemed forever.

"Thanks Jess!" said Nova warmly and he gave her an enriched smile.

"What for?" she said surprisingly.

"I've needed this, a bit of time to enjoy myself again!" he replied and she gave him a hug, showing how much he meant to her with a peck on his cheek again.

"Well the night is very young!" she gave him a smile and tugged him onward.

There was a faint breeze in the air as they walked down the country lane brimming with trees, all beginning to shed their leaves in preparation for autumn.

A chill came over Jess and she clung close to Nova, hugging him tighter than ever.

Nova stopped and Jess' perpetual grin dropped as she saw his worried look.

"What's wrong?"

"I dunno, maybe I'm feeling a bit guilty about letting him to go up to the site alone. Do you think we should go after him?"

"Leave him be. He can manage by himself. He said he'll call if he needs our help" she smiled again, "C'mon."

"Aye, but even so..." said Nova worriedly.

"Look, we'd better get a move on if we're to catch up with your friends!"

Nova caved in and walked on with Jess. He had an unusual feeling and it wasn't going to settle until he knew the Professor was going to be all right.

"Nova come on, he can take care of himself, you deserve a night off" she urged. Maybe she was right; after all the Professor would call if things got too much for him.

Nova joined arms with Jess again and grinned at her as they strode off down the road to the King's Rest.

Time-Ryder: Powerstone Book One

CHAPTER FIVE

The dig was in darkness as the Professor strolled up to the massive iron gates, noting they had been left open. The floodlights and security measures that should have been in place were non-existent and the worried old man took a step backward, not daring to confront anyone that may be lurking within the dark compound.
He wasn't frightened, but wasn't exactly a spring chicken and should there be anyone roaming around the site, just as the previous night, he wouldn't be able to handle it alone.
Quickly slipping his hand inside his tweed coat, he pulled out a slender black mobile phone and pressed a button, shoving it up to his ear.

When Nova and Jess appeared at the top of the road, Brian couldn't take his eyes off the sight of Nova's curly haired companion. Although he was holding tightly onto Brenda, it almost seemed as if the small redhead was practically invisible.
"Don't think I can't see you looking at her" scoffed Brenda, "look at her, Miss kinky knickers!"
Brian's face curled into a smile.
"At least she's wearing knickers!"
"Cheeky bastard, I am wearing knickers!" replied Brenda, gobby as ever and slapping his arm.
"Jealous much?" said Brian smugly.
She planted a kiss on his cheek.
"Just remember to look and don't touch, or you'll find I've got another use for my manicure set!"
From the top of the road Nova and Jess could see both of them under the row of olive trees, taking shelter from the faint flurry of rain that was starting to fall.

Time-Ryder: Powerstone Book One

Jess held onto Nova tightly.
"There they are!" she hissed reservedly.
"Just give them a chance. You might like them, well him.
Brenda's sort of a law unto herself."
Jess pursed her lips.
"I'll try, but if he tries to look up my skirt again, I'll floor him where he stands!"
"Unless Brenda gets to him first," Nova chuckled.
She gave a smile of contentment as they joined the others by the olive grove.
"Ready?" asked Nova.
Brian smiled, bearing his white teeth.
"Jess, looking lovely as ever" he said charmingly. Brenda poked him in the ribs and gave Jess a disapproving stare.
Brian pulled the main door of the King's Rest and entered the pub, taking off his jacket and putting it on the tall hat-stand; which proceeded to fall over from the unbalanced added weight. He quickly picked it up and draped the jacket back over his arm as he approached the bar, trying to look cool and collected as he made himself at home.
"Look at him, like he's won the lottery. You must be doing something right," Nova looked at Brenda.
She adjusted her top and stuck out her heaving bosom.
"Some of us have got it," she hissed, looking Jess up and down before moving off to join Brian at the bar.
Jess' jaw dropped.
"Hark at her, cheeky mare!"
"Don't worry about it. You're much better looking than her Jess. She knows it, that's her problem," Nova smiled, "Drink?"
"Em, yes" she stuttered at the compliment.
She'd known Nova for so long that if she didn't know any better, she'd swear he was flirting with her.

80

Nova made off to the bar and stepped away from the main door.
It was a different pub from the Lodge hotel, more intimate, cosy
and the large open coal fire in the main lounge made him want to
park himself beside it and toast some bread like he used to do
with Aunt Rose at home in Riverdale.
He looked to the exposed brickwork, the rows of old books lining
the shelves and the dark panelled wooden walls.
It reminded him of one of those swanky theme pubs in the big
cities with lots of junk plastered about precariously to make it
look authentic, but in this case it probably was the real thing.
His eyes led him over to the raised floor on the far side of the
room where the pool table was situated and Brian ever at the
ready was racking up as if he were getting ready for war.
He smiled in Brian's direction and turned back to the bar where,
true to his word Brian hadn't lied about this one.
The rather dishy barmaid currently serving had a cleavage that
would serve as a more than ample floatation device had she been
onboard the Titanic.

"Drink?" Nova asked again.

"Yeah, I'll have a coke!" replied Jess.

"Lightweight!" he retorted with a grin.

"Alright, I'll have a Bacardi and coke. I'll just pop to the loo" she
said with a smile and quickly sauntered off into the corner.

Nova shook his head and looked across the bar to the beaming
barmaid.

"Richard O'Sullivan" she smiled cheerily.

"Excuse me?" narrowed Nova.

"Your ringtone, your phone is ringing, 'Man about the house'
isn't it?" she commented on his chosen ring-tone.

"Oh Yeah" he smiled absently.

"A pint of Lager and a Bacardi and coke please, and one for
yourself!" he handed over the crisp Twenty and plucked the

phone from his pocket and held it open in his best Captain Kirk pose.

"Hello?" he stepped through the doors to listen as Brian had just piled a handful of tokens into the jukebox and it almost deafened him.

"Mr Mitchell, It's me" it was the Professor's voice, *"that offer of help would come in very handy right about now if you don't mind me intruding on your night"* he said, his voice clearly out of breath. It was hard for him to hear the Professor's voice, so he gave a quick answer.

"No probs Professor. I'm on my way!" he clicked the phone off and put it away in frustration at the noise.

Catching Brian's attention, he beckoned him closer.

"What? You're not leaving already? We just got here. I wanted to show you my new moves!" said his friend with a beaming grin.

"They're wasted on me Brian, use them on Brenda, I'm sure she'll appreciate them a lot better!" smiled Nova.

"Look I've got to nip out to help the Professor with something, tell Jess I won't be too long!"

Before he had a chance to object; Nova sped out of the door quickly, leaving Brian lusting over the delectable barmaid.

The Professor stood by the main gates pacing frantically.
He was worried.
The King's Rest was only a few minutes away, but he continued pacing until Nova showed up, clearly out of breath and he leaned over; his hands resting on his knees.

"You sounded urgent!" he wheezed.

"The main gates have been left open and all of the floodlights are out," answered the old man.

Time-Ryder: Powerstone Book One

"And you're sure it's not just another break-in?" Nova stepped forward the large iron gates and examined the padlock that was still looped around the large chain, although not fastened.
"Not a break-in then?"
"Just tread carefully Mr Mitchell, whoever it is may still be here!"
Nova stopped in mid-stride.
"I thought we just established that it wasn't a break-in?"
The Professor scratched his beard nervously.
"That doesn't rule out the possibility of someone coming in after Mr Jenkins opened the gates!"
"You've got a point there" Nova mused, stepping into the compound, "didn't you think about phoning the Police?"
"I would have, but it seems my credit has expired, I used my last to call you!"
"I've told you before about keeping that thing topped up, what if something was to happen. Like Aunt Rose said it's always handy to keep a spare fifty pence for the meter" hissed the young man.
"Do you want to call them?"
Nova smiled, showing that his interest was aroused.
"Maybe just a quick look, eh?"
He stepped into the compound, broken shards of glass crunching under his feet and a slight smell of burning plastic wafting under his nose. He sniffed and looked around, leading the Professor up to the porta-cabin.
Nova paused and his hand clasped around the door handle.

Settled nicely at the bar, having consumed Nova's pint, Brian pocketed the change while gazing heavenly down the cleavage of the barmaid, with Brenda sitting next to him.
She slapped his arm and stirred him out of his daze.
"Am I just an ornament here?" she snapped.

"Sorry!" said Brian dreamily, "don't often see big.... optics like these" he smiled as the barmaid made her way to the other side of the bar to collect up the empty glasses.
Brenda smiled
"Well keep your eyes off her...optics or you'll be in Stevie Wonder's Braille group by the time I'm finished with you."
The door to the ladies room eased open and Jess straightened her jacket as she rolled up to the bar beside the others, looking all around her, immediately alerted by her companion's absence.
"Where's Nova?"
"Oh, he said something about nipping out for a minute, I wasn't paying much attention to be honest" Brian returned.
She could see from his gaze that he was still eyeing up the barmaid.
"Grab a stool, he won't be long!"
"He wouldn't have just gone, what happened?" urged Jess.
Brenda wolfed into the bowl of crisps.
"He got a call!"
"Did he say who from? Come on Brian it's important!"
He shirked his shoulders.
"He just shot out of here like there were flames coming out of his ass."
"How long?" hissed Jess.
"Eh, I dunno. A few minutes, just after you went in the bog!" he grunted. Brenda smiled at him.
"You've got such a way with words!"
"Damn!" cursed Jess. She bolted to the door and almost pulled it from its hinges as she flew through like a mad woman.
Jess rushed outside the King's Rest, looking all around her as the faint beginnings of a shower of rain made themselves felt.
"It must have been Uncle Henry; it couldn't have been anyone else!"
She pulled out her phone and started walking back up the hill.

"That means he's gone to the dig!"
She touched the strange looking pad on her mobile and watched as the blue neon lights flashed all around the device, expanding the casing as it morphed into a slightly larger black device, still illuminating with life.
She put the device up to her ear and her face straightened.
"It's Jess," she sighed "We have a problem!"

Time-Ryder: Powerstone Book One

Time-Ryder: Powerstone Book One

CHAPTER SIX

It was a warm night, but a faint chill in the air made Professor Carlson curl up his collar as he crept behind Nova into the compound.
Nova's hand faltered on the door handle, and to his surprise it swung open with ease, revealing the bleak interior.
"Shouldn't that be locked?" said the young man softly, his eyes going to all corners of the room.
"And the floodlights should still be on!" returned the Professor. He moved up behind Nova and hesitated in the doorway.
"One lock perhaps, but two? That's no coincidence, and no sign of forced entry!"
"What are you? C.S.I. Riverdale?" Nova squinted.
"Only stating the obvious!" replied the old man.
"Right then Sherlock, what do you make of this?"
Nova flipped on the light-switch and was surprised when the room lit up. He looked out of the window, noting the shattered glass at the foot of every floodlight.
"Pretty expensive repair job" he muttered, "whatever caused it must have shorted out the system!" he looked over the debris.
"Maybe an external power surge" said the Professor.
He looked around for clues, like an errant detective trying to spot the cause, if indeed there was one.
Reaching inside one of the desk drawers, he produced a torch and tossed it to Nova, collecting another for himself.
Flipping the beam on, it danced around the floor and he stepped back into the compound.
"Weird!" said Nova softly, following closely behind the old man. He trained the beam upon the shattered glass.
"Weird?" asked the old man.
"If it was a power surge then the cabin lights wouldn't be working either. Did you check to see if all of the stuff we pulled

Time-Ryder: Powerstone Book One

out of the crypt was still there?"
Inhaling almost prematurely, the Professor re-entered the cabin and knelt down to the cupboard doors, unlocking them and making a quick inventory.
"Everything is still here, maybe not in the correct place, but all here as far as I can see."
"Would you say that someone's had a good rummage?" hissed Nova. He saw the old fashioned pistol on top of the table and studied it as the Professor guided his torch over the walls.
Nova stowed the pistol in his pocket for safe-keeping as he moved over to join the old man.
"Are you listening to me? A good rummage I said!" repeated the young man.
"Sorry, that would be one way to describe it!" said the Professor, wheezing as he climbed to his feet.
"Then they didn't find what they were looking for!" smiled Nova, "Why don't we check the pit?"
He rushed off before the Professor had time to object as the old man bumbled on behind him.
"They who?" asked the Professor.
"Whoever broke in, it can't be a coincidence two nights running, surely? He, she, they, damn, I never thought that there could be more than one of them!" muttered Nova.
As they reached the hole, the sound of the wind became more apparent as the tarpaulin flapped freely from the edge of the pit and clearly exposed what lay beneath.
Professor Carlson took an overlooking posture and rubbed his eyes, taken back by what he had found.
"Mr Mitchell, come here" he hissed softly in hesitation.
Nova stopped dawdling and brought the circlet of light over the edge of the deep pit.
There he saw the groundskeeper; his crumpled body resting in the mud on the half exposed stairs.

Nova immediately leapt into the hole, his fingers operating with lightning reflexes and checking the man's pulse.
He looked up to the Professor with a forlorn look of dismay and shook his head. The Professor slowly lowered himself into the hole beside Nova and began examining the body in closer detail. Rifling through the man's hair for signs of a wound or abrasion, Nova cringed at touch of his greasy hair.
"Bit too late for head & shoulders now mate," he hissed dryly, "no sign of a bang on the head and no marks on his face as far as I can see!"
"And no sign of a struggle either" commented the old man.
Nova straightened up beside him.
"We're overlooking the possibility that he's just been dumped in here," he said and cringed, realising that he was starting to sound like the Professor.
"But why?"
"You only have to look at him to see that. He's got a face like a welder's bench. See that scar down his cheek," answered the young man.
"He could have got that anywhere" spat the Professor, "but regardless of how colourful a life he might have led, no one deserves to die like that, all alone!"
"I suppose, but he's here now, what do we do about him?"
Nova shone the torch over the body, noting the man's drenched clothes and then something caught his eye.
A small glimmer resting under the mud, half exposed to the light of his torch-beam.
"What's this?" he looked down to the object embedded in the mud.
"Perhaps we should leave all this to the police, all this is effectively a crime scene!" said the old man softly, kneeling closer to the object.
Nova smirked, still eyeing the glimmer.

Time-Ryder: Powerstone Book One

"If this is a crime scene as you say, then all of this will no doubt end up in the back of some forensic filing cabinet until it's long forgotten!"

"That's a bit cynical," hissed the Professor.

Nova shook his head.

"Not cynical, just realistic!"

"What do you suppose he was doing down here?" Nova stepped carefully, trying his best to avoid treading upon any vital clues.

"Perhaps he heard something. I think he was being a little more cautious than usual, especially after the break in last night, in fact he was a little more than embarrassed by it," replied the old man waving the torch-beam around.

Nova smiled up at the Professor.

"Do you want to take a quick look? Seeing as we're here!"

The old man gave an excited smile and followed Nova through the broken aperture and down the few steps into the crypt.

"It's not so smelly in here now!" he remarked and waved his torch around carelessly.

Mr Patterson's team had been quite meticulous in their clean up, having removed all of the human remains, but for some reason they'd overlooked the half open stone sarcophagus that was the focus of the centre of the room.

Maybe it was the smell that had dissuaded them, or not relishing the idea of having the leftovers in the dinner tent. Their loss was the Professor and Nova's find as both archaeologists spied the elevated casket and moved in for a closer look.

"Hello, what have we here?" smiled the Professor.

The circle of light hovered over the open sarcophagus and he scurried over like an excited child, pointing the beam into the depths.

"A set of steps, that's weird!" Nova looked down into the sarcophagus.

"And not common for fifteenth century architecture!" hissed the Professor, "Maybe they were trying to hide something!"
"Or someone?" Nova added and looked at the Professor's confused expression.
"Well it is a crypt," scoffed Nova, "You know grave robbers and all that. Not exactly Burke and Hare I know but maybe there's something else down here that they didn't want anyone to get their hands on."
"Indeed, but it wasn't only the Egyptians that buried their valuables with their dead" commented the old man.
"Shall we take a look?"
Nova raised a brow.
"Aye, but if there's rats, I'm outta there!" he smiled, but the Professor knew he wasn't joking. For someone who chose to dig things up for a living, he was afraid of most insects and things with more legs than himself. Thankfully he hadn't seen the dead ones littered around them.
"Well, you can go first, I don't want to get stuck down there if you wedge the opening!" said Nova waiting patiently.
"I've lost four pounds this month thank you!" returned the old man with a stern gaze.
Professor Carlson smiled back and climbed over the edge, where he started to lower his frame into the stone coffin and he descended the steps into a much larger chamber below.

Outside in the main compound, a glow of torch light wandered over the ground as the source searched around the dig, slowly moving closer to the pit that led to the crypt.
Holding the torch up to his line of sight while he climbed precariously into the pit, the newcomer's face was lit up.
Somersby dropped onto the muddy surface and turned the beam

towards the broken aperture, scanning the area inside, before lowering himself into the crypt.

"So this is where you hid it MacEran!" he hissed, "Very clever, even for an old fool!" he drawled and moved over to the sarcophagus, listening to the echoing voices coming from below.

Following the old man down, Nova emerged into the enclosure and he looked around for anything out of character with the place.

The chamber was dark, although had a slight blue tinge and the Professor looked around, trying to see where the source of light was coming from.

His torch-beam settled on the walls where a set of intricate carvings stood out to him.

"What are they?" Nova asked, "They look a bit familiar!"

"Celtic runes" said the old man squinting at the walls, "it's a different alphabet to the one I'm familiar with, but some of the characters are the same"

"What does it say?"

The Professor scratched his beard and looked down his nose, squinting at the carved wall.

"It's a warning of sorts. I can't make out the last part, but. Oh heavens no…"

"What is it?"

"It's part of a prophecy about something called the Sphere of Ancients, something about its touch releasing a demon to ravage the world!"

Nova winced.

"Does it say what this Sphere looks like?"

"Spherical from the description" said the Professor glibly.

Time-Ryder: Powerstone Book One

"Oh you really are on top form today" drawled Nova looking around the crypt, "well there's nothing else down here, maybe we should go back up and decide what to do about Mr Jenkins."
The Professor gave him a solemn look and nodded in agreement, gazing around the walls as he followed the young man back up to the upper crypt.
He tripped over something on the ground and knelt to pick it up. It was Jenkins shotgun and the barrel was still warm.
Nova's gaze met the Professor's.
"It's been fired!" he hissed alarmingly.
Taking the weapon in a pincer grip, the old man took a last look around the interior.
"Fascinating discovery" he hissed to himself, still in awe of the building, but Nova had already gone elsewhere, removing his presence to the steps leading upward.

Sensing their return to the upper crypt, Somersby flipped off his torch and took position behind the sarcophagus, squeezing his thin frame down into the smallest of gaps. He crouched down as they both emerged from the lower part of the crypt.
"That smell is no better than this afternoon!" moaned Nova as he flipped over the edge onto the stone floor.
The Professor followed suit and they both came into the fresh air and their excited mood became a sullen one at the sight of Jenkins twisted frame once again.
Nova's attention was quickly grabbed by the embedded glimmer in the mud by the corpse and he knelt to take a closer look.
Puffing as he came out of the crypt behind Nova, the Professor narrowed at the young man and laid the shotgun down beside its owner.

Time-Ryder: Powerstone Book One

The Professor pointed to the object beneath the mud that had gripped the young man's attention so vividly.
"What is that?"
"I dunno" smirked Nova, "maybe it's some middle-age ashtray or something" he smirked and scooped the object out of the mud with a stray piece of wood and he began cleaning it off.
"Really Mr Mitchell, that's the kind of comment I expect from Mr Wilde" the Professor frowned in displeasure and squinted closer.
"It looks like a sceptre without the cross!" replied Nova.
"Or a Sphere?" said the old man alarmingly.
"It wouldn't look anything like this surely?" objected Nova, "I was half expecting something bigger."
As the Professor bent closer to have a better look at the sphere, he saw that his torch-beam was dimming and becoming somewhat redundant. He narrowed at the torch and shook it profusely in annoyance.
"I told Patterson to keep these things charged up at all times!" he rasped.
"Well if it makes you feel any better mine is just as bad!" said Nova, watching the light dim and an increasing red hue began to spread from the sphere on the ground.
The old man switched off his torch as the red glow soon encapsulated their vision.
He looked to Nova and the young man leaned over to pick it up, making the glow increase even more so as he got nearer.
"The warning did say not to touch it!"
"Come on, it's an old wives tale meant to scare the kids" voiced Nova, "it's not as if Beelzebub himself is going to put in a guest appearance is he? I mean half of Nostradamus' prophecies did turn out to be nonsense."
But he was cautious and listened to the old man for once.

Time-Ryder: Powerstone Book One

The Professor smiled, coming forward to see the glowing sphere more closely. He flipped the torch back on, amazed that it had full power again, if only for a few seconds.

"There are markings around the side" he shone the torch closer and the sphere started to emit a low whine, accompanying the dim red hue with a dull sound.

The Professor shot backward in shock.

"Do that again!" said Nova softly, his eyes widening.

The old man brought the circlet of light closer to the sphere and watched as the light began to shine brighter, sapping all the energy from the battery cells of the torch.

"It looks like there's something inside!"

"What? Like an egg?" Nova retracted, holding back, but his eyes were dazzled by the illuminating aura coming from the sphere, "or is it solar-powered or something?"

Professor Carlson nodded,

"That may be a roundabout way of putting it, yes!" he stood up and took a breath, "just leave it for a moment. Let me think."

Nova knew what the old man had said about the events surrounding Jenkins death, but he wasn't going to take any chances, and still he looked at the sphere, hypnotically drawn to it. He began to rise from the ground when the sphere suddenly moved.

"Did you see that?" Nova blinked.

He dipped his head closer in curiosity and the sphere shot from the ground involuntarily, leaping into his open hand and securing its outer shell to Nova's palm.

It started burrowing into his skin as if welding the glass shell to him.

"Get it off!" screamed Nova, "It's stinging!"

With the sphere attached to his hand, it started to glow brighter, a louder whine emitting from its body, piercing outward as the clouds above the dig started to darken and swirl.

Time-Ryder: Powerstone Book One

The Professor looked from the startled young man to the area above, hearing the thunderous sounds of the clouds crashing and shifting overhead.

The rain started to descend heavier, drenching the two men as the Professor stepped closer, his fingers reaching out to prise the sphere from Nova's grasp, but upon his touch, the sphere magnetically linked itself to the old man, just as it had done with Nova.

The radiance grew brighter; the whistling-whine louder and the area all around them started to fill with the expanding red light from the sphere.

Nova winced; his eyes slit-like and he felt the pain grow within his head. His body was weak, drained and numb from whatever the glass ball was doing to him, but his only concern was the old man opposite, bearing much of the same pain as he was.

"Switch it off!" wailed the Professor, screaming above the oscillating sound.

"I can't, I don't know how!" cried Nova.

The energy that the ball had absorbed from their bodies turned into light and spiralled upward in waves, channelling into the skies and creeping through the parting clouds and torrents of rain that lashed down upon them.

Much as Nova and the Professor tried to gaze upward, their eyes were pulled away by the cascading torrents.

Running through the village, Jess panted for breath as she stormed on towards the crossroads.

She stopped for the visible traffic and glanced up at the sky, seeing the strange aura of colour opening up the black clouds way above the archaeology dig.

"Shit!" she cursed and looked onward; her face so stern and gaunt, yet so concentrated and determined.

Time-Ryder: Powerstone Book One

As the traffic lights stopped her, Jess tore past them, stopping the cars with a screech as she made for the dig, running as fast as she could, hopefully before it was too late.

The clouds above continued to swirl, parting and making way for the rising light that crept on ever upward.
The rain continued to fall, cascading heavier and in the calamity, a whirlwind was born.
The tornado of sorts was slower and focussed on the singular point of the dig, more importantly upon the two men who were ensnared by the glass sphere and its unearthly attraction to them.
The light from the sphere bled out.
It flowed from its shell and fed upward to the clouds, stabilising the vortex that appeared above their heads.
As soon as the sphere had absorbed enough power from both men, a solid beam projected from the glass ball and spat upward, ripping through the remaining clouds with such force and severity.
The tornado turned slowly and both men watched the events as if time seemed to crawl by.
Nova looked at the Professor, who stood back just as frightened as the young man was.
They began to feel a pulling sensation, gripping their skin, their essence and finally their bodies.
With an abrupt flash of red energy, culminating in a singular blast of red light, the site was once more reduced to darkness.
All that was left was the desolate archaeological dig with the dead form of the groundskeeper's body firmly ensconced on the muddied steps, his dead eyes staring right ahead.

Time-Ryder: Powerstone Book One

Through the aftermath of the tornado, Jess rushed into the dig. The rain had gone, the wind and swarming clouds had all dispersed and the sky was clear once again.

Jess looked around the area of destruction, the broken glass, twisted gates and debris strewn all over from what had been fallout from the tornado.

There was no sign of Nova or the Professor, only the slightly muddied handkerchief that she had given Nova on the cliff-top. She picked it up with a worried look and pulled out a long black device from her coat.

Jess held it up to her ear and waited with a heavy exhalation of breath

"It's me!" she said gruffly with an air of disappointment, "I'm too late, it's already happened!"

She paused and looked around the site, her face wrought with anguish.

"No it couldn't be helped; I already told you what he was like. No matter what plans you put in place, it was always going to happen, I couldn't have prevented it," she shouted and shook her head.

"No way, we had a deal. I've done my part and made sure he was safe."

She closed the black device abruptly and shoved it in her jacket as she strode away from the site and through the twisted iron gates, leaving the dig empty once again.

She took a last saddened look backward with remorse and the faint beginnings of a tear began to roll down her unblemished cheek.

Jess took a breath and exhaled softly.

"Well Nova, you've done it now. I only hope you're prepared for what's to come!" she hissed softly and began to walk away towards the open gates and stopped in her tracks, lifting her hands up in front of her.

She felt a slight tingle and her eyes widened as she turned her palms in towards her.

"No, you can't!" she shrieked to the air, "It's not fair. You can't do this to me!"

Before her very eyes, Jess watched the tips of her fingers turn a burnt gold colour and start to shimmer in the air and fizzle into ash, her essence blowing away in the wind and bleeding into nothingness as her screams faded away with it.

Once the surrounding disturbance had cleared and the site was once again empty, a scrape of shifting wood sounded off and a few scraps of debris were thrown aside as Lord Somersby emerged from the crypt.

His scowling face showed that he was not best pleased and he made every effort to escape from the pit as fast as he could.

Taking out a handkerchief, he dusted down his hands and made for the gates before anyone else turned up.

And the archaeology dig was silent once more.

The waiting was finally over and the sphere had completed its task, but for Nova and the Professor it was only the beginning and it was about to change their lives forever.

Time-Ryder: Powerstone Book One

Time-Ryder: Powerstone Book One

CHAPTER SEVEN

Prising his eyes open, Nova Mitchell saw a blurry haze of whiteness surrounding him. His eyes were stinging and his ears were still hearing the oscillating whine that accompanied the flashing that came from the glass sphere. It began to lower to a dull thump until it diminished completely and his head returned to normal or as normal as he supposed it should be.

His head pounded severely and if he didn't know any better he'd swear that it was the after effects of an all night bender with his friend Brian, but at least then he would have had something that would alleviate a hangover. The after effects of this event left him confused and disorientated as he opened his eyes and squinted at the white glare all around him.

It was a white void; no significant marking that would indicate something familiar and definitely not the walls of a hospital as he had first thought. He motioned as if to speak, but his throat was a little tender and nothing came out.

Aside from his throat, Nova's chest ached with every movement. It too was tender, as if he had over-exerted his body and was now feeling the repercussions of his actions, but this was not the case as Nova's memory of the events leading up to his awakening was all too clear, even if the details were a little hazy. Wherever this was; Nova wasn't too happy about it.

If only he could gain the strength to rise from the smooth floor, then he could ascertain where he was, but his limbs were numb; the stabbing tingle of pins and needles coursing through them. Still lying face-down on the floor, Nova's blinked.

His face felt cold, icy cold.

His jaw was numb and then as he tried to move, he felt the sensation coming back to his body and there was the sudden realisation that he was flat out on a slab of pure ice.

Time-Ryder: Powerstone Book One

The ice was almost perfect, glistening like glass and it seemed to stretch on forever; or as far as his bleary vision would go.

It took him a pained few minutes to move, but as he strained to sit upright, he gazed around his surroundings and realised that he was inside a cave of sorts.

The rugged grey walls were tinged with faint trappings of snow, cascading down from an open gap in the ceiling above them.

The dark sky was devoid of any clouds; only the majestic pin lights of the stars beaming down.

Nova could hear a gale howling, swirling torrents of beautiful whiteness above him.

He had no idea how long the snowfall had been going on for, but his clothes were slightly damp and he patted the excess amount of flakes from his sleeve, wiping the dampness off his black trousers.

His first thought on coming around was the Professor.

Quickly looking around the cavern, he saw an irregular lump close to the farthest wall, moving slightly and it looked as if the snow-covered ground was breathing, slowly moving up and down.

But upon second glance, he noticed that it was the Professor's rotund frame; his body adorned by a fine layer of snow, covering up his rather battered checked suit.

It took much effort, but Nova rose to his feet and stumbled as the feeling slowly returned to his legs and he clambered drunkenly over the icy floor to where the Professor lay.

"Professor, are you all right?" he panicked, trying to rouse the old man.

He swept aside a layer of snow from the Professor's frame, almost as if he were unearthing another rare find.

The old man stirred with a groan as he emerged from his enforced slumber.

"Easy now Mr Mitchell, I'm not quite dead yet!" said the old man with a strained groan. Nova closed his eyes over in relief and rolled him over onto his back.

"Oh thank god! You scared the crap out of me" he exhaled, "How're you feeling?"

The old man removed his glasses that were frozen over and he sat up slowly. He blinked and started to clean them, peering through slit-like eyes at the concerned Nova.

"A blinder of a headache and a rather sore throat." he rubbed his windpipe and looked to the young man.

"And you?"

"The same; and a hell of a sore chest, as if Vanessa Feltz has been using me as a space hopper!" replied Nova, rubbing his aching chest profusely.

Professor Carlson put his glasses back on and looked at his surroundings, flicking stray specks of snow from his sleeves.

"And why am I covered in snow of all things?"

Nova pointed upward to the gaping orifice in the cavern ceiling where a faint powder trickled down.

"Do you think that the ground might have given way and we're inside the Eran mountain or something?" asked Nova, equally as confused as the Professor.

The old man shook his head.

"That wouldn't account for the snow, and the temperature down here is decidedly different from where we were at the dig!"

"Then how do you explain it?" narrowed Nova.

For the first time the answers eluded him and the Professor simply shrugged.

"I can't!" he waved his hands in the air and struggled to get up, puffing with every move.

And then he saw the object of their predicament

Resting under the blanket of snow on the icy floor was the source of all their problems.

Time-Ryder: Powerstone Book One

The glass sphere sat with the red indicator still flashing and still showing some resemblance of life, although now its power appeared to be waning and the light was receding rapidly.

"It has to be this!" pointed the old man, "there can be no other feasible explanation for it."

He moved to inspect it and cautiously; Nova tugged at the back of his jacket.

"Careful!"

The old man grinned and knelt to pick up the ball, carefully turning it over in his hands.

He screamed aloud to the air for a brief second and then his gaping mouth curled into a smile, and he tossed the gleaming ball in Nova's direction. The young archaeologist caught it and felt nothing; comparing it to the first time he'd felt it in his palm. He looked around and saw the Professor's inane grin staring back.

"That's not funny" Nova hissed, "You nearly gave me a heart attack!"

The Professor stood up, clearly amused and shook the rest of the snow from his clothes.

"Feel anything?"

Nova shook his head.

"Nope, it's dead now, nothing like what I felt when I first touched it."

"Just as I thought!" the Professor nodded, his mind already working overtime.

"In some way it must have extracted all of the necessary energy it needed to complete its programmed task and now it appears to have ceased functioning."

"I'm not following you" said Nova echoing the Professor's earlier words. He narrowed his brow, equally as confused to the explanation as he was to their new surroundings.

Time-Ryder: Powerstone Book One

"You remember the torch?" began the Professor.

He crossed to Nova and took the sphere from him.

"Remember how the light inside the ball grew when the torch came closer to it!"

"Aye, like it was draining the power from it. I felt the same when I touched it, like it was draining me. I felt totally exhausted after it and then I woke up here," he looked all around the icy cavern.

The old man nodded in agreement.

"Precisely, and I think that's what caused poor Mr Jenkins to die so suddenly!"

"Come again?"

"The sphere fed on him just as it did with you. It was only when I touched upon the ball that the sky seemed to come alive," sighed the old man, "the extra body heat generated from me seemed to enable it to finish its task. I suspect that Mr Jenkins struggled with the pain of the energy loss and collapsed as a result," the old man gasped and scratched his nose.

"Perhaps some mild form of a stroke or heart attack led to his death!"

"Aye but that still doesn't explain where we are. Does it?" Nova nodded. The old man looked around the bleak rugged walls for answers, or any form of inspiration.

"That I don't know, but I wouldn't be at all surprised if this place has some form of military applications to it," replied the Professor.

"What makes you think that?"

"This has experiment written all over it, confined space, lack of memory and it appears that we're the guinea pigs," snorted the old man. Nova grinned and thrust his hands in his pockets.

"There you go with your conspiracy theories again!" he scoffed and then turned curiously to the Professor.

"I thought you were the one who didn't make assumptions about people."

105

Time-Ryder: Powerstone Book One

"There are certain exceptions!" smiled the Professor, "although I'm not entirely sure if this warrants being one of them."
"You think this might be some sort of military base, and that thing knocked us out?"
"It's only a theory, but not one that should be discounted just yet!" he put the ball into his coat pocket, "the government are always involved in covert practices, I don't see how this can't simply be another one of them" declared the old man.
"Some of us look more like a guinea pig than others" retorted Nova with a smile and puffed out his cheeks.
Blushing slightly, the Professor closed his coat and buttoned it tight, trying his best to suck in his stomach.
"These constant aspersions towards my weight are becoming increasingly tiresome Mr Mitchell!"
"But you're such an easy target" Nova smiled and waved his hands out in the air.
"Well, we certainly won't find any answers languishing around here will we?" he replied and gave the young man a stern glare.
Nova looked at the dark passage that was their only exit except for the open ceiling above them and he gulped.
"You don't seriously want to go in there do you?"
"Well the answers certainly won't come to us Mr Mitchell, will they?" the Professor raised a brow and started off enthusiastically.
"Suppose not!" resigned the young man with a frown, "but..."
The Professor beamed and shirked aside the young man's fears.
"Come on then, a brisk walk will soon bring back our circulation and the exercise will do you the world of good."
Resigning himself with a heavy sigh, Nova fumbled off after the Professor.
"Just remember who looks like a guinea pig," replied Nova with a smile, disappearing into the darkness beyond the cavern entrance.

Time-Ryder: Powerstone Book One

CHAPTER EIGHT

Protected by the cavern walls, the two archaeologists had no idea of the extent of the soaring winds above them. The weather pattern was so severe, snowfall descending so rapidly that it slowed the progress of a large group of heavily protected people in the distance; who slowly trudged towards the open ground. Through the snowstorm, their visibility was poor, but they carried on with determination. Their target was a massive jagged peaked mountain that overshadowed them and it was the only part of the surrounding landscape that could be made out in the ensuing blizzard.

The wind ripped up so violently that it caused one of them to fall, and the others stopped briefly to scoop the exhausted man up from the snow, holding him steady until they started off again slowly. Carefully they progressed, fighting against the howling gale, but determined to reach their goal, however long it would take.

In another equally rugged and blinding white cavern, a black man in his mid-forties, dressed in a drab navy blue jumpsuit that was obviously a few sizes too large for him, tore through the caverns at an alarming rate.

Trayna's heart was beating so fast and the adrenaline rush was so high that he never realised the speed or distance that he had traversed in such a short a time, but the most alarming thing about Trayna was not the rate at which he progressed through the caverns, but the object that was held close to his chest.

It was another small, glass sphere; identical to the one that the Professor and Nova possessed, and much like the two errant archaeologists, he seemed to rely on the orb to provide answers;

namely how he came to be in these barren passages in the first place.
But he didn't dwell on the answers for too long; his first priority was getting somewhere warm, as he shivered and his teeth chattered noisily together.
The tunnel was filled with vapour, as if he had just stepped into the depths of a freezer, so he kept his arms folded close to his chest and plodded forward, his zest for speed having long since gone.
The new cavern was narrow with a high ceiling and showing all of the same trappings as every other carved wall within the subsystem.
It was dark, no illumination shining through the walls like all the previous ones, it was only the dim red hue coming from the top of the glass sphere that lit his way ahead.
His memory of the sphere was vague, yet it held the key to the answers he sought and he clung to it like a child refusing to share its favourite toy.
With a concerned stare, Trayna stopped to rest in the cavern and looked at the sphere determinedly trying to recollect what had happened to him.

Pulling up the zip of his black pilot jacket, Nova rubbed his hands together and looked cautiously all around him before moving to the Professor's side.
They'd been walking for some time, feeling that the tunnels and caverns were endless, all looking similar, with the exception of the myriad of colours that each individual cavern seemed to bestow.
The current stretch of tunnels were white; with slight overtones of a blue tinge bleeding from behind the walls as if they were glowing and alive somehow.

Time-Ryder: Powerstone Book One

"We should have stayed where we were," moaned Nova, "can't you feel it? It's getting colder the farther that we go down!"
"We'll never find out anything by staying in one place shall we?" chirped the Professor, "besides, there was no other way out of there. We were a little out of options."
Nova smiled and thrust his hands deep into his pockets as his cheeks suddenly became flushed.
"I could have been propped up at the end of the bar right now" he said, feeling sorry for himself, "and what about Jess? I completely forgot about her!"
The old man inhaled deeply and looked down his nose, over his dark rimmed glasses.
"If I know Jessica, she's already got the local services looking for us both."
Nova tugged at his zip, pulling it right up to his chin.
"Aye that sounds just like her," he laughed, "I bet Brian's still drooling over that barmaid."
The Professor trudged on ahead, his eyes scanning around the carved tunnels in fascination.
"Mr Wilde does tend to have an overactive imagination."
"Are you trying to say I'm being naive`?" Nova hissed.
"On the contrary, Mr Wilde is the master of manipulation. He simply used whatever means to get you out of your room. Even if his description was how you say 'a little colourful'!"
"Colourful isn't the word for his description this time, try 3DD" chuckled the young man at his own joke.
"I wouldn't be at all surprised if he over exaggerated the image of the barmaid to entice you out of your room"
"Brian might exaggerate sometimes, but not about women" clipped Nova, "he might tell the odd fib now and then but he doesn't rank up beside the likes of Baron Munchausen or Nick Clegg!"
The Professor smirked and carried on.

Time-Ryder: Powerstone Book One

"Hey I just had a thought!" exclaimed Nova, he started patting down his jacket and pulled out his mobile phone, to which he flipped on and started keying a number rapidly.

"Why'd I never think of this before?"

"Of course?" snapped the Professor with a smile. He stopped his advance and pulled out a rather battered first generation Nokia phone to which Nova sniggered.

"You'll be lucky to dial a number with that piece of crap" he joked, "you didn't even top it up remember?"

The Professor keyed one button and gave a smug grin.

"They don't charge you for emergency services!"

"What are you gonna tell them? Help I'm lost in the caves of mount doom!" scoffed Nova with a slight chuckle.

"More like Wookey Hole from the looks of it" replied the Professor, "minus the ice and snow of course."

With a frown of dismay, Nova gave up and turned his phone off.

"Maybe if we get to higher-ground we might get a signal, I mean we are going downward aren't we?"

Starting up his pace again, the Professor agreed, pocketed his phone and sniffed the air.

"The tunnel may open up another route the farther on we go" he said, trying to convince them both that his course of action was going to lead somewhere.

"And the temperature appears to be dropping the farther down that we go, but we have no alternative to press on, this is the only path."

Nova felt he had no choice but to follow on blindly as usual.

"Alright, but first pub we make it to, you're buying!"

Time-Ryder: Powerstone Book One

Clumps of ice and snow fell into the area where the Professor and Nova had awoken, followed by the heavy black booted feet of three heavily protected men in uniform.

The snow continued to fall and had masked the footprints, practically wiping out all trace of the two archaeologists presence there, but the swift movements of this highly alert team took no interest in the cavern itself, only the entrance that would lead them into the dark tunnels beyond.

The newcomers landed on a fresh layer of snow as the tallest of them took a commanding posture and stepped away from the others as more heavily armoured troops abseiled down into the cavern behind him, an array of large blue packing crates dropping down beside them.

Pulling back the large fur edged hood, he pushed up his peaked cap and lowered his yellow-rimmed snow goggles, revealing the slightly handsome face of a man in his early forties. A high forehead and a square jaw, he was definitely a force to be reckoned with.

He scratched his finely groomed goatee beard nervously and stepped forward, pulling out a strange black device that squealed as he waved it around the walls and surrounding area.

"Perimeter is secure Commander" grated a cheery voice behind him.

A young, black man in the same styled grey fatigues looked above to the trickling snow. He held an enormous chrome weapon with an elongated barrel, strapped over his shoulder and was poised and ready for whatever lay ahead.

Seconds later the enclosure was greeted by more men, each clad in the same garb, all armed and prepared for a serious undertaking.

"All present and correct?" asked the Commander lightly, his broad American voice booming out in the small enclosure.

Time-Ryder: Powerstone Book One

"Yes Sir!" replied the black man with a strange twang of an accent. Aside from the Commander, he was the only other American present, the others a mix of varying English, Irish and Welsh accents.

He stood at ease as the Commander continued his search with the small black scanner, running the device up and down the icy walls, evidently looking for something.

"Ships scans are confirmed, there's a high concentration of..." the Commander squinted "vast deposits of Velium in the main structure"

"Is that what the expedition team were here to find out sir?"

"No, they had a seismic operation to initiate, but I'd be weary Vane, the deposits might interfere with our communications. Which direction did your team enter the mines from?" he asked, closing the device and strapping it back to his thigh.

"The main hatch leading to the gantry, it's close to the old workings, but it's farther up the mountain. The Captain thought it was the right place to start," replied the black trooper.

The tall officer carried his thoughts for a moment and tapped his lip nervously, moving close to the arch leading to the tunnels and he peered into the darkness.

"Commander?" Vane tried to rouse him from his daze, "Commander Adams!"

He revolved silently to the on-looking troops and took a breath with a gruff exhalation of annoyance.

"We haven't got long before the weather pattern changes sir, maybe a few hours!"

Adams nodded.

"Good, then break out the VDU and get it set up. You and Mr Brooks set up a base of operations here. Owens and Barker, I want you to proceed to the gantry and plant explosives all around the hatch, with a remote detonator, just in case we need to cover our exit. Palmer and Madeley you're with me" he announced and pulled out his sidearm.

"If these mines are unstable, then I don't want anyone else entering after we leave!"

Adams pulled back the chamber on his pistol and looked at the shaft of the slender silver weapon. It was a curious piece of weaponry when compared to the firearms that the others bestowed, a trusted Beretta. He didn't trust the Field pistols and rifles that were the mainstay of the ships armoury, he felt more relaxed with something familiar and reliable and something that wasn't prone to jamming like the other weapons were.

"I want that tracking system up ASAP!"

The slightly untidy and churlish Trooper Brooks started unpacking the crates that had been lowered before Owens descent and he discarded the lids, pulling out the antiquated pieces of equipment, to which he started assembling them with Vane's help.

"Just try not to drop them this time Joe" he smiled at Vane.

Adams started doing up his leather gloves and held his pistol aloft.

"Ready?" he looked to both troopers beside him; who acknowledged with a brief nod.

"Everyone got their orders?" he looked across the cavern to the sullen Owens who stared on ahead in a constant state of disapproval.

"Have you got a problem with that Trooper?" he barked.

"No sir!" replied the Welshman sharply and he slowly turned to follow Barker out of the cavern sheepishly.

The broad shouldered Vane stood forward beside the Commander, watching them go.

"You're gonna have a problem with him sir" he hissed.

"If you mean he doesn't like the way I do things?" asked Adams as he paused, "then I don't care Vane. It's not a popularity contest, I'm here to do a quick job, find the Captain and get you all out safe. This place doesn't concern me."

He was taken aback by the Commander's sudden brash nature. Their contact prior to the journey through the snow had been brief and the Commander had all but kept to his own company. They didn't know the Commander, only his reputation for getting things done and if anyone could find the Captain it was him.

"Do you really think the Captain is still alive down there sir?" asked Brooks over the top of the small monitor he was adjusting.

"We can only assume so, the fact that he and Doctor Belder are the only two unaccounted for gives us hope!" he answered, "how long now Mr Brooks?"

"Only a few minutes to do a quick diagnostic and extensive perimeter scan sir!"

"Good, you can get me on comms should you have any problems. Try modulating frequencies if you have any difficulties" he said softly as Vane bent down to check the connections at the back of the VDU.

Adams spotted the pack of cards that were on top of the tower unit and he gave a whimsical smile.

He looked right over at Brooks.

"You do know those cards are marked don't you?" he said softly, but Brooks didn't look at all surprised.

"Course!" he whispered in return, "Who'd you think marked them?"

Adams smiled back and crossed to the arch. With a deep sigh of uncertainty he looked aloft to the falling specks of snow.

"Try to keep an eye out and inform me of anything out of the ordinary!" he hissed softly.

Before both troopers had any questions to interject, he spat through the archway with Palmer and Madeley in tow.

"What was that all about?" Brooks looked up to Vane.

Time-Ryder: Powerstone Book One

"I don't know, but he's keeping something from us. Just look at the way he's acting. He's been like that ever since he came on board" replied Vane, "I tell you Brooksy something about that guy just doesn't add up."

Brooks shifted his position and plugged in the last few connections.

"He's only been here a day, give the guy a break. Have you seen his record? He's got a hundred percent mission success rate."

"Yeah, and a high body-count to go with it!"

Vane made a grim face.

"Impressive sure, but I'm telling you Brooksy, I've got that strange feeling in my gut. And doesn't it seem weird that they only send one guy to take control, why not a full extraction team especially if there are a dozen dead crew members already?"

"You're thinking about this too much Joe."

Brooks hissed and put down his screwdriver.

Vane shook his head and pulled off his cap, revealing his bald dome. He felt the cold and placed the cap back on just as quickly.

"It doesn't add up Buddy. Did you ever think that there may be more to them wanting to re-open the mines after all this time? Maybe there's something else down there that they don't want too many people getting wind of!"

Brooks gave him a glance that showed he half-believed what he was saying.

"Pass me that micro-driver" he said and held out his hand to the trooper; who slipped the strange device into his open hand.

The stare was enough to shut him up for the moment, enough for Brooks to finish his work on the scanner screen, but he knew, once given time to think about it, Vane would have a whole new set of theories to probe him with.

He sighed and crouched down behind the monitor again, connecting the last few cables.

Time-Ryder: Powerstone Book One

CHAPTER NINE

The tunnels although dark and gloomy were not intimidating to Commander Adams as he pitched forward with only the bare light of the trooper's field-rifle scope-beam to guide him.
He made a swift pace with both troopers backing him up, yet he scanned the area ahead of him with caution, before stepping into the first open cavern ahead of him.
It was bright, incandescent ripples of green light filtering through the walls. Adams wanted to use his scanner on the substance to identify what it was, but maybe he'd let his curiosity rule him some other time. For now, he had another task to complete and he was damned sure he wasn't going to let anyone get in his way.
"Eyes open gents, keep a watch out for anything out of the ordinary" he warned, but Palmer and Madeley did a full sweep of the perimeter as they crossed the glowing cavern.
"No life signs in the vicinity sir!" Palmer strained his beady eyes to see the illuminated pad in his hand.
"There's another exit twelve o'clock sir"
Madeley stepped forward first, creeping to the darkness of the archway; he turned his rifle to the floor and his scope light showed up the indented set of footprints in the fine trail of snow.
"Sir, come and take a look at this."
Adams shifted away from his brief examination of the rock walls and stooped down to where the trooper was holding the light.
"Two sets of prints, very recent. And one of them heavier footed than the other" he frowned and stood up.
Palmer fumbled forward excitedly.
"Do you think it could be the Captain and Doctor Belder sir?"
"I can't be sure, but both their medical records state that their weight is under ten stone. These prints and the distribution of weight show it to be a much larger person," he answered grimly.

Time-Ryder: Powerstone Book One

"And it must have been something big to massacre over a dozen people, according to Trooper Vane's report!" he continued, giving both anxious men something more to think about.
"Keep your weapons primed!" said the Commander forcefully and he stepped up the pace, aiming for the archway on the other side of the cavern.

With his hands thrust deep into his pockets and trying to keep warm, Nova hunched forward and dawdled along behind the Professor. He was unusually quiet.
The Professor thought that he was still preoccupied with his thoughts of Barbara, but in regard of their present situation, he couldn't blame the young man for being so silent.
Deciding to break the tension, the Professor stopped and took out his small silver hip flask, taking a swift swig of brandy and offering it to Nova.
"Not quite the bar you were hoping for" smiled the old man, "but under the circumstances."
"No thanks!" refused the young man politely, "that's gut rot!"
"It'll warm you up!" he offered again.
With silence from Nova, he swigged again and slipped it back inside his coat.
Nova stopped for a second and exhaled slowly in annoyance as he stared after the Professor.
"When were you going to tell me?"
"Hmm?" the Professor cleaned his glasses and turned to him.
"About the letter" Nova declared softly, "before I came to Baleran, I went home to Riverdale. I saw the letter in your study!"
"Oh!" said the Professor simply, his face ashen and for once he was lost for words.

"Why didn't you tell me?" Nova looked up at him, "did you think I wouldn't be able to handle it?"
"You were a little hard to contact. You had been gone for some time" said the old man sheepishly.
"So spill it, what's going on?" Nova looked at him, half angry and the other half he wasn't quite sure what he was feeling.
The Professor stopped again, and took a breath to compose himself.
"It's nothing, I have been undergoing some tests, but I've been rather putting it off, work has been rather piling up of late."
Nova rolled his eyes.
"Did you just take a course of stupidity pills? Its cancer! Excuse my words, but that shit kills. That should be your first priority, not some bloody stupid archaeology dig!" thundered the young man.
He was angry that the old man seemed to be treating the news so flippantly.
"You don't understand what I'm involved in" hissed the old man, "the implications of the dig, it's all rather complicated."
Nova stopped in mid-stride and glared at the old man, he blinked as the realisation came to him.
"I knew you were hiding something" hissed the young man, pointing directly at the old man, "Did you know that sphere was there all along?"
The Professor was silent for a second, trying to think of how to put it.
"When we restored the village Tollbooth, we recovered a bunch of journals, there were scattered truths by the Marquis of Ravayne about the Castle and a fire that decimated the grounds," answered the old man, "a fragmented paragraph about something that was being protected by the MacEran Clan, not that I'd ever heard of such a clan before, I was just as surprised as you with the inscriptions in the crypt."

Time-Ryder: Powerstone Book One

Nova closed his eyes briefly.

"Don't sideswipe the question. What's this got to do with you not going for treatment?"

From the look on his face, Nova could tell that he was holding something back.

He stopped and looked at Nova with a solemn stare, his stomach turning with the thought of uttering the words that were teetering on his lips.

"There is no treatment" he said softly, "My cancer is inoperable. I have at best Six months to a year!"

Nova's face became ashen white, the colour dropping out of him rapidly. He stood on the spot almost ghost-like and lost for words.

"But you said that woman wanted you to extend your contract!"

Nova was somewhat confused; he couldn't understand the Professor wanting to work himself to death.

The silence was so awkward between the two of them that only the Professor dared speak.

"I don't like leaving a job half finished."

Nova was still lost for words, a small tear emerging from the corner of his eye. It had been a hard time lately; First Aunt Rose had passed and then Barbara's sudden death and now this.

He was beginning to feel that he was jinxed; maybe it would have been better if he didn't know and then the Professor's death would seem natural somehow, but then at least this way he would have some time to spend with him and make the most of it.

Unsure of what to say, he changed the subject and spoke softly, his voice almost child-like.

"Why is the dig so important to you?"

The old man exhaled a deep sigh, finally able to confide in the youngster.

Time-Ryder: Powerstone Book One

"It was only after the journals were documented officially that it all started to happen. The castle and surrounding grounds had been abandoned for centuries and the Trust got involved wishing to begin the restoration, then the sudden, if not curious appearance of Somersby with his documents stalled us when he filed the injunction and produced the documents for his claim. That was the first knowledge of the Clan MacEran."

"So you think he was after something buried at the dig?" asked Nova and then he suddenly became alarmed, "do you think he knew about this sphere? Could he even have been the one who broke into the dig last night?"

"That would be my first assumption, even more so when I discovered that his documents were fakes. If indeed he was after the sphere, he wouldn't have found it as you only uncovered the crypt today."

"When did you find out this?" Nova squinted.

The Professor gave a wry grin.

"Amusingly enough, just before we left the hotel. Timing is uncanny isn't it?"

Nova was trying to get his head around it and stopped against the wall; a perplexed look upon his face.

"So he faked the documents to get access to the dig?"

"The documents themselves were genuine enough, but the Marquis signature was a fake. If we hadn't recovered those documents from the tollbooth with the original signature I'd have been none the wiser!" exhaled the Professor.

"The strangest thing is that Somersby's signature on the documents to the council was identical to the ones on the original document."

Nova just looked at him, wondering what he thinking.

"What are you saying Professor?"

The old man took a breath and rubbed his bearded face.

"That either the documents were fake all along, or. No, it's just too ridiculous to even comprehend!"

He stepped away and gave a wide eyed look of amusement.

"What?" narrowed Nova, "It can't be too ridiculous if you are considering it, whatever it is?"

Nova knew that the Professor had a very rigid sense of reasoning, that there had to be a cause for every action, a lynchpin that obviously made him think of it, regardless if it was ridiculous or not.

"The ridiculous notion that this Somersby may have been knocking around for several hundred years in pursuit of the sphere, now that is ridiculous" he announced, "There, I told you it's not only ridiculous, it's ludicrous!"

"You're right it does sound ridiculous!" scoffed Nova, and he scratched the back of his head, "But just supposing it isn't as ridiculous as it sounds right? That sphere must be pretty important if he has been after it for centuries, ridiculously speaking of course!"

The old man nodded and pulled the glass sphere from the depths of his tweed coat.

"Whatever its purpose may be?"

Nova waved a hand out in front of the Professor dismissively.

"But just supposing it isn't ridiculous, how else did he find out it was there? Especially if these documents were only just discovered"

Professor Carlson dropped the ball back into his pocket and scratched his beard nervously.

"He must have had access to the Trust records room, or going by our ridiculous theory, he was at the Castle at the time of this undocumented battle."

"This sounds like the beginnings of one of your conspiracy theories," returned Nova.

"But only a theory, as theories go" smiled the old man, "come on I think I can see light ahead."

He moved as if to head down the tunnel when Nova grabbed his arm and held him back.

The Professor turned and saw the concern in the young man's eyes.

"You could have told me earlier today, you know," whispered the young man, and his eyes were still red.

Professor Carlson stepped forward and put his arms around him, pulling him close.

"For that I'm sorry," he said softly, "I never wanted you to find out like that!"

The Professor stepped back and held him by both shoulders and gave him a square look.

"Come on, better to get a move on" affirmed the Professor and he sauntered off towards the light.

Nova nodded in agreement and plodded on.

"I only hope it's warmer down there" he said thrusting his hands back in his pockets, "if it gets any colder I'll have another couple of crystal balls to contend with!"

Luckily out of earshot, the Professor didn't hear anything.

"I dunno, I'm wasting all my good ones on you" Nova frowned and followed the old man down the tunnel into the dark.

Time-Ryder: Powerstone Book One

CHAPTER TEN

The VDU station was fully operational. Troopers Brooks and Vane sat idly watching the display that operated much like a sophisticated radar device.
Vane looked to the gap in the open ceiling where they had entered from and watched the snow trickle down.
He could see the wind pattern change above, whooshing noisily and he turned up the temperature dial on the collar of his flight suit, pulling the fur lined hood around his face for comfort; clearly anticipating the worst.
Brooks narrowed his gaze, constantly frowning at the screen, scared in case he had missed anything, even though Vane knew that the Trooper was far too meticulous with his connections to have made any mistakes with the equipment.
The screen pinpointed each person within the tunnels and showed them as heat sources, but Brooks was confused as Vane counted the signatures upon the display.
"Are you sure everything is connected properly?" he asked, but a look from Brooks made him retract his statement, "Forget I just said that, course it is!"
"I'm the technical genius here remember," Brooks smirked smugly.
"Okay then smartass" said the American, "Why are there three more orange dots than there are supposed to be?"
Brooks tapped the screen and gulped.
"Could be a glitch in the system I suppose?"
Vane grinned inanely.
"Technology huh?"
He started to point out that the dots that were moving as Brooks cleaned the points of one of the cables and re-inserted them into the console again.

Time-Ryder: Powerstone Book One

"That's Owens and Barker at the gantry" Vane pointed to the screen, "and that's the Commander, Madeley and Palmer" Brooks nodded and Vane pointed to the glitch.
"Then who the hell is this?" he indicated the other two blobs and one other lone blob in the corner of the screen.
"That can't be right" stormed Brooks angrily.
"Is it Doctor Belder and the Captain maybe?" Vane shrieked and became worried, "Check the connections again!"
"I've already checked the circuits and the connection, it isn't a glitch on the screen Joe" stormed Brooks, looking alarmingly at his colleague.
"Then that could be the killers you're looking at!" Vane jabbed the screen, indicating the slow moving heat sensors.
Brooks raised his brow.
"Adams did say to check in with anything out of the ordinary!" But Vane already saw that he had the small hand communicator in his grasp, fumbling with the dial to no avail.
"There's no signal. It's that dammed Velium Ore. He said it might interfere with the systems," hissed Brooks, double-checking his calculations.
Vane exhaled annoyingly and narrowed at the VDU station.
"Do a quick system-scan to make sure it isn't a fault, if it's not then we need to tell the Commander, he could be walking into a trap just like the Captain did!"
Brooks threw his hands over the controls frantically as Vane looked on worriedly.
Impatient though he was and as much as he didn't like it, all Vane could do was watch and hope that his fears were not going to come true.

Trayna had stopped to catch his breath for too long and leaned over, resting his hand on his knee until his heart rate slowed

Time-Ryder: Powerstone Book One

down, but when he straightened up his vision was shadowed by a dark shape looming over him, watching him closely and tilting its head in curious observation.

The newcomer had no identifying features, only a ragged piece of black fabric draped across it with a makeshift hood obscuring its features.

From what Trayna could make out, the long dark robes stretched to the cavern floor, and gave its frame a very deathly image and was almost shadow-like.

Trayna looked upon the newcomer, confused; yet maybe this person had arrived in the same manner and was equally as bewildered as he was.

"Are you lost?" he asked softly and then he smiled.

"I'm lost," he declared with a smile, still clearly out of breath, "what is this place?"

And still the figure looked on, tilting its head like an inquisitive dog.

Trayna widened his eyes and straightened up at the non-responsive newcomer.

"Well if you're not going to answer, then I haven't got time to waste, if you'll excuse me I need to get a move on," he said politely and tried to move past the dark shape.

The figure stood its ground, unmoving; almost statuesque.

"Excuse me?" asked Trayna, anxious to pass the tall figure.

And still there was no response.

"Well I'm sorry, but I have to find some answers before I freeze to death!"

The first sign of life came from the towering giant, looking at Trayna's tunic, or what he had just concealed inside it.

As Trayna prepared to pass the tall figure, its hand emerged from beneath its drooping robes and a flash of green came before the man's eyes, so fast that he barely noticed it.

Time-Ryder: Powerstone Book One

The swish of movement was too quick for Trayna and he didn't know what he had just witnessed until he tried to speak; yet only a strained gargle came out.

He reached up to his throat, feeling the dampness and the sticky substance that started to weep between his fingers, stemming from an open wound across his windpipe.

A singular cut from a sharp object in the figure's grasp had severed his jugular and he thrashed desperately at the wound with his hands, dropping the glass ball onto the smooth finish of the cavern floor.

Trayna's blood was yellow, pungent and thick.

It distressed him seeing so much weep from his throat and it poured out rapidly like an uncontrolled gusher.

And still the figure didn't make any attempts to move, it just stood watching Trayna's every last movement, studying him closely.

With his balance affected, Trayna swayed and lost control and felt his life ebbing away slowly as he crashed to his knees.

With a sudden stab of movement, the figure glided over the barren ground, floating towards the wounded man, where it scooped up the glass sphere from the man's feet.

The dark shape clasped the sphere tightly; the faint flash of reptilian claws stretching around the gleaming ball and holding it close.

Trayna's eyes widened and he outstretched a hand to his retreating killer, but his strength was waning and the drop in temperature in the cavern seemed to speed on his demise.

With a last exhale of breath; Trayna was frozen to the spot, his body ceasing movement and his fate finally sealed.

The dark shape glided back over to him and slipped a small silver ringlet from its ragged robes, slowly easing it onto the head of the dead newcomer.

Time-Ryder: Powerstone Book One

It waited a few seconds until a miniscule band of green light rippled around the crown becoming solid and then pulsing momentarily before diminishing completely. Lifting the crown from Trayna's head, the killer quickly hid the crown beneath its ragged clothing and stepped away from the outstretched figure. Gliding off down the passage, the cloaked killer left the frozen victim with his hand forever reaching outward.

In another part of the seemingly endless myriad of tunnels, a large incongruous shape started to form on the snow-crested floor.

The orange body of light that enveloped the newly formed shape slowly dwindled until all that was left was a shining silver mass curled up on the tunnel floor.

After a few minutes, the ball unfurled and revealed a large flowing silver cloak, crowned off by a fur-lined hood that hid the face of the newcomer.

Stretching from its position, it eased backward, and the hood concealing the wearer fell back, revealing the beautiful, yet aristocratic face of a pale skinned young woman, long platinum locks framing her face and streaming down around her shoulders.

Her piercing green eyes darted around the cavern walls quizzically, brows drooping in confusion.

With the realisation that her surroundings were new; she rose from the ground and her long cloak clung tightly to her nimble frame.

She looked down to her feet and saw the object that had caused her shift in location. For a brief second, she was angry; the veins on her forehead pulsing until she felt a sudden surge of pain and she clutched an intricate silver bangle that hung around her left arm.

Time-Ryder: Powerstone Book One

It was unfamiliar to her and she looked at it angrily, tugging at the bangle that had begun to glow white, but it refused to budge and she exhaled exhaustedly, letting go of it in gruff annoyance. Looking back to the other object of curiosity, she stooped to collect it from the ground.

Resting on the fine layer of snow was yet another glass sphere; a match to the one in Nova's possession and just as dead and lifeless as his appeared to be.

She carefully prised it from the snow and looked at the object in her hands, sensing a familiarity with it, before quickly dismissing it and dropping it into one of the deep pockets of her flowing silver cloak.

Moving swiftly through each passage with ease, she seemed little out of breath, but daren't stop to try and find out where she was. As she stepped up her pace, it came to her that she was all alone and she finally accepted her loneliness and came to a stop, stepping into the next cavern.

It was much darker than those that she'd already traversed through and she moved cautiously forward, still that unnerving feeling that she was being watched came over her, even though there was no proof of that.

Thinking she had heard some errant noise behind her; she wheeled slowly and walked backward, but it was just the eerie wind whistling down the tunnels.

Her face was blank of all expression, yet she looked cold, unfeeling and emotionless as she peered all around her surroundings.

With a quick and clumsy movement; she tripped backwards over something hard on the cavern floor and she turned in mid-fall, twisting her frame and landing face-first upon the hard surface. Her hood followed on, and covered her beautiful features once again.

She spat out a faint powdering of snow that covered her face, but something was different. Her mouth tasted salty and she touched her tongue with her fingers, fearing she had bitten it.
At first she thought she was bleeding, but then she wiped her lip and found no cuts or abrasions.
It wasn't until she lowered her hood that she saw the mess all over her chest.
A crimson stain of pure blood adorned her silver cloak and she looked down onto the floor to see where it had come from.
As her eyes slowly adjusted to the dark cavern, she saw the twisted form of a poor unfortunate soul, its body savaged and bloody, but the most distressing thing was that it was missing its head.
She put her hand to her mouth aghast and edged backwards, her hands and body soaked in the richness of the bloody stain.
The body was still warm, which seemed unusual regarding the fluctuating temperature within the caverns, but she could feel the warmth of the blood on her fingertips and she cringed at the sight, even though the rising emotions inside her were saying different.
Her jaw trembled in shock at the disgusting sight and still she edged back from it until she stopped suddenly, thinking that she had reached the wall of the cavern.
Without turning around, her right hand flailed behind her and she patted the area, but instead of the wall as she had assumed, it was rough material, frayed and ragged to the touch.
She moved her hands slowly downward and stopped breathing momentarily.
Her fingers felt long arms behind her, sharp clawed fingers and as she withdrew her hand, tainted blood from the claws now on her own fingertips, although yellow, not the thick red stain that had spilled from the body in front of her.

Time-Ryder: Powerstone Book One

Wheeling quickly, she saw the tall dark shape behind her and screamed at the top of her voice.

As her shrill cry sounded off, the silver bracelet on her arm started to glow until it was white hot and shone in the darkness. With the bracelet providing illumination, she saw the dark figure in its entirety and she screamed again.

The killer, although obscured by the ragged clothing and hood, raised a clawed hand to shield its eyes from the intense glare of her bracelet.

The girl screamed at the discoloured green scales that were now visible upon the assailant's arm and she screamed yet again, only this time she saw the exit behind it and took the opportunity to run.

Time-Ryder: Powerstone Book One

CHAPTER ELEVEN

In the massive cavern that connected the gantry to the upper levels, Barker and Owens trod carefully down the green metal walkways on the first level. Looking over the rail, Owens could see that they were they were distanced from the ground by a great height and he craned his neck out and then up to the other three levels that towered above him and he gulped, while holding a secure grip upon his field rifle.

Barker kept a close eye on the tracking device strapped on top of his rifle as he moved forward slowly.

"So what about you Rhys, do you think the Captain's still alive?"

"He's dead!" replied the Welshman gruffly, "doesn't matter what Vane said, he can't remember much himself, can he?"

"Yeah, but funny that he and Doctor Belder haven't turned up yet" argued Barker, still keeping his eyes on the tracker.

"I doubt he made it out of here in one piece!" said Owens pessimistically.

"Vane did!" spat Barker.

"Vane's a different kind of creature, isn't he?" Owens continued to walk alongside Barker, his eyes going everywhere, "Survival is top of his list. You don't expect anything less of someone who survived earthquakes and landslides to be bumped off by a homicidal arsehole now do you?"

"So what are you saying about the Captain?"

"The Captain's just a nosy one. It wasn't down to him to come down here, he was just told to find the survivors of the expedition. His nose just got the better of him!" Owens shot back.

Barker understood what he was getting at and was about to reply when he heard a scream.

The warbling cry carried down the tunnels and seemed to reverberate within the gantry cavern, given that the colossal size of the cavern acted like a large echo chamber.

Time-Ryder: Powerstone Book One

He gave a shocked look to Owens and they both cocked their weapons, charging down the metal walkway to investigate the scream.

Satisfied that there was nothing wrong with the VDU station, Trooper Brooks leaned back on the overturned packing case that he had been perched upon and scratched his clump of untidy hair.
"I don't understand it. The diagnostic says everything is operational. All the connections are fine and no cable breakages. So it must be intruders."
In all the events that occurred since the Captain's disappearance, the dark skinned Vane always knew that there was something else going on in the tunnels, something that the Captain kept to himself. Vane was no genius, but even he knew when someone was concealing something.
"Wait a minute, what's that?" Vane's long finger wavered in front of the screen as the lone blob had disappeared, yet the other two remained.
"Hang on a minute I'm going to try something" Brooks gritted his teeth and swapped the cables down the back of the monitor and the screen turned from the green hue to a blue tinge.
"What did you do?"
"Turned it from a heat sensor to a motion sensor, just something I've been working on with the portable unit" answered Brooks, narrowing his eyes at the screen, "Trying to make the systems compatible with each other."
Vane leaned forward behind the seated trooper and watched as his hands moved over the controls like lightning and the screen fizzled, changing the picture until the motion sensor over-laid all of the tunnels within the mountain, but as the screen changed, Vane narrowed his eyes and pointed at the screen again.

Time-Ryder: Powerstone Book One

"Your machine must be screwed" scoffed the American, "there's another three dots just appeared" he pointed to another section of the map.

Brooks looked confused.

"But only one of them is showing a heat signature, the other two are only showing up on the motion detector."

"And look, the extra heat blob has just gone" said Vane bluntly, noting the fading signature on the screen.

"That can't be right," Brooks flipped the control and turned it back to heat mode, showing the screen as before but without the dots that newly appeared.

He looked directly to his friend in confusion and flipped the control back again, showing the new signatures on the display yet again.

Vane frowned, tried the comm unit again and tossed the handset onto the desk, not amused by the static interference that screamed in his ears.

"Have you tried changing frequencies?" snorted Brooks.

"Not that it would make much difference" said Vane negatively and rubbed his bald dome. He collected up his large rifle, slinging the strap over his shoulder as he prepared to move off.

"Whatever these new signatures are, they're not giving off body heat, could be why our team were ambushed down there if they can't be seen in range of a spectrometer."

Vane nodded and then finally came to a decision now that they knew the comm systems weren't working for them.

"Get your stuff; we need to let him know before anything else happens!"

Brooks lifted up his weapon and scanning equipment.

For a bright man he didn't understand what his friend was getting at. Vane cocked the large barrelled silver field cannon and pushed back his cap.

"Hurry up Brooksy!"

Time-Ryder: Powerstone Book One

Nova pushed past the old man into the wide-open space and noticed the contrast in colour between the new cavern and the old one.

He was beginning to see the Professor's fascination in the beauty of the glistening colours as the walls were almost fully crystallized, sparkling with the fresh tinge of ice weathering upon them.

Nova thought that it must have something to do with the level at which they had descended, as this particular passage into the cavern ahead seemed marginally colder than the previous one.

He noted the glistening green substance of the walls, as if a river of ice was moving steadily behind it. His hand gently caressed the wall and then shot back to the warm comforts of his jacket pocket.

"Hey Professor, it's gorgeous in here, check out the walls, it's like they're glowing!"

The old man dawdled on behind absentmindedly, scanning their surroundings as he entered until he saw something in the far corner. He put a hand on Nova's shoulder, pulling him back slightly and he and pointed in the direction of the unconformity.

It was a crouched figure facing away from them, but it delighted Nova greatly and he beamed up at the old man.

"See I told you we weren't here alone Professor" smiled the young man with a gasp of delight.

"Hey mate. Do you know where we are? We're a little lost" he laughed, "Who am I kidding? We're a lot lost."

Nova began to approach the figure, but it was hard to see in the fluctuating light of the cavern. Whatever it was appeared to be dark and hunched over, and when Nova moved closer, he saw that the man was on his knees and he narrowed his eyes to the Professor.

"Is he praying or something?" he whispered softly, "Is that why he isn't answering?"

Time-Ryder: Powerstone Book One

As he moved closer, Nova saw the face of the newcomer and capped his mouth in disgust, turning away and closing his eyes briefly.

After a pregnant pause, he looked up to the Professor with a glum expression and the old man came to his side.

Frozen to the spot where he had been slain; his hand reaching out ahead of him was Trayna. The ghastly sight told the two archaeologists everything.

The Professor put his handkerchief to his mouth. The sight of the distended veins and tendons hanging from the open tear in the man's throat was disturbing enough, but the fact that he was frozen to the spot in such a pose filled him with fear.

Nova knelt in front of Trayna, holding back his disgust, but managing to look upon the frozen corpse with a morbid fascination. He looked back up to the old man by his side.

"Just when you thought we didn't have enough to worry about," he hissed.

"Aside from our late friend here it certainly proves that we are not here alone!" said the old man coldly. He continued to stare at the frozen corpse.

"Aye, but who'd do a thing like this and why?" drawled Nova, "I mean it's just pure sick to leave the guy out here like that!"

The Professor nodded.

"The temperature down here seems to be in a state of flux," he said, looking at his visible breath.

"It's as if some parts of the tunnels are naturally warmer than others," said the old man, looking for answers.

"That's not my main worry, his blood is still fresh" interrupted Nova, eying the old man, "If that's what you call blood. Look its yellow!" he declared.

"I don't like this Professor, I wasn't a fan of this place before, but now there's someone killing people and that's not a good thing!"

Time-Ryder: Powerstone Book One

he said gruffly, "especially when we're practically stuck down here!"

"Certainly not!" agreed the old man.

"Then maybe we'd better move on before we get caught and blamed for this," pointed out Nova.

"I had overlooked that possibility," hissed the Professor.

"Aye well I didn't." Nova began to rise from his knees and his eyes suddenly went wide as he felt the cold steel of a cylindrical object nudging the back of his head.

Having emerging quietly from the cavern behind them, Commander Adams and his two troopers levelled their weapons and armed them with a sharp click.

Nova closed his eyes over and sighed.

"I'd say our problems have just doubled!"

Time-Ryder: Powerstone Book One

CHAPTER TWELVE

The dark shape was practically impossible to see in the shadows of the gloomy cavern that the girl was tearing through.

She kept up her pace, passing each set of tunnels and multicoloured caverns at such a rate that she traversed through half the lower levels in mere minutes.

Confident that she had eluded whatever had killed the fallen corpse; she stopped and brought out the glass sphere from her cloak, holding it in her grasp and peering into the red misty realms.

It was clouded, mysterious and posed so many questions, but it opened up very few answers.

In her heart, she knew that what was contained within the sphere would explain everything, if only she could get it open, but that was proving harder than she anticipated.

Parting her blonde locks, she pulled back her fur-lined hood and clasped the ball tightly, letting her long fingernails touch the edges of its shining surface and trying to pierce the barely visible seam that ran down the side of the ball.

She knew that this was the only way to open the sphere if at all possible. Grimacing in annoyance; she abandoned all attempts with a gruff sigh of displeasure.

It was only when she saw her bloodstained fingers that she withdrew her attention from the orb and scrambled in the snow at her feet, trying to rid the crimson stain from her fingertips.

Panting and out of breath, Troopers Owens and Barker followed the direction of scream that had echoed through the gantry. They attempted a brisk jog through the ice tunnels and into the blackest chamber where the girl had come across the dark shape.

Time-Ryder: Powerstone Book One

Owens pointed his rifle to the floor, the light-scope his only means of illumination, but he saw nothing as it danced over the snowy surface.

"There's nothing here!" shrieked Barker, nervously moving around his comrade quickly.

He could feel the icy chill whistling down the passage ahead of them, and it made the hairs on the back of his neck stand erect. His cat-like senses made his head snap around in the direction of the gust of wind, the twin beams of his scope light checking out the opening ahead of them.

"This is where it came from isn't it?" Owens replied, still scanning the cavern floor with his scope.

The column of light moved across the uneven ground until he noticed the deep red trail in the powdered remains of the snow at their feet.

Following the trail, it led him to the ghastly sight of the headless body and Barker cocked his weapon, pointing it directly at the corpse.

Owens knelt cautiously and pulled out a light rod from his pack, snapping it and throwing it to the floor at once. Almost immediately the rock walled room was filled with a burst of green luminescent light that left no stone unturned.

They could see everything before them, the corpse wearing the same fatigues as they were, but not the hovering dark shape that clung to the ceiling way above their heads.

"It's disgusting!" croaked the Welshman, he cringed back from the body, yet still had to identify it.

"Is it the Captain?" Barker whispered, tipping his rifle forward to the mess.

Reluctantly, Owens knelt down and started rifling through the pockets and pulled out the rank and insignia on a chain. He shook his head.

"No, it's Belder!" he hissed.

Barker gulped and pushed back the cap, revealing his scruffy mop of dark hair.

"What are we going to do Rhys?"

"We have to report it, what else?" answered Owens.

The ground below their feet began to tremble and the oncoming shudder of the cavern made Barker hold onto the wall as Rhys looked up to the ceiling and shrieked as he saw the large incongruous shape lingering above their heads.

Loosening its grip from the jagged ceiling, the dark figure revolved in mid air, showing a gaping maw of serrated teeth; salivating wide and it dropped down on top of them before the troopers had a chance to get a shot off.

The attempts of both troopers to fire upon the creature failed miserably and their violent deaths were soon followed by a dragged out wail and a horrific scream that sounded off, echoing down the tunnels until all was silent once again.

And very gradually the artificial green luminescence of the light stick in the cavern started to diminish until darkness enveloped the tunnel once more.

Still kneeling in the snow and facing the gruesome sight of Trayna, Nova tried not to look at the discarded remains of the corpse. The throat had been split and the repulsive sight spilled out onto his tunic and frozen to the fabric of his jumpsuit was more than the young man had expected to see.

But the foremost thing on Nova's mind was the gun pointed directly to the back of his head, the cold steel unnerving him, as if it wasn't cold enough in the cavern.

"Not one move!" hissed Adams, his long finger wavering on the trigger.

Nova blinked and gulped, his breathing becoming sparse.

Time-Ryder: Powerstone Book One

"Are you kidding? I'm about as frozen stiff as this stiff!" he exclaimed in a gasp, nodding in the direction of the frozen corpse.

"You're Scottish!" exclaimed the Commander in amazement, "then you're from..."

"Scotland?" Nova said sarcastically, "Mensa didn't half miss out on you for a member!"

Adams face became stern, angrily staring at the young man as Madeley called out.

"Commander, have a look at this!" Madeley noticed something and darted forward to take close inspection behind the body, indicating the deep prints in the snow.

Palmer concentrated his field rifle upon Nova and the old man as the Commander joined the inquisitive Trooper by the imprints.

"Strange!" the tall officer fingered the depth of the print and frowned, "not the same pattern as before, these are more heavily indented."

Nova coughed and cleared his throat, trying to attract the attention of the newcomers.

"We know it's not Scotland that's for sure. Unless you've found some way to speed the weather on by a few months" echoed Nova, "or somehow dropped us off at Aviemore!"

He saw the armed trooper, concentrating the weapon on himself and the Professor.

Nova raised his hands into the air, as did the old man.

"I know what it looks like, but we never killed him. We just found him like this!" blurted out Nova in his best way of offering a defence, before any accusation was made.

Pulling away from the imprint, Adams looked at his small black scanning device and ran it over the area above the indented pattern.

"Since you are the only ones here, you'll forgive me if I don't believe you" hissed the Commander.

Time-Ryder: Powerstone Book One

The Professor coughed disapprovingly at the attitude of the tall uniformed man.
"I would like to know who is accusing us?"
Adams revolved quickly, his face stern and accusing.
"Tom Adams, PCA intelligence," he announced in all but a bark; "On your feet!"
Nova rolled his eyes and shrugged his shoulders; his hands still aloft and stretching up, over-eager to show they meant no harm.
"How can we get up if we're not supposed to move?"
"Get up" barked Madeley, grabbing Nova by the scruff of his neck and dragging the young man to his feet.
"Start talking!" barked Adams.
"About what?" Nova shivered with the cold, "that we're lost, freezing cold, bored and..." he looked at the Professor, "And sober!" he drawled.
"Is it really the time for this?" the Professor frowned upon him.
The old man revolved slowly and faced the Commander.
"If we're trespassing Commander then we apologise. We don't exactly know where we are. It's all rather confusing."
Adams looked at the old man's choice of clothing and narrowed, even more confused by the young man's attire. They were clearly not dressed for the present climate and the shivering that the youngster seemed to be emitting showed that all too clearly.
He sidestepped the Professor and took a glance at the grotesque remains behind Nova and then noticed the discarded shell of the sphere by Trayna's frozen form.
"Is this why you killed him?"
"We never killed anyone" protested Nova, "told you, we just found him like this and if you looked at his throat you'll see that it's been ripped out" he held out his hands and showed him his shorn nails, "It wasn't me, I'm a biter!" he said quite pleased with himself, the fingertips covered in the yellow gunk that was Trayna's excuse for blood.

Time-Ryder: Powerstone Book One

"Would you mind telling us where we are?" asked the old man impatiently, "our arrival was a bit hazy at best."
"Search them!" Adams straightened up.
Both troopers proceeded to strip the archaeologists of their belongings and dropped them onto the cavern floor, including Nova's penknife and the antique pistol he had acquired at the dig.
"Nothing Sir, only this!" Madeley picked up the weapon and showed it to the Commander.
"It's a..." the Professor coughed before being cut off by the Commander.
"Antique!" answered the Commander "Where did you get it?" he eyed it strangely.
"We found it at an archaeology dig" clipped Nova and he received an odd look from the Professor to which he shrugged, "Comes with the Job."
The old man's gaze was disapproving to say the least.
"What? I wanted a closer look at it so I shoved it in my pocket until we checked out the pit" he lied, not apologising for himself, "I didn't expect the whole trip to Oz, whirlwind included!" he exclaimed.
"And yours!" Palmer pulled out the Professor's belongings from his coat pockets, endless coils of string, a boiled sweet covered in fluff and his antiquated mobile phone.
"You carry about some junk!" exclaimed Nova.
Adams narrowed his gaze, the objects looked even more confusing than the pistol that he held in his hands. Then Palmer pulled out the last object and held it out to the tall officer.
"And then there's this sir" he hissed softly
In his gloved hands was the dormant glass sphere, having returned to its original opaque colour.
Adams stared in awe at the ball, resisting the temptation to touch its surface and he just stared on blindly.

Time-Ryder: Powerstone Book One

"We don't know what it is, but it certainly poses a lot of questions" said the old man, "one of them being how we got here, and where exactly here is."

"That's two questions!" stated Nova, only to have a look of annoyance from the Professor, but the Commander wasn't convinced, something about these two didn't add up; their sudden appearance in the tunnels, the body and an intact sphere.

"You really have no idea where you are?"

"Do you think we'd be asking if we did?" snapped Nova.

Palmer stood forward to let the Commander see the glass ball in his hands.

"It's the first intact one we've come across sir. Where did you get it?" Palmer looked at the two strangers.

"At an archaeological dig in Scotland, heaven knows how it got there. Why? Do you know what it is?" asked the old man, seeing the Commander's continual interest in the sphere.

"Every one that has been found so far has been empty, whatever was inside appeared to have gone, all of them very close to a corpse just like this one" replied the tall officer.

"Then whoever is bumping them off is taking the kinder toy inside," said Nova softly, "I told you there was something inside it."

"But seeing as you are the only ones with an intact sphere, you seem to have put yourselves in the direct firing line!" accused the Commander, still gripping his pistol tightly and circling the two men as he looked them up and down.

"Absolute rot!" spat the Professor, "accusing us of a crime when that is your only evidence. If that's the case, where are the contents of this poor fellow's sphere, Hmmm?"

"You tell him Professor!" said Nova lowering his hands.

The old man looked up accusingly as Madeley threw the empty shell to his feet and he frowned.

Time-Ryder: Powerstone Book One

"You've already searched me already, if I took whatever was inside it, surely it would be here!" he said logically.

Palmer tipped his rifle at Nova and he quickly raised his hands again as Madeley shook his head and took the Commander's arm, drawing him away from the others, barely out of earshot.

"Commander what the hell is going on? First that guy with a century old Astro suit and now these two. The old man's clothes look like they stepped out of a damned museum," declared the trooper in a shrill voice.

Adams nodded as he thought about it a bit more.

"I know. It doesn't make any sense!" he eyeballed the Trooper with a steely gaze.

"They're hardly dressed for this place are they?"

The Professor coughed interrupting them both and the Commander turned his attention towards the old man.

"You're still not telling us where we are Commander, have we wandered into some top secret base of some sort? Not that we can remember."

Nova shook his head.

"It looks a bit too remote for a base, but then I suppose that's the whole point if it is a secret if it's remote" he said, confused by his own outburst.

"You're in the Penithe mines, but then you already know that, otherwise we wouldn't be having this pointless conversation," hissed the Commander accusingly as if he had little time for them.

"Where is your transport? Is it close by?"

"The Oregon never detected anything in the vicinity sir," announced Palmer.

"Then you've got a vessel with stealth technology?"

"The only vessel we've got is that hip flask the Professor's keeping close to his chest," retorted Nova with a smile.

Time-Ryder: Powerstone Book One

Adams was silent, still thinking, but keeping his thoughts to himself.
Tipping his weapon to Nova, Palmer prompted him to empty the rest of his pockets, much to the Professor's amusement.
"And you said I carry junk?" he sniggered.
"Ha, ha" scoffed Nova, "these are essentials!"
He turned out his jacket, felling the chill as he unzipped it. Pulling out his belongings, Nova laid them out to the bemused Trooper. His phone, wallet, keys, ipod, penknife, glass vials, notebook and a small cloth package that was unfurled, containing various brushes and a small metal tool with a clawed end.
Adams reached out to the wallet and opened it.
"I've got twenty quid in there, so don't bother nicking it!" he pointed to the Commander.
Adams pulled out Nova's driving licence and turned the plastic card over as he studied it closely and his eyes widened.
"What is it sir?" Palmer asked, noting his shocked state.
"Put your weapons down" he hissed and looked at the old man with a solemn gaze.
"Your Name?" he asked the Professor.
"Professor Henry Carlson" said the old man hesitantly and his brow drooped, "Why?"
"Can you tell me the date Professor?" pressed the Commander.
Henry gave Nova a strange look and then turned to the officer with a pregnant pause.
"Thursday September the Twelfth!" he exclaimed, "I'll ask again. Why?" he raised his brow.
"And the year?"
"Now you really are being preposterous young man!" thundered the Professor, "Where are we?"
"The year, please Professor? It is important!"

Time-Ryder: Powerstone Book One

"Two thousand and Thirteen" interjected Nova, "What's this all about?"

Palmer sided back beside the Commander, both he and Madeley looking confused as they faced the Commander.

"Sir?" hissed Palmer.

"You're sure about the date?" said the Commander in a concerned tone, but one that the old man sensed had distress and confusion.

"Of course he's sure. He's a bit doddery, but he's still got all his marbles. Well most of them" spat Nova, "Anyway it's my birthday tomorrow. How could he forget that, eh?"

He looked at the Professor in alarm.

"You didn't forget it did you?"

"As if I could, not with you constantly reminding me every five minutes," the old man gave him a wry grin, "Just like your Aunt Rose!"

Adams folded up Nova's wallet and returned it to him in silence.

"You're in for a bit of a shock gentlemen" he hissed softly, "this isn't Scotland."

"We'd figured that out for ourselves!" spat Nova.

Adams gave a long pause as he tried to think of the best way to inform them where they were.

"And this isn't Earth!"

"Not on Earth, what are you drivelling about man!" snorted the Professor, his voice elevating slightly in his retort.

The Commander lowered his pistol and holstered it gingerly.

"You're a long way from home" he said coldly and took in a deep breath. "You're in the Velium mines on the Southern side of the planet Penithe."

Time-Ryder: Powerstone Book One

CHAPTER THIRTEEN

There was a brief silence at the Commander's revelation. The only obvious factor was Nova's dropping jaw.

"Are you taking the piss?" he blurted out.

The Professor gave him a glare of disapproval at his use of language.

"Professor I think under the circumstances, I think a wee sweary word is allowed," Nova smiled wryly.

The simplicity of the details on Nova's driving licence were barely enough for the Commander to see that there was some semblance of truth in what they were saying and the evidence of the murder before them showed him clearly that they weren't the killers, and it gave some credibility to the theory that there was something much fiercer in the mine.

The imprints in the snow told him that there was something very much larger and far more dangerous then these two could ever be.

"There is another piece of news that might be a bit hard for you to take in, if you are telling the truth!" said the American officer sharply.

"Of course we're telling the truth, what is your problem man?" Nova shrieked.

Adams pulled out his weapon and pushed the young man back against the wall, pressing the nib right into his throat.

"You know any other man wouldn't hesitate to pull the trigger upon finding two intruders at a crime scene," snarled the Commander; his fingered wavered upon the weapon as his weight held the young man back.

Nova's eyes widened in panic and he glared at the gun.

"If we knew what was going on down here we'd tell you, no need to go all Dirty Harry on us!" scoffed Nova and looked at the gun again.

Time-Ryder: Powerstone Book One

"Do I look amused?" narrowed the Commander.

"Constipated maybe!" sniped Nova cheerily and then the Commander pushed him back across the cavern where Nova slammed into the wall again.

"That was uncalled for!" barked the Professor, rushing forward to his aid, "You really aren't helping things" he said to Nova under his breath.

"Aye, well this boring exchange of questions isn't getting us anywhere Professor!" replied the young man.

Adams turned away from the young man, composing himself and straightening his flight-suit as Nova zipped up his coat.

"We've got twelve dead crewmembers" he hissed in a shrill tone, "Most of the expedition team dead and our Captain and Chief Medical officer are MIA"

"And how were we supposed to know? We didn't kill them," shrieked Nova and then he saw the look upon the Commander's face, but he wasn't letting on.

"But you already know that don't you?" said the young man, not backing down this time.

The look in the Commander's eyes told Nova everything he needed to know, there was more to this man than the simple mission he was on, something personal.

Nova took a step back from the troopers and their guns, seeing something vulnerable in the Commander's disposition.

Adams sighed, took a breath and calmed down, re-holstering his weapon.

"No I don't think you killed him or any of them" he sighed.

"Then you believe us?" asked the Professor in a hiss.

"Let's just say I don't disbelieve you, but your presence here does need to be explained!" Adams looked solemnly at the old man.

"We can't really help you with that Commander, but the sphere is the key, everything changed after we both touched it."

Time-Ryder: Powerstone Book One

The Commander shook his head and looked at the sphere; fascinated by it.

"What does it do?" Nova asked.

Adams leaned forward to the two men and frowned, scratching his moustache nervously.

Even the Professor could see how secretive he was, whether it was his orders or not, it was going to take a lot for him to tell them what was going on.

Nova looked at the Professor, seeing the old man deep in thought, at times like these he usually left the old man alone, but this time he was in the same position, thinking along the same lines.

"How many of these things have you found?" asked Nova.

He took a breath.

"Five so far. Why?"

The Professor cleared his throat.

"And all very close to one of these poor dead fellows?"

Adams nodded briefly, wondering where the line of questioning was going.

"And are all the corpses slightly out of your own time?" asked the old man.

"How the hell could you possibly know that?"

A brief pause of smugness on the Professor's behalf ended as he stepped closer to the Commander.

"I may be old and past it as Mr Mitchell constantly reminds me, but my hearing is still in good working order. A century old Astro suit he said" the Professor quoted Madeley, "that and the certain questions you've been asking, it's all slotting into place."

Nova, like the Commander was silent for once, he listened to the Professor's ramblings, but it made little sense to him, he was just waiting to see how it played out.

"So there you have it Commander" continued the old man, "our story and a little of yours, very intermixed. Just one thing I'd like to get clear if we're going to assist you!"
Adams folded his arms.
"And what might that be?"
The Professor made a face as he scratched his thick white beard and he looked away from the Commander; he couldn't quite believe what he was about to utter.
"Exactly what year is this?"

The communication blackout had caused Troopers Vane and Brooks to abandon the VDU station and travel into the depths of the maze of glacial caverns. No matter how many times Vane stepped into a new chamber, he couldn't help but gape in awe at the enormity of the high ceilings and the hanging stalactites drooping down like the elongated teeth of some long dead dinosaur.
He couldn't believe the size, or the fact that so many chambers were crammed into the whole mountain area. It really was no surprise that it was a mine with all of the tunnels and passages spread all over.
Vane looked back at Brooks and stepped up the pace, holding the elongated black tracker in front of him, until he clipped it onto his field cannon. He trudged forward with the short form of the anxious Brooks covering his rear.
"Which way are you heading Joe?"
Vane sniffed the air as they came to a fork in the tunnels. He looked to the ceiling where a series of small lamps were linked from one end of the tunnel to the other.
"This way!" he indicated the right path.

"If we go through the gantry we can meet up with Owens and Barker. Safety in numbers buddy," he smiled back at the other trooper.
"Do you reckon it might be the Captain? Do you think he's found him?" Brooks spluttered, still keeping his eyes on the tiny tracker screen.
"No, and No!" retorted Vane, walking calmly forward.
"Why not?"
The bald trooper stopped in his tracks annoyingly and held back, tipping his field cannon to the air.
"If the Commander had found him, he'd have made it back to the rendezvous point by now, so I reckon there's something else down here."
"The killer?" asked Brooks, his eyes wide.
"Maybe, but this Commander is two strikes down, he's not going to give up till he's made a full run!" said the American sternly.
"Joe, we've known each other for well over a year now, and I still don't get half of your Baseball metaphors!" Brooks gulped and still couldn't take his eyes off the tracker strapped to his rifle.
"What I mean is. This is his last chance. I don't know if it's gone past you Brooksy, but there aren't a lot of crewmen left after Blackthorne's encounter in the mine."
"Yeah, but you got out all right!" shrieked Brooks.
"Oh yeah and that just makes the poster-boy for suspicion in Lieutenant Everett's eyes" replied Vane.
Brooks could tell by the tone of his voice that he had a slight dislike of Lieutenant Everett.
"Is she still on your case?'"
"Nothing I can't handle" smiled the bald trooper, edging forward.
As they carried on down the track, the ground became more rugged, until it smoothed out onto a slippery glass floor and then

stretched out to the next dark cavern to which both troopers gave an anxious glance to each other.

"After you!" whispered Brooks to which Vane cocked back the large silver muzzle-shaped barrel of his field cannon and trudged carefully across the glass floor to the opening.

The interior was clouded, dark and foreboding yet Vane moved slowly into the opening; the smell of death apparent and overwhelming as he took a pause and stepped backward before composing himself for re-entry.

"Brooksy get in here with that scope light" he hissed.

Brooks tipped back his black cap and followed the tall trooper into the dark; the smell hitting him almost immediately.

"That's disgusting, what is it?"

"Circle the floor, and watch your step!"

The cautious Vane followed the light on the end of Brooks' rifle and saw the gory mess all over the floor of the cavern.

He turned his head away upon sight of the bloodied area and the corpses that were torn apart.

Limbs, intestines and all manner of organs were strewn from one corner of the cavern to the other and the blood splatter was all over the walls as if someone had dipped a paint roller in the redness and had begun to decorate the walls.

"I think I'm going to hurl" Vane capped his mouth and returned to the opening.

Brooks on the other hand had a strong stomach and a very unusual sense of smell. He almost ignored it and stepped through the bloody mess to where the fabric of the bodies could be seen. On the floor in amongst the varying array of detached limbs, he could see a small plasti-card name badge and the small Identifit photo of Owens and very close by was the card belonging to Barker, equally as tarred in the crimson stain.

Brooks could see from the type of uniform that the third corpse was Doctor Belder, minus his head; yet didn't seem as mutilated as the troopers' bodies were.

"Joe... It's Owens and Barker," he paused and with no response from Vane, still being sick at the cavern entrance, he carried on. "And Doctor Belder, what's left of him anyway!"

Vane composed himself and entered the cavern gingerly, stepping lightly through the gore to join his friend.

"What do you mean, what's left of him?"

"Joe, his head's gone. There's no sign of it at all!"

Brooks held out a restraining hand to the American.

"What?"

"Sshh, listen, did you hear that?" whispered Brooks, he cocked his ear in the direction of the other entrance to the cavern.

"Nope" said Vane bluntly, "anything on the scope?"

"No" hissed Brooks in a shrill tone.

"Well what did it sound like?"

"I dunno, a scream I suppose!"

"A manly scream or a girly scream? Or a man doing a girly scream?" Vane smiled wryly

"A girly scream, Sshh, listen," whispered Brooks again.

"You've been in deep space too long, need a bit of shore-leave," retorted the tall trooper, wiping his mouth.

"I'm telling you it was a woman. A definite scream and it wasn't my imagination!"

"Then let's check it out" said Vane, already marching through the archway.

Brooks stooped to collect Barker's identification disc and plasticard, stowing them with Owens card and making for the archway somewhat reluctantly.

Time-Ryder: Powerstone Book One

Time-Ryder: Powerstone Book One

CHAPTER FOURTEEN

Frightened as she was, the blonde haired girl in the silver cloak had eluded the killer for some time, but it had eventually caught up with her in the lower part of the tunnel system.
She backed away from the hooded shape, still looking upon it, but afraid to take her eyes away from the enormous hulk.
She screamed again and again, retreating from its advance until it stopped in its tracks.
Even though it kept its stance, she was still scared to death.
Her heartbeat increased so much that she became hot; her head was on fire, and her pulse raced feverishly.
Along with her increasing heartbeat and panting breath, she felt a sudden tingle of pain coming from her arm again and she pulled back the sleeve of her elegant glistening cloak to reveal the silver bangle that was firmly clamped around her wrist.
It began to glow with intensity again, shining until it was white hot. It was the source of all her pain, her head, and her racing pulse all seemed to be connected to this mysterious object that she had never laid her eyes upon before, even though it felt vaguely familiar.
Gritting her teeth, she tried to ease the bangle over her wrist, but it seemed to contract onto her skin as if it were alive, and still it continued to glow.
As if in a robotic jerk of movement, the shape strode across the cavern floor, bound for the object at her feet. The glass sphere, the very cause of her newfound surroundings was resting on a thin layer of snow.
She looked down at it curiously, trying to remember.
Her memory still hazy from her emergence and every time she tried to remember, her head was filled with a horrendous pain. Unlike the agony that she felt from the bangle, it stabbed at back of her head and spread across her skull; filling her cranium with

severe rush of agony that seemed to intensify as she tried to concentrate upon her lost memories.

She looked down and saw the powdered snow surrounding the glass ball before turning back to the advancing shape that lumbered forward, its gaping maw wide and salivating as it came nearer.

Still the bangle glowed brighter until it soon encapsulated her vision and she had to close her eyes from the brightness.

The light grew brighter with intensity until the monstrous shape emitted a shrill whine of discomfort and backed off, almost animal-like in its movement.

It retreated from her, moving sluggishly backward and holding its clawed hand out to mask the brightness from its eyes.

Darting out of the cavern, it left behind what it had pursued the girl for as it bled back into the darkness in retreat.

As the pain and the glow of the bangle reached breaking point, the girl felt the sensation ripple up her arm, crossing over her chest and her breathing became faster.

Her back arched as the glow spread over her body and her arms soared backward, the bright light filling the whole chamber.

But it was too much for her and she collapsed to the ground; the light finally fading and retracting back inside the bangle, where it returned to its natural state.

She lay unconscious on the ground, the sphere nestling close to her body. Once again, just as she had arrived, she was alone.

The cloaked shape retreated through the tunnels, moving faster; its clawed hands reaching out to touch the walls, feeling them for support and clutching them as a guide.

The light had such an overwhelming effect upon it, that it had been blinded and its massive hands touched the ragged walls,

feeling them for the next opening and guiding its massive form along by touch.
The killer was frightened and still pushed on through the mine, not realising what damage the intense light had done to it, but the blindness was only temporary.
It was still enough to scare it away from ever going near the girl in the near future. As its sight slowly returned, the shape slowed its progress and lowered its long arms to the side, fumbling inside for the large silver crown once again.
Holding it in a tight grip, the shape backtracked slowly and swept aside the snow at its feet, bound for the gantry in search of any more intruders within the mine

Nova's mouth had been open for such a long time as he gaped in disbelief and wondered if they were playing a joke at his expense. The Commander's statement left him stunned, but could he believe what he'd been told?
"Twenty One Ninety Six!" he exclaimed, "Are you shitting me?"
The Professor gave him the usual disapproving glare at his choice of words, but he was beginning to give up hope.
"Oh that's a really good one, did Brian put you up to this?" he grinned, "Bet he's down in the King's Rest laughing his ass off" blurted out the young man, but his grin vanished quickly when he noticed no one else found the situation as amusing as he was. He looked at the Professor.
"You don't seriously believe them about all this future stuff, do you?"
"In the words of the Commander, I don't disbelieve them," said the Professor softly, a statement that truly rocked his reasoning. He took off his glasses as the troopers behind Adams primed their weapons and levelled them upon him.

Time-Ryder: Powerstone Book One

"Just cleaning them!" he pressed his glasses back on over his nose and held his hands aloft again.

"Why?" Nova asked, but he knew the Professor would have an explanation for his thinking.

"Keen detection Mr Mitchell. Take a look at their uniforms, the insignia, the weapons and all these strange devices attached to their belts."

"Aye well I didn't think we were at a Batman convention," he said sarcastically.

The old man gave him that look again.

"Doesn't it seem a little odd that he might ask such a question such as that? And look at the sphere, doesn't it seem slightly otherworldly to you?"

"Nah, I just thought it was like one of those cheap fibre optic lamps that you used to have" retorted the young archaeologist.

Sighing at his attempt at humour, the old man continued.

"And yet the Commander doesn't seem at all surprised that we know so much about it, do you Commander?"

Adams raised his head and turned back to face them.

"You seem too much at ease that we might come from another century," said the Professor turning the tables.

"There's something you aren't telling us? Isn't there Commander?"

Palmer and Madeley said nothing, for they had noticed the signs themselves, the strangeness of his behaviour and the absentmindedness. They waited to see if the Commander would open up, but it would be a good deal longer than they thought.

"Twelve dead you say?" the Professor held out his hands, waving off the two gun toting troopers, "Including that poor fellow down there?"

In all of the confusion, Adams and his troopers had overlooked the prone form of Trayna frozen behind them.

"He's not one of ours," said the tall man in all but a hiss.

Palmer almost gagged at the disgusting sight and the blood splattered tunic.

"Commander whoever committed this atrocity can't be far away," interceded the Professor, "the blood is still relatively warm, even at these remarkably low temperatures."

"And from the look on his face, he seemed shocked at the sight of his killer!"

Adams lowered his pistol slightly.

"So he either knows his killer or was shocked by their appearance. It stands to reason that it can't be either of us!" the old man said after a breath and lowered his hands, retreating to the rock for a breather.

"I dunno though," Nova grinned at the Professor "that tie is a bit of a shocker!" he smiled at the old man, who straightened his tie and frowned with displeasure.

"This isn't funny Mr Mitchell, death isn't, doesn't matter who it is on the receiving end. You of all people should know that!"

"Aye, I'm sorry," mumbled the young man, "I was just trying to lighten the mood!"

The Professor sat upright and then rose, circling the corpse, still being watched by the troopers.

"What are you going to do about him? You surely can't just leave him there like that?"

Adams eyed Trayna's contorted form again and rifled inside his backpack for a second, pulling out a silver field pistol, it was a smaller hand held version of the weapons that the troopers bore. He didn't like using these things at the best of times, but kept one handy as a back-up.

He stepped closer to the corpse and braced himself with his hand pointing toward the frozen form.

"Just a minute!" said the Professor sharply, "Mr Mitchell, a vial please!" he said and outstretched his hand. Nova passed over the glass tube from his pocket.

"What are you doing Professor?" Adams stooped closer, narrowing his eyes in confusion.

"Something I noticed earlier" the Professor took the top of his pen and scraped a few green flakes from the open wound into the vial and sealed the top with the rubber stopper.

"There, that should do it!" he smiled forlornly and nodded to the Commander and then paused as he revolved to see the back of the man's head. At the nape of his neck, just beneath the skull were three small pinpricks directly in line with his spinal column.

"What do you make of this?" he asked the Commander.

Adams pushed back his cap and leaned closer for inspection.

"It looks fresh, but what caused it? An insect bite maybe?"

"No, the temperature down here is too low. You haven't seen any bugs have you?" said the old man softly.

Thinking nothing more of it, the Professor stepped away from the body and Adams took his stance again and fired the pistol.

Watching as the blue burst of energy from the weapon bathed the corpse and slowly it disintegrated to nothingness as the old man gave a remorseful sniff.

The Commander put the pistol away in his bag and snatched the comm unit, trying it again, adjusting the channel and attempting to contact anyone within range, but he heard no reply, only the droned out garbled scrape of interference.

Nova; who had been silent throughout their disposal of the corpse suddenly spoke up and looked at Adams who saw that he was deep in thought.

"If all this future stuff is true, which I'm still not believing by the way" he said in a pessimistic retort, "then why did it bring us here of all places? There has to be a reasonable explanation for that!"

"What do you mean?" Adams turned slowly

Nova gave him a steely gaze.

For someone with such a flippant outlook on life, he had moments of pure clarity and saw things that the others around him had often overlooked.

The Professor looked on in amusement.

"Go on, I'm eager to hear what you have to say," he said cheerily.

"We know that sphere brought us and others here, right? But what's inside it? That's what whoever is doing the killing is after. He's just tossing aside the shells and taking what's inside. What's its purpose? Especially if it's killing to get the surprise inside," he looked pensively at the others.

There was a brief period of silence to which the Professor crossed to the Commander and looked at him with a curious gaze.

"It might put us a step closer to finding out how to get us back!" he continued, "Then there is another thing that we've overlooked Commander," Nova hissed softly to which all of the surrounding men turned to look at him strangely and he made the most obvious statement that all of them had overlooked.

"If this intact sphere is so important, then won't the killer be coming after it?"

Time-Ryder: Powerstone Book One

Time-Ryder: Powerstone Book One

CHAPTER FIFTEEN

Vane's disgust of the scene of death was making him angry and tense; it reminded him of the massacre in the mine when he crawled to safety and hid under the pile of crewmen's corpses to get away from the killer. The unknown assailant had left him for dead, and he eventually fled; making it back to the ship some time later.

The smell of death brought it all back, and had unsettled his stomach, but the chamber was silent. They couldn't hear the scream that had attracted them to the bodies, yet both troopers heard an oscillating whine that echoed towards them, coming louder and louder from beyond the opening.

Brooks tipped his rifle, turning the twin beams of his scope lights on the archway ahead as a lone figure shuffled into the opening, casting a shadow over them.

It was over seven foot tall, the frayed robes flapping in the wind behind it as the mist clouded around its feet. Vane pointed the large silver barrel of the field cannon in the direction of the newcomer and aimed at the deathly figure.

Its size was enormous and he didn't think even the mighty firepower that the cannon had would be enough to stop it. Whatever the shape was, it didn't see the troopers until Vane cocked the weapon loudly and its massive head snapped around in his direction; although squinting, unsure of what it was seeing. Still dazed with blindness from the girl's bangle, the shape was vulnerable; if only the troopers knew that.

Its mouth stretched wide, bearing the endless row of salivating teeth and Vane prepared to fire.

From out of the figure's mouth, a long flex extended like lightning, wrapping around Vane's throat and slowly dragged him closer.

Time-Ryder: Powerstone Book One

The bald trooper dropped the cannon immediately and clawed his hands to his throat; desperately trying to free the tight grip that whatever the shape was had on him.

It reeled him in; pulling him closer until Vane saw the extent of the creature's appearance. His eyes went wide in panic as Brooks dropped the field rifle and crawled desperately forward to seize the larger field cannon.

He lifted the heavy silver weapon that was not unlike a large projectile launcher; albeit a little larger and he fired towards the creature.

Luckily for Vane, the shot of energy missed and careered into the wall close by the figure's head. The shape held Vane close as the trooper fumbled about his side and he slipped a long slender blade into the air, severing the creature's slippery tongue and relaxing the grip around his throat.

The bald trooper dropped to the floor as Brooks took a defensive stance once again and released the trigger on the cannon, but this time it was a direct hit and the blast eradicated the figure, leaving only a smoking corpse or rather the lower half of one.

The blast had decimated the creature with only its lower limbs standing erect and the faint remnants of clothing surrounding the smoking frame.

Brooks just stood in shock; his mouth gaping at the extent of the weapon's firepower and he quickly relinquished it to Vane; who more than welcomed the return of his beloved weapon as he unfurled the rubbery flex from around his throat and he wheezed for breath.

He moved to inspect what was left of the corpse and squinted to the object in the powdery snow at the feet of the creature's remains.

It had clearly dropped from the beast's robes and nestled on the floor like a penny that had spun on the ground. It was a large silver ring, but resembled a halo with strange symbols around the outer facing.

"What the hell is it?" Brooks fumbled forward to his friend's side.

Vane lifted the silver crown device and held it up into the air.
"Beats me, but I reckon it's important!" croaked the bald trooper, still massaging his windpipe.

"What do you think it was?" hissed Brooks, looking over the charred remains.

"I suppose it was the thing that killed everyone, but we don't need to worry anymore," gasped Vane with delight.

Quickly putting the silver crown into his flight-suit; he cocked the cannon again.

"C'mon, let's find the Commander, give him the good news!"
Brooks looked glum and shifted nervously around the remains, following Vane out into the white tunnel beyond the chamber.
He just prayed that things were going to be that easy.

The girl still lay where she had collapsed, curled into a ball beneath the silver sheen of her almighty cloak, unaware that her pursuer had been dealt with.

The approach of footsteps into the chamber roused her slightly and she began to stretch beneath the sea of silver material.

Her long hood clouded her face, obscuring her beautiful features as the newcomers entered the chamber and she began to retreat slowly.

She wept slightly as a hand reached forward and tugged back the hood gently and she saw the bearded face of Professor Carlson beaming down upon her.

"Now what do we have here?" he said cheerily, but almost frightening the terrified girl.

Time-Ryder: Powerstone Book One

The group behind him had come to a sudden standstill as he leaned over and scooped the young woman up from the floor and patted the snow from her cloak.

"What's the hold up?" shrieked Nova, edging past the two troopers to see the beautiful, yet slightly marred features of the girl. Professor Carlson saw her tear-stained and reddened face; her shaking hands, and he moved slowly forward.

"It's alright, no one will harm you!" he tried to reassure her, "Do you have a name my dear?"

She shook her head as Nova crouched down beside her and smiled, clearing away the small specks of white powder from her platinum locks.

She saw the innocence in his face and the kindness he was showing; yet she still held back with fear.

"Can you talk?" whispered Nova softly.

Commander Adams looked over the young man's shoulder and saw her tunic and fingernails tainted with blood.

He withdrew his pistol and levelled it directly at her head.

The girl recoiled in fear; hiding behind Nova, her hands shaking and he protected her; his brows narrowing at the Commander's behaviour.

"Alright Serpico, put that thing away! Can't you see she's harmless?" spat Nova in disgust.

"Look at her fingernails" snapped the Commander.

"A little blood... How d'you know it's not hers? Look at the state of her," retorted the young man.

He turned back to the frightened girl and inhaled deeply.

"Hey, it's alright. No one's going to hurt you. Here come and take a seat," Nova held her up by the elbows and helped her over to the rocks that stemmed from the wall.

"It's alright my dear, bit of a rest and then you can tell us everything" said the Professor, but he didn't mean it to sound so patronising. As she reluctantly took her seat; her cloak opened

and Nova noticed the body-hugging silver jumpsuit, with much the same design as her cloak, clearly showing off all her attributes.
It was then that Nova noticed the series of letters and numbers on her left breast, clearly stencilled in black.
"Valana 359" he whispered, "Is that your name?" he looked into her deep blue eyes.
"I, I, can't remember!" She finally uttered a word and stammered softly, her voice quiet and frightened to the core.
Nova continued to stare at her beauty and he looked back to her breast and then realised what he was doing. He blushed.
"Sorry I wasn't staring at your...bits" he said looking for a better word.
"Look I'll call you Valana until you can remember your name, is that alright?" he said softly, "we can't keep calling you she, can we?"
She smiled at his kindness again, yet still said nothing.
"Sorry, I'm Nova, that's the Professor and the one with big chin is called Adams!" smiled the young man, trying his best to put the girl at ease. He could see she was trembling, her hands shaking.
Adams raised his hand to his bearded chin for a second in a peak of vanity and then realised that Nova was just teasing him, or so he hoped.
"Where are you from?" he said bluntly, looking down on the girl.
She looked back up, her jade coloured eyes almost giving him the puppy dog treatment. He saw how teary she was and stood back, not expecting an answer.
"She's in shock!" hissed the Commander.
Nova rolled his eyes.
"Aye, thanks for that Sigmund. Even I can see that!"
Valana sniffed and wiped her nose with the Professor's outstretched handkerchief.

"That Th..Th..Thing. I think it killed those poor men!" she stuttered, holding back her breath and trying to compose herself.
"Try to relax" Nova said softly and put a hand on her shoulder.
"This thing, what did it look like?" Adams stepped closer.
Both troopers behind him looked at each other as she tried to get the words out.
"It was big. Covered in black robes with a long hood over its face, but I saw under the hood," she stammered again, her posh voice clear and calming down.
The Professor's eyes widened as he leaned over.
"And?"
"Easy now, take a deep breath" reassured Nova, rubbing her shoulder.
"I'll never forget that face," she hissed coldly, "and those teeth, teeth like a wild animal and its eyes. Green and glowing"
"Anything else?" pressed the Commander.
Nova squinted.
"Isn't that enough to go on?" he spat.
"I didn't stay around to find out. I ran out of there as fast as I could!" said the girl softly.
Adams snapped his head around to the two troopers.
"You two scout ahead and report if you find anything" he pointed his pistol to the tunnel where the girl had entered from.
Palmer exchanged looks with Madeley and then the Commander before they tore off quickly into the dark, leaving the girl to finish her story.
The Professor rose to face him and thrust his hands into his deep pockets, peering over his glasses at him.
"Well Commander? Do you believe us now?"
Sheepishly Adams felt his face flush and he gave the quietest of apologies.
"Sorry I didn't hear that?" snapped Nova loud enough for all to hear.

"Under the circumstances, you can see where I was coming from," continued Adams.

"Under the circumstances, Under the circumstances?" began Nova and then saw where the officer was coming from and decided to drop it, "I suppose under the circumstances you were only doing what you thought was right."

Professor Carlson nodded and thought of the frozen corpse in the other chamber that the Commander had disposed of, thankfully Valana hadn't seen it; otherwise it might have made her worse.

"Commander a minute please?" the Professor asked, and stood back beside him, as Nova continued to comfort the girl.

He indicated to the Commander and he moved swiftly over to join the officer by the wall.

But Adams was staring into space, not hearing the old man's words and after several attempts he finally acknowledged the Professor.

"What is it?"

"Perhaps if you explain to us what is really going on here, we might be able to help?" offered the old man.

"You're two hundred years out of time Professor, what can you possibly do to help the situation?" replied the tall officer, somewhat rashly.

"Try me?' returned the old man, standing his ground.

He folded his arms and looked directly at him, refusing to budge until he conceded.

"Why not? It's not as if I'm under orders not to disclose anything." Adams shrugged.

He perched on the outcrop of rocks and took a deep breath.

"I hope you have plenty of time Professor!"

The old man smiled and held out his hands.

"I'm not going anywhere and call me Henry please!"

Adams smiled, feeling quite at ease in the Professor's company.

"Well Henry, it's all a bit complicated."

Nova rolled his eyes and looked up from Valana.
"Can't be any more complicated than our lives have already become today" he chuckled.
The Professor took a seat beside Adams and inhaled deeply; he had a feeling that it was going to take a while.

CHAPTER SIXTEEN

In the darkness of some long, forgotten chamber, there was a constant flicker of light.
The illumination was very poor, but it served the purposes of the inhabitants; patiently tapping away at a series of keypads that stretched over an extensive workspace in what seemed to be some sort of vast operations centre.
The walls were lined with screens; mostly dormant, yet only a few were filled with power, and only those with a trained and keen eye could see what was on them.
The chamber looked as if it hadn't seen the light of day for some foreseeable time or the services of a cleaner as the corners were thick with cobwebs; dust gathering so much that they outlined the webs and made them stand out in the dark.
A small figure hunched over the controls, coughing sparingly; his small clawed fingers clicking away and watching in keen observation at the screens before opening his mouth to speak.
His head was covered by a darkened cowl, shrouding his appearance like the hooded killer in the tunnels.
Whether it was vanity or disgust, only he knew, but he pulled the hood down slightly over his eye-line as he stared at the screens in front of him.
"The one sent to the lower levels is dead!" he hissed softly over his shoulder; his words in all but a whisper.
His statement was directed towards another mutually concealed being that hid in the darkness far behind him.
The slow movements of a larger occupant shuffling forward to the workstation were accompanied by an oversized hand clamping down upon the shoulder of the smaller being, the claws sharp and elongated, almost like a birds; yet his hand coursed with faint traces of reptilian markings.

The skin and scales were intermixed, smooth, and yet shiny and appeared charred and blackened.

"Show me!" hissed the coarse voice of the taller being.

The smaller one's hands crept across the keyboard lightly and one of the screens showed the faded image of what was left of the creature that had been disposed of by the field cannon; its remains still charred and smoking.

"I told you they'd come back with more troops Kersey, I warned you," said the small one.

"And it looks like they've got sufficient firepower to try and stop us" answered Kersey politely, still holding himself in the darkness and appearing like a disembodied voice, apart from the visibility of his clawed hand.

"What do you want to do? He had the endower on him and there are four spheres still to track."

There was a brief silence to which Kersey removed himself from the screens and paraded the darkness, deep in thought.

The smaller one continued to look at the screens, switching the control and watching the tunnels for signs of the intruders; turning his hand to the various cameras that spanned the upper sections of the vast mining system.

"Have all the spheres been returned to the mines?" asked Kersey.

"All but one, the recollection device hasn't tracked its signal yet, but it's just a matter of time."

With a resigned sigh, Kersey stepped back to the workspace, clamping his massive hand down upon it.

"With the troops added firepower we can't take any chance of not completing our task. We will have to step up our plans. We have no alternative but to release the rest of the specimens from the vault. Is there any news from the other?" he rasped.

The smaller creature checked the readings on the sophisticated computer, waiting patiently before answering with a resounding "No!"

"No, I didn't think there would be!"
"His communication device is offline," replied the small one, "it might be unavoidable!"
"Then release the specimens," barked Kersey in resignation.
The smaller creature slid back a panel and pressed his clawed thumb into the recess as the lights surrounding another screen turned red and spurts of gas started to surround the area.
"It's done!" he sighed, disappointingly.
"Good, now send the commands to their remote processors and then we can begin!"
The smaller creature still hunched over the controls, tapping its clawed hand down impatiently upon the keypad.
"Will they do as the processor commands them?"
Kersey coughed; his breathing worsening as he shuffled forward again.
"The Bio-mechanical implants will give them no choice, if they decide to disobey their commands; it'll administer a shock that will shut down their vital systems."
"That sounds barbaric, even for you Kersey!" rasped the smaller creature.
"Then you should be thankful you don't have a neural implant Gage, otherwise the Restoration would be mine and mine only!"
Gage felt as if he was betraying the others like him, but he activated the control, sending the information to the implants that the specimens had grafted into their minds; implants that would hopefully enable them to complete their tasks, but he was dubious of the technology, and if it would succeed at all.
"Are you sure you should have released them all? They haven't had sufficient time for the cryo process to wear off; they might become unstable when they emerge."
Kersey straightened and the smaller creature could hear the pains as he tried to stand erect.

Time-Ryder: Powerstone Book One

"Whatever it takes to achieve restoration, the cost does not matter," said Kersey bluntly.
"Even if the rest of the specimens may be volatile?"
"As long as they do what is asked of them I don't care, you do want Restoration don't you?" asked Kersey, his coarse voice elevating slightly.
"Of, of course!" the smaller creature stammered.
"Good, the time for a guilty conscience is long since past, another few deaths need not matter!"
The smaller creature was weary, nervous and sat watching the screens, waiting for the specimens to make their presence in the tunnels known.

Slipping the small silver Coronet out of his flight suit, Trooper Vane stopped in his tracks as Brooks looked on, equally intrigued about the device as he was.
Both troopers couldn't believe that the killer was dead, or had been killed so easily, but then maybe if they'd brought the field cannon with them upon entry into the mines the first time around, then all of the casualties wouldn't have happened and the Captain wouldn't be missing - presumed dead.
"What do you think it is?"
Vane turned the object over, eyeing the strange symbols and glyphs that marked the areas around the rim, he took note of the illuminated band that spanned its whole length and he looked confused.
"Some sort of crown I reckon," said the American softly.
He demonstrated by hovering it over Brooks' mop of hair, showing his friend that it would fit on an average head and even the slightly oversized one it was hanging above at the moment.
"Yeah, but what is it for?"

"I dunno, you're the technical one, you figure it out!" spat Vane, idly passing the silver crown into the welcoming hands of his friend.

Brooks looked at it in more detail and saw the strange triangular symbol on its face, slightly more elevated than the other symbols and he touched it lightly with his fingertips.

Almost immediately three black rod-like stems protruded from the inside of the crown, reaching out for something until Vane craned closer and pointed at one of them.

The first rod made contact with his gloved finger and bit deep, to which Vane retracted his hand instantaneously. He looked at his gloved hand and saw the hole, almost burn-like and he removed the glove, seeing the slight scorch on his fingertip.

The rods continued to flail around the inner ring of the coronet until the triangular symbol flashed with a green flurry of light and they slowly returned home to the silver rim.

"What was that?" shrieked Brooks.

"I dunno, but don't do it again, it stings like a mother!" snorted Vane, "maybe the Commander will know what it is."

"I suppose," Brooks said offhandedly, "but what was that thing doing with it?"

Vane hid the crown beneath his flight-suit and held the bulky silver field cannon tightly, beckoning his friend to follow him into the tunnels ahead.

"Well whatever it is, it's ours for the taking!" said the bald trooper.

Brooks nodded as they passed under the archway into the network of tunnels, bypassing the overturned mine carts and discarded machinery. Unnoticed as they left the chamber, a small shining red crystal lay at the remains of the creature's feet, nestling neatly in the fine layer of snow, yet totally overlooked by the two anxious and half-frightened troopers.

Time-Ryder: Powerstone Book One

Deep in another part of the mine, in the coldest reaches that had been long forgotten, the craggy grey walls blended into a smooth white finish leading into an adapted area that was entirely walled off with glass, the reflection long since gone.

Only the frosted tracks of some form of animal were present, stemming from a vacant chamber; almost like a cubicle, yet it was empty.

The glass walls hid more chambers; each had been fashioned into sections almost like small cells, concealing what lay inside.

The contents were in deep hibernation and sleeping for eternity.

Three of the large chambers were empty, the doors long since opened, yet another six remained tightly sealed, each holding a dark secret inside, ready to be unleashed.

High up on top of the chambers were a set of controls and symbols, undecipherable to the human eye. Only the great architects of this domain would know what they meant, but they started to fill with light, until power flowed into the circuits and the transparent glass doors that hemmed the occupants inside started to rise.

Five of the cubicles began to open, releasing streaming jets of cold gas that dispersed throughout the small confines of this new room, although the temperature in the corridor remained a constant, yet the sixth chamber did not budge.

It was fastened tightly and showed no signs that the occupant was going to put in an appearance any time soon.

As the icy air cleared, the newcomers emerged from the cubicles, given a new lease on life and taking their first steps into the white void beyond.

The new creatures recoiled briefly from the bright light above, cowering slightly from the imposing rays before exiting their cubicles slowly.

Their dark clothes were ragged, just as the others were, stitched together loosely and draped over their bodies, some fitting better

than others, yet still concealing whatever creature may dwell beneath them.
For who knows what other horrors these creatures were.
They craned their heads to the side, hearing the inaudible signal and received their commands through the remote processors they had been conditioned with; giving them their orders, before they shuffled into the white corridor ahead, bound for the mine tunnels and the tasks that lay before them.

Time-Ryder: Powerstone Book One

Time-Ryder: Powerstone Book One

CHAPTER SEVENTEEN

Nova was perched on an overturned rock with the girl he'd christened Valana, as Adams and the Professor were still deep in conversation. She still hadn't said much to him, but he could tell by her body language that she'd calmed down a great deal since they'd first met.

He couldn't help but stare at her beauty, reminded much of Barbara by her long flowing locks, but he did his best to put those memories away and at least try to concentrate upon everything that was happening here.

Valana looked up at the young man with puppy-dog eyes, and pulled out the small glass sphere from her cloak.

"I want to show you this!" she said softly, showing it off to him.

Nova's eyes widened. Normally when girls wanted to show him anything, the surroundings were a little more relaxed and clothing was optional.

He smiled at her wryly.

"This is all I had when I arrived here, do you know what it is?" she said softly, her voice quiet and less panicky as it had been.

He pushed himself back on the rock, edging away from the glass sphere as if frightened somehow. His reaction disturbed Valana but she kept a tight grip on the object.

"Em, Professor" he paused for a second, "Come and see this," he exclaimed as his brows lifted in surprise.

"In a moment Mr Mitchell" came the gruff reply as the old man concentrated on what the Commander was saying.

"No Professor, you really need to see this like now!" he said forcefully and in a tone that the old man recognised.

The Professor tore away from the Commander and turned to see Nova's startled expression and in the girl's outstretched hand was the glass sphere identical to their own.

Time-Ryder: Powerstone Book One

Patting his pockets down, the Professor checked to see that he still had their own sphere in his possession and he tapped the Commander to attention.

Adams tipped his cap backward and looked over curiously.

"Two intact spheres, now that is something" said the American officer.

He edged off his makeshift seat and followed the inquisitive old man over to the girl who was still holding onto the ball for dear life.

The Professor eased his sphere out of his battered coat and showed it to the girl; who didn't seem at all frightened by it. She looked curiously at the identical sphere and then up to the old man.

"You have one too?" she exclaimed, startled by the appearance of another, "Do you know what it is?"

Shaking his head, Adams stared at the sphere, but Henry noticed his uneasiness, yet kept a silent vigil for the moment.

The Professor began to pace nervously up and down the cavern in deep thought, tapping his lip nervously with his finger.

"D'you mind not doing that? It's starting to annoy me" drawled Nova, pulling the zip of his black jacket up under his chin.

"It helps me think!" whispered the old man and he came to a stop to the amazement of the others upon seeing his beaming smile.

"You know I've only just realised!" exclaimed the Professor out loud.

"That you're getting on my nerves" snapped Nova, "I could have told you that a while ago and saved you some shoe leather."

"No, I've only begun to realise how incredibly dumb I am" spat the Professor in delight, smiling at his own insult.

Nova's brows drooped.

"For a guy that can speak nine languages, I'd hardly call you dumb!"

"Why do you think you're dumb Professor?" Adams was equally as confused and he looked at the old man squarely.

"This creature seems to be after these things" he waved the ball in front of them, "and every one your people have found them next to a corpse."

"Aye, I think we already established that," Nova drawled, "So?"

"So why don't we arrange a trade for our safe passage out of here? Theoretically speaking of course" offered back the old man.

"Now you are being incredibly dumb" spat Nova, "This thing, whatever it is, is skewering everyone like kebabs and you think it'll just agree to your terms?"

"It's worth a try!" said the Professor. He was prepared to do anything possible to spare their lives.

Nova nodded sarcastically, if such a thing was possible.

"Aye and when we get home I'm buying you six rolls of rubber wallpaper for Christmas!" said Nova dryly.

"He's got a point Professor" interjected Adams. The idea sounded idiotic and totally out of character for the Professor, or so Nova thought.

"Please call me Henry!" reinforced the old man again.

"Well he's got a point Henry. Whatever this thing is, it's killed well over a dozen people so far, what makes you think it'll stop at us. It's collecting these things for a reason, I hardly expect they're for mounting on its mantle"

"We don't even know what's inside it" said Nova as he started to rise from the ground.

"I've been trying to open it, without much luck" said Valana softly, feeling confident enough to enter the conversation.

"If only I had something sharp I might be able to prise it open" she continued.

Crossing to Nova, the Professor held out his hand.

"Let me see your tools"

Nova's blank face looked up.

"I do have a life outside of work you know, what makes you so sure I've got them on me, eh?"
But the Professor knew him only too well to know how meticulous the young man was, something he'd taught him many years ago, and thankfully it had rubbed off on him.
"C'mon give them over!" he held out his hand again.
Nova conceded, and produced the small wrapping that Palmer had unnecessarily unfolded while turning out the young man's pockets.
He handed it over somewhat reluctantly to the Professor.
"Does he always carry a set of tools with him?" Adams folded his arms and looked on as the Professor unfurled the brown bundle and produced the small set of tools wrapped inside.
"Mark of a good archaeologist to be prepared" said the Professor promptly.
"I thought that was the boy scouts?" asked the Commander.
Nova grinned widely to himself.
"And if you knew me, you'd know that I ain't no boy scout" drawled the young man.
Professor Carlson took the small wire pick tool and passed it into Valana's soft hands and she began to slide it into the groove that was barely visible on her own glass ball.
After a few moments, the glass housing clicked and fell apart in Valana's grasp. Within the small sphere was a sight of beauty that enveloped their eyes, making them gaze dazedly at the shining construct in the belly of the sphere.
A gleaming ruby-red crystal reflected all the light in the cavern to the varying corners, shining in all directions for them to see.
Valana pulled the stone from its lodging point and gazed at it dreamily, she couldn't believe that it was the cause of her spatial displacement.
"It's beautiful!" she gasped.
"Indeed!" agreed the Professor

Time-Ryder: Powerstone Book One

"Right then Einstein, what are we going to do now?" asked Nova.
The Professor took the gem from Valana, gazing deep into the misty red depths of the gleaming crystal; he pocketed it quickly and scooped up the open sphere, closing it firmly with a sharp click.
Suddenly Valana realised what he was doing and for the first time she smiled. Her smile was something Nova like.
The way her mouth curled at the edges and it made him smile too.
"You're going to bluff it aren't you?" said the girl softly.
"Of course I am!" affirmed the old man with a smug grin, "you didn't think I was just going to hand it over willy-nilly did you?" he looked around at the blank faces of the Commander and Nova, "Oh ye of little faith!"
Both of them looked equally as sheepish as they frowned at each other in displeasure.
"This crystal may be the only link we have to get us home!"
Nova was still confused.
"But what makes you think you can get away with it, surely it'll realise that there's nothing inside?"
The Professor took out his sphere, the unopened one and then Valana's one with the crystal removed. He passed them both into Nova's inquisitive hands.
"Well?"
Nova narrowed his brow, "Well what?"
"Do you feel any difference?"
Nova still looked confused, he looked to the Commander; who simply shrugged.
"Should I?"
"Do you notice any difference in the weight?"
Strangely enough, Nova felt that both spheres felt the same and he simply shook his head.

Time-Ryder: Powerstone Book One

Adams saw what the Professor was getting at and nodded.
"And all we have to do is create a distraction long enough for it to get away and avoid opening it in front of us."
"Aye, like that's going to work!" said Nova pessimistically.
"We have the firepower to back it up, why not?" Adams hissed and looked to the girl, "can you open it again?"
She gave the smallest of smiles and took the glass ball from Nova again as he gave the other one back to the Professor for safekeeping.
Valana prised open the empty sphere and looked up to the Commander, offering the vacant ball to him, wondering why he wanted it open again.
He graciously accepted it and took a small green sliver of plastic film from a pouch on his flight suit sleeve, inserting it in the shell before snapping it shut once again.
"What's that?" asked Nova bluntly, voicing what everyone else was thinking.
"A little insurance!" he replied, "It's a tracking device that might lead us to their base of operations. If they have Captain Blackthorne, I assume that's where he'll be."
Nova grinned and thought that the Commander was quite clever in his deviousness and he was pretty impressed by him.
"You mean it's like a Trojan horse, it'll lead you to them without them knowing" he smiled wryly, "You know you're not the square jawed gorilla I had you down for."
Adams was unsure if this was a compliment or not, but took it as one and dismissed the young man just as quickly.
"If it does its job, then you might get home sooner than you think," retorted the American officer gruffly.
Valana who had been quiet throughout suddenly broke her silence, her observations giving her time to think.
"But what makes you think it'll take the bait?" she said pessimistically.

"Pure luck my dear, and a little bravado from the Commander!" said the Professor with a smile.
Nova rubbed his hands together.
"Don't you think we've given your two goons enough time already? They've been gone for ages!"
Adams nodded and stood upright.
"He's right, we should start making our way to the gantry and back to the ship, I have to get you lot to safety, providing we don't run into this thing!"
Nova stood beside him and eyed him squarely as the Professor and Valana rose from the outcrop of ragged rocks.
"I don't know about you lot, but something's not right about this place, can't you feel it?"
"Only the cold Mr Mitchell" said the old man softly, "Come on before we freeze to death!"
As Adams led the way into the next passage, Valana held back beside Nova and put her arm through his, holding on for safety. She felt secure next to him, there was something protective in his manner that made her feel safe, and until they exited the caves, she wasn't going to stray too far from him.
Nova felt her grip, but Valana's body was cold, almost icy to the touch, still he held onto her and followed the others into the tunnel ahead, his eyes falling back to the dark passage behind them.
"I'm telling you Val, something's not right about this," he warned her.
She smiled and pulled upon his arm as he continued his awkward stare.
But Nova knew that everything had been quiet for too long. It wouldn't take long before the creature tracked them down and then the fireworks would really begin.

Time-Ryder: Powerstone Book One

Time-Ryder: Powerstone Book One

CHAPTER EIGHTEEN

Heading through the caves in search of this elusive creature that the girl had described, Palmer and Madeley weren't that eager to meet it, regarding what it had done to the expedition team and the Captain's troopers. They kept their eyes sharp and their weapons primed and ready; unwilling to be the next victims if they could help it. Palmer fumbled forward nervously, carefully treading up the slippery track; his feet trembling with every step.
"I don't like this Bob, not one bit!" he hissed, feeling the chill of fear and cowardice rippling down his spine.
He wasn't normally a cowardly man, but the prospect of running into a seven-foot tall lizard, didn't fill him with warm thoughts, now that they knew what it was.
"Neither do I, but we've got our orders and if I see it I'm shooting to kill," rasped Madeley in return, following behind the smaller man.
"What do you suppose it is? I mean a lizard in the ice caves, not exactly normal is it?"
"I couldn't care less Pete, all I know is if I get it in my sights, it's gone. You saw what was left of Romero and Carpenter"
"You aren't making this any easier Bob!"
Madeley rolled his eyes and turned back to his friend and he took a breath, trying not to lose his temper at Palmer's fear.
"Look we'll just take a quick look around and report back to the Commander. We won't go far, I swear!"
It was supposed to make the scared trooper feel better, but it didn't. Madeley pushed Palmer's field rifle up to his chest and looked into his eyes.
"Just watch my back, I'll go first this time" he said softly and crept into the tunnel ahead. Palmer followed; his finger teetering on the trigger, fearful of what lay beyond the darkness of the tunnel.

Time-Ryder: Powerstone Book One

Having given up on waiting for the two troopers to return, Commander Adams gathered everyone together and started off into the tunnels, making way for the gantry.

The tunnel in which they were traversing was a route for the automated railcars, like the others, these were tipped out, rock fragments and ore spilled onto the tunnel floor to which they sidestepped and carried on towards the light ahead.

Cautious as ever, Adams gripped his pistol tightly and led the way with the Professor close behind and Nova close to Valana, covering the rear.

"So tell me a bit about you Henry!" said Adams, trying to make the time pass more easily.

The old man shuffled closely behind him, scratching his beard and wiping the back of his neck with his handkerchief. The caves had suddenly become so hot, or at least this part of them, a pleasing thought to Nova; who opened his jacket fully and panted as his brow coursed with sweat.

"What is there to tell?" said the Professor.

He didn't like talking about himself at the best of times. Too many things had happened in his life and he bottled it all up inside.

"Family, surely you have family?" asked the Commander, still keeping his attention ahead of him.

"Apart from the boy, no. I lost my wife a couple of years ago. He is the only family I have left."

"I'm sorry" apologised the Commander, taking a breath, "No Brothers, sisters, nieces, nephews?"

The old man chuckled; the thought of an extended family would have pleased him so much, a house overrun with laughter.

He thought of the number of times that he and Rose had wished for children, but nature had not been kind to either of them.

His only saving grace was caring for Nova after his parents' untimely demise, and with the inclusion of Jessica as part of his

extended family, he remembered that there was always laughter in his Riverdale home and he smiled fondly. But Nova was an only child and Henry's two remaining sisters had no family.
"I have two sisters, but, the least said about them the better," he chuckled.
"The boy is the closest one to me!"
Adams nodded; he thought about his own family and wished he felt that way about his daughter. A messy divorce had forced him to take a step backward, not through his own choice. He had buried himself deeply into his career; which seemed to have taken over his life and push him farther away from her.
"You seem very close to him!"
Henry smiled, his whiskered beard curling up at the edges.
"I've looked after him since he was young!" declared the old man, "Protected him all his life, but I suppose all things must come to an end."
"That sounds almost like a final statement Henry!" Adams narrowed and looked at the old man squarely.
"I can't protect him forever Commander, I'm ill you see" he took a deep breath and smiled almost in resignation.
It was almost a relief telling a stranger, so much easier than it had been for him to tell Nova in the first place.
"The things I've seen would make your hair curl. That boy is special Commander, if anything happens to me he must be protected!" hissed the Professor.
"From what?"
Adams was in a state of shock. Firstly from the Professor's morbid declaration that his time was possibly limited and now that there may be some threat to the young man's life.
"Just make sure the boy will be alright Commander!" he looked across at the two young people in conversation, both of them smiling at each other and Nova doing his best to keep her spirits up.

Time-Ryder: Powerstone Book One

"Promise me?"
Adams nodded, but was lost for words momentarily.
"Of, of course!" he stammered, but didn't know what he was getting himself into.
Like the snap of his fingers, the Professor's mood uplifted and he changed his tone.
"And you Commander, any family?"
Adams stopped for a second and looked at the fork in the tunnels, choosing the right hand passage.
He was a bit taken back by what the old man had said and would have to question him further when he got the chance and they weren't so distracted by everything here. but he answered politely.
"I have a daughter that I haven't seen for four years, she'll be almost fifteen by now."
He suddenly fell silent and changed the subject as he looked on ahead to the craggy tunnel ahead that widened out.
"There's a light ahead" he motioned forward with his pistol, "can't you see it?"
The Professor squinted.
"It may be a reflection of the cave walls, it's flickering!"
Adams raised his brow almost cheerily, yet the mention of his daughter stiffened his attitude, and his smile soon vanished.
"I suppose there's only one way to find out" he moved fast to the flickering light and stopped in his tracks, gazing ahead of him.

Slipping through the mines with ease, one of the cloaked creatures crept up to the remains of its fallen comrade. It was the charred remains of the creature that had been repelled by the force of Trooper Vane's field Cannon.
It moved with ease around what was left of the lizard creature, until it spied what had been overlooked by the troopers.

Time-Ryder: Powerstone Book One

The red gem nestling in the snow shone and caught the creature's eye. It knelt slowly and its long talons wrapped around the crystal, lifting it into the air, but it was not with the same scaled appendage that its fallen comrade had shown.
Its massive appendage was a black barbed arm, covered in fine wispy hairs that stretched up its whole length.
Carefully holding the gem; it moved into the darkness with its prize, overlooking the dead bodies of the troopers that the reptilian creature had killed.
It fumbled around in the powdered snow, searching for the silver ring and then finally gave up, moving off into the darkness ahead.

They'd been searching through the mines for some time, but now Vane and Brooks had come to the assumption that the Commander had gone off route, taking some other way to the rendezvous point at the gantry, even though no other route showed up on the extensive schematic of the mine-works.
Brooks looked constantly from side to side, trying to keep focussed as he followed Vane onward. It was never ending; the tunnels stretching on forever, and for one crazy second he thought that they had double backed and were passing through the same passage yet again until Vane stopped and stooped forward, his intuition telling him that something was wrong here.
"Why've you stopped?" said Brooks in annoyance.
Vane crouched by the floor and indicated his friend over with a beckoning finger.
"Tracks!" he hissed.
"Yeah...so?"

"Heavy footed and recent," continued the bald trooper. If he had any hairs on the back of his neck they'd be standing up right now.

"Recent?" Brooks just saw the outline of an overly large footprint. "Too big for a human foot and look at the weight distribution, it's larger than that thing you off'd"

He was starting to get worried now. The prospect of something larger and far more dangerous didn't fill him with joy and he straightened up, nervously checking the levels on his field cannon just in case he needed it again.

"So it could be another one of those things?" Brooks panicked.

Vane raised his brow. Thinking such a thing was disturbing enough, what was going to actually happen when they came across it was a different matter; he hoped that it wasn't so soon.

"I didn't think it would be on its own, things like that normally hunt in pairs," Vane announced vaguely and remembered what had happened when the first creature had struck Blackthorne's rescue team. It had killed them and moved so fast, it now seemed more logical that there was more than one of them, but how many that's what disturbed him.

"C'mon, let's get a move on and wait for the Commander, maybe he'll be able to explain what's going on!"

Brooks narrowed his brow.

"What about those extra signatures we saw on the monitor, shouldn't we at least try and tell him about them?"

"Can't do much if the comms are down, and if the mine is going through a geological shift, we'd best get to the one place that's safe" answered Vane, "That's where he'll try to get to as well."

"The gantry?"

Vane nodded and started off, but Brooks didn't show his enthusiasm.

He gripped the field rifle tight and fumbled after his friend, paranoia making him turn to face the rear every five seconds.

"You'd better be right Joe" he hissed and followed him to the next passage.

CHAPTER NINETEEN

Time-Ryder: Powerstone Book One

Palmer stepped up the slippery path, craning his eyes at the opening ahead. Madeley couldn't believe what was before them; but edged closer, his eyes narrowing.

Stretched across the archway ahead of them was a thin wispy wire-like substance that resembled a web.

As intricate and beautiful as it was, it seemed a little out of place in the mine, laced with ice and the glistening trail of the frost illuminating the normally shrouded seams of the web.

The Trooper's weapon was pointing ahead, yet the inquisitive Madeley crept slowly with Palmer, edging close behind him.

"What the hell is going on Pete?"

Palmer reached out to clear the fine substance away, wiping his gloved hands upon the walls from the semi-sticky remnants of web.

"I thought that girl said it was a reptile or something?"

"That's what she said," hissed Madeley, "nothing about a spider!"

Palmer primed his weapon and straightened his face, trying not to appear as frightened looking as he had been, but as he edged through the archway and into the vast tunnel ahead, he stopped in his tracks.

"Bob, look at this!"

Madeley followed him into the dark tunnel and gasped. The whole length of the passage was covered with webs, the faint trappings of ice adorning each fine line and illuminating them in the darkness like the others they had just torn down. Regardless of how anxious Palmer was feeling, Madeley gaped at the beauty and Pete squinted back at his friend.

"Are you really sure we should be going this way?"

Madeley gave him a look and reluctantly started wiping away the webs; disappointed that he was destroying such a beautiful thing.

"It's the closest passage to the gantry!" he hissed coldly and then suddenly became excited, "C'mon I want to see what's in the next one!"

He swept away the webs and made his way through, the cautious Palmer following; yet still frightened as ever.

Sitting in a hunched position at the cavern wall beside Valana, Nova looked at his watch; which seemed redundant, he could only use it a basis for how long they'd been in the mine; which seemed longer than the few hours that had passed since they'd arrived.

"Fine conversation this eh?" he smiled to her, "You can't remember anything at all, so I can't ask you about anything!" he murmured.

She returned the smile, wincing from the bruise upon her cheek she must have sustained in her fall.

"I do remember something, but it's a bit of a blur" she answered, "It feels more like a dream than a memory"

Valana tried to cast her memory back before her arrival on Penithe.

"Like I said, it's all really hazy!" she shirked it off and hoped that her memory would begin to return soon.

Nova knew the feeling only too well, it sounded exactly like his method of travel to the caves and he sympathised with her loss of memory.

"What about you?" she said politely and in such a way that Nova thought her upper class accent made him smile.

"Me?" Nova blushed.

"Yes, did you leave anyone behind? Someone close to you maybe?"

Then he shrugged.

"Sort of, but that seems like a long time ago" he chuckled at his little joke. Two hundred years did seem a long time, even though it was only a few hours in reality.
"What about you, are you feeling alright after your tussle with that big whatever it was?" he asked.
"Thanks for reminding me!" she said, although from her it didn't sound as sarcastic as his comments usually were.
He saw the glare under her cloak and saw the bangle on her wrist.
"What's that?"
"I have no idea!" she stammered, and pulled back the folds of the cloak to let him see the intricate markings on the bracelet that she wore.
"Whatever it is, it won't come off and I've tried. It contracts every time I try to prise it free."
"I wouldn't worry about it, it looks really good on you" Nova shirked it off, felt the bangle and then her arm.
"You're freezing cold! Almost as cold as me" he shivered and pulled the garment back down over her arms.
"I don't really feel the cold!" she replied and he patted her arm affectionately.
"Well I don't suppose we'll be down her for too long. He'll find us a way out" Nova nodded towards Adams, "He might come across as a bit of a prat, but I think he's got his head screwed on the right way!"
He could see from the few hours that he'd been in the mine that Adams was a good sort of guy, the kind who could take control and limit the possible damage to any situation.
"You don't like him do you?" she narrowed. But Nova wasn't sure. His initial impression of the Commander had solidified his opinion, but it was slowly changing, noting that he had a protective and lighter side.

Time-Ryder: Powerstone Book One

"I've only known him a little longer than you, and he does annoy me a bit, but I still think he'll get us out of here in one piece."
"If we survive that long!" she replied pessimistically.
Valana started clawing at her head, the tips of her nails really digging into her scalp.
"What's wrong?" Nova leaned closer.
Her hands burrowed through the mass of fine locks, trying to find what was disturbing her.
"It itches, feels like something's biting me!"
"Here, let me see," Nova watched as her head drooped forward and her blonde hair swayed. It reminded him so much of Barbara, but he shook it off and started rifling through her soft hair, until his finger touched upon an irregularity.
"What is it?" she panicked and tried to sit up.
"No hold still a minute" he asked.
"Professor, could you take a look at this?"
The old man dawdled over and craned his neck closer, seeing what Nova had found.
Deep within Valana's scalp, grafted into the flesh and close to the base of her neck was a small piece of circuitry. Metal and wiring burrowing deep into her flesh and causing the irritation that she was feeling.
"What is it?" she shrieked again.
"Something of a mystery my dear, but I think we may have discovered what is causing your memory loss" said the Professor, stooping further.
"It may be possible that it can be removed!"
Valana sat bolt upright, her face thunderous and her bangle starting to glow.
"You're removing nothing!"
"I only said could!" the Professor backed off, "with the proper tools, we might be able to inspect it farther."

"Then for the moment it stays exactly where it is!" she thundered, "I can handle the irritation."
The Professor held his hands up in apology and backed off, rejoining the Commander as Nova looked concerned.
"He really was only trying to help!" he said softly.
"I know I'm just angry about my memory. I want to know who I am, or what I am!"
Nova's eyebrows raised in surprise.
"That's a pretty odd thing to say!"
"I'd be happy just to know my name" she smiled back, "But I think Valana will do for now!"

The dim lights in the darkened control chamber flickered in succession as the surrounding illumination that lit up the consoles struggled to sustain their power reserves.
Shuffling out of the darkness, Kersey stretched his robes out, gently touching the fine white beam that dominated the centre of the room.
Kersey kept his back to Gage; who was hunched at the controls and he hissed softly; harsh breath exhaling with a vibrating grate. He was clearly in pain, struggling with every breath and his voice so garbled and croaky, that he did his best to disguise it from his companion.
The chamber was graced with the presence of one of the newly released specimens, yet the shape of this one was inherently different to the construction of Kersey, his companion and the other reptilian creature that had scoured the mines.
"Did you find the crystal?"
From under the robes that the creature wore, it produced an appendage, covered in dark bristles, jagged and almost thorn like in appearance. Within its grasp was the gleaming red stone that the other creature had so much difficulty in retrieving.

Kersey's scorched hand reached out and took the red gem, his hoarse voice almost elevating in excitement.

And the creature within the light finally spoke, its tones buzzing, just like an insect.

"But I failed to reclaim the endower!"

It was then that Kersey flew into a raging frenzy, his anger taking control and he smashed his blackened clawed fingers onto the workspace before struggling to regain his composure and his balance.

"It was not with the other," hissed the creature, "the crystal was all that I could find!"

After his outburst, Kersey was silent, calming down as he thought carefully and steadied his breathing.

"If it wasn't in the surrounding area then one of those troops must have it" he glided across to the beam, daring to look into the glare, even though it pained his eyes to do so.

"I want you to return to the gantry and make sure they don't leave the mines alive!" he broke off as an alarm sounded off from the workstation that Gage was monitoring.

"The detection wave has just traced two spheres that were activated earlier," he rasped.

Kersey was excited, shuffling forward, his clawed hand tingling with glee.

"How close are they?"

Gage's clawed hands rattled across the controls.

"On the same level as the gantry, approximately two hundred metres from it"

"Good!" hissed Kersey, his voice elated.

He turned quickly to the unmoving figure by his side.

"Go now and keep a low profile, don't let them see you, but don't let them leave" he commanded and watched as the cloaked creature quickly slipped away into the dark.

"Restoration is coming soon Gage, and no one is going to be able to stop us!"
He turned back to the far wall where a small bald-headed, dark bearded man lay bound and unconscious, leaning against the smooth metal finish of the chamber wall.
"Isn't that right?" he hissed, "Captain!"

Time-Ryder: Powerstone Book One

Time-Ryder: Powerstone Book One

CHAPTER TWENTY

Her eyes were closed tight in concentration, a grimace spreading over her pleasant features and yet Valana as frustrated that she was could not recall anything prior to her arrival on Penithe. The tiny micro sized chip on the back of her head itched and much as she'd like to, she resisted the urge to pry it from her mass of hair and cease the constant irritation it was causing. She had a feeling that the Professor was right in his assumption that it was causing her amnesia, but it didn't help her feelings of anxiety decrease any less.

Nova could see from her expression that she was troubled and he thought less of his own predicament and put an arm around her as they huddled under the cloak for warmth. He gave a smile; trying to reassure her, but it wasn't having much effect.

They'd stopped for a rest so that Adams could reset the black scanner unit and re-affirm their location.

He'd told them a few times that they were close to the exit point where the gantry was, but they didn't believe him. So much that Nova could swear they'd passed through this particular tunnel before.

It would be a complete cliché` to say that all the tunnels looked the same, but from Nova's point of view, they were, all too similar, save for the different colours that some of them seemed to bestow.

The only one that didn't seem at all phased by their predicament was Professor Carlson; who was slightly amused and cast his eyes over the iced walls in deep fascination, completely unperturbed, unlike the Commander.

Adams wasn't having much luck with the scanner either.

He thought that the device was being interfered with, just like the comm unit and the Velium in the rocks, so he decided to strip it down and clear the receptors.

Time-Ryder: Powerstone Book One

Perched on one of the overturned mine carts, Adams creased his eyes and looked narrowly into the innards of the black scanner. He looked concerned and the Professor had noticed it, peering over the Commander's shoulder with curiosity.

"Will these adjustments take long?" exhaled the old man, trying to see what the Commander was doing, not that he would have understood a bit of it.

"It's not so much the adjustments Henry, it's this place!" hissed Adams, "You know I've got the weirdest feeling that we've gone down this tunnel already!"

"I thought that a while back," spat Nova, "but I just thought your gizmo was on the fritz and making us go round in circles!"

"There you see!" said the American, "I'm not the only one who imagined it!"

The Professor nodded and with a sigh, he leaned on the wall for a rest.

And then he vanished.

Nova's jaw dropped and he looked to the Commander almost immediately as Valana looked on, her mouth gaping just as Nova's was.

"Did you see that?" asked the Valana. She emerged from the silver cloak and approached the wall; moving her hand over the same section that the Professor had leaned upon.

She put her hand out to touch the rugged wall face, and it seemed to blur and shimmer beneath her caress.

"Boo!" said a mischievous voice from the wall and she jumped backward with fright as the disembodied head of the Professor shimmered into existence and protruded from the rugged section of wall.

He gave an increasing beaming child-like grin of mischievousness. Valana gasped and stooped forward, almost pulling Nova down.

Adams lifted his head as did Nova; watching the Professor stepping through the wall as if he were doing his best imitation of Jacob Marley.

Ever so slightly amused by his vanishing act, the Professor stood back from the wall to allow the Commander to see for himself. Instead of running his hand over the rugged surface, Adams reached forward and forced his hand onto the wall.

Like the Professor's, his hand didn't touch upon the rugged peaks that met his own gaze, but his arm passed all the way through and touched upon a smooth metallic finish beneath.

"What the Funk?" began Nova.

He received another look from the Professor to which he simply shrugged and stood up, still shivering ever so slightly.

"It's a veil!" hissed Adams, "A holographic veil, masking what the wall looks like underneath!"

"For what purpose?" said Valana coldly.

The Professor, ever thoughtful stood back from the wall face and watched it blur back into shape.

"I imagine they don't want us reaching the exit until they have our crystals!"

Adams saw the logic of it and stood back from the wall. It seemed very strange that this type of technology would be active on a facility that had been all but abandoned for thirty years.

"Maybe we have been going round in circles, if they've been deploying holographic technology; who knows how far we really are from the gantry!"

Nova cleared his throat.

"Can't you use your black box to find the right way out of here?"

Adams scratched his beard nervously and took the device from his belt again.

"I can tune it to send out a five second pulse that should detect false structures, that way we'll know if the paths are clear or we're about to walk into a holographic wall."

Time-Ryder: Powerstone Book One

Nova wrinkled his stubby nose.
"I suppose worse things could happen!" he said and hoped he didn't live to regret saying it.

The mood in the control chamber was a tenuous one, the smaller of the two cloaked beings still hunched over the array of monochrome screens, constantly watching the fizzled images and looking for some sign of life in the vast network of tunnels within the mine.
Far behind him, Kersey strode back and forward impatiently; his tattered robes collecting dust on the smooth floor.
His mind was in turmoil, desperately racking his brain to advance the state of things. Time was running out for him and he coughed; his coarse voice more pained than ever.
Kersey shuffled across the floor more slowly and he wheeled to the forward station where Gage was carefully watching the progress of the monitors.
"Power levels are at sixty percent and stable. Do you want me to connect the crystal now?" hissed Gage, not that his cloaked friend was listening to him.
Behind Kersey, resting against the wall was the bald, bearded and slightly impish form of Captain Blackthorne, his clothes blackened and slightly dishevelled.
He was still unconscious, and inert, save for the uneven inflation of his chest that was the only indication that he was still alive.
After a pregnant pause, Kersey glided over to the controls, hovering over the nervous Gage.
"Are there any signs of the others?"
"Did you really think there would be?" asked Gage flippantly, "the process was speeded up; you released them from cryo-sleep without enough time for them to adjust. They might not have

received orders from the transponder; if their minds are still viable enough to process it. I did warn you about that Kersey!"
Kersey said nothing and pushed himself off the console in annoyance. He looked over to the Captain, bound and chained up like a wild animal.
"Then activate the light cage!" he hissed coldly, "maybe he does have some answers after all!"
"He'd have told you already" spat Gage, "the Endower has his brain pattern. It'll just take some time for the information to be processed,"
"Once we find the rest of the crystals they'll speed up the process," hissed the smaller creature, a slight sigh of frustration at Kersey's impatient nature passing his lips.
"Do it!" snarled Kersey.
"There's no need to kill him. You're not a monster Kersey; at least you didn't used to be!"
Kersey stalled in mid-stride.
"Do it!" he hissed again.
He watched as somewhat reluctantly Gage flipped one of the antiquated copper switches and a thick white beam of light centred the darkened control chamber.
The light flickered in succession as the surrounding dim lights that made up the consoles struggled to sustain their power reserves.
The power was being diverted so that the light cage could function, although not to its fullest effect.
Gage was becoming concerned by the power reserves and watched in annoyance as they dropped, sustaining the beam.
Shuffling out of the darkness, Kersey stretched his robes out, gently touching the fine white beam that dominated the centre of the room and he slowly made his way over to the Captain, ready to heave the unconscious man into the light-cage.

He kept his back to the smaller creature at the controls and hissed softly, his harsh breath exhaling with a vibrating grate as he coughed. Masking his cough with a clawed hand, Kersey withdrew it from his mouth and looked into it, the faint smudges of darkened blood in his palm.

He disregarded it and wiped the blood on his cloak, gliding over to where Blackthorne lay.

"Kersey the levels are dropping, do you want the crystal installed or not?"

He'd half listened to Gage, his mind addled by his throat, the pain increasing and affecting his thinking.

"Do it!" he rasped in return and he kept his eye upon Blackthorne, watching the unconscious man wearily.

Gage opened a section of the elaborate console, pulling down what appeared to be a bulky service hatch and bathing the dark room in a red aura, much like the colour of the crystal in his grasp.

Wrestling his claws in the air, Gage shoved his hand into the glowing recess and uncoupled the source of light, ready to affix the new gem to the one attached to the machine.

Spinning on its axis in the centre of the hatch was a much larger crystal, sharp and irregular.

Its edges were uneven and it was almost as if it was incomplete and awaiting the final pieces to appreciate its full shape.

Gage took the larger crystal from its holding and brought it into the open.

Immediately all power within the chamber ceased, the consoles and monitors were left blank and lifeless as his monstrous hands held the large chunk of crystal tightly.

He took the smaller one that he had just been given and held them together until the edges blurred together and melded into one crystal, albeit a larger and slightly more wholesome shape.

Satisfied with his task, Gage replaced it inside the service hatch and the chamber was once again filled with light, only brighter. Many of the previously inoperative systems that had been dormant for decades were now functioning and the systems were working faster and harder as the processing speed began to flow through each connectable unit and bind them all together.
"It should speed up now!" hissed Gage, turning his full attention back to the console.
The light cage had sprung to life in the centre of the room again, filling the chamber with bright light and making Kersey recoil from the glare ever so slightly.
It was almost as if he was afraid of the brightness and he kept his distance, only looking at it when he had to.
The console flashed fiercely and Gage gripped the edges of the workstation, pulling his castor driven chair closer to the stretch of monitors.
"The locator has focussed on two crystal signatures," he hissed, almost as excited as Kersey was.
Kersey moved past the light beam to where Gage was stationed and tried to follow what was being revealed upon the screens, even though he didn't understand the complexity of the locator. He left all of the technical matters to Gage and didn't realise how much he depended upon him.
"Is the holo-generator still working?" hissed Kersey.
"It is, but it won't hold them for long, one of them has a visibility detector!" replied Gage.
"Then give the others time to stop them!" rasped Kersey, "They may be newly released from cryo-sleep, but they're still conditioned to obey!"
Gage flicked his clawed talons over the controls.
"That what worries me!" he hissed softly to himself
But Kersey was growing impatient, hissing with contempt under his breath and didn't hear what he'd uttered.

And at the back of the control room, Blackthorne opened one eye slyly; having listened carefully to everything, yet keeping an eye on things and with a slight grin; he listened further, biding his time.

Time-Ryder: Powerstone Book One

CHAPTER TWENTY ONE

The web-coated tunnels that Palmer and Madeley were passing through were unnerving them, Palmer more than his comrade. It clearly showed by his constant reluctance to be the first one into a new chamber and one that had not gone unnoticed by Madeley.

He kept his field weapon close to his chest, his fingers trembling as he tip-toed behind Madeley; who kept a silent vigil, fascinated by the glistening beauty of the webs and their appearance in the cold.

"There's no sign of this creature she was talking about!" objected Palmer, his jittery behaviour annoying the other trooper.

"If there was a creature at all!" said Madeley with a sharp crisp hiss in his voice.

Palmer stopped in his tracks and relaxed slightly.

"Do you think she was making it up?"

Madeley raised his brow and kept onward.

"It wouldn't be the first time for a murderer to shift the blame away from themselves!" he snorted.

Palmer narrowed his brow, his mouth curling in confusion.

"How do you explain the webs? She couldn't have lied about that!"

"We don't know how long the webs have been here, anyway she never mentioned webs, she said whatever it was had glowing green eyes and had big teeth or something!" Madeley began to sow the seeds of doubt within the confused mind of his friend, even though he was on the fence regarding the girl's innocent demeanour.

"Do you think we should turn back, if there's a chance that the Commander might be in danger?" Palmer stuttered.

His friend held his composure and pressed on ahead.

"We haven't found Owens or Barker yet, if she was telling the truth about that!" Madeley trod forward into the dark tunnel, sweeping away the webs with the tip of his rifle.

"I think we should go as far as the gantry and clear the way at least!" he suggested, not that Palmer was likely to object, "And then report back to the Commander. Who knows, we might get the comms working on higher ground" he said optimistically.

Palmer followed obediently, still scared of his own shadow; his eyes darting all around him.

He followed Madeley into the dark mine tunnel, nervously turning and watching all around him as they made their slow progress forward. Looking to the torn webs as they passed through them, Palmer hoped that they had been there for some time and their creator wasn't still alive, given the size of the web. He tried not to dwell upon it and hurriedly shuffled on after Madeley as a shiver passed down his spine.

There was a strange rumbling within the walls of the mine. The ground shook as if a tremor was passing through the tunnels; so much that the Commander and his strange entourage held their ground as he moved the black device around the walls that seemed to shimmer and blur. The rock face vanished, revealing the sleek black design of polished walls under the rugged holographic representation that they'd become used to.

Nova craned his eyes to the ceiling and all around him, the slightest twang of an electrical hum could be heard and the hairs on the back of his neck stood up making him shudder.

"What is that?"

Adams moved around, trying to ascertain which path to take.

"The tremors must be having an effect on the holographic generator, which means we must be close to where it's operating from. If only I can isolate the signal!" he looked all around him and Valana drew away from Nova, her aristocratic beak tipped into the air, inhaling deeply.

"What is it?" Nova said and tried to smell, but his runny nose prevented him from sensing anything.

She sniffed again, inhaling and closing her eyes in deep concentration.

"It's musty, like old oil, can't you smell it?" she looked around them all, "It's really potent!"

The Professor attempted to comply, but he too couldn't pick up anything, neither could the Commander who continued to glare at his black scanner device in deep concentration.

"Machinery!" she declared, inhaling again.

She stood silent for a second as the Commander tried to get his bearings and he wheeled to one particular wall and crossed toward it.

"This way!" he motioned to the wall.

"Are you nuts?" declared Nova, "You can't just walk through a wall!"

But his statement became void when Adams turned on heel and stepped into the wall that blurred all around him and he passed through freely like a ghost, just as the Professor had already proved before.

Nova gaped in awe, an expression of shock upon his face and he turned it into a grin.

"That is just so cool!" he said, totally impressed with a smile, "very suave in your Patrick Swayze-ness!"

He looked fleetingly at the nervous Valana and gripped her hand, pulling her through the wall, but still closing his eyes for fear that sods law wouldn't let it work for him.

Time-Ryder: Powerstone Book One

Troopers Palmer and Madeley had stopped in one particular chamber. Their guns had drooped to their sides as their faces fell and they saw the repulsive sight in front of them.

There was a silence between them both, even though they both knew what each other thought.

The bodies of Owens, Barker and the headless Doctor Belder lay at their feet; the snow laden ground tainted by the rich crimson stain that had been left in the wake of their dying bodies.

"At least she didn't lie about that!" said Palmer softly, beginning to wonder if the girl was telling the truth after all.

In spite of all that had happened and the murders surrounding the Oregon crew and those of the mining survey team, he was beginning to think that the girl was a victim of circumstance, much like the Commander; who accused the two archaeologists that had suddenly appeared from out of nowhere.

Madeley of course had extensive knowledge of the planet Penithe, clearly having done a little homework prior to their arrival on the ice-world. It was his feeble attempt to show an interest in each mission and with any luck his eagerness and quick thinking might lead to a promotion from a meagre Trooper.

"It's some bloody mess!" Madeley checked his field rifle and stepped over their bodies, about to make way into the chamber beyond the arch when a familiar sight crossed them both.

The bald dome of Joe Vane poked out of the darkness, his dark skin almost standing out compared to the white surroundings of the iced walls.

"You found them then?" hissed the American softly.

Brooks bumbled out of the archway, almost knocking Vane into the room and then he saw the sight of the dead bodies, about to set Vane off again.

He capped his mouth and turned away, but the potent smell still unnerved him a little.

"Did you just come from the gantry?" Madeley relaxed the grip on his weapon as Vane moved closer.

"Yeah, it's completely deserted!" his eyes cast all around him in confusion, "Where's the Commander?"

Palmer took in a breath; he was feeling his stomach turning, just as Brooks was.

"He's back a little bit, asked us to check out the story of some big monster down here, got a girl with him, says she saw this thing kill these two," he pointed down at the corpses and then he turned away again.

"You haven't seen anything weird down here, have you?" hissed Madeley.

Rather pleased with himself, Vane grinned.

"We killed it!" he declared and saw that Brooks was about to be sick again.

"Look behind you!" he pointed into the corner where the gruesome half remains of the creature lay in the darkness, easily missed by the two troopers.

"That's what's left of it," hissed the American softly.

"Yeah, amazing what a field cannon can do!" scoffed Brooks briefly before he removed himself to be sick yet again. Palmer clutched his mouth for fear that he might do the same.

Madeley and Vane simply looked on and shook their heads.

"You said he had a girl with him!" said Vane, wondering if she might be one of the extra life-signs they had pinpointed on the VDU screen.

Madeley checked his rifle.

"The Commander's got another two with him and get this, they're from the 21st century!" he declared.

"No vesh?" shrieked Vane.

"No vesh!" returned Madeley, "You should see their clothes" he sniggered, "like they've just stepped out of a bloody museum!"

Time-Ryder: Powerstone Book One

It didn't make much sense to Vane as to how they got here, but it certainly explained how they came to appear upon the heat sensor from virtually nowhere.

"The Commander wanted us to scout ahead and check the way to the gantry was clear in case this thing tried to stop us!" Palmer said, returning from the tunnel entrance.

"Do you want us to go back with you and double check?" Vane asked.

Now that the extra sensor dots had more or less been explained, he felt less anxious to report in to the Commander, especially since the creature had been taken care of.

Madeley nodded and they moved back in the direction that Brooks and Vane had entered from.

Palmer held his rifle tightly and looked at the remains of the creature, giving it a kick as he went past.

"Not so tough now are you?" he said smugly and courageously now that it was dead.

The free standing legs fell backward to the ground and he nearly jumped out of his skin; scampering quickly after the others.

A shadow glided from the other entrance and slithered into the tunnel, the black, thorny hand turning over the scorched fabric of the dead creature's cloak as it fumbled around the remains in a thorough search. With no success, the cloaked creature tailed off, pursuing the troopers to the gantry.

Plodding on through the mine behind the others, Nova Mitchell was still curled up in Valana's cloak and feeling the benefit from the warmth that it was giving.

They moved forward arm in arm and he gazed at her beauty, totally enamoured by her aristocratic nose and high cheekbones. He even thought her slightly soft upper class accent was attractive.

Nova snuggled in so tightly to such a point that she seemed to huddle comfortably back into the young man and she even gave him the smallest of smiles.

"You're not saying much Val, what do you make of all this?" he said, half wondering about the question himself.

Her lack of memory reinforced her innocence and may have been the defining factor in her silence, but Nova was convinced that it was the result of whatever the chip was doing to her.

She smiled shyly and pulled him closer, almost whispering in his ear.

"I'm too terrified to think of it. That thing scared the life out of me!"

Her soft breath tingled his ear and tickled, if he wasn't so concerned with thoughts of this creature, he might have thought the situation would lead somewhere else, but he had to think about practical matters first and wracked his mind, collating together all of the information that they had about the creature so far, even though he was having trouble making sense of whatever it was.

"They're taking all of these crystals right?" he whispered softly.

Valana nodded, listening intently.

"So they've obviously got some form of intelligence and aren't just animals killing for the hunt. But could they be the ones responsible for bringing us here?" he theorised.

She stopped in her tracks, never having thought that the ones chasing them may not have brought them here in the first place. She recalled her memory prior to her transference and looked at the young man strangely.

"That ball was on display!" she narrowed her brow and looked at him as she remembered it and she gave him a smile.

"I remember it!" she exclaimed.

Nova raised his brow.

"Anything else?"

"I was running, I hid in this dark place, but I don't know what it was!" she said softly trying to recall the details. Her head pounded as she closed her eyes and tried to picture it; trying to get it to manifest.

"It was filled with all these strange objects, vases, paintings, hanging tapestries, priceless works of art!"

Nova braced her by the shoulders as she remembered it, vividly describing her surroundings. She could almost smell the aroma in the room as her memory carried her back to it.

"There were rich marble floors and dark mahogany woodwork and then there was the sphere."

Valana prised her eyes open, she didn't need to concentrate. She could remember the brief period before her emergence in the mine tunnels.

"It was mounted upon a dais, encased in a glass and on display for all to see."

"Who were you running from?" asked Nova softly, he gripped her arm as she smiled back, elated that she could recall something, even if it wasn't her identity it was still something and gave her hope that the rest would return in time.

"There was a noise all around. An alarm I think!" she closed her eyes briefly.

"They were chasing me, shooting everywhere and I fell backward and smashed into the glass case."

"It shattered into a thousand pieces and in amongst the broken glass was sphere. It called out to me, drawing me closer. I reached out to touch the ball and then..." she gulped, "Then I was here."

She took a slow breath.

"It was in a sealed glass case and I knocked it over." Valana stopped and gave Nova a square look.

"It could have been anyone who was brought here, if anyone had touched the sphere it would have happened to them!"

It never occurred to her how long it had been on display, or where it had come from, she just remembered the magnetic attraction that it had, as if she had been drawn uncontrollably to it.

"It was the same with us." Nova agreed with her, "We found it next to Jenkins our groundskeeper. We reckon it tried to use him to power the ball, but his body couldn't take it. It took the two of us to get it to work, but it only took you to operate yours!" he spat, "That's weird!"

"Some of us are more resilient than others" smiled Valana.

"A woman's touch eh?" he smiled.

The more that he thought about it, it pure luck that he and the Professor ended up here, just as Valana did. He thought about poor Jessica, probably wondering where he had gone. He didn't even get a chance to say goodbye. The only hope of getting back home would be to uncover what the creature was up to and maybe reverse the process, if it was at all possible.

The best chance he had of accomplishing that was to stick close to Adams; who seemed to be looking for answers in the mine, but wasn't too forthcoming about revealing what he was after.

Nova looked at his watch.

"We've been here about three hours" he hissed, "here, are you sure you know the way out of here?" he asked the Commander, his voice echoing ahead of him.

"The gantry isn't too far now Nova!" replied the tall officer.

Nova sighed and gave an exasperated exhalation.

"That's what you said ten minutes ago!" he retorted.

"The next intersection is just ahead and it's just beyond that," Adams said, holding the black scanning unit in front of him. It showed the basic schematic of the tunnels from the virtual maps he had been given, even though not all of the chambers were documented.

Time-Ryder: Powerstone Book One

The Professor could see something glistening ahead and assumed that it was the silvery content embedded in the icy walls until Adams stepped in front of him with the tracker panning the air. Ahead of them, Adams saw the fine silvery web glistening across the open passage.

It barred their way and he gave a curious look to the Professor before reaching out his gloved hand to clear the path ahead.

"Doesn't that seem a little odd?" asked the old man.

"Nothing down here surprises me now Henry. C'mon, let's get a move on!"

The opening was clear and Nova clung to Valana as they shuffled behind the others into the new chamber. It looked strange to them. There were no indented marks in the floor that provided the runners for the automated rail cars and the floor was smooth, shining, almost like crystal.

Nova's smile spread across his face as they glided into the chamber.

"It's amazing!" he exclaimed as the colour of the chamber seemed to mix between green and red, blending together and then separating again. The colour behind the walls glowed as the shining content inside pulsed as if the chamber walls were alive somehow.

Nova looked down to the floor.

He could see the levels below them, travelling on and on as far as his vision would go, but he was a little disturbed that the floor might be fragile and he pulled Valana back to the walls; carefully navigating their way along the edges to the opening on the other side.

Adams turned in amusement.

"What's wrong with you two?"

"It doesn't look exactly safe" Nova drawled.

"Rubbish, it'll hold!" retorted the Commander.

"I'll stick to the edge all the same" hissed the young man in return. Valana stuck close to him and they moved slowly around surface of the wall, but the Professor was looking all around him, his eyes wandering around the green chamber.

He felt uneasy and it wasn't just the glass floor, something else unnerved him and he was surprised that Valana didn't pick it up with the heightened senses that she seemed to possess.

From out of nowhere a flash of black clothing crossed their path, knocking Nova and the girl to the floor.

They fell back instantly, Valana's silver cloak covering over them and blocking out the view of the intruder.

Adams barely had time to draw his weapon when the cloaked beast enveloped him; forcing him to the floor and shattering the smooth glass finish beneath his feet.

And he fell.

Time-Ryder: Powerstone Book One

Time-Ryder: Powerstone Book One

CHAPTER TWENTY TWO

The Commander soared through the air, propelled through three levels of glass floor surfaces until he crashed onto the smooth floor on one of the lower levels, and he looked up in agony from the fall; still held in the intruder's tight grip.

Professor Carlson could do nothing but watch as Nova and Valana unfurled themselves from the cloak and scrambled over to the shattered aperture, gazing down to see the Commander writhing with the black cloak smothering all over him.

Nova peered over the edge and blinked, his eyes widened as he caught a flash of the creature below. It was way different from what Valana had described.

"Is that what I think it is?"

His fingers curled around the rim of the ragged hole and he pulled himself closer, taking in full view of the beast. He had to squint as it was so far away, and the lower levels were darker, but he could clearly see what it was.

"It is!" he shrieked, "It's a funking bat!"

Professor Carlson narrowed his gaze and looked on, trying to ascertain Nova's conclusion by viewing the beast's appearance, but found it hard to see in the darkness of the levels below.

Still pained and held tightly on the lower level, Adams thrashed about violently, lifted bodily by the cloaked creature and slammed into the jagged wall.

Like the reptilian, it had an overly large upright bi-pedal shape, but very few characteristics between the bat and a human. The only similarity with the previous creature was its increased strength, something that the Commander was about to find out.

Reaching for his weapon, Adams gripped it tightly and posed to fire when the creature forced his hand backward to the wall, stuck tight as the strength of the colossal beast pinned him to the rugged facing and it didn't do any help to his already throbbing back. Nova gaped at the cloaked creature.

"What the funk?" he said in amazement again and slunk back from the aperture, fumbling nervously about his person.

Valana pulled back, her eyes wide and wondering what he was doing.

"What are you looking for?"

"It's here somewhere!" he mumbled, rifling through his untidy clothes.

"What is it?" she shrieked again, watching him rummage through his black coat and the holes inside his deep pockets.

"My Ipod, it's slipped inside the lining!" he smiled.

Professor Carlson frowned and looked back from the cracked floor.

"This is hardly time for the 'Spice Girls'" retorted the old man.

Nova looked up to the old man.

"Hey, I was only seven, and that was a long time ago!" he spat and then his face lifted with an expression of glee.

"Found it, you sweet little bugger!" he exclaimed to which he pulled out the slim black device and kissed it, much to the confusion of Valana.

The Professor pushed back from the edge, narrowing his gaze to see what he had in mind, but Nova's face was filled with delight as he elbowed his way across the floor to the ragged aperture and peered down to where the Commander was being overwhelmed by the creature.

"It's a bat. Right?" he said.

The Professor joined him and looked over the crack again.

"We had noticed!" his tone verging on the sarcastic.

Valana peered over, her eyes watching the horrific sight of the creature wrestling below them.

"And bats are susceptible to high frequencies?"

The old man nodded.

Time-Ryder: Powerstone Book One

"I don't see what relevance this has Mr Mitchell!"
Nova smiled smugly and held his ipod over the crack.
"I just need to tweak the volume!" he said, gritting his teeth as he adjusted the slider, "Plug in my mini-speakers and Mr Bat, say hello to Mr Hendrix!" he tapped the play button on the device and watched as it erupted into the air.
Their ears were suddenly filled with noise, high-pitched guitar wailings soaring above them.
He looked down to see the bat starting to release the Commander as it was tortured by the deafening wail.
"See how you like Star Spangled Banner!" smiled Nova.
Adams was immediately released, the dark cloak that enveloped him suddenly retracting until they saw that it wasn't a cloak, but the thick leathery wings of the creature that took flight and soared up through the opening towards them.
Valana shrunk back with a squeak of displeasure as the creature broke through the remainder of the cracked floor, gliding high above their heads.
Nova smiled and re-directed the device up into the air, as if warding the creature off like a crucifix to a vampire as it retreated and shied away.
"It worked!" shrieked the girl.
Nova raised his brow and his mile curled into a mild frown.
"Of course it worked. You don't mess with Jimi!"
The Professor was almost impressed and scurried back over to the hole, overlooking the Commander.
"Are you alright down there?"
A rather shaken Tom Adams picked himself up from the ice floor and stood dazedly as he still gripped his pistol, scouring his surroundings for an exit point.
"I'm fine Henry. Make your way forward and I'll meet you at the next juncture point!" he capped his hands around his mouth and bellowed, and the pointed to the wall ahead.

Time-Ryder: Powerstone Book One

The Professor nodded as Nova stood, pleased with his listening device.
"Of course it worked!" snorted the young man arrogantly and he slipped it back into his jacket again.

The pretence of being unconscious that Blackthorne had displayed while chained at the back of the control chamber had served its purpose.
He'd listened closely to the plans of the two creatures and had taken note of what technology they possessed during his deception, but now that he had some of the information he needed; it seemed the ideal opportunity to shed his ruse and ask some real questions in person.
He gave a strained groan noisily and stirred, giving the illusion that he was waking from his supposed slumber and putting across the most pitiful pantomime performance.
Kersey lifted his cowled head and swept over the floor to where the Captain was bound, standing arrogantly over the small man's downed position.
"You're awake!" he hissed, almost with a degree of concern.
Blackthorne shifted in his position, his rear end numb from the cold floor.
"Very observant of you!" he said sarcastically, his tone quiet and trying not to provoke the seven-foot tall-cloaked creature.
The small dark-bearded man looked through the gloom to the array of computer screens, trying to see anything of consequence on them.
"What I don't understand is why I'm still alive?" spat the small man inquisitively; "You already used that device on my head, so why keep me alive?"
"And technically you should be dead after undergoing the Endower, but you have more than one purpose Captain, access to

your ship for one thing!" clipped Kersey, being just that little bit forthcoming, but just as mysterious.

"Once our plans are complete, we'll need a way to escape this barren rock!"

"And what did you do with Doctor Belder?"

Kersey glided away from the Captain, returning again to the sporadic array of screens that Gage was still busy analysing.

"Hopefully his medical training will have served its purpose, just as he did!" said the creature, "but that will all be clear very soon, once we have the full systems up and running!"

Blackthorne felt the irritation on the back of his neck and lifted his chained hands to feel it, touching the raised section of skin that felt like three distinct wounds that were still fresh.

He winced upon their touch and narrowed his gaze at Kersey. Although he'd been pretending to be unconscious, part of his memory was hazy and he couldn't recollect how he had had become wounded in the first place.

"And all of this because you're collecting the stones inside those spheres!" declared the Captain, "Why?"

Gage turned from the console and looked up at his fellow creature.

"He knows a hell of a lot for a freighter Captain!"

Kersey swept away from the console, returning to hover over the small man once again.

"He does, doesn't he?" he hissed, peering down on him with an overbearing glance "far too much!"

Blackthorne cleared his throat and looked at the creature sharply.

"It didn't take a genius to notice the empty shells of the spheres in the mine!" he said, trying not to let them see that he knew more than he was letting on.

"What we're doing shouldn't concern you!" rasped the tall creature.

"It shouldn't, but it does. You've killed a large number of my crew, and the survey team. It won't be long before the PCA send another rescue team!"

Blackthorne tested the chains that bound him to the floor, but they were too strong, even the bracelets that bound his wrists were just too small for him to slip his hands out.

He was using the conversation to buy some time and could see that his questions just weren't leading anywhere. Kersey was just too secretive; fearing that his plans might go awry should he reveal them.

"You think a pitiful bunch of soldiers will be able to stop us?" rasped Kersey arrogantly "how many of your people are dead?"

Blackthorne was silent; he knew all too well the answer.

"All these needless deaths were caused by only one of us. Imagine the carnage if all of my brothers were left to roam free!"

"Needless deaths?" spat the Captain, "You caused them!"

"The deaths were just unfortunate, the survey team were just accidents!" hissed Kersey, "But we didn't make the first act of violence!"

"So you originally chose not to kill, is that what you are saying?" asked the Captain.

"It was merely self preservation!" snapped Kersey.

"And what if I help you, will you spare everyone else that's trapped here in the mine?" Blackthorne made the offer but wasn't sure what he was letting himself into.

"It's too late for that. There are two of the crystals in the tunnels, but they are being guarded by some of your troops!" Gage interrupted, giving him more information than Kersey had.

"But what are the stones for?"

"They're the power source for the central hub, once that's activated we'll be closer to restoration!" continued Gage.

"That's enough!" hissed Kersey sharply. He didn't want the Captain to learn too much.

Blackthorne looked around the bleak control chamber, wondering what was going to happen when all of the power was fully integrated into the systems and restoration was achieved. Clearly the creatures were dangerous, regarding the number of lives that had been lost, but what were they really up to, what was their whole purpose here?
He waited patiently as Kersey turned his back on the small man and returned to the console, he'd find out sooner or later, it was just a case of paying attention a little longer.

The bat creature had retreated to the endless shafts and mine-tunnels that stemmed from the centre of the core of the mountain.
It soared above the heads of the unsuspecting troopers and flew past them into the gantry; taking refuge high up above the metal green girders and affixing its massive winged frame to the highest point where it hung upside down.
Below on the ground a flicker of shadows was the first sign of the approach of the four inquisitive troopers; who stepped into the massive cavern.
With the display of his scanner attachment bleeping ferociously, Trooper Brooks looked to the three, weapon-bearing troopers around him and stepped away from them fanning the device in the air and taking readings from all around him.
They'd finally reached the gantry cavern where the massive steel platform and stanchions met with the ragged wall; four large darkened vents leading into the rock face from each level, each stemming off inside the mountain to the endless labyrinth of mine shafts.
The cavern was almost a hundred feet high and behind the metal work of walkways, large cogs and remnants of machinery lay in

the dark corners next to a pair of large metal doors that almost dominated one entire side of the wall.

From what Brooks could see, it looked as if it was a hub of operations for the defunct mining works, many of the tunnels that spanned out from the gigantic cavern were still littered with long discarded tools and rocks that had been carried along by the automated mining carts which were also upturned and derailed.

"Are you sure it came in here?" Vane hissed.

"The readings say that something over two metres tall came in here just ahead of us," drawled Brooks.

"So there is more than one of those things?" asked Palmer, curiously narrowing his brow, yet his eyes darted all around the cavern, with his weapon held tightly to his chest.

From up above they could see the crack in the metal girders as if some weight was causing the stresses to weaken and crack.

Palmer turned nervously and fired, his automatic weapon unleashing a volley of projectiles in the direction of the noise.

A scream from another section made Madeley wheel, he too fired upon the echo even though he couldn't see what was causing the din.

A movement of shadows forced them all to open fire and cause the chaos that was soon to erupt.

Time-Ryder: Powerstone Book One

CHAPTER TWENTY THREE

The scanner in the Commander's grasp wasn't making any sense. He moved cautiously through the gleaming ice tunnel three levels below the Professor, Nova and Valana; but it seemed to wind around almost in a spiral and come to the bottom of a slope with a long, straight passage leading upward.

The screen showed that there was a juncture point ahead that would allow him to meet up with the travellers and save him the extensive walk that he wasn't too enamoured by, but it seemed to him that there were no holographic walls on his present level, nor any evidence of the minerals that the survey team claimed had interfered with their communications.

Adams began to wonder if the reports were entirely accurate regarding the survey team's entry into the mines, and he narrowed his brow as he trod onward carefully, looking for any sign that might disprove what he was thinking.

But if the survey team didn't declare the exact truth as to their intentions or outcome in the mines, then it only posed another set of unanswered questions for him.

Deciding that he was just tying his mind in knots, the Commander kept up his pace, moving the scanner across the walls as he looked all around him.

Tom pushed back his cap as he stared at the display, watching as a red blip suddenly appeared upon its face. He tapped the device and illuminated it, focussing in on the blip and turning to where the signal was coming from.

Reaching out to touch the wall, he felt that it was solid and pursed his lips annoyingly. He rubbed the face of the gleaming wall and looked through the glass to what lay beyond.

Whatever the object was, it was inaccessible from this point and he stared intently through the gleaming wall face.

Time-Ryder: Powerstone Book One

It was almost hexagonal in shape, mahogany face plates with strange switches and controls spread across it, burnished brass edges, and large enough to be held with two hands.

There were four distinct handgrips on either side, yet there appeared to be something missing from the middle section where a glass dome was housed, holding only a few thin wires that should have been connected to a vital component, or so he assumed.

Tom thumped the wall in frustration and heard voices coming from the passage ahead.

He sighed reservedly and took a last glance to whatever it was and chased on after the voices; reluctant to leave it behind as he had the feeling that it was something important.

So severe was the barrage of weapon-fire that had been released from the over-eager troopers; the gantry had begun to crumble, veering away as the large supporting struts that held the walkway to the rock wall and were weakened as the supports started to give way under the strain.

The thunderous sounds of destruction forced Palmer, Brooks and Vane away from the ensuing dust and debris that coupled the falling metalwork.

"Where's Madeley?" Palmer hissed, his eyes scanning the debris and wafting aside plumes of powdered dust.

"I'm over here," croaked the Trooper's voice.

As the dust began to settle, Madeley's form could be made out more clearly, neatly harnessed between two officious looking boulders that held him trapped by a pile of the fallen gantry walkway.

"My legs are trapped, I can't move," he hissed softly; trying not to let the others see the extent of his pain, but he was failing miserably.

"I'll put the rifle on a higher setting, that'll cut the rock away and get you out" Palmer prepared to level the rifle and screwed up his eye, taking aim.

"Like hell you will!" spat Madeley, "Let Joe do it. He's a better aim than you" he said, wincing in pain.

Vane gave a smug smile to Palmer and set down his field cannon, reaching out for the Trooper's rifle, but as Palmer prepared to prime the rifle and hand it over, the area above them gave a rumble with a thunderous crash and the rest of the metal gantry started to give way.

Vane pulled Brooks and Palmer free; almost throwing them across the cavern to the archway as the debris from above showered down, the ground rumbling in its wake.

After the crashing sounds subsided and the smoking remnants were lifted into the air, Vane wafted aside the clouds of dust, coughing as he creased up his eyes and stepped carefully through the flotsam of twisted metal and bent girders.

He looked through the dust to see Madeley, practically untouched by the falling metal, although covered in thin white powder and residue of ice that had formed on the walls of the freezing cold gantry, but as the dust settled, Madeley looked up in horror.

Falling from the highest point of the fourth level vent; a dirty green girder shot toward him like a spear, impaling him to the spot and covering him in blood.

Vane stepped back, aghast as Madeley coughed up a mass of blood, pouring from his mouth and dribbling down his chin.

He gave a pained look back to the others, trying to lift his arm to gesture out towards Palmer until his arm drooped one last time and all life was gone.

A long silence ensued and Palmer gently stumbled forward to his fallen partner; his mouth lost for words and gaping wide at the monstrous sight before him.

Time-Ryder: Powerstone Book One

Vane tried to pull him back, but Palmer shirked off his arm and he crept forward to Madeley's decimated body.
The girder had penetrated the Trooper's chest and had shot through with such severity that it was embedded into the ground.
"He didn't stand a chance," Brooks said softly.
Palmer said nothing but kept his vacant stare as if he couldn't believe what was before his eyes and yet he still crept closer and something crunched under his feet. He looked down as a slight reflection caught his eyes.
Palmer knelt down and picked up the shattered piece of metal and plastic, holding the scarred remains of circuitry tightly between his fingertips.
"What've you got there?" said Vane softly, craning over the Trooper's shoulder. He noticed what it was and joined Palmer by his side.
"That's part of a detonator!"
Brooks joined them both, taking the circuit from the Trooper's grasp and eyeing it closely.
"Owens and Barker were ordered to secure the hatch and place charges, but not around the gantry itself' he narrowed his brow.
"Unless they got sidetracked and chased that creature into the mine!" said Vane, the voice of reason.
"Then how do you count for them going off?" Brooks looked equally confused. Vane gave him a blank look and Palmer still said nothing.
He continued to gaze upon Madeley's fallen form and crept closer, closing the dead Trooper's eyes over.
Staring down at the dead trooper, Palmer couldn't believe what had just happened.
The gruesome sight of Owens and Barker had been enough, but he had seen this as it happened and it shocked him into silence.

Time-Ryder: Powerstone Book One

Vane tried to pull him back up, his hand resting on the distraught trooper's shoulder.

"C'mon buddy, we need to get out of here and report it to the Commander" said the American softly and trying to be as sympathetic as he could, but Palmer wrestled him free, his face torn and teary.

"Joe!" said Brooks softly.

He caught the black trooper's attention and wheeled to the opening of the massive gantry chamber.

There stood the Commander, his appearance slightly weathered, his clothes a little ragged and covered in rock dust, but at least he was alive.

Standing just behind him were the huddled figures of Nova and Valana with the larger form of the Professor bringing up the rear and gazing around him in awe at the height of the cavern.

Adams gaze moved past the troopers to the main wall where the torn shards of metal from the gantry still jutted out from it.

His plan of a quick and easy escape wasn't going to go as smoothly as he had anticipated, but his mind was working overtime on a plan for their extraction.

With a gruff sigh he pushed back his cap, tightened his leather gloves as he removed his backpack and threw it to the ground brashly.

He strode away from the opening, taking in all the destruction and trying to see a way out of the situation as he looked up to the wall facing where the gantry had once been attached.

"What the hell has been going on here?"

"It looks like the charges went off sir, but the remote detonator hasn't been activated!" exclaimed Brooks stepping closer to the tall officer.

"It's taken out half of the main structure, but I don't know if the hatch has been affected!"

"I can see that!" clipped the American, "was it a malfunction in the detonator itself?"
"I can't tell sir. There isn't enough detonator debris to determine if it was a fault or not!" Brooks sounded disappointed, normally he'd have relished the idea of getting into the guts of the debris, but their situation wasn't ideal. The Commander's first task was to get everyone up to the main hatch and to the safety of the ship. He trod forward carefully through the debris and looked over Madeley.
"I'm sorry Palmer," he said softly to which there was a brief silence and the trooper slowly rose, taking refuge by the far wall in remorse.
Nova shuffled forward, still shivering and he gazed up at the Commander, looking slightly lost, but anxious to get out, not that the wet clothing wasn't enough a reminder for him.
"So what are we going to do now?"
Adams looked up and sniffed, his face frowning again.
"We improvise Nova. Mr Vane, break out the portable gel pack and get it set up, these young people are freezing!"
"Sir!" replied the trooper, edging over to Nova with his hand reaching out.
"Joe Vane!" he gave a briefest smile under the circumstances.
Nova accepted it somewhat reluctantly.
"Nova Mitchell!" he smiled in return.
"You've got a pretty strong grip there buddy" smiled Vane back and relinquished the grip, sizing the young man up and noting that his clothes weren't as shocking as the other had made out.
"You're an American!" Nova raised his brow and wrinkled his nose.
"You're catching on Kid!" warmed the dark skinned trooper.
Nova immediately felt the trooper's sense of humour and smiled.
"It's alright, I won't hold that against you!" he joked.

Time-Ryder: Powerstone Book One

Vane smiled back at his sense of humour and almost at once he knew he was going to like him.

"Where are you from?" Nova pressed him for an answer, if only to distract him from being so cold.

"Detroit!" Vane raised his brow, "You?"

"Riverdale, I'm not surprised if you've never heard of it. The village is so small it's almost like it only surfaces every hundred years" he joked again, "I mean you only need to look at the Professor's dress sense to see that!"

"I heard that Mr Mitchell!" came the whisper of an echo from behind them.

Nova grinned again.

"Did he say you've got a heater?"

Brooks was already one step ahead of them and had set up the gel cylinder. It was an elongated cylindrical drum, transparent, but with a gelatinous green substance bubbling away inside and providing a suitable amount of warmth that Nova soon found himself huddled around.

Adams approached the wall with the Professor close behind his back; both looking upward to the vents above, his hands feeling the surface of the wall.

"What are you thinking?" asked the Professor, afraid of what the answer might be.

The Commander looked away from the wall and smiled forlornly.

"That's the only way out now, we're going to have to scale the wall!" he grated, much to the old man's dismay.

"In case it's escaped your notice Commander, I'm not exactly twenty-one!" said the Professor in a strained strop of protestation, but when he thought about it, he probably wouldn't have managed it even if he was twenty-one.

His frame over the years was something of a constant; Nova put it down to his affection for macaroon bars.

Time-Ryder: Powerstone Book One

The Professor wasn't so much of a physically active man; it was only his mind that worked overtime.

The Commander was half-listening; his eyes wandering over the whole wall face, scanning for anything that might elevate the situation.

He crossed to the far end of the cavern where the pile of twisted metal had accumulated and he peered over the green girders to the dark recesses. The large pair of iron doors came into view and he climbed over the wreckage to inspect them, tugging on both handles.

"Vane, give me a hand with this!" he called out and within seconds Joe joined him by the rustic looking barriers.

He eyed the Commander sternly and knew what he was planning. Both of them gripped the handles tightly, heaving with all their strength, but the doors were sealed tight.

Adams pulled out his scanner and ran the device over the seam between the two doors.

"It's locked from the other side!" he hissed and gave his beard an annoying scratch.

Looking sideways, beyond the mass of twisted iron and frayed metal were the workings of some type of machinery. Adams slowly scaled over the rest of the broken gantry to the far corner and almost smiled at the find.

There was a rectangular box, affixed to the floor of the cavern with an extensive metal framework hemmed all around it and stretching way up to the heavens of the cavern and drifting into the realms of the fourth level.

He circled around it and approached the door of the cage-like box, pulling it open to reveal a small cramped space within, yet enough for half a dozen or so people.

It was the main base for an elevator shaft.

Taking a look inside, his eyes narrowed and he looked up to the top. He could see the bottom of the elevator cage, way up on the highest level and he grimaced.

Adams closed the cage door and looked to the activation panel at the side where the metal runners stemmed upward to the higher levels. The activator itself was damaged; the glass screen covering the panel was shattered; small fragments of glass still embedded in the panel housing.

He cleared out the fragments and pressed the activator and then every button on its face, but there was no result.

Adams gritted his teeth in annoyance and pulled out his black scanner, running the device over the panel as he studied the results. At least the connections were still intact and it was still operational, even after all the years of non use-age.

He gave himself a small smile of self-satisfaction and climbed back over the girders to where the others were crowded with Trooper Vane following, but confused as to what he was planning.

Valana was now at Nova's side, warming herself by the generator as close as she could get, although the young man appeared to be hogging the majority of the warmth for himself.

"There's a service elevator in the corner, it's still functional, but there must be a working control panel on the higher level!" announced the Commander.

Henry breathed a sigh of relief and smiled, almost chuckling to himself.

"I had the most impossible thought that you really did expect us to scale the wall!"

Adams smiled back as he looked upward again.

"You still might if I can't get the elevator operational!" he replied and began unfurling coils of wire from within his black backpack. With a beaming smile, Nova relinquished his crouching position and flopped out on the floor, his hands still hovering in front of the gel cylinder and feeling the warmth flow through his fingertips.

It reminded him of the fireplace at home in Riverdale where he used to sit with his back against the fire-guard and risk getting a tartan patterned tan on his skin.

It was either that or give up the much-desired position in front of the fire and let the Professor's dog Jake take the dominant place on the rug.

"You're not seriously going to climb up that rock face are you? Look how high it is!" shrieked Nova, stretching his neck to see the very top, "surely there's another way?"

"I wish there were Nova, but the elevator cage is up on the fourth level, and that's where we need to get to. Don't worry. Once I'm up there I'll send it down and we'll all be out of here soon!"

He slapped the young man's arm in reassurance and gave his best smile.

Adams, ever the optimist took out a long, slender piton gun from the emergency pack and filled the barrel with a sharpened metal shard, attaching the thin coiled black wire onto the end.

He took a retreating step and aimed up to the highest level, creasing his eyes shut before releasing the trigger.

The whole group watched as the piton soared into the air and it struck the rock face, jamming hard onto the surface and embedding itself tightly to the white iced wall.

The Commander pulled upon the wire, testing his weight upon it and giving a smile, as he was satisfied with the fixing.

He harnessed the black-coiled wire-like rope around himself and began to hoist his frame up the rugged wall, carefully pegging pitons into the rock face as he ascended.

Adams had taken a starting point directly below the first vent leading to the first level and moved so fast that he had almost passed it by in minutes.

The others looked on warily, watching his ascent and not one of them envious by the task he was undertaking.

Vane and Brooks kept their weapons tilted to the air, covering the Commander's back as Palmer absentmindedly gazed into the bubbling goo inside the gel container.

Nova looked to the forlorn trooper, yet said nothing. The last thing he would want is comfort from some stranger, not that Nova would know what he was comforting him for, but he had an idea after seeing Madeley's corpse that the two of them were close.

Within minutes, Adams had passed by the second vent and was making a speedy progress upward, clipping in the metal shards with the piton gun and quickly hooking the coiled wire through each loop with careful precision and ease.

It wasn't until the Commander approached the third level that he noticed the surface of the rocks were loose.

Sweeping the surface with his gloved hands, he decided to move under the third level vent, crossing horizontally until he came up the left side of the opening. Quickly pegging the way, he clambered up until he was inches away from the fourth level and he took a moments rest to gather together the last few remaining pitons that would bring his task to completion.

From out of the dark vent above him came a series of small winged creatures, each as terrifying as the next and he smiled at being frightened by such a small group of harmless animals.

He leaned closer with the piton gun, about to strike another metal shard when the massive hulk of the bat creature soared out; narrowly missing his head as he shrunk down to avoid being struck by the beast.

Adams revolved on the line; his back slamming against the rugged wall face and the spider creature ejected its frame from the vent, spinning a glistening web into the air, before landing upon it and making its way rapidly downward.

And lastly, the large elongated claws of a reptilian snapped out of the black void, aiming directly towards the Commander.
He froze; his mouth gaping at the colossal size of the beast and believing for the first time the stories that the girl had told him of its monstrous appearance, yet he was unprepared for the arrival of two other equally disturbing creatures.
Glaring at the creature as it came closer to him; Adams looked through slit-like eyes as it approached rapidly, hissing under its blackened robes and advancing with severity, its teeth snapping in his direction.
His hand wrestled with his pistol, aiming directly at the creature's hood, his eye creasing in concentration and he fired.
But the gun clicked.

Time-Ryder: Powerstone Book One

CHAPTER TWENTY FOUR

Watching the events on the small bank of monitors, Gage hovered closely over the console, masking the view from Kersey and the Captain at the back of the control chamber. He kept a close watch over the power levels and was more in control of the situation than Kersey was; even though Kersey was giving all the orders.

The readout on the console showed that the database was almost at eighty percent decryption, but they still needed the power from the remaining crystals to maintain the output in order that restoration could be completed.

Much as he wanted restoration; he didn't approve of Kersey's methods, and preferred it that he didn't see what was on the screens if only for the sake of the humans in the mine.

There had been too many deaths, and Kersey made it all seem flippant as he offhandedly dismissed it.

As far as he was concerned, the ends justified the means.

Gage took a fleeting glance in the direction of Kersey and saw the tall creature hovering over Blackthorne; who looked up with a disappointed glare.

Turning back towards the small monochrome screen, as he watched the Commander hanging on the line, and waited to see what was about to happen.

The Commander swung on the line, disbelieving the fact that the pistol was not firing for him.

He checked the chamber and reloaded the clip, but it still would not fire and he couldn't see any reason for it to fail, but rather than dwelling upon it and giving the creature the advantage, he fumbled inside his tunic: putting the useless weapon away and saw that he had no other alternative to save his life.

Time-Ryder: Powerstone Book One

With an almighty surge of strength, he bent his knees, pushed himself away from the wall and sprung backwards.

Each of the embedded pitons ejected from it's fixing as his weight pulled them free and he soared backwards through the air.

The creature's talons lashed out, but narrowly missed him as he fell through the air in a backward swan dive.

The others could do nothing but look on and gasp; Nova's mouth gaped as Valana covered her eyes and hugged him tightly, not wishing to look on any further, but the Commander's flight was short-lived and the black cord snapped taught, bringing him back to the wall; spiralling as he crashed back into the wall face, hovering just inches above the second level vent.

The long talons extended as the creature left the fourth vent and grasped the wall, dragging its cloaked body of across the rock face and clinging to the surface as it crawled spider-like toward the Commander.

As soon as he'd stopped spinning, Adams saw the oncoming beast and reached for the piton gun that hung from the makeshift cord around his neck.

He aimed nervously, trying to hold the butt still, gripping the metallic piton gun tightly and he fired.

The gun recoiled with such force, throwing out a sharpened piton instantaneously as the Commander rocked on the suspended line.

The shard of metal flew through the air and struck the greyed flesh beneath the creature's hood.

A scaled hand flew back to the piton, clawing desperately to free the metal fragment from its head as the dark hood fell back and the creature pierced the Commander's eardrums with a bloodcurdling howl.

Clinging to the wall with its one remaining free limb, the creature was still for the moment.

Time-Ryder: Powerstone Book One

The group on the cavern floor looked up in shock and surprise, but the Commander's predicament was the least of their worries. The soaring bat swept down, narrowly avoiding Valana as she ducked from its reach and it flew back up above her head. Nova pulled her down beside him as the Professor took refuge by the archway and both Brooks and Vane aimed their weapons, but the creature was too quick for them to get a target.

Palmer was not so lucky.

In his attempt to stand back from the gel heater and aim his weapon into the air, he was snatched from the ground amid a contorted series of wails.

The spider creature had spiralled down on its web and plucked him from the cavern floor, spinning him away into the heavens as he continued to scream; his echoing wails becoming quieter the farther away that he climbed.

Vane took aim and drew a breath, waiting for the right moment and he fired off one shot, winging the bat creature that quickly lost its trajectory and barrelled into the third level vent, vanishing from their sight with a heightened squeal.

With two of the creatures injured, Brooks looked aloft to try and locate the Spider creature, but the misty realms at the top of the massive cavern were too far away to see, so he kept a close eye and a finger upon the trigger of his rifle.

Valana cringed and cowered back, holding onto Nova; who for the first time was lost for words. His eyes widened as an object fell out of the air above him and landed directly in front of them both.

Valana took one shocked look and let out an almighty scream. Resting inches away from her feet was the bloodied and horrific head that had belonged to Trooper Palmer; shorn clean off, just as Doctor Belder's had been.

Time-Ryder: Powerstone Book One

A volley of shots fired off into the air, the noise deafening as Nova crouched down and cupped his ears, Valana following his example.

Hoping that a random shot might wound the spider creature before it returned again, Brooks screamed loudly as he let the whole chamber of his field weapon discharge until it powered down with a wheeze.

With no sign of the Bat or the more elusive spider, the surviving troopers concentrated their weapons upon the creature that was about to terrorise the Commander again.

Its head was exposed to the light and letting them see its features in its entirety. It bore its long fangs wide, screaming to the top of its voice in a deathly bellow.

The creature's face was almost skeleton-like; the construction of its jaw-line jutting out like the mouth of a mountain lion, yet its greyed skin and scaled features were almost snake like.

The fierce roar of the beast continued and Nova looked up to Adams in concern, he recognised the sound from many a national geographic documentary and he turned to the Professor quickly.

"It's sending out a distress call, listen!" he hissed.

"How can you be sure?" Vane narrowed on him.

Nova furrowed his brow.

"He's right, listen!"

The howl carried down the tunnels, reverberating in every passage as it echoed on.

"Well it's either that or a mating call Joe, and somehow I don't think it wants to buy you dinner first!" retorted the archaeologist and he quickly jumped back from the portable gel chamber.

Nova's shoulders shirked off the comfort of Valana's cloak and he let it fall to the ground as he prepared himself with the small glass ball firmly in his grasp.

"Stand back!" he hissed.

Arching back his arm, he threw the glass orb, and watched it sail through the air, straight into the fourth level vent.

He smiled with a subtle grin of arrogance that he was on target.

The creature had seen the soaring sphere carry way above its head, but concentrated upon the Commander flailing on the black line.

"What did you do?" asked Valana worriedly.

Nova flinched.

"I thought it would take the bait!" he sighed gruffly in return.

His arrogance at assuming the creature would go for the sphere only made them realise that Adams was its next target.

Disregarding what the old man had said, they couldn't take the chance that this creature would dispose of another ranking officer.

The old man pointed up and saw the creature recoil, its yellow eyes reacting to the light in the glacial cavern and it quickly coiled its head back under the hood.

"Its light sensitive!" shrieked the Professor; he stood back as the two troopers opened fire.

"Aim for the ledge above its head!" he announced, "Softly now, we don't want to kill it"

Brooks looked at the Professor as if he had gone mad.

"This thing could kill all of us, we've got the perfect opportunity to get rid of it and you want to let it get away!" he barked above the rifle-fire.

"Precisely!" coughed the old man, "the Commander has placed a tracker inside the sphere, it may be the only way to find where it is operating from and that may be where your Captain is."

Vane understood and stowed away the large field cannon; picking up the discarded field rifle from where Palmer had dropped it.

The two troopers saw the old man's point and raised their massive weapons; firing on the ledge above the creature's head. They watched as the rough surface began to crumble and powdery fragments of the grimy substance showered down and scattered over the watchful group.

The Commander managed to fire off a couple more shots from the piton gun before the beast conceded defeat and started to back off; trailing away to the fourth level vent that it had crawled out of, but Adams wasn't going to let it go without a fight.

He began clipping the black line back onto the pitons and pegged into the wall rapidly before sliding his weight over the edge of the vent.

With nothing to grasp onto, the creature was forced into a retreat as the Professor had hoped, disappearing into the fourth level vent.

Commander Adams stabilised himself and began climbing the wall again, pulling his tall frame over the edge of the third and soon the fourth vent. He tore a knife quickly through the harness, pulled out his pistol and bled into the darkness quickly.

The others looked on as the torn harness and black coil fell from the fourth vent and swung loosely.

Vane and Brooks gave each other a shocked glance as the Professor grinned wildly and looked up to the fourth level vent, hoping that the Commander knew what he was doing.

"Is he off his head?" Nova shrieked.

Brooks began collecting up their belongings.

"Come on; let's get over to the lift in case he makes it!"

Once again Nova was huddled under Valana's cloak as they crossed the flotsam and destroyed gantry to the staging area on the far side where they lay in wait for the elevator cage to descend.

Crawling off deliriously into the tunnels that spanned from the fourth vent, the creature's shaking claws gripped the protruding piton tightly. Squealing in pain, its clumsy fingers finally seized the climbing tool and gradually began to pull it from the grey infested layers of scales.

The blood flow had restricted and began to congeal all around the wound as the regeneration process that the creature possessed was beginning to take full effect.

Much like any other type of reptilian this creature possessed many of the strengths. Self-repair and more importantly regeneration was one of them. The ability to grow back any limb, which would prove to be stronger than before, was an important part to the make up of these creatures, but it worked faster than before and the wound began to heal instantaneously.

Tossing the bloodied piton aside, it staggered, flailing through the dark tunnels and holding its blood-tainted claw out to the wall as its robes flapped in the faint breeze coming from ahead. Little had the creature known, but its mark had been left in a blood soaked print adorning the tunnel wall; a mark that would make it easier for the Commander to trace.

The creature could hear the shuffling noise of the Commander pursuing it in the tunnels and gave a long exasperated hiss as it turned back to the tunnel ahead, but just before the shape retreated, its gaze rested upon the prize that it had been sent to retrieve.

On the ice crested tunnel floor was the shining glass ball that Nova had tossed into the air to attract the creature away from the Commander. Quickly grasping it tightly, the creature lumbered off ahead before the Commander followed on.

Reaching the end of the tunnel, Adams re-loaded his pistol and held it high, not knowing if the creature might be lurking nearby or indeed if the pistol would work this time, but he was all out of pitons and it was his only option, with the exception of the small knife he carried, and it wouldn't do much against the colossal beast.

He edged himself around the corner warily and flung his weight to the wall, keeping his back to the cold surface; his heart pounding like mad, but his breathing slow and controlled, as if he were used to situations such as this.

It was a really stupid move to pursue the creature, but the elevator cage was also on this level and it was doubtful that the creature was going in the same direction.

Scanning the area warily, Adams focussed on the elevator cage that sat at one end of the tunnel.

Half smiling, he knew that he was close to getting his people out, but still had no clues to the Captain's fate or how the strange device embedded in the ice wall earlier had anything to do with the situation. He approached the cage and pressed the activation slider, to no avail and shook the square display box, pulling it free of the wire cage that I was draped against, but it proved useless.

With one last thought: he slammed the butt of his pistol into the panel, activating the long disused device and illuminating the pad. He gritted his teeth with a wide grin of satisfaction and picked out the shards of cracked glass before pressing the activation sequence.

With a series of clunks and clicks, the cogs of the old service lift began to turn for the first time in decades, bringing a faint wispy odour of oil to the Commander's nose.

Adams grinned in delight and stepped into the cramped cage, feeling slightly anxious at the small confines of the lift.

He breathed slowly and then noticed that the construction of the metal surfaces were just as old as the girder that had impaled poor Madeley. Pressing the switch to take it to the lower levels, he took a step backward out of the cage and let the lift go on course for the ground level.

Time-Ryder: Powerstone Book One

CHAPTER TWENTY FIVE

The service elevator squealed down the runners of the cage and gently touched down on the ground floor, giving a rattle as it settled unsteadily.

Trooper Brooks trod carefully forward to the metal shutter, his hand teetering on the handle as he approached the cage door, totally bewildered; holding his field rifle upright and poised to attack whatever may be inside, if it wasn't the Commander.

"He made it!" shrieked Valana and it made him almost jump on the spot with fright.

Brooks took a breath and looked back, Nova giving him a grin of amusement, but Valana's face simply mouthed and apology.

Nova pulled her back, being over cautious and she looked at him strangely as he stood in front of her.

Brooks was suspicious of the lift, thinking that it was all too quick for the Commander to have completed his task.

His hand reached out to the handle again and he slowly pulled it down, turning it with a sharp tug.

The door opened with a restrained squeal of its un-oiled hinges and Brooks took a step back, his finger back on the trigger of the rifle and ready to open fire.

He half imagined the creature to come lumbering out of the lift, ready to slit the throats of the on-looking group, but his eyes eased open and glared into the dingy emptiness of the interior.

Valana sighed in relief as she looked on behind the armed troopers.

Creeping past the wreckage of the gantry, the Professor stepped over stray pieces of metal as he approached the cage and looked all around the structure.

"I don't get it, why didn't he come down on the lift?" said Nova aloud.

Valana looked into the cage.

"There doesn't look as if there's enough room for all of us" Professor Carlson furrowed his brow.

"I've just had a terrible thought. What if the creature is up there waiting for us? There's nowhere we can go of we're all trapped inside this little box" he said sceptically.

The others knew what he meant, but they were too anxious to get out of the mountain to care.

"That's why Mr Multi-purpose gun is here" scoffed Nova, slapping the dark skinned trooper on the back.

"And exactly why he's going to be placed directly in front of the cage door, aren't you Joe?"

"Watch it kid!" he hissed back.

The group of five crammed themselves into the tiny lift and waited as Vane, being nearest to the door, pressed the activation panel, forcing the lift to ascend.

The motor grinded and crunched as the occupants held on tight, awaiting arrival on the fourth level.

"What is this lift for?" began Valana.

A beaming grin spread across Brooks' face, failing to contain his amusement as Nova simply answered.

"For lifting things" he said sarcastically to which Valana gave him a look, "Sorry force of habit!"

"I mean the purpose for it!" she thundered, noting his humour with a wry smile.

The elevator slowly began to rise up past the first level, grinding as the old machinery wound the cable around a large cog-like drum at the top of the cavern.

It passed the second and third levels, before finally settling on the Fourth.

The occupants of the cage eyed each other in the grim silence until Nova spoke up.

"Go on then"' he shoved Vane forward to the metal plated door and he gave an unwilling gaze to the young archaeologist.

The metal shutter creaked open slowly and the group looked out to see Commander Adams, bearing his pistol on them as the Professor exhaled a heavy sigh of relief.

Nova could see the muscles on the Professor's face relax and droop once again, unburdened by the prospect of his life shortening any further than it was already. He mopped his head with a handkerchief and smiled inwardly, trying not to let the others really see how worried he was.

The Commander coughed as they slowly began to exit.

"I think that thing took the sphere!" spat Nova.

Adams gaped in surprise.

"Good!" his face straightened as his brows dropped.

"Aye, I threw it up to distract it from going after you!"

"Good shot all the same!" Adams was pleased that the young man's apparent dislike of him didn't appear to be as strong as it once was.

"Not really, I was trying to twat its head!" frowned Nova.

Professor Carlson stooped forward as he stepped out of the cage.

"From what we could see it disappeared back into the fourth level after it"

"And that's exactly what we want it to do!" thundered Adams, "When we come back with the proper protection then we can track it to its lair!"

There was a silence as all those around turned to him as if he had scratched his nails down a blackboard to get attention.

Nova's eyes widened in disbelief and he shook his head.

"Did I just hear you right?"

The Professor cleared his throat with a deep-rooted cough.

"I think we're all curious about that Commander!" he hissed coldly.

"Henry you know this isn't finished. With Blackthorne still missing, my mission still stands!" replied Adams, "and these things won't stop until they have every single crystal, remember we have two of them!"

Nova stood away from him in disgust.

"You're totally off your head, that's just asking for trouble!" he thundered. The more that Nova thought about it, he was opening up other lines of questioning. Blackthorne must have been important, had some information or something on his possession to warrant such a suicidal task. There was more to Adams than he was letting on and he suspected that the Professor felt the same and maybe knew a little more than he did. They'd spent time chatting to each other in the caves; maybe he'd let something slip to the old man. He knew the Professor well enough to know that he wouldn't be able to keep it to himself. Adams pursed his lips, wishing he could tell them more, but his orders were specific.

"Once I get you to the safety of the ship then I'll come back to finish what I started, alone if I have to!"

But Nova's disgust at the Commander's cavalier attitude towards his life could almost be regarded as concern. He swept ahead of the group into the open, standing in the centre of the tunnel, letting his anger completely override his sense of judgement. All the others cautiously kept to the safety of the wall, pressing their backs against the jagged tips of the surface.

Along the dark passage came a flash of darkness, so quick that they barely noticed it until they heard the objecting voice of Nova trailing off into the distance.

Swept off his feet by the large bat creature; it carried Nova along the tunnel and he smashed his fists into the thick leathery wings as they flew the length of the passage; not that his attack did any damage to the creature.

Vane stepped out and brought up the heavy cylindrical silver cannon, looking carefully through the sights.

Time-Ryder: Powerstone Book One

Adams pushed the barrel down and narrowed his eyes, taking off in the direction of the young archaeologist.
"The space is too confined Vane, you'll hit the kid for sure!"
The Professor looked anxious, his eyes staring down the tunnel.
"Commander please, we have to do something!" he gasped, prepared to pursue until the Commander held out a hand and looked over to Brooks.
"Get them to the hatch. I'm going after the boy," he replied softly and looked into the Professor's anguished eyes, "Don't worry Henry, I'll bring him back safe."
With a look to the bald trooper, Vane knew what was coming and slid back the arming device on the cannon.
"Vane you're with me!" hissed the Commander, already making way forward.
Trooper Vane brought the heavy weapon from his shoulder and held it up, ready to follow Adams into the dark as Brooks shuffled slowly in the opposite direction with the Professor and Valana close behind, stepping up the pace as they warily made their way towards the hatch.

Still in flight, the bat held Nova in a vice-like grip.
Its long wings extended and almost took up the whole width of the tunnel as it soared through the entire length of the mine system, bound for god knows where.
Its logical course would be to take the young man and his crystal in the direction of the control chamber; but its orders were to keep its location concealed, especially with the Commander's group in such close proximity to it, so the creature soared on; aiming for the next possible entry point, but Nova wasn't going to give up so easily.

Time-Ryder: Powerstone Book One

He gritted his teeth and looked over the creature's wingspan where he could see the torn skin; the impact point of one of the troopers weapons and he wrestled about.

The creature contracted its limbs, holding him tighter and making it harder to breathe, but it still wasn't going to stop him. Nova had managed to free his hand and slip it into his jacket, scouring the deep pockets until he found his tool-kit. He took out the small knife and jabbed it hard into the area where the creature had already been wounded.

It let out a shrill cry and reacted at once, careering into the iced wall ahead, smashing the aperture and knocking itself and the young Mr Mitchell unconscious.

The iced wall had split; the slab of ice shattered and leaving a gaping hole into the area beyond. And just beyond the orifice was the object that the Commander had been separated from earlier.

It was the strangely shaped device with the curiously placed hand clamps resting just within arms` reach of the young man, but as Nova lay unconscious and defenceless, the creature began to stir.

Time-Ryder: Powerstone Book One

CHAPTER TWENTY SIX

Brooks reset the power level on his own rifle and trod carefully, leading the old man and Valana down the long stretch of the tunnel leading to the hatch. Gazing back down the tunnel, the Professor still shuffled forward; clearly concerned and very out of breath.

Valana tugged at his arm as they reached the set of rungs leading up to a circular hatch set into the ceiling that was twenty feet above them. Close by the edge of the heavy metal ring was a small oval shaped black device with a smooth finish.

A tiny red light flashed in succession and a worried Brooks hung tentatively at the bottom rung, gazing up at the bomb which like the others could go off at any given moment.

"Come here Miss!" Brooks curled his finger to Valana, beckoning her closer. He passed the field rifle into her hands and told her to keep it trained upon the tunnel ahead.

"If any one of those things makes a move this way, pull your finger back on the trigger and don't let go for anything!"

The Professor craned his neck at the device Brooks pulled from his thigh; quickly flipping the wings open and watching as they flapped collecting data.

"What are you doing?" he hissed and gripped the rungs for support, feeling slightly queasy.

Brooks pointed to the charge way above their heads and the old man simply gave him a blank look.

"Oh!"

Charging down the passage at full throttle, Adams was amazed at the distance that the creature had traversed in so short a time, but regarding the wingspan that it had, he wasn't surprised how far it had glided.

Time-Ryder: Powerstone Book One

Its flight had carried Nova way from the top level, down through some slippery slopes and on a downward angle to the coldest reaches of the mine.

Vane kept the light-scope on the front of his cannon set for maximum yield and it illuminated as much as the small lights were able to.

He creased his eyes tight and called the Commander over to the jagged wall.

"Sir, look at this!"

The bloodied claw print on the wall told the Commander that this was the reptilian creature he had injured and he stopped to examine it.

"Just keep your eyes open Vane!" he hissed.

Nova's head was cloudy, his vision even more so.

Every time he tried to move, he felt like one of those old cartoons where the victim's head was continuously squashed by two very large cymbals and tiny birds flew all around him.

He pulled out his glasses and wedged them on the tip of his nose; thankfully it helped his eyesight a little, until he saw his abductor beginning to awaken.

Nova saw the opportunity and jumped upon the bat, smashing his fist down upon its head and forcibly making it go back to sleep. The creature squealed but eventually conceded to slumber and the young man stood erect, with a dominant smile spreading over him.

"Two-One, Two-One, Two-One, Two-One!" he echoed giving a smug football chant to himself as he towered over the beast and then he saw the open aperture in the wall.

The shining glint of whatever the device was had captured his vision and he stepped closer, scooping the odd shaped thing into his hands.

Time-Ryder: Powerstone Book One

He grabbed it by the handles and turned it over, noticing that the section in the middle was effectively missing something.
Nova shirked it off and shoved it into his deep pocket, revolving on heel as Adams puffed out of the dark tunnel towards him, with Vane lagging behind.
"You ok Kid?" asked Vane.
He trained the silver cannon on the unmoving form of the bat creature and Adams stooped over and turned it onto its back.
"Aye, I'm fine. And stop calling me kid, you're not much older than me!" Nova gave a gruff retort.
The Commander prodded the creature with his boot and narrowed his vision.
"Is it dead?"
"I think I just winged it!" Nova grinned at his bad joke.
He leaned over and tore a piece of its ragged wing, holding the leathery skin into the air.
"What are you gonna do with that?" Vane asked.
Nova frowned and stashed it away in one of his small poly sleeves in his jacket.
"I dunno, I could do with a new wallet!" he said bluntly and rose from the ground slowly.
Adams knelt down beside the creature and looked at it closely. Aside from the wings and the bat-like facial features it looked more or less humanoid. It was dark in colour, a heavily built upper body and toned muscular frame draped in the ragged clothing the same as the other creatures, but its hands were tipped with claws, a fine pointed barb on each one.
Pained and exhausted Nova turned to both men.
"Is everyone else ok?"
Adams nodded and looked around the area that seemed so familiar to him. Nova was already making his way back up the tunnel with Vane looking down on the Commander.
"Everything alright sir?"

Time-Ryder: Powerstone Book One

He studied the cracked wall and shook his head absently.
"Everything's fine Vane. Let's get back to the others."
"What about that thing sir, do you want me to kill it?"
"Just leave it Vane, I think its dead already!" Adams hissed and rose from the ground, looking all around, slightly confused.
Vane turned on heel and followed on after Nova, but the Commander continued to look at the broken aperture. After a few minutes he moved on after the others, yet thought that he was missing something.
The creature wasn't dead as Adams had thought, but under the folds of its massive leathery wing was one of the red crystals, clumsily dropped out of Nova's coat in the collision with the wall.

The darkened tunnel whistled as the wind the constantly ripped down the passageways, giving an eerie feeling to Valana who stood tentatively with the field rifle in her shaking hands.
"Are you almost done?" she whispered; her aristocratic voice lifting as she shrieked.
"Nearly there!" exclaimed the small trooper, easing up the ladder carefully to the top of the high wall. He looked up curiously to the small black metal disc that was stuck next to the hatch.
"Wait, won't you need to deactivate the explosive charge?" hissed the Professor.
Brooks rolled his eyes, but from his position the Professor couldn't see.
"That's what I'm up here for!"
"I don't like this, they've been gone too long!" complained the old man.
"I shouldn't worry Professor, the Commander'll bring him back in one piece, that's what he's best at!" mumbled Brooks.

He hung from the top rung, inches below the heavy metal hatch and tried to connect his scanning device to the explosive.

"Have you known him long?" the old man rubbed his hands together for warmth, despite this being the highest point in the system, it was one of the coldest, he surmised that it must be because they were close to the hatch.

"The Commander, No, he's only here on short assignment. Only been here a couple of days but with his mission success rate, something tells me that he'll be back soon, don't worry about it!"

The sound of shuffling came from the far end of the tunnel and Valana shook as she looked to the Professor nervously and followed her gaze as she pulled the butt of the rifle tightly into her shoulder and waited.

Valana's finger wavered on the trigger, gently squeezing as a figure lumbered out of the darkness.

Adams and Vane helped the pained young archaeologist along and the Professor shoved the rifle aside as Valana fired; the shot bathing the tunnel in blue light and the Commander acted with lightning reflexes, drawing his pistol in front of him at once.

"It's alright Commander it's only us!" cried out the old man and he relaxed, holstering his pistol at the sound of the Professor's voice.

He quickly joined them at the foot of the ladder and Valana relinquished the weapon to trooper Vane as she closed in on Nova.

"Are you hurt?"

"I'm alright, honestly!" he said with a grin, "no need to fuss!" he said, even though he was loving the attention.

Brooks was still dangling from the ladder and looked down on them all.

"There's still a charge here Commander" he echoed, "I'm having difficulty disarming it!"

Time-Ryder: Powerstone Book One

"I wonder why it never went off?" Adams narrowed his vision to see the device and the trooper descended to get the rest of his tools and then climbed back up to continue his disarming task. Finally the device clicked and the small pin-like red indicator went dark; Brooks sighing with relief and quickly slipping back down the ladder to join the others again.

Vane was becoming impatient and took up the challenge.

He climbed the ladders quickly and reached up to turn the wheel that held the heavy metal hatch in place.

He pulled the wheel with all of his might, it gave way with a strained creak, and he pushed the circular hatch out where it gave a clang on the outside.

Snow poured into the gloomy corridor as the coarse winds ripped up from above; howling with the torrent of the colossal storm that brewed outside the safety of the mining complex.

The trooper pulled himself into the open, gasping heavily at the abundance of fresh air.

Clamping his eyes shut from the bright illumination outside, he felt the tiny pinpricks of snow kiss his cheek and he tugged at his collar, adjusting the temperature dial once again.

One by one, the visitors shuffled up the ladder followed by the Commander, watching over the vast reaches that the mountain stretched out onto.

Valana stood on the mountaintop, gazing over the beauty of the breathtaking landscape.

She breathed in slowly; taking in the first breaths of fresh air since she had first arrived on the snow-blistered world and she let her silver cloak cling to her nimble frame.

Adams pulled himself into the opening where Vane stood surveying the area with his spectrometer.

He felt the cold chill touch his cheek as he stood up into the path of the oncoming blizzard; over-looking the trooper's shoulder and eyeing the spectrometer device in his hand.

Time-Ryder: Powerstone Book One

"It's getting pretty wild now," he announced and turned to help Trooper Brooks out of the hatch.

He reached down and pulled the trooper's hand and then lunged forward as Brooks shot back inside the hole. Adams toppled forward to the opening as Brooks sank back into the gloomy interior, still gripping his hand and vanishing from view.

"What's going on?" Nova creased his brow and shot over beside the Commander, peering into the darkened depths.

With a struggle, Brooks tried to keep his grip on the Commander's gloved hand; squeezing tightly as the tall officer strained to pull him upward.

Nova looked down into the hatch and saw the glowing eyes of the bat creature staring back at him. The beast had pulled the Trooper down and positioned itself between Brooks and the Commander as it tried to emerge from the interior and pull Adams inside the hatch.

"I thought you said it was dead!" hissed Nova in annoyance.

The Beast wriggled and writhed as it got to the top of the ladder, tugging upon the trooper's leg.

Adams craned his neck around and looked to Nova with pain in his eyes, straining to keep Brooks grip, but the strength of the creature was immense and he felt that he wouldn't be able to hold out for too long.

He gritted his teeth and tried to pull back once again, burdened by the Trooper's weight.

"Help me!" Adams hissed, straining under the beast's pull.

"Me?" Nova shrieked, "What can I do?"

As he looked on, he could see the veiled head of the beast beginning to protrude from the hatch, its claws ready to ensnare the Commander and pull him down.

"Anything!" said the officer bluntly, "Just do something Nova."

The frightened archaeologist stepped forward nervously and looked all around him for something to help him ward off the creature, and then his eyes feasted upon the Commander's sidearm. Much as he didn't like weapons, he removed the Commander's pistol from his side and leaned forward into the hole with the nib of the pistol tipped forward as he spied his target.

Pointing the weapon down into the cavern, he fired; jerkily moving backward by the uncontrolled backlash from the weapon. His brow deepened, holding it in the correct manner this time and he stood forward to the hole.

Nova's hand shook as he fired again, strengthening his grip on the gun and becoming less stolid. The whine of the beast echoed out of the hatch and alarmed the faces of the on-looking group. He poked his head into the dark hole and saw that Trooper Brooks had fallen the full length of the ladder and he rolled aside, avoiding the embittered bullets thrashing down upon his assailant.

The creature flailed to the bottom of the steps while Nova continued to pour the contents of the clip into it as Adams peered down, outstretching a hand and beckoning Brooks to ascend the ladder once again.

Convulsing on the floor, the creature was defenceless as Brooks looked on in disgust; he wasn't that keen on bats at the best of times, but the seven-foot tall specimen unnerved him even more so. The beast's blood was oozing onto the gleaming floor and the wound made him cringe.

Frightened as he was, Brooks scrambled across the floor reluctantly and delivered a blow to the wound on the creature's head, making it squeal once more and tainting his fist with the it's blood.

He hobbled over to the rungs of the ladder, hopping up them as fast as he could.

Howling in torment, the creature gave a deathly wail that

sounded like a war cry; to which the Professor stooped forward to the hatch, catching Adams frightened stare.

"That does sound like a distress call, now that you mention it" he looked to Nova and urged the others to retreat from the hatch.

He pushed himself back as the whine of Vane's weapon powered up and the rays of energy pumped into the creature.

Ceasing fire, Vane stepped back allowing Brooks his chance of escape.

The creature uttered a deathly howl as it flailed on the floor and Brooks scurried up the ladder despite his limp and he toppled out onto the fresh snow.

Resting his field rifle on the snow, Vane lurched forward into the hatch, his head just peering inside briefly, his arm stretching inside.

He turned to the left and flipped the switch back on the explosive charge, slamming the hatch shut behind him and turning the cog, screwing the seal back into place again.

"Quick, give me a hand with it!" cried the Commander; already bombarding the hatch with large rocks, piling them into a neat and heavy blockade, should the creature try to get out of the mine below.

"Commander, get back from the hatch!" warned Vane, flipping the small handset into the air as the officer's eyes widened and he took a retreating stance from the hatch.

"Everybody down!" he roared.

Vane fell back to the snow and produced a small control unit, sliding out the small antennae from the control box.

He cowered behind a large rock and thumbed the flip-switch.

The hatch gave a thunderous response as the explosion that ensued deafened all of them, the circular metal hatch itself propelled far into the air as the area was decimated with rocks and debris, most of them falling into what had been the only safe entry point into the mines.

Brooks lay back in the snow with a tearful grin beaming from one side of his face to the other, as the Commander stood tall and gasped for air at his side.

"I'm glad you find this so funny Brooks"

He smiled back.

"Sorry sir. I'm just glad to get out in one piece," said the relieved Trooper.

"You can have this back!" Nova held the weapon in a pincer grip and looked at it with disgust, "I don't like guns" he hissed, relinquishing the pistol back to the Commander and he moved back beside Valana, huddling together and conserving their heat.

The young archaeologist's eyes sharpened, focussing on the peaks of the mountainside, but when he looked at the snow it seemed to disorientate him. Nova shook himself.

"What's that big blue thing down there?" he asked, his eyes adjusting to the snow falling on his glasses.

"That's the ship," exclaimed Vane; he gestured to the distance, way beyond the mountain; where their craft was berthed on the snow crested landing bay.

Screwing up their eyes, the group looked down to see the massive navy blue misshapen blob that was the spacecraft they'd heard so much of.

Nova laughed at the sight of the large ship.

The explosion had caused the systems in the dark control chamber to glitch. Gage sped fast, trying to get them back online as Kersey screamed at the top of his voice behind him.

"Not having a good day at all are you?" commented Blackthorne with a small chuckle of satisfaction.

Kersey snapped around to the controls, wheezing as he glided over to Gage.

Time-Ryder: Powerstone Book One

"The outer hatch has been sealed," said Gage over his shoulder.
Kersey hissed under his breath in annoyance at the constant downturn of events.

"If they've escaped with the crystals they'll be heading back to their ship."

"And with the internal defences, you'll have no chance of getting on board!" said the Captain with glee.

But he thought that it was a little early to try and underestimate Kersey and he watched, hoping that the others would get away safely.

Kersey's clawed fingers writhed in the air as a sticky green substance began to drip from the tips of his claws.

He whisked his hand back immediately and looked at it in concern, clenching a fist as he tore back to the screens with determination.

Time-Ryder: Powerstone Book One

Time-Ryder: Powerstone Book One

CHAPTER TWENTY SEVEN

The space freighter Oregon was built like a large misshapen tin dustbin, cobbled together with all types of metal. The hull was a mish-mash of separate pieces all hemmed together, yet no effort had been made to disguise the repaired parts of the hull with paint. It seemed to Nova as if the people that owned the ship were a bit tight with their cash and scraped what they could together to keep the ship space-worthy.

Parts of the ship had been beaten into an irregular shape and there were various protrusions, aerials and satellite dishes on the upper sections of the hull.

The landing struts were silver and stemmed out from the front and an extending ramp that jutted out, gently kissing the edge of the landing strip.

As they descended from the high peaks, Nova could make out the ships tiny lights; sparkling out like a cheap seventies fibre optic lamp.

"That's really your ship?" he smirked with his eyebrows raised.

Vane nodded as Nova rolled his eyes.

"Jesus, and they said Thunderbird three looked tacky" he chuckled, unable to take his eyes off the misshapen blue craft, "are you sure it can fly?"

"It'll get us off this rock, that I'll tell you," declared Brooks feeling slightly off put. He began to straighten up with the help of Vane and the Commander.

Valana looked to the left where a series of small domes in the distance were interconnected with a series of tunnels, making it look like the legs of a spider surrounding the giant dome in the centre, but there was another lone building, stretching all the way to the foot of the mine.

"What's that?"

She stood firm, her hands firmly wrapped under her cloak.

Time-Ryder: Powerstone Book One

"Oh that!" breathed Vane adjusting to the high altitude, "that's the bio-sphere encampment; it's where the mining crew were based. It's been closed since the mines were sealed off."
She nodded briefly and scuttled off to join Nova.
Commander Adams helped the injured Trooper Brooks and followed the others on the scattered trail to the ship, turning briefly to the hatch where Brooks lowered his brow strangely, casting a weary eye over the metal covering.
"What's wrong?" roared the Commander over the howling wind.
Brooks hobbled over to where the metal hatch covering had landed and stared at the edges. Reaching out his gloved hands, he felt around the edges of the heavy entrance.
"It's all chipped. Like the hatch had been forced open already, I never noticed it before" alerted the trooper, he indicated the scored markings that adorned the central covering.
"Never mind that now, we'll have to get back to the Oregon before the wind takes hold, c'mon I'll give you a hand!"
Brooks had given the officer something more to think about, but he rejoined the Commander and followed the others carefully down the mountain track.

From a tiny porthole on board the massive blue craft, a lone figure watched the descending team emerging from the splitting seams of tracks running down the side of the mountain mine.
A strong hand leaned on the grey surface of the porthole interior wall and with a gruff sigh of disappointment he slammed a clenched fist into the porthole rim in anger.

Although it seemed to them that the weather was fierce, Nova, Valana and the Professor had no idea that the gales were only just gearing up.

Time-Ryder: Powerstone Book One

The worst of the storms were about to hit and Commander Adams was glad that his team were soon going to be back in the safety and comfort of the Oregon.

They traversed the path from the mountain and made their way through the snow slowly until they reached the landing strip. Adams helped the hobbling Brooks along as Vane made a quick inspection of the struts, before ascending the gangplank to the airlock.

Brooks limped along painfully, leaning his weight upon his superior as Nova looked back to the darkened night sky as the snow continued to fall.

It seemed no different to the sky that he had been looking upon hours before when he and the Professor had stood at the gates to the Baleran dig.

He huddled into Valana as they looked above to the underside of the massive craft. Assorted pieces of metal made up the hull, and the exposed innards could be seen through the gaps where the landing struts would recoil into.

"That's really your ship?" he said to Adams.

"That's the Oregon" smiled back the officer, somewhat proud of the hotchpotch vessel.

Nova gave a strained look as his eyes cast to the underside of the massive craft.

Adams stepped up to the airlock hatch that would allow them entry to the cargo sections of the ship. He paused hesitantly and pulled out a small cylindrical ident key, coded with his DNA and he slipped it into a hole behind the external access panel. The door glided up with a strained hiss of pressure upon the pistons that regulated it and it stuck halfway, only for Vane to assist the Commander in pushing it up fully.

Once it was accomplished, they stepped into the warmth of the Oregon's airlock, the slightest glimmer of heat clearly pleasing Nova, as he was the first one directly behind the Commander.

He stopped and looked at the plexi-glass bulkhead in front of them; where a tall muscular man in uniform leered back and almost frightened him half to death.

The only difference between him and any other man was that he had pale blue skin and a glorious dome of a baldhead with a few ridges stemming down behind his ears. His eyes were a steely blue and he glared down at the young man; his face blank and emotionless.

Seconds later the outer door started to glide down behind all of them, hemming the close-knit group in between the inner and outer bulkheads

"Denton, what are you waiting for? Open the inner bulkhead door," voiced the Commander forcefully, but the tall blue giant showed no signs of acknowledgement as he depressed a control by the activation pad and the enclosure between both bulkheads started filling with a mist that soon enveloped them.

A robotic female voice echoed above their heads.

"Decontamination process initiated!"

Nova pricked up his ears and looked to the Commander with a worried glare.

"Who's contaminated?"

A gas-like mist started to cloud around them as Nova felt himself becoming drowsy and light on his feet.

Valana's bangle began to react; but before it got a chance to enlighten, she toppled to the floor in a heap; the Professor collapsing next in line. Nova looked up to the tall blue giant before it all went dark and he passed out, falling beside Valana, his arm draping over her protectively.

"Denton, what the hell is going on? This isn't part of the decontamination process!" Adams clung onto the door edge as long as he could, but began to feel weak as he clambered against the plexi-glass window.

Time-Ryder: Powerstone Book One

He felt his vision begin to cloud over and he dropped to the floor beside the others as the tall blue-skinned officer looked on, joined by a small, hard-faced young woman with blonde bobbed hair.
"Is it done?" she hissed coldly in an Australian accent.
"Yes ma'am, I mixed in the anaesthasine with the decontamination vapour. They should wake in about an hour."
She nodded and looked down with a displeasing grimace.
"Have them taken to the Medibay and have 'The Commander' sent to a holding cell!" she hissed with a frown.
The tall blue-skinned Denton purged the bulkhead area of the vapour once it was clear that they were all unconscious and he stepped back, folding his arms over.
As the glass barrier rose with an electronic hum, a few troopers entered the small enclosure and began carrying the Commander's group into the interior of the ship.
The small blonde haired Lieutenant looked on as Adams was heaved inside.
She stared down accusingly as he was carried past her.
"Maybe now we'll find out who the hell you really are!"

Time-Ryder: Powerstone Book One

Time-Ryder: Powerstone Book One

CHAPTER TWENTY EIGHT

The small blonde haired Lieutenant who had purposely knocked out the Commander's party sat in a small bleak room. With only one tiny riveted porthole on the rear wall, she leaned on the edge of the window sill, gazing out onto the blizzard that had exceeded the forecast of the ship's computer.

She watched it soar higher, and was thankful that she was safely indoors, anyone outside wouldn't survive too long in the temperature along with the fierce nature that accompanied the lashing torrents of snow.

She turned back from the porthole and slid into the dark red leather chair; resting back on the high headrest for a moment, exhausted and weary.

But she wasn't one for lazing around, even though the battered black desk in front of her was littered with her belongings; she found it hard to concentrate with the Captain still missing.

Stacks of documents, papers and small electronic computer tablets were strewn about the surface of the desk, all having been there for some time; but she just didn't have the time or patience to sort them out or stow away the packing boxes that littered up the corner of the room.

She leaned forward and scooped up a wooden picture frame from the edge of her desk and looked at the firm image of herself in a stiff navy blue military uniform with ceremonial braid and high epaulettes. Underneath the image was a small brass plaque with an inscription.

"Commendation for Bravery awarded to 2nd Lieutenant Kara Everett June 6th 2195"

Kara gave a smile of amusement at the photo and inhaled deeply. She sifted through some of the papers on top of the desk and thumbed over the nearest one.

Time-Ryder: Powerstone Book One

The file inside contained information about the Captain, details of his career, a profile and a photograph that didn't do him any justice.

She lost herself in the details when a rap of knuckles on the doorframe sounded off and she wheeled to the half open door as a young woman peered into the office, her impish face, forlorn and uneasy at the thought of disturbing the Lieutenant.

"Lieutenant, Doctor Gennero just informed us, he's awake!" she announced softly, her rough Geordie accent coming over very clearly compared to the Lieutenant's brash Australian tones.

Kara nodded with a smile.

"Holding room two!" said the woman softly as she retreated back through the door.

"Thanks Sergeant!" Kara welcomed the news, maybe now she would get some of the answers she was desperately seeking, but she had a feeling that she was going to get more than she had bargained for.

Kara laid the frame down gently and took a deep breath.

She'd only been stationed on board the Oregon for a week and was still settling in; the mess on her desk reinforcing that.

Some of the previous first officer's belongings were still in the office, pictures of the tall thin man with the short dumpy figure of the Captain.

Kara crossed to the door, where the picture was hung and she looked upon it with contempt.

"Where the hell are you? You Bastard!" she hissed.

Finding himself in the confines of a detention cell was not what Commander Adams had anticipated. He cradled his head in his hands and rubbed his ruffled hair.

Leaning back in the padded chair, he concentrated on the small opening in the top section of the cell door. waiting intently for a pair of elusive eyes to appear in the opening and explain to him why he had been detained, although he had his suspicions why. He knew that Lieutenant Everett had her doubts about him, ever since he had come on board. Aside from that, he was quite at ease with her constant sneering looks, then again that was the way she looked at everyone.

Adams rubbed his eyes and stared continuously at the tiny gap in the door.

Silently, the door edged open slowly and hanging in the threshold was the thin form of Kara Everett, her hand clamped firmly on her hip whilst her other hand gripped the door rim. Although she was small, she was very sure of herself and very formidable.

Adams had clashed with her on his initial arrival and she was opposed to his entry into the mine, despite her wanting to find the Captain as much as he had been.

Kara gestured to the door with the nod of her head, keeping her eyes firmly trained upon the Commander, and still she said nothing.

Stripped of all of his belongings, Adams was held to the chair by a magnetic belt around his waist, constricting his movement and binding him to the spot.

"Would you like to explain yourself Lieutenant?" he said brashly and narrowed his eyes at her.

She slowly took the seat opposite him and turned it around, dropping herself into it and leaning forward upon the backrest.

"I could ask the same of you Commander?" she snapped, her Australian accent lifting slightly as she became angry and her tone verging on sarcasm.

"But we both know you aren't Tom Adams, Don't we?"

He said nothing, but listened intently to her.

Time-Ryder: Powerstone Book One

"We were feeding your DNA sample into the system and big surprise, because it didn't match up with the bio-data in your ident key and there's no file on record for the DNA you supplied. I wonder why that is?" she hissed and rose from the chair, starting to circle the seated Commander.

"So that leaves me with two options, you're either a spy for the Tandaren conglomerate, or your identity goes that far up you're hidden from view, and that's an entirely insane idea," she shifted in her chair and pushed herself back, "So which is it? Huh!"

He was quiet and the small woman studied him closely, waiting or an answer of some sort.

"Regardless that four of our troopers are dead, the only saving grace is that you've returned two of the others alive, even if you brought a bunch of strays back with you!" continued Kara.

He opened his mouth to speak, but Kara held her hand up, halting him as his mouth gaped open.

"Be careful about the first words you say, I'd think about it carefully," She said calmly, "If you want to get out of this holding cell, you're gonna have to make it pretty convincing."

There was a long silence, a drawn out pause that made him consider what was happening all around him.

"If it makes it any easier, Brooks and Vane vouched for you, they said you saved their lives a couple of times" said the blonde woman softly.

She was cocky and clever; but a little too cocky he thought. Adams bit his lip. Could he confide in her? Maybe he would have to if it meant it was the only way off the ship and finish what he started.

"It would be beneficial to both of us if you let me out of here!" he replied softly, "I've read your file Lieutenant. I know why you requested a transfer to the Oregon. We have one thing in common!"

Kara's brow drooped and she took a seat again.

Time-Ryder: Powerstone Book One

"I'm listening!"
"Blackthorne!" he said simply and her brows arched.
"I'm here to find him, exactly the same as you and for exactly the same reason, Information!"
Now she was intrigued.
"And I also know that the Captain is the only link you have in finding out who your real parents are!"
Kara shrugged.
"How the hell do you know that? It's not on my record!"
"I have my sources!" he said bluntly.
"And with him gone, the search is over!" she hissed.
"Not if he isn't gone. There was no body Lieutenant and a reputation such as his does strike me as someone who has been in a scrape or two, and knows how to keep himself alive" replied the Commander, trying to shift in his chair and feeling uncomfortable by the binding belt.
"That doesn't explain why you're so interested and who you really are!" she snapped.
"I knew Tom Adams at the Academy and I assumed his identity to get on board; he was the only PCA officer I knew that had this level of clearance to become a trouble-shooter. The SOS call from the Oregon didn't make it back to Central Bank. Someone jammed it at the source, but I've been looking for Blackthorne for some time and monitored every frequency for even the mention of his name. I took a sample of Adams DNA and imprinted myself with a crystal lattice retina and fingerprint resurfacing" he shirked nervously.
"It must have worn off. I boarded a private shuttle past Ganymede and piggybacked on a frontier drop-ship just to get here."
Kara looked up, it seemed to add up, but he was keeping quiet about his identity for some reason.

"That does seem like a pretty outlandish way of achieving your ends whatever they are!" she exclaimed, "But it still doesn't explain who you are? Why does this mean so much to you?"
Adams cleared his throat and eyed her sharply.
"How do I know if I can trust you?"
"You don't, but if you want out of here, you're going to have to give me something" she replied.
Adams took in a deep breath and looked into her eyes. He could help her, but not from the confines of the cell, maybe it was time to trust someone, but was it her. He had no choice but to take the chance.
"Have you ever heard of Professor Charles Ryder?"
She looked confused, having heard the name somewhere and then she remembered a vague reference to him.
"He's been doing experiments with Quantum manipulation, time experiments, hasn't he?"
Adams nodded.
"It was funded by the Macarthur/Bettany group. He developed a new wave of time-folding technology and supposedly completed his experiments three weeks ago. But all the Data, blueprints and work logs have been either removed or deleted and he's gone missing, Blackthorne was the last one known to have seen him."
"That's impossible. Blackthorne's been on the Oregon, the ship hasn't journeyed back to Earth sector for six months!" objected Kara.
"I have a time stamped video link showing him in the Professor's lab. It is him, I can assure you!" said the American.
Kara was getting confused and she rose to the door, touching it lightly before turning back to the Commander.
"But what is all of this to you?"
"If you access the GSA records and compare it with my DNA, it'll verify my identity, but use a secure connection!" he said mysteriously.

Time-Ryder: Powerstone Book One

He looked at her squarely.
"Lieutenant, if you're genuine about finding Blackthorne you'll do it discreetly. I can help you, but you need to trust me too, then I'll tell you everything!"
"You could be saying all of this just to get out of here!" said Kara dryly, half convinced.
"Of course I'm saying it to get out of here, but it is the truth, so what have you got to lose?" he said softly.
She could see his point, as it was she was no closer to discovering what had happened to the Captain or indeed his whereabouts, maybe she should trust him.
It was a double-edged sword; both of them unsure about each other, but neither of had been prepared to give up the chance. Maybe the Commander's statement would convince her.
"What assurances do I have?"
"My goal here is to find Professor Ryder. To do that I need Blackthorne, I'll help you find him and we both win!"
There was something dark in what he was saying, something that she wasn't quite sure of, but he was her only hope.
"We've already got a sample of your DNA, tell me your name and I'll see it goes no further. I'm trusting you on this, whoever you are!" she gulped.
"The DNA profile will tell you and prove I'm telling the truth!"
She nodded graciously and banged on the door.
"Ok then. I'll be back just shortly. Don't go anywhere!" she smiled.
He raised his brow and smiled.
"She does have a sense of humour after all"

Time-Ryder: Powerstone Book One

Time-Ryder: Powerstone Book One

CHAPTER TWENTY NINE

Kara left the murky holding cells and nodded to the trooper standing guard; who snapped to attention and she travelled up the corridor quickly.

The corridor was like all of the others over the ship, festooned with multicoloured pipes overhead, the dark grey walls and wires very feebly concealed behind the pipe-work.

The ship was a hotchpotch of cobbled technology, all held together with whatever could be found to repair it. Kara wouldn't be at all surprised if there was duct tape holding half of the engineering section together; not that she ever ventured down there that often

She trawled through the dull grey corridor and came to the end, which had the only illuminating point of the ship. The passage to the upper deck was a glorious white spiral staircase that crept up, twisting through every deck and seemingly never ending.

She quickly moved up through the levels and eventually emerged onto A-deck, coming to a small set of steps that led up to a pair of glass, silver-rimmed doors that parted upon her approach.

Kara stepped onto the impressive flight deck, normally a hub of activity; but with half of the crew gone, she was thankful for the few who remained, pulling a second shift on duty.

She moved over the threshold to the yellow railings and overlooked the flight deck from a high balcony.

It was an enormous centre of operations, slightly industrial in construction with long metal grilled walkways around the upper floor.

She stood on what could be taken as a balcony that spanned the length of the rear end of the flight deck, stretching to the Captain's office at the opposite end to her left and then coiling around in a sharp right turn to another walkway that would lead on to the first officers office.

A set of steps folded down in front of her, twisting left the bottom to the grey metal colour of the technician's pit.

A large shining black octagonal table graced the centre of the raised area; a series of screens built into tabletop. A couple of steps farther forward led down into a much larger area in the forward section with an extensively long console in front of an enormous window, surrounded by much smaller monitors all spread around it.

Kara gripped the rails and grimaced as she looked over and quickly turned to her left and making for the first officer's office to unravel her dilemma.

The door parted and she entered, locking it with the wave of her ident key over the lock.

Impatiently, she moved to the other side of the desk and touched the glass facing on the top, activating it with her thumb-scan.

A small screen started to rise from the depths large silver computer block on the old battered desk and unfurled the databank link to the ship's computer.

"Request access to data files, encrypt with an alpha signature and relay to this station," she said aloud as the clouded screen began to clear and show her the ship's internal memory bank.

Her hands flew over the silver tablet, operating it like a keyboard and she looked to the display as it fizzled with data.

"Input query. Request all known information on Professor Charles Ryder and cross reference with the GSA."

She sat back in the chair and poured a coffee from the dispenser behind her and sipped from the poly-form cup, the feel of the cup putting her off her coffee, which she spat back into the cup and almost gagged.

"*Access granted,*" droned the computer voice.

"Good, now overlay the DNA sample from subject one" she replied and waited moments for a response.
The screen started filling with information, showing his full medical data and an image of Adams in military uniform, or the man she had first known as Adams. She looked through his service record and gaped at what she saw. Her eyes glazed over the whole screen, following it down with her finger.
"Now that does explain a lot!" she remarked and gave a sigh, "Why didn't he just tell me? Course I wouldn't have believed him!" she spoke away to herself.
It made a certain sense to her now and she knew what she had to do.
"Delete all input history and close this terminal!" she said softly to the computer and watched as the screen descended back into the realms of the silver block once again.
Swiftly leaving her seat, she paused in the doorway, for the first time a glimmer of hope stretching across her sullen face.
Turning from the doorway, she jumped with fright, careering into a tall dark haired man, invading her space ever so slightly.
His hair was swept back in a ponytail and a devilish black beard capping off his features and making him look like a stereotypical pantomime villain.
"Lieutenant, I was just looking for you" he began. His voice was soft, a curl in his accent and a slight hiss in his tone.
"Craven, what brings you up to the flight deck?" she said, her voice showed that there was an instant distrust of his intentions, whatever they may be.
He was the sole survivor of the expedition into the mines and the one who sent the SOS to the PCA. But something didn't ring right about him; Kara always felt very on edge in his presence. She felt that he was being too familiar and slippery, almost like one of the reptiles that Vane had told her about in the mines.

Time-Ryder: Powerstone Book One

"I was wondering if there was any progress now that the team has returned?" he hissed, "I still have a survey to complete."
"The Commander will be doing a briefing in an hour. We can't do anything about the mine until the storms subside" she lied. It would do no good to reveal who the Commander really was until they decided on a plan of action.
Keeping Craven out of the loop about the Commander's identity seemed right, at least until she had spoken to him.
"Very good Lieutenant!" he replied in a slightly sleazy tone.
Kara looked at him and he moved out of the way as she rushed past, bound for the holding cells again.
He watched after her with a hawk-like stance and then turned to lean on the yellow railings overlooking the whole flight deck and observing the few crewmembers that remained on station.
With a frown, he turned to the door, keeping a distance, but following the Lieutenant down into the lower decks.

Nova woke to the white surroundings.
It was a little like déjà vu, his bleary eyes adjusting to what was around him, but instead of the white ice laced caverns that had first greeted him on arrival, he was in a pristine white room and it was warm.
He sat up slowly; his head thumping until an Auburn-haired woman in green medical fatigues eased him back down on the comfy bed.
"Take it easy, it's a side effect of the anaesthasine, it'll clear in a few minutes!" she said softly, "Here drink this!" she passed him a glass with a strange blue swirling liquid that looked as if something was moving inside it.
She gave him a smile and nodded for him to drink.
Nova turned up his nose and quickly gulped it back, looking rather queasy as he put the glass down.

Time-Ryder: Powerstone Book One

"It takes more than a swift drink to butter me up!" he announced.
She beamed, finding him a breath of fresh air, compared to the doom and gloom from the rest of the crew.
The woman was in her early forties, of average build, with a beautiful, yet stern and serious face.
Nova looked over at her warm smile, her fair skin, high cheekbones and flowing auburn locks. From the looks of her, Nova saw that she was clearly a physician of some sort, regarding her relaxed fatigues, yet she was slightly nervous in some way.
He rubbed his eyes and tried to look around himself, taking in the surroundings, all colourless and empty somehow. He smirked to himself that even the NHS in his time would have shelled out for the odd pot plant to make it more homely.
"It's a bit of a cliché to say, but where am I?"
"You're in the Medibay. Standard procedure for toxicology tests after the decontamination process!"
She replied and seemed perfectly genuine; her voice had a strange lilt, almost the faint remnants of a French accent.
"How are you feeling?"
"My head hurts like a bitch!" he drawled.
"Of which you constantly moan about" came another voice from the other side of the room, "must you use such appalling language?"
From the gruffness and disgust at his profanity, he knew that it was Professor Carlson.
"I see you're alright then Professor!" ventured Nova.
"Yes Mr Mitchell. And my head is just as tender as yours," he smiled up as the Doctor leaned over him.
Nova capped his mouth and pointed to his hand, indicating the old man behind it.
"Secret drinker!" he mouthed silently with a smile.
She managed a snigger and moved over to the other bed.

Time-Ryder: Powerstone Book One

"I'm Henry Carlson!" hissed the Professor, cradling his head and trying to speak softly.

"Elizabeth Gennero!" she returned and straightened up as Valana stretched on the other Medibed at the opposite end of the bay.

The Medibay was not nearly as large as was needed, a fact that Doctor Belder had always conveyed to the Captain; not that he ever listened to what was being said. It seemed for the moment that the Medibay was Doctor Gennero's domain, now that she had assumed the mantle of CMO since Belder's disappearance and now his apparent demise.

Elizabeth was a geneticist on a three-month stint aboard the Oregon to prepare her for a leap into a new position as head of the institute for disease control.

She had basic medical knowledge, although was not a practicing physician; but in light of what happened to Belder, she had to step in and take over, at least until they returned to Earth.

Elizabeth turned away from the medical console as the doors behind her glided open and the tall blue skinned officer they had seen through the plexi-glass windows strolled in.

"Lieutenant, a pleasure as always!" she beamed.

Denton didn't speak to that many people on board and tended to keep his own company, but he had an ongoing medical condition that made him frequent the Medibay more regular than anyone else, to the point that there was a familiarity between them and were relaxed in each other's company.

She withdrew to the console and scanned over the screen briefly.

"The toxicology reports have come back clear. No apparent threats!" she announced and wheeled to the tall blue giant, "I'm clearing them to have access to the rest of the ship!"

Denton's face was solid and he gave a more stiffened frown than usual.

"This is Lieutenant Denton, he'll show you to temporary quarters" she said softly, quickly moving away to her workstation to check her readings on the computer screen.
Denton stood to his full height, trying to ignore the awkward stare that he was being given by Nova; who did everything but gape his mouth in the tall man's direction.
"Is there something wrong sir?" asked the Lieutenant with a downward stare.
The Professor stepped forward, away from his bed.
"You'll have to excuse him Lieutenant, he's never seen a non-human before" stated the old man and then he remembered the stranger in the tunnels with the yellow blood.
"In fact none of us have" he shook the tall man's hand graciously and beamed at him.
It was then that Nova realised he was staring and he broke off, almost stuttering.
"You're blue!" apologised Nova, shaking his head, a wide grin bearing across his face.
"I had noticed that!" replied Denton, his face solid.
"I'm sorry," stuttered Nova nervously, "Where I come from you don't normally get people with pale blue skin, I mean you're like a cross between the Hulk and grumpy Smurf!"
Denton's frown told him that his descriptive was very accurate and the young man smiled wide.
From their arrival into the future and the clash with the different species in the mine, Nova wasn't surprised that there were other with alternate skin pigments, but he didn't quite expect to meet one so soon.
"Nova Mitchell" the young man offered his rather shaky hand and Denton accepted, closing his webbed hand in a clamp-like fashion around the archaeologists petite appendage.
"This is the Professor and Valana" he pointed a rather shaky hand to the others.

Time-Ryder: Powerstone Book One

"Are you an Alien?" Nova whispered, leaning forward, but the tall blue-skinned man stooped over to return the whisper.
"No, I'm Denton!" he replied.
Leaving the others to their introductions, Professor Carlson edged off the bed, feeling slightly dizzy and clutching the bed for support.
Elizabeth stooped forward and grabbed his elbow steadying him as he perched himself back upon the bed.
"Are you ok?"
"Just a bout of dizziness!" he replied as she stepped back, but she knew the signs and folded her arms.
"When did you last eat?"
The Professor raised his brow and put his finger to his lips, trying to keep out of Nova's earshot.
The Doctor nodded in his direction and wheeled to the tall blue-skinned Lieutenant.
"Denton I'm all finished here, you can take the others to their quarters now!"
They all turned to them both as Elizabeth gave a false smile.
"The Professor is going to stay here to help me with something, he'll join you just shortly" she lied.
With a blank look, Nova eyed the old man.
"It's alright; I'm going to go through the vials with the Doctor here. You two go on ahead!" he whispered, trying not to sound out of breath.
"See what you make of this then!"
Nova pulled out a small plastic sleeve with the section of the Bat's wing he had appropriated and handed it to the Professor.
He shrugged his shoulders and smiled at Valana, holding his hand out to the doorway.
Denton escorted them quickly out of the Medibay, leaving both of them alone.

Without looking at him, Elizabeth perched herself back upon her stool.
"Care to tell me what that was all about?"
He fished out the small vials he had been given from Nova and laid them out in front of her.
"I'll tell you everything, but I have a favour to ask. I have a few samples from one of the bodies I would like you to take a look at."
It sparked the Doctor's interest and she took them from him, turning away to the equipment on the far counter.
Henry winced in pain and then gave a false smile as she turned back to him.

Time-Ryder: Powerstone Book One

Time-Ryder: Powerstone Book One

CHAPTER THIRTY

The door to the holding cell opened and Kara slipped in, she circled around the prisoner, trying to make out what he was planning and then stood in front of him, her arms folded.
"You read the file?" said Adams.
"You might have said you were a Colonel with Global Security!" shrieked the Australian, "It makes sense why your files are off the grid."
"So you believe me?"
Kara nodded.
"Colonel Jack..." she began to introduce him but he cut her off abruptly.
"Ex Colonel" he rasped, correcting her, "I've been AWOL since they refused my leave to investigate my father's disappearance, that's why I don't want you to contact Earth Lieutenant. They'll send an extraction team to drag my ass back, and I'm in this till we find Blackthorne!"
"Yeah, I caught the footnotes. You're Professor Ryder's son!" drawled Kara, quickly slipping around him.
Kara unlocked the binding belt and released him from the restraints, she unbuckled the magnetic-lock pinning him to the seat.
Jack Ryder stretched and rose from his chair slowly.
"We haven't got much time!" he breathed slowly and flexed his arms as she looked up to him.
"What do you mean?" she sat on the edge of the table; still gazing up at him, but seeing him in a new light, feeling that there was hope in finding the Captain.
She just hoped that she was doing the right thing.
"Whoever sent that SOS put it on a carrier wave that wouldn't stretch back to the relay station. There was no way it was ever going to get back to Earth!" answered Jack.

Time-Ryder: Powerstone Book One

"Craven's the only one who survived the expedition, he never denied that he sent the SOS!" argued Kara, much as she didn't trust the creep, she didn't see that the accusation led anywhere.
"Not the original SOS!" he objected, "The one sent from the Oregon requesting help after Blackthorne's team were massacred. That's the one I intercepted!" Jack folded his arms. "Someone purposely didn't want any more help sent!"
"How do you want to play this...Colonel?" she said unsure of what to call him.
"Straight up!" he replied, "And it's just Jack, or maybe better still be the Commander for the time being. I'd like to keep it between us for the moment. I suspect that Henry has an idea that I'm not showing all my cards!"
"The old man? Can you trust him?"
Jack shrugged and straightened his flight suit.
"I've no reason not to, he's not part of the grand plan, doesn't come from around here, so I suppose I can trust him. He does have a vested interest in sticking with us, coming from the past and all. All his hopes of getting home lie in that mountain too!"
Kara agreed with him, keeping his identity secret for the moment was the best thing to do, especially if there was a possible link between Craven, Blackthorne and Professor Ryder.
"Do you think he'll help us?"
"I don't see why not. He'll do anything for the boy. He's his nephew"
"What about the others you brought back with you. Are you going to tell them who you really are?"
"Nova and the girl?" he thought about it, "No, let's just keep it between the three of us!"
She made an awkward grimace.
"About that, Sorry but the only one I've told is Denton, he's totally trustworthy to the point of obedience, I'd swear he was a dog in another life" rasped Kara with a chuckle.

"Just the four of us then!" he gave an exasperated hiss.
"So what's your plan?"
Jack rubbed his wrists.
"I've got a few other things up my sleeve that might help us out. Are you up for it Lieutenant?"
"If it means finding the Captain, then hell yeah!" shrieked the Australian in delight.
He reached out to grab the door handle.
"Then first stop is Blackthorne's office. C'mon, I'll tell you the rest on the way!"

Pressing his eyes tightly against the microscope, Professor Carlson watched the flow of genetic material on the glass slide below. Leaning over his shoulder, Elizabeth looked at the microscope.
"May I?" she gestured, feeling awkward about asking to use her own equipment.
The old man moved aside, letting the Doctor have free reign.
"Strange!" she murmured and narrowed her eyes, adjusting the focus of the scope.
"You've found something?" exclaimed the Professor, straightening his bow tie and leaning closer.
"Maybe!" she answered removing the slide before he got a chance to take a second look.
She took the strip of glass to the computer and keyed in a sequence, opening the particle analyser.
"This might give us some better answers!" she replied with a smile.
The Professor could hear some slightly accented French tones in her voice occasionally, although her English was very good, he knew that she had been brought up in a different climate.

Time-Ryder: Powerstone Book One

Elizabeth dropped the glass slide into a small open drawer and watched as it closed and they waited for the computer to return the findings.

"I gather you're used to this sort of thing!" spoke up the old man, noting all the varied pieces of equipment splayed over the workstations in the room. Although even in his own time, he wouldn't have understood such machinery.

The dark-haired Doctor's eyes darted back to the screen, taking in the images that were presented before them.

"I've only been doubling as CMO since Doctor Belder disappeared" she announced.

"Genetics is my main field!" she exhaled softly and sat back as the screen visualiser showed them the results.

"Here we are!" exclaimed the Doctor; she fingered the fluctuating scale that dominated the upper half of the complex computer screen on the wall.

"I'm sorry Doctor, even in my own time I had trouble comprehending these blasted things!" wavered the old man.

Elizabeth narrowed her eyes, concentrating on the screen.

"It's quite an unusual strain!" she spoke softly and craned her eyes closer.

Seeing only the wiggling lines on the screen that he couldn't interpret, the Professor awaited the Doctor's diagnosis.

"This part indicates the genetic content!" she explained, showing him the longest part of the diagram. Moving her finger along to another, she held her finger in place while her other hand demonstrated the difference to the other lines.

"I'll need some more time to process it!"

She cast her hands into the air and the Professor narrowed his eyes, wondering what she was up to.

"And the other sample that Mr Mitchell gave us?"

She nodded and exhaled deeply.

"It's much the same as the reptilian strain, but obviously from another animal!"

Elizabeth skidded backward on the chair, propelling the castor driven seat to the other side of the room; where she withdrew a drawer full of platelets and sped back across to rejoin the old man.

"There weren't many people that returned from the rescue team. Trooper Vane made it out with Stratton and Lieutenant Larson, but they didn't survive long!" she hissed coldly and began to organise the glass slides from the cold storage box.

"I took a few samples from their bodies, but none of them were in an advanced state such as this!" she put the first slide in the analyser and turned to the screen.

"This is Stratton's blood sample!" she said coldly, "You'll see the rapid decay of his red blood cells, the venom from his wound was soaked into his system almost like a sponge and started to affect him. He died of respiratory failure shortly after. But the venom continued to work in his body even after death!" she paused for a second as the Professor sat back in his chair intrigued.

"System, please display visual record of Trooper Stratton at the beginning of the autopsy!"

The screen showed the bald trooper in his mid thirties, the green slash from the creature's claws stretching across this throat.

"It really is quite unfortunate isn't it?" said the old man in disgust.

"System, please show the visual display at the end of the autopsy!" continued the Doctor.

The screen shimmered and showed the same man, his chest showing seam-like incision marks that had been sealed up by the dermal-grafter, but the Professor saw no difference in the man's body.

"What am I supposed to be looking at Doctor?"

Time-Ryder: Powerstone Book One

"Zoom in on grid reference three point one five" she said aloud to the air again.

The image focussed on Stratton's throat, namely the area that had been ravaged by the creature's claws.

But what the Professor saw was a miracle act.

The claw marks and green luminescent scarring that had ended the poor trooper's life had gone.

"I didn't seal the wound, it did it of its own accord!" she declared, "Now I'm beginning to see why!"

But the Professor still wasn't following.

"I did a few preliminary tests after the autopsy and used Lieutenant Larson as a case study and I found that the venom has a regenerative quality about it. I tried to synthesise it, but every attempt led to a breakdown. Do you know what this means?"

The Professor was beginning to realise the connotations of the creatures in the caverns.

"Somehow they've harnessed the ability to accelerate the regenerated tissue. If we could duplicate the findings then it'd be a medical breakthrough!" she exclaimed excitedly.

But the old man was thinking something entirely different and he took a breath, scratched his thick white beard and pushed himself back in his chair.

"What if these creatures thought the same thing? But the venom or DNA went that step farther and overtook them, turning them into these creatures!"

Elizabeth nodded in agreement.

"Under controlled circumstances I suppose the results could theoretically be achieved!" she hissed, "If only I could get a look at their documentation, or see the body of their work!"

"That's all just supposition Doctor" he hissed and rubbed his eyes. Elizabeth could see how tired he was and didn't want to keep him back from getting some rest. She rose from the stool as he stopped her.

"Do you seriously think the Commander will let anyone go back to the mines?"

He didn't relish the possibility himself, but the answer to getting home still lay within the craggy walls of the mine.

Elizabeth stripped off her long green lab coat and draped it over her chair.

"There's only one way to find out. Are you coming?" she smiled.

Half-excited and half-forlorn, the old man shot off his perch and joined her; bound for the flight deck.

Time-Ryder: Powerstone Book One

Time-Ryder: Powerstone Book One

CHAPTER THIRTY ONE

The Captain's office was an absolute mess.
Papers were strewn all over the floor and the desk. Books and documents had been pulled from their shelves, all in the search for answers, to which none had been found.
Jack was stretched back in the tough old red leather chair; his eyes mulling his eyes over the ceiling. He put his hand up to his face to tap his lip and scratched his thatch of a beard in a nervous gesture. Kara stood by the door, rather disappointed in the search, her frowning face telling all.
"You said there would be answers here!" she waved her hands in the air dramatically.
"And there should be. It doesn't make any sense!" he shot up from the chair and looked all around the Captain's office,
"He couldn't have been so careful to conceal everything. There has to be something here, unless..."
"Unless what?" Kara's brow drooped again.
"Unless he has another hiding place on board? Think Kara. Is there anywhere else on the ship that only he would go?"
"Apart from his quarters? No. He kept to himself, although I've only been on board for a week and haven't really studied his comings and goings!"
Jack resigned himself to a sigh, a gruff expulsion of air and frustration to which he looked at Kara squarely.
"I've got to get back into that mine. hopefully the tracking device will provide some answers!"
Kara felt panicked and unsure; she was starting to warm to him or rather the thought that he might lead her to the Captain.
"Why the mine?"
He looked up and sat back on the edge of the desk.

Time-Ryder: Powerstone Book One

"I saw something there that further proves my father's link to Blackthorne and the mine itself. Do you still have my stuff in storage?"

"Just a minute!" she exhaled and backed off to the door that opened with a restrained hiss.

"Sergeant Bailey, can you get Denton to retrieve the Commander's things from the hold?"

The small woman nodded in return and Kara rejoined him in the office.

"What are you looking for?"

He closed his eyes tightly and tried to concentrate as she stared at him intently, wondering if she did the right thing in setting him free.

"It has to be here somewhere!"

"What has to be here?" she narrowed.

"A link. Something that connects my father, the Captain and this planet. It can't be a coincidence that the Oregon was the one to answer the SOS call!" he was trying to piece it all together, thinking that the Captain may have left some kind of a paper trail or a journal, a diary perhaps.

"Are you thinking that Craven directed the SOS specifically at the Oregon, as if it had been planned all along?" She asked, thinking about Craven's involvement in all of this.

"Or Blackthorne has been monitoring events surrounding this planet and manoeuvred the ship into position once it became clear that an expedition was sent to check out the mines!"

Jack rested his rear on the edge of the desk beside Kara, both of them equally as disturbed by their theories.

"If that's true then he might have anticipated that all of this was going to happen!" exclaimed Kara.

She shot up quickly and moved to the door that opened upon her approach.

"Or there's another explanation!" began Jack.

Time-Ryder: Powerstone Book One

Kara never replied; she simply raised her brow inquisitively.
"There's the possibility that he knew those things were in the mine!"
Behind her in the doorway to the flight deck balcony stood Elizabeth and the Professor, looking as if they had just walked in on something. Henry smiled forward and straightened his bow tie.
"Did we miss something?" he looked to the Lieutenant and Jack and gave a fleeting glance to the Doctor; who was just as confused.
"Come in Henry and close the door, we're just about to get started!"
With an awkward glance between them both, Elizabeth and the Professor stepped into the office and the door glided shut behind them.

Looking up from the ops table on the flight deck, the dark-haired Craven kept his beady little eyes upon the door to the Captain's office. From the lower section on the flight deck, Sgt Bailey looked up to the ops table where Craven stretched his hands out over the black glass face of the display.
"You alright up there Mr Craven?" she asked.
He gave a wry grin, yet kept his gaze upon the balcony.
"Oh everything's fine Sergeant, thanks!" he said warmly, if somewhat slippery.
"Everything's starting to come together!" he hissed to himself and kept his eye on the Captain's door.

The door to the ship's recreation centre opened and Lieutenant Denton stepped into the opening.

"Lights!" he said aloft to the vacant room. The room remained a blissful shadow haven despite his vocal commands and he gave it a second to register.

Lifting his arm, Denton slammed the butt of his blue fist into the wall panel and at once the deck was showered in a bright aura of light. The tall man ushered Nova and Valana into the empty space, pointing to the various corners of the vast centre of entertainment.

"Down to the far left there's a recreation room, showers and changing areas to the right," he motioned.

Nova followed his finger with his wavering eyes.

"Exercise simulator!" he indicated the complex machinery that dwelled in the corner of the room.

"Through the door at the end and there you have the ships..."

Nova's eyes lit up, cutting the Lieutenant off as he shrieked.

"A bar, you've got a bar, then there is a god!" he shrieked with a smile. The bald man nodded as Valana looked on in amusement at the young man's delight.

"We have everything to cater for the crew's entertainment needs. We need them on the long term contracts!" said the tall blue giant, "the ship is fully equipped. We have a cinema, squash courts, swimming pool and even a bowling alley!"

"Fully equipped?" scoffed Nova, "where's your karaoke machine then? Eh?" he snorted.

Denton raised his brow.

"I have in fact studied several of Earth's languages, isn't that a Chinese form of self defence?"

Nova gave a wry grin and didn't know if Denton's bad joke was intentional.

"Not unless you bludgeon your attacker with the microphone or deafen them with your singing. Believe me, I've seen it happen!" he smiled, "I think that's Karate you mean Denton!"

Time-Ryder: Powerstone Book One

He looked all around the deck with dismay and remembered the lounge in the King's rest where he'd last seen Jessica.
"You haven't even got a pool table!" he moaned flinging his arms wide.
"Most of the decks are sealed off. A lot of the furnishings have been removed. The ship was due to be refitted when we return to Earth. Most of the unnecessary equipment has been stripped out!" replied Denton.
Nova gave a frown.
"So your bar isn't likely to be stocked?"
A chime sounded above their heads, followed by Bailey's unique accent.
"Lieutenant Denton please report to the Captain's office ASAP!"
"Oh yes, full bar, but no barman, Murray is on leave. Once we're finished with here, we're likely to be recalled to begin the refit. Excuse me while I get that!" he crossed to the small box on the wall and slid his finger over the surface.
"Denton to flight deck. Receive?" he hissed.
"Sgt Bailey here sir!" crackled the woman's voice.
"What is it Sergeant?"
"Lieutenant Everett requests you bring the Commander's pack to the Captain's office, you've to make it Priority One sir, she needs you up here right away!" continued Bailey.
He nodded to the wall with a frown of frustration.
"Understood, Denton out!" he backed off from the wall and rejoined the two youngsters.
Valana surveyed the room behind them both, scanning the walls and ceiling in silence, she glided over to them both.
"What is it you do here? I mean what is this ship's purpose?"
"We're one of twelve ships in the conglomerate" answered Denton, "The ship was originally designed for deep space exploratory mining detail and ore processing, but more recently

Time-Ryder: Powerstone Book One

we've been collecting space debris, salvaging derelicts and carrying freight!"
"Salvage as in scrap metal?" asked Nova; "So you're like an intergalactic Steptoe & Son?" he smiled.
Denton didn't understand any of what the young man had said, but he simply smiled politely.
"If you follow me, I'll show you where you can change!"
Nova ran his hands over one of the surfaces and collected dust on his fingertips.
"Someone really needs to have a word with your decorator" he joked, looking around the drab grey interior that seemed to be the mainstay of decor all over the whole ship.
Denton showed them into the changing facility where he proposed to open a few lockers and show the contents to Nova, much to his disgust.
"Haven't you got anything else?" he asked as Valana smiled at the choice of clothes that were obviously far too big for the young man.
Nova pulled out one of the white boiler suits from the open locker and modelled it upon himself.
"Well I think I've got three choices Denton" he coughed, "either I start to clean your toilets, I get ready to go to an Elvis convention or..." he put the boiler suit back and held his dirty clothes out in a pincer grip.
"Or I get these washed!" he smiled.
"You could make use of some of Palmer's old clothes; you look around the same size. If you'll follow me I'll show you to his quarters!"
Valana crept behind the tall man as Nova looked back to the locker, closing it over. He held his arm up in his best Elvis impersonation and curled his lip.
"Thank you very much!"

Time-Ryder: Powerstone Book One

There was a state of silence in the Captain's office, words had been exchanged, secrets revealed and it left them in a state of shock and surprise. Henry settled down in the sofa under the small porthole beside Elizabeth.
Jack hadn't counted upon her being brought into the fold, but it wouldn't harm things if one other person were let into the loop.
"I knew something wasn't right when we were in the mine. You were too distracted and reluctant to leave," spat the Professor.
Jack looked across the room to the old man and the Doctor.
"Which is half of the reason why I want to go back!" he pulled out an electronic pad with a brief sketch of what the device he discovered in the caves. Henry took it from him and showed it to the Doctor.
"Is this your father's device?"
"I can't be sure, all of his research and documents are missing. I'd never seen it before, but he kept me informed of his progress!"
"Then it can hardly be a coincidence for the ship to be here!" reinforced the Doctor.
It seemed that they were all on the same page and had more or less the same theories about the situation.
Kara stiffened, leaning back against the bookshelves.
"What's your plan?"
Jack took a breath and stood beside her.
"We have to make things look as normal as ever, if Craven intentionally dragged the Oregon here, we can limit the damage by keeping things quiet. I'll take a small party into the mines, try and retrieve the device and find out where they're operating from!" he announced.
"What about Vane?" Kara hissed, "I'm still not convinced he isn't involved somehow, he's too shifty!"
Jack tapped his lip nervously and looked at the small blonde officer.
"You could always lock him up and see how you go from there!"

Time-Ryder: Powerstone Book One

"And if Craven is innocent?" Kara was trying to look at it from all directions, not that she thought he was.

"If he's innocent, then there's no harm done. If not it let him might think the suspicion is drawing away from him and he might let his guard down!"

Kara was unsure of Jack's motives, but she trusted that he knew what he was doing.

"And I'll check around here, Doctor you can search the archives, while I do a physical search? I can use the DNA detector to see if there's anywhere the Captain has gone in the last seventy-two hours. It might help us!"

"Then I'd like to come back to the mountain with you Commander!" said the Professor softly. He felt so out of place and helping out would make him feel useful somehow. At least if he was in the mine he would have a chance to discover why they were brought here.

"Just call me Jack. Look I can't take responsibility for your safety when I go back into the mine Henry!"

Jack's patronising manner got the Professor brewing, his temper on the very edge of exploding. Anyone that knew him knew that it was safer on your eardrums to stay well out of his way.

"Now see here young man, I take full responsibility for myself. If there is any possible way to send Mr Mitchell and myself home, I can't sit idly by and do nothing!" he argued his case. It wasn't the first time that he'd seen the aggressive side of the old man and knew how passionate he was, so he conceded if not for his own sake then for the sake of his hearing. Jack caved in quickly and nodded, he understood the old man's frustration, much as he was about his own father.

"Well if you're so insistent Henry, I can't argue with you, but we'll be better prepared this time!"

Time-Ryder: Powerstone Book One

Kara and Elizabeth had taken a back seat ever so slightly, letting both men thrash it out and the Doctor had no idea what she had just walked in on.

"I need only one more member for my team then we can get prepared!" Jack said, just as the door to the Captain's office gave way with an expulsion of compressed gas.

In the doorway stood the tall, blue-skinned Lieutenant Denton, carrying the backpack and looking rather confused by the looks he was receiving from the occupants.

Jack smiled at him widely.

"I think we've just found the third member of our team!"

Time-Ryder: Powerstone Book One

Time-Ryder: Powerstone Book One

CHAPTER THIRTY TWO

Barely a few hours had passed, but Jack knew that everyone involved in the rescue attempt in the mines were all exhausted. The stresses of the expedition had taken its toll on some of them and while he still assumed his guise as Commander Adams; he thought it only right to order everyone to get some rest before the return journey to the mines, under the guidance from Kara; at least until the weather improved.

Nova's head nestled into the soft fluffy pillows in the guest quarters he had been allocated to.

He was curled up in a ball, happy in warm clothing and in the safety and comfort that the ship provided.

The sheets and duvet were so warm that the memory of the cold in the mines was miles away from him and he looked forward to a restful sleep without the fear of the very promiscuous Mrs Norman trying to ravage him in the middle of the night.

He looked across the large double bed to see Valana resting peacefully beside him. And she, like him, was having just as much difficulty sleeping.

She turned to face him, her head caressing the pillow gently and looking into his tired and heavy eyes.

"You look like you're having about as much trouble sleeping as I am!" said Nova softly, gazing back at her.

Her eyes batted as she smiled.

In the short time that she'd known him, he'd always made her smile, he had a pleasant disposition that made her relax.

"I'd like to say that I've a lot on my mind, but there's not much there!" she replied, joking at her own expense.

Nova's mouth curled into a smile.

"If I didn't know about the whole memory thing I'd probably say - typical blonde!" he gave a small laugh.

Valana pulled the pillow out from under her head and struck him with it.

"Hey you!"

Nova grinned inanely and held out his hands for her to stop. She laughed and settled back down onto the bed again.

"Careful now. A beautiful girl in my bedroom starting a pillow fight, you don't know what images I'm conjuring up in my head right now!"

She stopped and gave him back the pillow.

"Thanks for letting me bed down here tonight. I just didn't relish the idea of being alone. This place is kind of creepy!"

"Hey, no bother. I'm not exactly a fan of strange places myself so I'm happy for the company. But in saying that, you could have put a night-shirt on or something, you must be uncomfortable in that running man outfit!" he said softly, eyeing her silvery suit.

He could sense the nervousness in her, coupled with awkwardness.

"I thought it might make you uncomfortable!"

"Don't mind me, I probably won't sleep tonight anyway!" he smiled and then panicked at the thought he had probably just inserted into her head.

"Not that I have plans for doing anything else!" he didn't want to give her the wrong impression.

It was Valana's turn to smile at his awkwardness.

"You really don't mind me sleeping here?" her eyes widened and beamed at him.

It was a face he couldn't say no to.

"Nah, course not, but if you hog the covers, you can billet back in the bunk room!" he said with a smile, "I heard that Sgt Bailey likes the top bunk and she's got a certain expulsion problem, all that Newcastle brown ale I expect!"

Valana grinned and slipped off the edge of the bed, vanishing into the en-suite bathroom to change.

Time-Ryder: Powerstone Book One

There was one thing about the ship Nova thought. It had a pretty drab interior and design, but was more than made up for by the luxurious private quarters that catered for their every need, right down to the comfortable sofa and vid-screen that stretched across the whole of the wall on the far end of the room.

He considered that the crew probably needed their comfort if their missions were months at a time, as Denton had explained.

Valana glided back into the room with a thin lilac nightgown draped over her, tastefully showing off her physique. She slipped into bed and felt the benefit of the soft sheets, the instant touch of the cold silk almost chilling her to the bone.

"Better?" asked Nova softly.

She gave the briefest nod and he saw that twinkle in her eye again.

"Good, then go to sleep. We've got a long day tomorrow!" Nova closed his eyes over tightly and snuggled into the pillow, ready to try and get some well-earned rest.

"Nova!"

His eyes sprang open again, his narrowing gaze asking her the obvious question.

"Do you think we'll ever find a way home?" said the girl in a whisper.

"Ask me again in the morning, then I'll know if this is a dream or not!" he closed his eyes and started to drift off, wishing he were back in his own bed at home in Riverdale.

It had been hard for him since Aunt Rose passed away; so much that he'd barely spent a few nights in the house. He always found some reason to take a trip, or often used Barbara as an excuse to avoid being at home, but strangely enough, home was where he was thinking of right now.

Valana watched him try to get to sleep, wondering if she would drift off soon. She closed her eyes tight and within moments she was gone.

Time-Ryder: Powerstone Book One

There was a peace in the quarters, a peace soon shattered by the snorting snore like a spluttering school bus sitting in neutral gear. It roused Nova from his rest and he opened one eye to see the girl fast asleep; clearly the sources of the unsettling din.

"Poor thing is exhausted!" he remarked and saw that the bangle on her arm had begun to glow, illuminating the whole room.

"Oh great," Nova rolled his eyes, "Amnesia Barbie comes accessorised with her own night-light!"

He closed his eyes and frowned into his top pillow, pulling it over his head to block out the light.

And five minutes later, he was snoring just as loudly as Valana was. And resting safely under his bottom pillow was the strange looking device that he'd found in the mine.

In one of the other guest quarters, Professor Carlson wasn't catching up on the sleep like the others. Something was clearly on his mind and he paced the small room frantically.

He'd been heavily unsettled since their arrival onto the snow-blistered world, but it seemed to stem back long before that.

He thought of the sphere's prophecy and hoped that he and Nova hadn't become part of the foretelling.

Henry had stripped off his battered checked coat and was down to his white shirt and burgundy waistcoat, clearly feeling the benefit of the heating system that the ship had to offer. His eyes glazed over the desk again, stretched out underneath the extensive bay window, showing the grand view of the beautiful yet heavy snowfall outside.

But he was more concerned with what was on the desk, rather than the beautiful sight of the mountain landscape heavily deposited by the constant snowfall.

Folded out on the desk was a set of documents. Some of which he'd had about his person prior to his arrival on Penithe and others that were given him by Colonel Ryder in the attempt to unravel part of what was going on.

It was going to be strange adjusting to the Commander's new identity, yet still keeping it a secret from the others, but the old man smiled that he wasn't being paranoid and his suspicions about Jack were not totally unfounded after all.

He took a seat in the bonded plastic chair and pulled it closer to the table, peering at the documents with amusement, but they still clearly perturbed him.

The faked papers that the council had been submitted by Somersby showed all the hallmarks of authenticity, yet something as stupid as a forged signature had unravelled all of whatever the pretending Laird had sought. It all seemed so pointless now, but if he ever managed to get back home, he'd have the great pleasure of unmasking Somersby for the fraud that he was.

Henry loosened his tie and pulled out the small pill bottle from his pocket, taking out a couple of capsules and downing them with some water, tossing the bottle onto the desk absentmindedly.

He gave an exhausted sigh and arched back his neck before leaning forward and then something caught his eye.

In amongst the papers was a stretch of parchment that he had already translated from the Celtic runes, like the ones he and Nova had discovered on the walls of the lower crypt at Baleran. In a smudged scrawl on a piece of blank paper was the warning and somehow he was taking it slightly more literally than he usually would have, but the lower portion of the text had not been translated and it was bothering him.

Now was not the time for deliberation or going off on a tangent, he could decipher the remainder of the text when things were a little less frantic.

Time-Ryder: Powerstone Book One

Henry leaned forward, his eyes creasing shut as he gripped the desk, clearly in pain, but not wanting to dwell on what was bothering him.

He fought it back and bore the pain, trying to stand erect again as the chair shot backwards.

As the pain decreased, he breathed out slowly, his eyes easing open and he glared down to the desk.

The documents given to him by Jack were spread out to his right, detailed reports of the mission to the mines and all the surrounding data concerning the situation.

If he was going to be of any use to the Colonel, it seemed only right that he knew exactly what was going on. He didn't think that Jack would have trusted him with all of the information, but was taken aback when he thrust the files into the old man's possession.

His desk at home was always untidy, much like this one, but he didn't see the photo sticking out from under the brown file that he'd been given and it slipped under the desk, floating away out of his sight.

The Professor withdrew from the desk with a sigh of frustration and resigned himself to sleep.

He retired to the bed, leaning back on the headrest where he gradually drifted off into sleep.

The upturned monochrome photo lay on the floor under the desk and was swept over by a gust of wind as the door to the guest quarters opened and a pair of heavy intrusive boots lumbered into the room.

The upturned photo settled on the floor, facing upright once more and strangely enough it was an image of Captain Blackthorne.

Time-Ryder: Powerstone Book One

Much as Nova had given warnings of Sgt Bailey's amazing rumoured feats of wind, she was stationed on the flight deck for part of the night shift.

The lighting was low, the blue-grey colour of the decor looking less dazzling than it usually did. Half of the monitors stemming either side of the massive window were powered down, most of the regular stations non-operational.

All of the functions had been re-routed and were available at the forward station desk where she sat, leaning on the smooth glass display.

Although she was alone, there were voices still being carried forth, carried in argument, even though she couldn't make out what was being said.

She looked up at the red digital display of the flight deck clock above the main screen and sighed as the minute digit flipped forward and the clock had finally reached midnight. It wouldn't be long until her shift changed and then some other poor exhausted soul would assume her watch.

The voices grew in volume again and Janice Bailey lifted her head to the balcony; where the elevated voices streamed from the Captain's office.

She gave a sigh and turned back to her station.

As much as Janice thought she was alone, she was far from it. In the gloom at the back of the flight deck, shrouded in the shadow of the balcony, Craven kept to the darkness, listening and trying to piece together what little was being said above him. He continued looking upward as the voices elevated still.

Time-Ryder: Powerstone Book One

Time-Ryder: Powerstone Book One

CHAPTER THIRTY THREE

It was a heated exchange in the Captain's office, both Jack and Kara clearly opposed to the plans of the next day; their tempers flaring and clearly clashing with each other's ideas.

Jack had to contain himself, remembering the fact that Kara was in charge; even though he thought she was a little out of her depth.

"You're the most stubborn and arrogant man I've ever known. You do know you're walking into a trap!" she spat angrily.

"Flattering me won't change my mind Lieutenant!" scoffed Jack.

"I'm being serious Jack. You walk back into that mine without proper back up and you're as good as dead, and anyone else that is dumb enough to go with you!"

He rolled his eyes.

"Look I've got it all planned out. We can't go back in the same way, Vane blew apart the hatch," announced the American, "but there must be another way in!"

"There is, even if it is a bit unconventional" she replied.

Kara had gone over the reports and the brief details surrounding their escape and had studied the plans of the mines.

"Aside from my original entry point which has probably been swallowed up by the shifting ground, I don't see how!" he retorted and then saw the sly glint she had in her eye, "What did you have in mind?"

She'd taken a great deal of time to research the mines before they had arrived and used whatever resources, some of which had now been added to with the information and outlay from his Spectrometer.

"Leave it to me," she said softly, "I'll work on it," she looked around and crossed to the door.

"Have a nice sleep Lieutenant!" he said and buried his head back into the documents, just like the Professor.

"Just don't stay up too late Jack!" she smiled and left him to it, "The watch should be changing shortly!" she announced as the door parted for her.

Kara yawned as she entered the flight deck, looking down to the tech pit to see Sgt Bailey was still draped over the front console and doing her best to keep up the appearance that she was fully awake.

"Anything to report?" she shuffled along the balcony.

"Just lots more snow!" remarked the Sergeant, "And there's some wind too ma'am!" replied the woman glibly.

Kara smiled as she reached the end of the balcony and she wavered outside the large silver rimmed doors.

"Night Janice!" she managed a smile of amusement before shuffling through the doors.

Bailey returned the grin and perched over the station, her eyes beginning to cloud over again.

Still cowering under the balcony, shrouded in darkness, Craven narrowed his brow in confusion and looked aloft to the balcony, his face still perplexed.

"Who the hell is Jack?" he whispered softly.

He shirked it off and edged his way over to the left, where the lower side doors to the flight deck led out onto the outer deck that ran the whole length of the ship. Quickly making an abrupt exit, he slipped through as Janice awoke from the whoosh of the parting doors.

Thinking that it was just her imagination, she shook her head, smiled and concentrated back on the screen in front of her and drifted back off to sleep again.

In the Medibay, Elizabeth was putting the final touches to her work before she turned in for the night.

Time-Ryder: Powerstone Book One

She gave a sigh and stretched, walking over to the doorway when the screen on the workstation illuminated and grabbed her attention.

Bleary eyed, she tried to keep her eyes open, and she sauntered back over, just in case it was anything important.

She gave another long sigh and pulled off her long white lab coat, throwing it over the nearest Medibed.

Pulling up a chair, Elizabeth rubbed her eyes and planted herself in front of the screen and she stared at it for a few seconds before screwing up her face and squinting at it again.

"System, increase room illumination to full!" she said aloud.

The room was filled with bright light and Elizabeth almost strained from the brightness.

"Transfer the display of station one to main screen!"

The large screen on the main wall of the Medibay showed what she had been startled by, although in greater detail.

It was an overlaid image of Trooper Stratton's post mortem, but there was something that was puzzling her, so she'd prepared for a full scan and had waited patiently for the results. The image on screen was essentially what could be determined as an X-ray, but looked more complex and almost resembled the blue prints of a building. The bones, muscles, veins and surrounding tissue were all illuminated by varying colours and easy to omit from the scan readings.

The Doctor waved her hand in front of the screen and it slid the image to the side, showing another from another angle.

"I knew it!" she hissed in a shrill expulsion of air.

"System, enhance the image around the base of the skull!"

The blueprint zoomed in on the area where the brain stem connected to his neck and she narrowed curiously, stepping closer to the screen.

She turned her fingers over in the air in front of her and the image revolved to give her a better view.

Time-Ryder: Powerstone Book One

How she had overlooked it before was unclear, but the scan had picked up every single detail.

There were three puncture marks at the base of the neck and an intruding set of marks, leading into the brain.

"It's leading right into the hippocampus, but why?"

"Problem?" echoed a voice behind her.

Elizabeth nearly jumped out of her skin with fright and revolved to see Jack looming in the doorway.

"I'm not sure, I can't make any sense out of this!" she replied.

She continued glaring at the screen and he sided up to her, trying to see what she was looking at.

"What are we looking at?"

"It's a full spectral scan of Trooper Stratton's body, there were abrasions all around his neck with small incisions around the base, but I couldn't see any reason for them."

The blueprint of Stratton reverse-zoomed and Jack saw where the indentations were.

"Have you checked the rest of the bodies?"

Elizabeth shook her head.

"I didn't see the point; their deaths were caused by severe lacerations to the throat. Stratton was the only one I was concerned with as he survived the attack until he came back on board!"

There was a brief pause and Elizabeth squinted and turned to look at him.

"Why?"

Jack folded his arms.

"When I first met the Professor and Nova in the mines, we found a body with the same marks on the base of his neck, just like those!"

"But what would be the purpose?" she narrowed and looked back to the screen once again.

"You're the Medic, you tell me?" he retorted and then narrowed his eyes in thought,
"What part of the brain does it enter?" he looked closer at the screen, but had no idea what he was looking for.
"The hippocampus!"
"And what's its function?" Jack pointed to the image.
"It's part of the Medial Temporal lobe, the area of the brain that's associated with memory!"
Tired as she was, this seemed to bring her back to life, she didn't like puzzles getting the better of her and this looked like it was going to get the better of her for a long while yet.
Elizabeth gave an even longer sigh of desperation, meaning that she was going to have a lot more work to contend with.
"It looks like I'll have to scan the other bodies, and I was so looking forward to a good night sleep!"
He gave her a gentle pat on the shoulder and stepped away again.
"It can wait till morning Doctor, go get some sleep!" he yawned and on a sombre note he leaned forward, "When you get the chance, can you take a look at Henry?"
Her brows met and she looked at him strangely.
"Is he alright? Maybe he's just a bit exhausted!"
Jack bit his lip, unsure of how to put it, but if there was any way of finding out what was wrong with him, Elizabeth was the logical first step.
"It's just something he said in the mine, he's ill, but he never said what was wrong with him. Can you take a discreet look at him without him knowing?"
"A little medical espionage?" she gave him a smile and resigned herself to a nod of agreement.
"I suppose everything else can wait, even if the questions are going to keep me up all night!"
"Questions?" Jack raised his brow.

"Of course. If whatever it was, was trying to access the memory centres of the brain, what information were they after and how were they going to access the information and process it. Do they have the technology to even do that and why?"

Jack rolled his eyes and retreated backwards.

"You do realise I'm going to get very little sleep after that information don't you Doctor?"

"You started it!" she smiled back at him wryly.

He frowned and moved out into the hall, leaving her alone in the Medibay.

"And I have the feeling I'm going to regret it!"

Returning to her quarters for the night, First officer Kara Everett stepped through the opening door, her eyes nearly closed over with fatigue as she fumbled through the room and unzipped her flight-suit, letting the garment drape needlessly around her waist.

She took a few steps into the en-suite and shoved a glass under the tap. The automatic sensors kicked in and the glass filled up rapidly. Kara swigged the water back, almost as if it was a shot glass and she felt the cool liquid course down her throat, relieving her instantly.

The room was surprisingly hot and she shuffled over to the temperature control unit by the door to see if the levels had risen. Strangely enough they were the same as they always were and she disregarded it, pulling the lower half of her suit down and flopping out onto the comfy bed before her.

The small blonde woman was exhausted and it didn't take long for her to sleep as she drifted off where she lay.

In the shadows of the gloomy quarters, something moved slowly, coming closer to the bed and hovering over the sleeping Lieutenant's form.

Time-Ryder: Powerstone Book One

A gloved hand shot out into the area above her head, a small silver device in its grip and it coughed out a small puff of gas. The mist enveloped her and she deeply breathed the vapour in. After a few seconds the gloved hand lifted her arm and tried to rouse her from her sleep, but Kara was out cold.
Returning to the shadows, the unknown intruder started rifling through her things, opening drawers and sifting through the papers that were piled upon her desk. The intruder carried on the search, and still Kara slept unawares.

Nova's eyes eased open.
He felt refreshed and took in a long deep breath, waking with a smile and then his eyes went wide.
Not in panic, but in surprise. A long slender arm was curled around his chest; hugging tight and holding him close, not that he was complaining.
Valana was snuggled in behind him and even though she was unusually cold, she drew the heat from him. Nova gave a small smile and closed his eyes again, settling back down into the warm duvet and putting his arm over her hand for comfort.
With lightning reflexes, the blonde haired girl withdrew her hand and sat bolt upright, drawing the duvet up over her chest and covering herself.
"Are you alright?"
Nova looked slightly amused as he turned to face her and saw the alarming look on her face.
It took a few minutes and then she started to remember. Valana's face relaxed as she looked into his eyes.
"I'm sorry, I seemed to lose myself there for a bit!" she became slightly shy and withdrawn as Nova sat up in concern.
"You do look a bit off, have you remembered anything?"

Time-Ryder: Powerstone Book One

"Unsettling dreams that's all!" she said softly with a hiss, "I didn't do anything out of the ordinary did I?"
He looked at her with a cheeky smile, thinking of winding her up, but decided that he wasn't that cruel.
"Besides turning into a cuddle monster during the night? No!"
She gave him a smile and blushed.
It was the first restful sleep he'd had in months and the first time that he hadn't been constantly dreaming about Barbara.
It was a consolation that he hadn't dreamt about her as usually they turned into bad dreams and he'd find himself awake for the rest of the night.
"Maybe I should get dressed!" she replied, slightly embarrassed.
Her skin was so pale, that it was totally obvious that she was blushing as she withdrew to the bathroom.
Nova turned back over, pulling the warm cover over his head and he faded back off to sleep with a beaming smile.

In much less the same position as she had fallen asleep in, Kara Everett groggily lifted her head from the soft sheet of her bed.
Her head was pounding and her vision slightly blurry, but aside from that she was well rested and ready for the day ahead, or would be after her first few cups of coffee.
She gently eased off the bed, gathering up her flight-suit from her ankles and pulling it off her feet. Kara staggered towards the en-suite, her eyes still half closed over and she flipped on the steam shower.
The bathroom was soon clouded up so much that she couldn't see two feet ahead of her, but she managed to guide herself into the bathtub and stood under the warm torrents that made her feel so alive.

Time-Ryder: Powerstone Book One

Kara closed her eyes over and smiled absently as she washed herself down. Her head quickly snapped around as a noise came from the adjoining room.
"Is there anyone there?" she echoed, but there was no reply. Shutting off the shower, she shuffled back into the room and narrowed her brow, gazing around the room as she gripped the towel tightly around her nimble frame.
"I must be hearing things!" she murmured and slipped back into the bathroom again.

It was much the same in the rest of the ship. Those that were rising for the new day were taking over from the night crew and slipping back into the daily routine, not that the last few days was any means near a routine day, but there still had to be duties to perform, systems to check and procedures put into place.
One such individual was Doctor Gennero. She'd barely had any sleep, the quandary over the skeletal scans perturbing her during the night, so she went straight back to work. On her fifth mug of coffee, she sat at the workstation; ready to growl at anyone that would dare intervene.
Elizabeth had completed the scans and was waiting for System to correlate them and see if there were any similarities between the dead. It was going to be a long wait.
Her attention was skewed as Jack Ryder gave a small cough and announced his presence in the doorway.
"Any luck?" he offered a smile.
She spun around in her chair, a wiry pair of glasses balanced on the end of her thin nose. A smile was all he was going to get and he moved warily closer to the workstation.
"I've completed the scans!" she replied in a brash tone, the coffee clearly getting the better of her, but something was bothering her.

Time-Ryder: Powerstone Book One

She flashed her hand in front of the screen and the charts and details swept to the side, clearing the monitor.
She tapped the air in front of her as if using a keyboard and another file opened.
"What's that?"
She sniffed and tapped the air, bringing the image closer.
"It's your report on what happened yesterday, something's not quite right about it!" she answered.
"It's quite detailed, I can assure you!" objected the American.
Elizabeth shook her head.
"No, that's not it!" she snorted, "You described that Doctor Belder's body was found, minus his head!"
Jack nodded, not seeing what she was getting at.
"And no sign of the head in the surrounding area?" she asked.
"Not that we could see, but there was quite a bit of ground to cover in the mine Doctor!"
She turned back to him, taking her glasses off to have a better view of him.
He was clean-shaven, except for his goatee and was freshly dressed, but still slightly rugged; Elizabeth put it down to his disposition.
"So he's been decapitated!" she mused.
"Yeah Doc, that's usually what happens when you get your head cut off!" he sniped sarcastically, smiling at her.
Elizabeth shrugged again and narrowed her brow. She tossed her glasses on the workstation and looked into his eyes.
"So where's his head?"

Time-Ryder: Powerstone Book One

CHAPTER THIRTY FOUR

Kara Everett was fully dressed in a pristine navy-blue shirt and trousers, finely pressed and immaculate.
The only thing wrong about her was the perplexed look upon her face. Something was wrong in her quarters. Everything seemed to be in place, yet it still didn't feel right.
She had a sudden sense of insecurity, as if a presence had been stalking around her and watching her every move.
Kara narrowed her brow and took a look around; her hand hovering over the table underneath the large bay window.
She saw that there was a fine line of dust, showing the outline of where her picture frame took place in the centre of the table, yet had been moved slightly. It pricked-up her senses; making her paranoid that someone had entered the room without her knowing.
"System, initiate a full spectral scan of my quarters!" she announced to the air; her eyes creasing as she tried to look for any other unconformities.
"Understood Lieutenant. That procedure will take approximately thirty minutes for a complete composite scan!" said the droning voice.
"Good, keep me apprised of the findings, I'll be on the Flight-Deck!"
Kara took another look around and left the room as a green hue of the scan wave began to touch out to the walls and eclipse the room.

Still in his clothes from the previous night, Professor Carlson had fallen asleep at the desk in his quarters.
He roused with a groan and an embittered yawn as he dazedly lifted his head and stretched out.

Time-Ryder: Powerstone Book One

Although he enjoyed his brief slumber, he immediately jumped as the door chime sounded off and he crossed to the opening, waving his palm in front of the sensor as he had been shown. The door parted quietly and Jack stood in the doorway, alert, pensive and inquisitive.

"Come in Commander!" hissed Henry quietly, "Sorry Colonel!" he said, still trying to get used to the American's true identity.

"Doctor Gennero has asked to see you!" Jack smiled.

"If you give me some time to freshen up!" replied the old man.

Jack eyed his dishevelled clothes and moved over to the large box-like cabinet on the far side of the room.

He slid his finger up the front of the surface and a digitised panel appeared on the outer face of the cabinet. He pressed a couple of settings and stood back as a door slowly descended like a drawbridge.

"If you put your clothes in here, the re-dryer will have them ready in five minutes."

Henry smiled in amusement and moved closer, peering inside the box curiously.

"Have you any idea why the good Doctor would like to see me?" Jack had already retreated to the door, his mind eager to get the plans of the return to the mines underway.

"Something about the samples you took yesterday," he replied, "She said it'd make more sense to you, but she'd rather tell you in person!"

"Of course!" he snapped his fingers and suddenly became alert. Jack left him to it and the old man started filling the re-dryer machine with his clothes, returning to the desk where the documents were laid out.

He lifted the battered scrawl of Celtic runes and stared at it for a second, his mind turning over and over.

He closed his eyes, took off his glasses and tossed them onto the desk.

Time-Ryder: Powerstone Book One

Henry had dreaded that this day was going to come and a small tear emerged from the corner of his eye as he dropped into the chair, still staring at the runes and he pulled out a pencil, ready to complete the translation.

Alone on the flight deck, save for a few on duty guards and technicians, Kara strode around the ops table, looking at the display, a small portable device in her hand which she kept flicking her hand across.
She looked from the device to the larger image on the display before her and gently let the small hand tablet rest upon its surface.
"Lieutenant, initial scans of your quarters have been completed. A detailed report of the findings is being relayed to your ops station!" finished the computer's sullen voice.
Immediately Kara leapt to the station in front of her, her hands spread wide over its surface as she looked over the vital information. She ran her finger down the list of items and came to a stop, with a smile of contentment spreading over her.
"I bloody knew it!" she cursed and ran her finger over the slider on the ops desk.
"Lieutenant Everett to Master at Arms, have a security team report to the flight deck!" she rasped and straightened up with satisfaction. Her suspicions had been confirmed, not that she was happy about being right. She looked at the details on the screen ahead once again, just to confirm her insecurities and then closed it off, turning the screen black once more.
Kara took a slow breath and wheeled as the two, armed security guards emerged from the lower doors and she moved over to greet them with a sullen disposition. Standing in the doorway of Nova's quarters, and looking like he didn't need any sleep whatsoever, Lieutenant Denton waited for the door to open.

Time-Ryder: Powerstone Book One

It eased open and Nova glared up at him, still slightly shocked by his skin colour, but slightly amused by it. He was still picturing the giant in a pair of white spandex trousers and a white, floppy 'Mr Noddy' hat.

The youngsters fixed their own attire and followed him into the drab hallway, both bound for the commissary and the anticipated feast that lay ahead for morning breakfast.

It had been a day since they'd first met the tall blue-skinned officer, yet it didn't stop Nova from gazing at the tall man's pale complexion and the crescent shaped gills that stemmed each side of his bald head, occasionally opening and absorbing a fresh intake of air.

"So Denton, where do you come from?" declared Nova, trying to make a start to an awkward situation. He was happy to be back in his own clean clothes, having discovered the joys of the re-dryer in his quarters.

Valana shuffled slowly behind them, her eyes wandering the walls, checking out the varied pipes, conduits and computer interfaces stations.

She wasn't as anxious or nervous as she had been the previous day; perhaps it was Nova's company that made her relax.

Whatever it was, she was letting it take her mind off her memory loss.

The tall giant was silent as they continued their brisk walk, almost increasing in pace as he continued to stare right ahead, focussed on his current task.

"Not even a little answer?" teased Nova, trying to get some information out of him, "Are you the only one of your kind on board!"

Denton halted, and for a second Nova thought that he'd said something wrong, to which he took a retreating step back beside Valana.

Time-Ryder: Powerstone Book One

"You don't have to answer that, I'm just trying to pass the time!" said Nova nervously, "Small talk you know Dents!" he smiled up at the tall giant who looked down, his face as stiff as stone.
After a long pause, Denton pursed his blue lips and spoke ever so softly.
"I am the only one of my kind!" he hissed softly.
Nova's eyes widened.
"What completely?"
"My species cannot propagate; we were the cloned results of the..." he broke off his sentence, not wishing to say anymore.
It didn't make any sense to Nova, but at least he was getting the big guy to speak to him. Valana looked at Nova awkwardly as the tall man started off down the corridor again.
They came to a wide set of double doors that glided open and stuck midway, the tall lieutenant offering assistance and shoving the doors home.
"Thanks Denton!" welcomed Nova stepping through into the bustle of activity.

Elizabeth Gennero was hard at work in the Medibay.
Her mind still awash with questions about the entry points into Stratton's and every other victim's brains.
It seemed that she had devoted so much time to the problem that she barely noticed the lingering form of Henry Carlson in the doorway. He stood silently, not wishing to interrupt, until she wheeled her chair around and almost frightened herself to death. She eased back in the chair and smiled.
"Henry!" she gasped and then fetched a smile.
He stood in his finest; his clothes clean, neat and unblemished with no signs of their extremities from the previous day with the exception of a few holes in his jacket.

Time-Ryder: Powerstone Book One

"The Colonel told me you had something to show me!" he said gruffly and started his way over towards her. His face stiffened and he tried to quell the signs of discomfort, but Elizabeth watched him like a hawk.

"Henry, what is it?"

"Nothing for you to concern yourself Doctor, thank you!" he said politely, biting back the pain.

She could see that he was in pain, but respected his wishes and beckoned him closer.

"I wanted to show you this before I told Lieutenant Everett and Commander..." she stopped herself and looked at the old man as she reclaimed her seat in front of the console.

He placed a hand on her shoulder and managed a smile.

"I know Doctor, it is a bit confusing!" he said softly, "Please show me what you have!"

Henry pulled a stool over and hunched behind Elizabeth, looking over her shoulder at the screen.

She tapped the board and the screen came to life, illuminating the specimens she had been interested in.

"These are the samples you gave me yesterday, they look like everyday scales from a reptile, but I looked a bit further and guess what I found?" she said smugly, even though the baffled old man had no idea where she was going with it.

"Do enlighten me please!" he hissed and straightened back in his chair, a slight air of sarcasm coming from him.

She rose from the console and crossed to the other workstation, slipping a small white scanning device under her long green coat. She re-took her position behind the Professor and ran the device inches away from his back, unseen by the old man.

Elizabeth leaned over him and tapped the screen, zooming in on the green scales and taking the image as far as she could go with the mass spectrometer.

Time-Ryder: Powerstone Book One

Satisfied with the operation of the small device in her hand, she stowed it away inside her pocket and moved in front of him, resuming her posture in front of the main workstation desk. Elizabeth touched the pad to the side and it brought up the DNA sequence for the sample on a separate screen.

"Voila!" she said pleased with herself, yet the old man was far from impressed.

"Doctor, I'm from the 21st century, you might need to elaborate your findings somewhat!" he said softly.

"Oh!" she pushed her glasses back on over the bridge of her nose and gulped.

"The sample you brought back isn't a basic DNA strand!" she announced and turned to face the Professor, "Every strand has a double helix, this one doesn't!"

She snapped her neck back around to the screen where the complex DNA sequence was revolving and she zoomed in on it.

"I've never seen anything like this in....ever!" she said in amazement, "It's never been documented before!"

"You're babbling Doctor; just tell me what it is!"

"Henry, what you're looking at is a triple Helix, it's never been heard of before. The third DNA strand has been genetically augmented and attached to the existing pair. This third strand is fighting for dominance, trying to convert the other strands into the same. It's like a parasite!" continued as the Doctor as the old man tried to follow her.

The Professor shifted uneasily in his seat, he was starting to get a wider picture; he frowned as he peered closer to the screen with the revolving data.

"It's an aggressive strain, but I managed to create an Antigen that inhibits the third strand and has enabled me to remove it!"

Elizabeth was so excited; this was what she was trained for, not merely cataloguing the dead for the morgue.

She tapped away at the pad once again and the main screen fizzled to life with a similar looking DNA profile.
"What's this?" Henry asked as she wheeled to face him again.
"This is the sample that I used the Antigen on; it's taken it back to a base pair sequence. This is what the DNA was like before the third strand was added!" She almost shrieked with delight at telling him.
"But what is it?" the Professor looked closer and could see a few distinct differences between the two screens.
Elizabeth took a breath and removed her glasses, her big brown eyes looking past the Professor's scratched lenses and into his eyes.
"It's Human!"

Hoisted up by the scruff of his shoulders, a confused and bewildered Trooper Vane was dragged down to the holding cells by two overly large troopers, both armed and prepared.
He was hand-cuffed and held tight, but Vane wasn't struggling. His only objections were vocal as the door creaked open and he was thrust inside.
"What? No refreshments?" the American joked.
Joe looked around the bleak and dirty walls before giving in and dropping into the nearby chair in the centre of the room.
His mind was going in all directions wondering why he had been apprehended, although he had some inkling of a suspicion why.
He was the only survivor of the first rescue expedition into the mines, a fact that Lieutenant Everett had always been quite vocal about and he wondered when more accusations would come up and bite him in the ass.
Joe took an elongated sigh and leaned back in the chair.
With nothing better to do, he leaned forward onto the rugged excuse for a desk, closed his eyes and tried to go to sleep.

Time-Ryder: Powerstone Book One

CHAPTER THIRTY FIVE

After a hearty breakfast, Nova had left Valana in the commissary and wandered through the decks, following the signs carefully in his unique yet bumbling curiosity. He'd listened to Adams at breakfast and as much as he disagreed with some of his plans; they made sense in a strange way.

He drew upward through the drab hallway to the elaborate white spiral staircase that swept upwards and slowly his black-booted feet clanked upon the metal as he climbed upward.

The spiral brought him out onto a white corridor and still the ceiling was festooned with pipes jutting out from the walls; some only half concealed by makeshift pipe enclosures.

Nova stepped up to the glass doors, thinly framed by a silver/chrome finish. Upon his approach they parted with a strained expulsion of compressed gas.

He entered the flight deck and was quite impressed by what he saw. When compared to the randomness of the cobbled together hull and exposed pipes and innards that he'd seen on the way up to the control hub of the immense craft, he didn't hide his amazement.

As he stepped to the top of the main entrance, he gazed over the enormity of the flight deck. It's sleek finish, state of the art computer systems and displays and massive suspended view-screen at the far end of the room, surrounded by many other little screens that showed various parts of the largely spacious craft.

There was a balcony just in front of him; yellow railings finely polished and a spectacular stairway leading down to his right in a slight left turn to the technician's pit where a large operations table showed the main focus of the latest mission.

Standing in front of the table was the slim form of the blonde haired young woman who he'd glanced at briefly through the clear bulkhead doors in the cargo bay.

Kara turned slowly; her cherubic face giving a faint smile, yet he saw sadness in her big brown eyes.

He glided down the stairs, his hand automatically outstretching as if hypnotically drawn to hers.

With a smile, he felt himself about to stutter, although hadn't yet uttered a word.

"Eh, hello" he faltered, "I'm Nova," he stuttered, "Nova Mitchell!"

She looked at him with intrigue, strangely mesmerised with him as much as he was with her.

"Kara Everett!" she announced softly, her eyes drawing over his face and memorising every inch.

"I saw you through the airlock doors, before you knocked us all out!" he said, trying to sound not as straight-faced as it came out.

She smiled back awkwardly.

"Yeah, sorry about that, didn't handle it as best as I should have!"

Nova made a frowning face, but somehow knew that it was the closest thing to an apology that she was going to make.

Their hands finally met and she shook, feeling the slight tingle of what could only be described as an electrical shock.

Kara withdrew almost instantly, smiling in a nervous reaction as Nova recoiled.

"Static!" she murmured, "Ship's full of it, half of the systems are buggered, whole bloody thing needs mothballed of you ask me!"

Nova was in awe of the small Lieutenant. She was no bigger than he was, of slim build and her hair in an unusually short bob that hung barely over the bottom of her ear-line, but it suited her somehow.

Nova still felt the tingle on his hand and gave an unusual grimace. He rubbed his hands, still feeling an after effect of the static charge.

Time-Ryder: Powerstone Book One

"What are you doing up here on your own?" she asked accusingly, "This area is off-limits!"

The approach of two troopers advancing to their position made him shrink back and Kara stepped forward in a defensive posture in front of the young man.

"It's alright, he'll be fine with me!" she backed them off and returned to the Nova with a smile.

Nova smiled back and looked all around him.

"The others are on their way, that Commander of yours wants a big pow-wow with all of us."

Kara nodded.

"He filled me in with all your details, how are you adjusting?"

Nova shirked and relaxed as the gorillas retreated back to their position at the lower doors.

"Not too well. But as soon as this is all sorted, the Professor and me are out of here. Don't get me wrong your ship is pretty cool for something that looks like a meccano pet project, but I don't plan to be sticking around any longer than I have to!"

She held out her hand to the stood by the table and he eased into it as she joined him; her eyes still wandering over the schematic on the display.

Nova took a glance to the surface and she closed the details, turning to him slowly.

"Just say that you can't get home, what will you do?"

Nova's eyes widened, taken aback. It was not something he'd considered. His main focus was getting back home and trying to slide back into as much of a normal life as possible, even if it was a life without Barbara and an uncertain future with the sudden news of the Professor's prognosis. It was more than he could possibly think about right now, but at least getting home gave him a focus and something to aim for.

"I don't know Kara, but the answers are all in that mountain and if that Commander thinks I'm staying behind then he's got another thing coming!"
She looked at him with concern.
"Let's just see what he has to say first!"
Nova gave a frown and looked into her eyes. He had a sense that things weren't going to go as he thought and but had the strangest feeling that he was inclined to trust her.
He'd wait to see what was going on and see if he was included. Adams had surprised him once already, who was to say he wasn't going to do it again.

Time had been going by so slowly for Joe Vane. He was finding his time in the holding cell very tedious, even more so that he didn't know why he had been detained in the first place. He had an idea that it had something to do with his involvement in the first rescue mission that led to the multiple deaths and the disappearance of Captain Blackthorne.
Now that Doctor Belder had turned up, sans his head, he knew that there would be more questions to be answered, but it was all just a waiting game and one that he was sure Lieutenant Everett was going to stretch this out for as long as possible.
He sat back in his chair, content to wait, his eyes wandering to the door, in the hope that all of this would be over sooner than later.

Jack paced the floor frantically in the Captain's office.
He paused momentarily and stared at his only companion. Kara stood with her arms folded, an expression of amusement and annoyance on her face.
She looked back at him with a slight sigh.

Time-Ryder: Powerstone Book One

"You need to stop worrying, everything's going to be alright!" she reassured him, but he didn't feel it.

She held out a hand to the door and he tried to get out of his slump.

"I don't like lying to them, they've been straight with me since I met them!" he hissed and gave his beard a frustrating scratch.

"You lied to me!" Kara stared back at him.

"But that didn't put you in any danger, this might! It's a big gamble we're taking here Lieutenant," he said coldly.

Kara move closer to him and looked up, he was at least a foot and a half taller than her and she seemed almost dinky when in comparison; even more so when compared to Denton.

"I'll make sure no harm comes to them while they're here, you just need to concentrate on finding Blackthorne, for both of us!"

There was something in what she said that rung true, a soft sense of reasoning that he seemed to filter out all of the dark thoughts and made him panic, just a little less than he would have done. Despite their brief time together, he was going to miss working alongside her, if circumstances had been very different, he could see the two of them becoming firm friends.

"Jack, they're all waiting!" she said softly as the door glided open with its usual hiss of movement.

He stepped through onto the balcony and overlooked the flight deck; his hands gripping the yellow rails nervously.

Everyone was settled.

The rag-tag band of technicians, officers, archaeologists and whatever Valana was, were all surrounding the large black ops table on the in the centre of the tech pit.

Each of the eager faces were looking forward to what Jack had to say, although only a very few of them knew what he was actually planning; only a few of them actually cared.

Jack looked around the group, like the attendees of a witch-hunt and quickly moved along the balcony to descend the main stairs,

Kara closely following behind him and he closed his eyes for a second to prepare himself.

He paused for a brief moment and reached the bottom of the stairs, ready to begin.

CHAPTER THIRTY SIX

"For the benefit of Mr Craven; who is representing the Company's interests in the mine. I have to report that the structure of the mines is unstable. There is a major geological fault that is in a state of constant flux and making it difficult to ascertain the accessibility of certain sections of the mine, I will be sending a report, reccomending that it remains closed until further notice," announced Jack.

Craven almost bounded from his chair in rage.

"That's preposterous. There is no evidence to state that the fault is the cause of the structure deficiencies!" he spat.

Jack leaned over the table and eyeballed the sullen man.

"We have the varied scans taken from my own and Mr Vane's spectrometers from separate points of the mine indicating that the tremors are the result of the fault shifting!" returned Jack calmly, yet so eager to raise his voice.

"But this is all conjecture. We've confirmed that the killer in the mine is not operating alone. There are a group of creatures that may be indigenous to the lower levels!" he continued "And as a result of this, there will only be a small party returning to the mines to attempt to locate Captain Blackthorne!"

Nova looked across the table from where he sat, he could see the veins on Craven's head were beginning to pulse and he stared on in amusement at the thought he was about to blow his top.

"I am restricting the team to a party of five!" announced Jack, "The team will comprise of myself, Professor Carlson, Lieutenant Denton and Troopers Dervish and Hoffman!"

Craven was livid, yet again he had been left out of the mix, but he wasn't going to stop there.

"Commander, I must insist on returning to the mine to mount a proper investigation!"

Jack stretched his hands wide over smooth finish of the table top.

"This is a snatch and grab job, we're not going for anything else, our job is to locate the Captain and get him out. I won't endanger anyone else's lives. Those on the team are on a voluntary basis!" Craven's mood wasn't going to improve as the bulbous vein continued to pulse.

Nova sniggered slightly and Valana tugged at him for being so rude, but Craven saw this and targeted his rage.

"And why are there children here Commander? This is official business!" he stormed.

Nova slid off his perch and stood to his full height.

"You'll get my child-sized boot up your backside if you keep it up Smiler!" he goaded Craven.

"This is conglomerate business, the Company doesn't govern what goes on here!" snapped Jack, "And my decision is final, consider yourself confined to the ship Mr Craven!" he thundered.

The scowl on the bearded man's face became slightly pointy and devilish as he narrowed his eyes at Jack.

"This is ridiculous!" shrieked Craven, already backing off from the table.

"Do you want me to have you confined to quarters as well?" asked Jack, but the wiry man declined an answer.

Nova looked nervously across the room at Craven; who he'd taken an instant dislike to, his manner and forcefulness really annoyed him to a certain extent and really pissed him off.

He just realised what had been said in his absentmindedness and narrowed in on Jack.

"What do you mean you're restricting the team?" he hissed.

Craven couldn't help but give a smile of satisfaction that the young man was also being omitted from the team.

"I'm sorry Nova, but I'm keeping the team to a bare minimum!" answered Jack; he folded his arms and stood back, "Any other objections?"

Time-Ryder: Powerstone Book One

"Fair enough!" chirped Nova and he sunk back down onto his stool, "It was worth a try though" he finished.

Henry fixed him with a peculiar gaze. It wasn't like the young man to give in so easily. He gave him with a defining stare, observing his every move and would pick him up on it when the meeting was over and there were less people around.

There was an unusual silence of no further interruptions and then Kara took the show.

"The main objective is to penetrate the mine at the least conspicuous point!" she'd been doing her research and had come up with an alternative route that had been overlooked on the initial intervention into the mountain.

She tapped the air above the black desk and the face filled with light, a 3d visualisation of the surrounding area, the spaceport, adjacent buildings and the domed structures of the old mining camp.

Kara moved her hand aside and it showed a hidden tunnel leading from under the domed city to the very base of the mountain.

"The Commander's team will enter from here," she pointed to the dome, "there is approximately a mile of tunnel between the main dome and the mountain. Provided that it is clear, it shouldn't take you long to get in there!"

Jack looked closely at the 3d image, narrowing his gaze slightly in annoyance.

"Why wasn't this route privy to the Captain or my mission brief?"

Kara sidestepped and moved past Nova to join the tall American. "We didn't know about it. I had System boot up the dome data banks by remote last night. It took this long; just to download the data from there!"

The rest of the group just looked on, never contributing, although there was so much more to be said. Elizabeth and the Professor

Time-Ryder: Powerstone Book One

kept close to each other, whispering softly to such a point that he made her giggle. The Doctor gave a wide beaming smile that Nova noticed and he elbowed Valana.

"Check out Hugh Heffner!" he scoffed.

If he didn't know better he'd swear that the old man was flirting with the Doctor, and after only one day, Nova was quite proud of that and happy to see him smile at something other than an eager find at an archaeology dig.

Kara looked around the table at all the anxious faces and some not so happy ones, she turned her back on the group and eyed Jack closely, trying to get his contact with her eyes, but he caught the subtle gesture and folded his arms.

"Does anyone have anything else they'd like to say?" he spoke up, looking around the table.

"I have a great deal more to say!" stormed Craven angrily.

"Don't you think you've said enough!" hissed Nova from his perch; he gave the bearded man a sly look.

"Who is this person?" shrieked Craven loudly.

Jack had overlooked the introductions; they all new each other, but the Professor, Valana and Nova hadn't met the structural engineer yet.

"Apologies Mr Craven, this is Nova, Professor Carlson and Valana. They came back from the mine with us. They'll be our guests for the foreseeable future!"

"Do they have any relevance for being here?" narrowed craven, feeling he was being sidelined.

"Their presence in the mine is what helped us get out safely!" spat Jack, "and I have approved that the Professor is joining the team!"

"And what about the children?" Craven pursed his lips.

Nova gave him a look, his foot hovering off the floor and he pointed to it.

"Still here," he said, "And just waiting!" he threatened.

Time-Ryder: Powerstone Book One

Jack held back his amusement and stepped back, letting Kara have the lead again.

She gave Craven a strange look again and he cleared his throat, stroking his beard nervously.

"There was an incident on board last night, a violation of one of the officer's quarters!" she announced and saw a faint smile begin to creep over Craven's face.

"Found the culprit then have you?" he asked with a rather smug grin.

The sullen faced man stared at Jack with all of the arrogance that he possessed. Neatly folding his arms he glared at the new arrivals and then back to the Commander.

"The creature that has been killing the crew and your team was helped by someone. We are conducting an investigation and a suspect is being interrogated as we speak," announced Jack in a soft lilt.

Craven smiled wryly.

"I don't suppose you could tell us who it is?"

He could tell that every one of the key members of crew were in attendance, but felt that someone was missing. Bursting the whodunit bubble was something he wished the entire group to hear.

"I'm not at liberty to say until we have completed the line of questioning. And might I remind you Craven are here as a liaison to the Company, I'm not required to inform you of every detail of internal ship security!" snapped Jack, fixing a dagger-like stare upon the bearded man.

Nova liked the word questioning better than interrogation, it somehow didn't sum up images of thumbscrews and often-repeated episodes of old police dramas.

Denton had been silent throughout the discussion stood firm, watching over the group of people from his perch at the back of the flight deck. The tall blue skinned man coughed, and announced his presence, but he wasn't too subtle with his cough. It sounded more like the below of an animal.

And it seemed to grab everyone's attention.

"If these creatures are seeking these crystals as you say Commander. Would it not be wiser to withdraw from the planet and deprive them of what they want?" he leaned back against the computer terminal on the back wall and looked over them all as they turned to gaze at the blue giant.

Jack gripped the edge of the desk; he hadn't exactly told the crew everything that had gone on in the mines.

"As I've said before, we can't rule out the possibility that the Captain may be still alive down there! We can't let these things roam wild, supposing they get on board the ship. We don't know how many of these things there are, but we can't take the chance of letting them get off the planet!"

"What are you implying sir?" Denton stood forceful; the ridges on his head began to flap.

Jack looked to Kara and then around the rest of the watchful faces.

"I'm going to blow up the mine!"

Craven threw himself up onto his feet in anger, his smug attitude soon subdued.

"You can't do that!" he thundered, his hands spread out onto the table in front of him and his devil like stare directed right at the American.

"I think you'll find I can. Article five of the Universal constitution states that any Colony in danger of enemy insurgence will be forfeit to whatever means necessary to protect not only Universal, but Global security!" Jack glared right back at him and it was enough to rattle the small man.

Craven took to his feet and stared across the table at Jack, his eyes on fire with anger.

"I'm going above your head; I want to contact central bank. You have no right to order the destruction of the mine without consultation!" he thundered.
Nova grinned widely and leaned back on the back of his stool.
"Article five Knobhead, weren't you listening?" he hissed and the Professor gave him a glare, but then gave up on his protestations. But Jack was ready for him, splaying his palms wide on the sleek table and leaning forward, looking at Craven face on.
"As the ranking officer on board, it is my call to impose a communication blackout!"
Craven's face went white. It was enough to tip the bearded man over the edge and he shot through the side doors of the flight deck in temper to which Nova followed him with his eyes.
"Well something's got his frillys in a tangle!" he remarked as Jack gave the order for them to dismiss.
"Not entirely what you were expecting was it?" Henry raised his brow as Elizabeth joined them.
"His reaction was exactly as I thought Henry," replied the American and he turned to Elizabeth, "how did your scans pan out Doctor?"
"Actually that's what we want to talk to you about!" interrupted the Professor and he sidestepped, letting the Doctor tell her story. She went into great detail, telling them about the DNA strands and the Antigen serum that she had been concocting in the lab, but her knowledge of the marks on the bodies of the dead had come to a standstill. Without anything further to go on, she couldn't offer any more insight into the situation.
Kara put down her data tablet, her last details of the re-entry into the mines finally complete.
"Are there any more measures to be put in place before the team moves in?" she asked.
"I could inject you with the antitoxin in case you come into contact with any of those creatures you spoke of. Even a scratch

might infect you, the toxin won't stop it completely, but it will slow it down!" declared the Doctor.
Jack nodded and turned to Kara at his side.
"What are you going to do while we're gone?"
She crossed to the ops table and waved her hand over the face, bringing it online.
A 3d representation of the crown that Vane had discovered in the mine hovered above the surface of the desk.
"I thought I might take a look at this, it might provide some answers!" she said, "And there's still a few repairs to be completed!" rasped the Australian.
"Good!" smiled Jack and he clasped his hands together.
For the first time he had a smile on his face and a happy disposition for a change.
Nova watched him as the Professor withdrew from their company and the Doctor quickly ambled off the flight deck, bound for the lab.
Henry sauntered over to both youngsters, a curling smile beginning to form. He thought of any number of ways to begin the conversation, but they all would have the same outcome.
"What are you up to Mr Mitchell?"
Nova fidgeted with his stool, adjusting his position.
"What do you mean?"
But Valana knew exactly what the old man was meaning, in the short time they'd known each other she was starting to pick up on little things that made the young man very unique.
"Ok I'll say it in a manner that you fully might understand!" said the old man softly, "What's your game?"
Nova almost laughed at the Professor's choice of words.
"Come now Mr Mitchell, I'm not stupid. You gave in far too easily, even I could see that!"
He gave a shrug of his shoulders as a response.

Time-Ryder: Powerstone Book One

"The Almighty chin already vetoed who's going on the team, so why fight it?" said Nova, but even to Valana; she knew that he had given up too quickly.

With his ruse rumbled, Nova exhaled deeply and finally gave in. "C'mon Professor, you know I can't stay here, I'll get bored stupid" he shrieked, leaned closer and whispered, "They haven't even got a telly or a pool table!"

The old man knew Nova far too well; he put a reassuring arm around his shoulder and spoke to him softly in a gentle whisper.

"You have to do as the Commander asks. It's in your best interest. Trust me!" he shrugged and yet Nova knew that there was more in the Professor's reply than what he had just said. The old man wanted him to stay for a reason and he smiled back.

"What are we going to do while you're gone?"

The old man smiled at them both and turned away.

"I'm sure you'll think of something!"

He left them both by the side of the ops table and rejoined Jack at the forward console, eager to get their plans under way.

But Nova's perturbed face gave Valana cause for concern.

"What is it?" she said softly, her arm snaking around his for reassurance.

"Something's still not right about this Val!" he hissed and turned to her and looked around the flight deck, recalling the attendees of the meeting, "I'm getting that same vibe I had back in the mine," he said and she looked on worriedly.

"Somebody's missing!" he said coldly, his eyes scanning the deck.

Elizabeth had already gone back to the lab; Denton was lingering at the back, standing hawk-like over them all. Kara, Jack and the Professor were whispering at the forward station and Brooks was recovering in the Medibay from his ankle injury.

Valana looked around the flight deck, seeing only a few stationed troopers at the exits and she turned to him quickly and they both spoke out at the same time.

"Vane!" they chorused.

Nova narrowed strangely and then looked at the blonde girl.

"He's not seriously the suspect they're holding surely?"

Valana shirked and scanned the room again, noting that they were being watched by the blue-skinned Lieutenant at the rear.

"He was only a trooper, but was quite involved with what went on in the mines; surely it would have made sense to have him here at the briefing?"

"You'd think so wouldn't you?" drawled Nova.

Time-Ryder: Powerstone Book One

CHAPTER THIRTY SEVEN

Frustrated and angry, Craven stormed down the corridors of G deck, heading for the guest quarters and not masking his attitude from any of the technicians that he passed by.

He came up to his room door and slid his thumb over the silver slider; waiting impatiently as the doors parted with a slow movement. His quarters were identical to Nova's, very elaborate and extensive. The only difference was the pile of computer tablets on the desk, laid out before a large screen and desktop display.

"System, access the updated schematic of the mine-system and overlay the details from Commander Adams and Trooper Vane's Spectrometers!" he rasped, pacing the room as if he were in the need of a fix.

The computer showed him the detailed map of the mine and the stress points that had been keyed in by the Commander's device. He studied the screen, moving his fingers and highlighting one particular area at the very foot of the mountain.

He looked at the readings closely.

"System, are these readings accurate?" he asked sharply, clearly impatient.

"The readings are correspondent with a point three variance. Approximately Ninety-Nine point Nine accuracy!" droned the voice of the computer.

Craven smashed his hand down upon the desk, smashing the glass desktop.

He paced the room again, trying to find another way around the problem and took a seat in front of the console, where he began to rattle away at the keyboard again.

Time-Ryder: Powerstone Book One

Having left Henry to contend with Denton and the small procedures that he needed to know for their return trip into the mine, Jack had sailed off to the Medibay to have a quick word with the Doctor.

As soon as he entered the serene environment, he caught sight of Elizabeth hard at work with the test samples and he joined her, making her almost shriek with fright at his sudden appearance. She pulled of her micro headphones and gave him a curious gaze that finally curled into a smile of amusement at her own frightened nature.

"Any progress Doctor?" he asked softly.

She offered him the stool beside her and he accepted, thinking it was better that he'd take a seat if it were bad news after all.

"I took the scans while he wasn't looking; it's taken a while to process them. He is dying Jack. It's an accelerated form of Cancer; it might have been treatable if it had been caught in time. The curious thing is that he has been subjected to a high burst of radiation recently which has gone right through his system!"

It was a bit of a blow to him. He'd only known Henry for such a short time, but had gotten to know him very well and he was the only one who he had really connected with on this mission, the only one he'd come very close to discussing his family with.

"How long has he got, medically speaking?"

Elizabeth pulled off her glasses and looked him directly in the eye.

"It's hard to say, but at the rate of the disease spreading, I'd say a matter of weeks, two months at most. Do you think he knows how far it has progressed?" she said softly.

"I think he has an idea!" Jack paused and gave the Doctor a forlorn smile of thanks.

"Is there nothing you can do for him?"

Elizabeth turned back to the screen and flipped the monitor back on, looking over her research.

"There are a few drug trials, but it will only prolong him for a short while and give pain relief, there's nothing that can be done, it's advanced too far for surgery and with his age, a DNA graft is out of the question. His best bet would be the facility on Senterra Seven, they're specialising in treatment of advanced cases with some surprising results!"

Jack nodded briefly and rose from his seat.

"I'm sorry Jack; I wish I had more positive news for you!"

"Thanks for trying Doc!" he said softly.

She turned back from the workstation and rose from her chair, placing a hand on his arm.

"It really wasn't any bother, I've grown quite fond of him myself!" she replied, "But I won't give up on him just yet!"

Jack took a deep breath to compose himself, and he stood away from the stool.

"And your other project Doctor, have you made any advances with it?"

She wiggled her finger in the air with delight.

"I've managed to separate the key enzymes that bind the third strand to the helix and created an antigen that will allow me to remove it. It takes away the dominant factor of the third strand and relaxes its grip on the parent DNA. Letting the antibodies fight back and regain control!"

"In English Doc!" he drawled.

"Essentially if these creatures are augments of humans as I suspected, the antigen will reverse the process and make them fully human again. But it's at an experimental stage, I'm still trying to perfect it at the moment!" she answered with a derivation of something that he would understand.

He still gave a frown, thinking about the Professor and made his way toward the door.

"I've completed a set of test inoculations for you, in case any of you become scratched or wounded by the creatures. It will stop the infection of any DNA spreading throughout your system!" announced the Doctor, just before he left and he wheeled on the spot.

"Tell me that it's past the testing point?"

She nodded and gave him a smile, trying her best to lift his mood.

"It is ready for injection!" she replied and before he could answer, he took off into the corridors as another thought had occurred to him.

Elizabeth turned back to her duties, looking at the results once again. She gave a small sniff of remorse that she couldn't do anything to help the Professor and then she sealed the file shut, returning to the Antigen problem. She revolved on her stool and waited for the testing samples to finish turning on the large tumbler. The device bleeped and she stopped the machine, pulling off the lid and extracting the samples for testing.

Elizabeth lifted the green vials and inserted her syringe into the first one, taking a droplet and putting it on a glass slide for examination.

She placed the syringe on the stand by the machine and looked deep into the microscope.

Taking Valana by the hand, Nova pulled her down the corridor on G deck to the quarters they had been allocated to. He felt like an excited teenager trying to sneak a girl into his bedroom.

"What's the urgency?" she shrieked as they stepped through the doors into the room.

"I've got something to show you!" he said excitedly, yet nervous, "They've got all their stuff going on, but there's something even they don't know about."

He slid his hand under the pillow and pulled out the gold device.

Time-Ryder: Powerstone Book One

"What is it?" she asked and he handed it to her as she made a quick inspection of it.

"I dunno, it was hidden behind the ice wall, after that big bat thing took me on a night flight!" he drawled.

Valana turned it over, scanning the odd shaped object. It was clear that it had some purpose and she stared at the vacant section in the middle, almost as if something should be harnessed inside. There were small wire-like protrusions from the main body that drooped needlessly in the centre as if they should be connected to something.

"What is it?"

Nova saw the strange, curious look in her eye.

She narrowed at the device and held it out to him and he gripped the handle, yet Valana kept hold of the opposite one.

They both could feel that their positions and stance, holding the device seemed totally natural, but the gap in the centre of it was clearly on both of their minds.

"Look at the centre of it Nova. There's something missing, it's as if the heart has been taken out!"

Nova's eyes met hers and they widened.

"Or a power source?" he hissed softly, "Here hold it for a minute!"

He fumbled around inside the many pockets of his coat, pulling out all of his belongings.

Valana looked curiously at the device and lifted one of the flexible rods with her finger, the tiniest fragment of redness in the cracks of the clamp.

Turning the pockets outright, he looked up at Valana in shock.

"It's not here!" he shrieked in a panic and removed the jacket, feeling about it fully.

"The crystal, I had it before we left the mine!" he patted the jacket again in case it had slipped down inside the lining.

Valana straightened up and let the device droop by her side.

"You think that it might power this thing?" she said, thinking of the small sliver of red.
"Hey, why not? This thing was found in the mine and it seems pretty clear that these spheres are more or less battery cells!" he replied, but his face was still unclear of what they should do next.
"We have to tell someone about this!" Valana waved the device at the young man.
Nova put his hands on the device and looked at her, staring deeply into her green eyes.
"About this thing, No way!" he patted the wooden and brass object and still kept his gaze on hers.
"Well you have to tell them about the crystal at least, we can keep this thing quiet for now. Until we can work out what's going on."
"And what about the Professor?" she said softly, "You can't keep it from him!"
Nova bit his lip, chewing over the idea of telling the old man and he shook his head.
"He's become a bit chummy with that Adams and there's something about that guy. I can't put my finger on it, but there's something he's not telling us about all of this."
Nova sighed and took the device from her, stowing it back under the pillow.
"But I suppose I'd better own up about the crystal, eh?" he asked her.
Valana looked up and pursed her lips. She slipped her hand into his and pulled him reluctantly over to the door and off to tell them about the crystal.

Lieutenant Denton was an unusual man. Aside from his outward appearance, his blue skin and inflating gills that made him strides apart from any other crewmember, he had a very quiet

Time-Ryder: Powerstone Book One

disposition. The only person on board that seemed to maintain a conversation with him for more than one sentence was Elizabeth Gennero, only from his frequent visits into the Medibay.

His face was sullen and stern, very rarely smiling, yet Denton did have a sense of humour, not so as you'd noticed.

He crossed the threshold into the extensive flight deck and turned abruptly to his left, making way for the Captain's office, his face full of conviction and concentration.

His hand rose to the thumb-plate and his webbed fingers ran over the surface, sounding off the door chime.

"Come in!" echoed the voice from within and the automatic locks opened the door.

Denton passed through the opening doors and stood before the desk; where Jack Ryder looked out of the small porthole, an electronic tablet held tightly in his grasp.

He wheeled to the approaching man and held his hand out to welcome him forward.

"Denton, Just the man I was thinking of" he began and then saw the Lieutenant's stolid features, "But I can see you have something on your mind already. What can I help you with?" he asked, intrigued.

He hadn't had much contact with the Lieutenant since he came on board, only fleetingly looking at his service record to familiarise himself with the blue skinned man's background and abilities.

Denton held his hands behind his back, clasped tightly, his posture almost rigid and stern as his face was.

"I have a few concerns I would like to address you with!" he announced, almost officially.

Jack dropped the pad on the desk and folded his arms, leaning back with a small smile.

"What's on your mind?"

Time-Ryder: Powerstone Book One

"Lieutenant Everett informed me of your predicament and your intentions sir. My concern is the way you compromised security to get on board the Oregon!" said the blue giant coldly.

Jack had figured as much. He wouldn't be much of a security officer if he hadn't brought these concerns to the Lieutenant Everett's attention.

"I understand where you are coming from Denton. I wasn't my intent to deceive you all. I only wanted to find the Captain and see what he knows about my father!"

He pulled back the Captain's chair and gently slid into it, holding a hand out to the opposite chair.

"Take a seat Lieutenant!" offered Jack, but the giant straightened and refused, preferring to stand.

"Is that your only concern Denton, or do you think I had another agenda for getting on board the Oregon?"

It was almost as if Jack had read him like a book, even though Denton's rigid facial features gave him the perfect poker face.

"It has been on my mind sir!"

"Then you can set your mind at rest Denton. No one has been harmed by what I have done, except the deaths of those troopers in the mine and that was out of my control. I have no other plans; I only want the Captain's safe return. He's of no use to me dead."

Denton took a breath, his gills flapping in a brief inhalation.

"You know the Captain well. What's he like?" asked Jack.

He watched the tall blue skinned man closely.

"I don't understand the question sir!" he said coldly.

"What kind of a man is he? There isn't much to go on in his service record and it seems that he's avoided taking the annual psych test for over a decade."

Denton took a breath again, feeling that he was betraying the Captain if he said anything that might be construed as a lack of loyalty. He owed the Captain his life.

Time-Ryder: Powerstone Book One

If it would help to find the Captain, even for the sake of helping out Lieutenant Everett, he knew that he had to open up.

"He is a very quiet man. Very secretive!" answered the giant, not that it told the Colonel anything.

Jack nodded, his mind clearly perturbed by his perplexed expression.

"Do you know much about his movements? The places he went on the ship, anywhere secluded that he liked to go?"

Denton inhaled and his nostrils flared, he gazed down at the Colonel.

"There was one place on the ship he liked to frequent, but most of the crew did," answered Denton, straightening his back yet again.

Jack was listening, waiting for the blue skinned man to reveal.

"The Commissary and Recreation centre sir!"

Jack leaned forward and smiled slightly.

"Everyone has to eat Lieutenant!" he said and then saw his defining stare.

"Not the Commissary itself sir, he spent a lot of time in the kitchen stores with Murray. The two of them were quite close!"

"Were they now?" Jack mused and tapped his lip, "well maybe we should pay the stores a visit. How do you fancy a reconnaissance mission Lieutenant?"

Denton stiffened, but Jack was already halfway around the desk and heading for the door.

He wheeled to join the Colonel and followed him out of the door like a greyhound.

Time-Ryder: Powerstone Book One

Time-Ryder: Powerstone Book One

CHAPTER THIRTY EIGHT

Kara had practically given the new-comers free reign of the ship below G deck. Most of the vital systems were locked out and many of the other crucial systems were on the higher decks, all of which needed access through the crew's ident keys so they couldn't do any damage or compromise security.

But Nova and Valana were making for M Deck; the entire run of that particular deck was dedicated to the Medibay, science labs and the Morgue.

It seemed the logical place where the Professor would be, regarding the fact that he thought the old man and Elizabeth had become very chummy indeed.

"How do you think he's going to take it?" Valana asked, keeping up the increased pace that Nova maintained.

"With his usual calm attitude probably!" he smiled wryly, never remembering for one moment that the Professor had ever raised his voice at him or his Aunt Rose for that matter. If he was frustrated, he usually took it out on a multipack of macaroon bars, which Nova proposed added to his overall weight.

He hot-footed it to the large white spiral and spun down the few decks to the Medibay and then slowed down apprehensively.

"He might not say anything, but what about the Commander?" He didn't know Adams or like his methods, but he knew he wasn't going to be best pleased with what had happened.

"He's going to find out sometime, it might be better coming from you!"

Nova faltered again, just outside the doorway to the Medibay, he poked his head around the edge of the door and could see them both hovering over the workstation.

"They're busy, I'll come back later!" he backed off and Valana grabbed his arm, pulling him back the other way.

"It won't go away Nova!" she said softly, "I'm here with you!"

Time-Ryder: Powerstone Book One

He could see that she was right and he strode into the Medibay, into the beaming faces of the Professor and Elizabeth.

Nova gave a false grin, almost verging upon a grimace with the pretence of a smile and he looked at Valana who made the same face back and gave him a gentle shove in their direction.

He looked back to her and gave her a silent, yet rather sarcastic. "Thank you!"

Concerned as he was with ship's security, Denton followed Jack down through the decks to the commissary. They passed through the battleship grey corridors, past the repair crews at the maintenance lockers and through the wide doors that brought them to the food court.

It was desolate, dingy and lifeless, giving no sign that anyone had been here since breakfast, yet it was immaculately clean.

Everything was in place from what Jack could see, not that he was interested in the main staging area where everyone would gather to eat.

He was more interested in the storage area where the Captain spent a good deal of his time with this Murray person.

Denton drew over to the right corner and around the shaped counter area to the kitchen. There were various shelving stacks, each lined with pots and pans of all types. Other shelves had every kitchen utensil ever created and a set of chopping knives and meat cleavers suspended from the ceiling.

Jack gave the smallest of smiles, thinking that they would make a good addition to someone's weapons cache.

"It's through here sir!" said Denton softly.

"Denton you don't have to keep calling me Sir, it's just Jack!" he clipped, pursuing the blue giant through the stacks.

"You do outrank me sir, it would be improper to address you as anything else!"

Time-Ryder: Powerstone Book One

Jack decided it was best not to argue with him and followed him on to the storage area at the back of the room.

"This is it Sir, I don't know what you hope to find down here?" he asked, his steely blue eyes locked in stern concentration at the Colonel.

The locker at the back was massive, almost like the vault to a bank. The thickness seemed overly ambitious for a food storage area.

"Can you open it?" hissed Jack.

Denton already had his hand-held spectrometer out; the wings of the device flapping profusely as he tried to connect it to the main lock. With a stern look, Denton reached forward and opened the concealed panel by the door and took two small wires out of the Spectrometer to which he connected to the panel.

The blue giant ran his webbed fingers over the display pad and the door began to give way, edging open just enough for them to venture inside.

Jack coughed.

He could smell fresh flour, smell the potency of sugar and then there were the spices, Oregano, cinnamon, coriander and many others, the odour so potent that it almost made his stomach yearn for lunch time.

There were roots, dried barks; anything that Murray thought might give flavour to an otherwise drab dish and all the odours were lifted into the air and affecting the Colonel, much like any chef wanted an avid connoisseur of food to do so.

But this was not what they were looking for, whatever it was had to be here, amid this amalgamation of smells.

"Take a look over there Denton; I'll check this section down here!"

Jack left the tall blue giant to it, and scoured the left section of the massive storage room. He sifted through the many shelves of

ingredients and half opened packets, but couldn't find anything out of the ordinary.
"Down here sir!" Denton whispered.
Jack scurried around to join him, crouching down as Denton waved the spectrometer over the floor, pulling back some heavy sacks from where his tracker was giving off a piercing sound and going wild.
"What is it?" hissed Jack, craning closer.

The declaration by Nova that the crystal was missing didn't please the old man, and there was nothing they could do about it. But Nova thought he knew exactly where he had lost it and was cursing the tussle that he had with the bat creature; wishing he had disposed of the beast while he had the time and then his conscience would have kicked in, and he'd have felt guilty about the whole affair.
The Professor gave him a smile, reassuring him that they still had the other Sphere they had brought back with them. Valana was concerned that it would only be a matter of time before the creatures made their way out of the mountain once they discovered that it was on board the ship and in their possession. She looked around the white-walled Medibay for inspiration; yet couldn't find any. Her only saving grace was that they were all safe and as far away from the creatures as they could possibly be for the moment, as if that wasn't far enough.
Professor Carlson sat by Elizabeth: each of them peering over their glasses like a pair of pensioners with the Sunday crossword. As both young people tried to stoop forward, they saw Doctor Gennero and the Professor hovering over the glass ball set upon a stand, but none of them could work out how to penetrate the shell.

Time-Ryder: Powerstone Book One

Nova gave a smug smile and straightened up beside his young friend and he held out his hand for her to assist.

"If you would do the honours my dear!" said the old man politely as Elizabeth looked on.

Valana scooped up the ball and already Nova had the same tool she had used before in the mine and within seconds the shell was open and the beauty of the gem was on display for all to see.

Elizabeth took the jewel from the open ball and her eyes were already ablaze with beauty for the object.

"Typical girl, it always takes a big rock to make them smile!" said Nova rather cynically, but Elizabeth was fascinated for another reason as she pushed her glasses back for a better look.

"Look at the refraction points!" she exclaimed.

She pointed to the many surfaces of the red gem, her mouth still open with surprise.

"Yeah fascinating!" drawled Nova, the beauty of the gem having long since worn off, "Look we'll just leave you two to it!"

He pulled Valana by the hand out of the Medibay and she looked at him curiously.

"What was that all about?"

"They'll be at this for hours!" he said with a smile.

"Where are you going?" Valana still held his hand, but felt uneasy moving so freely around the ship, with all of the armed troopers stationed at junction points.

"Come on, I want to take another look at that thing!" he said and tugged her hand, pulling her down the corridor. Valana's face morphed from a surprised expression to an excited grin as she kept up his pace and they made off for their quarters.

With the silver Coronet in her hands, Kara Everett stared at the symbols as she sat back in the chair in the Captain's office. She laid it down on the old desk, looking at it with concern.

There was something unique about it from the very moment that she touched it, the feel of it, the shape and the material that it was constructed from, even though it was unknown to her.

She had a feeling that it was a major part to what was going on in the mines.

With a determined look, she snatched the silver ring from the battered desk and bounded for the door, making headway along the balcony on the flight deck and through the doors at the top of the stair.

Kara gripped the crown so tightly, she didn't dare let it go and she moved through the empty decks to the detention block on D deck.

There was still a wiry trooper stationed at the first door and she nodded to him and he sidestepped, flashing a card over the door sensor and opening it for the small Lieutenant.

Kara pushed open the door and slid in quickly as the trooper on guard pulled the door shut and sealed her in.

Vane still sat in the chair, his head resting on the table, but he wasn't asleep.

"I figured it wouldn't be long before you came down here!" he said, without lifting his head from the surface, "What do you want Lieutenant?" he hissed with contempt.

"What can you tell me about this?" Kara waved the coronet in front of him and he raised his bald dome from the table.

"What makes you think I'm going to tell you?" he sneered, "You've locked me up in here without any evidence!"

She moved over and took the opposite seat, dropping down into it and placing the crown on the table.

"It would go a long way to prove you had nothing to do with all of this!" she replied and leaned back as he looked from her optimistic face to the silver ring. She was even more determined to prove his guilt than she was at believing Jack's innocence, yet it didn't seem to concern her.

Time-Ryder: Powerstone Book One

It was as if her judgement was clouded and she was eager to get this whole thing rounded up.
He exhaled in a deep hiss and took the device into his hands, running his fingers over the slightly raised surface.
"It fell out of that creature's robes!" he said softly, never taking his gaze off it, "I've already put it in my report Lieutenant!"
But Kara had a feeling that he knew more and pointed to the symbols upon its face.
"The time stamp on your report shows that there was a significant time you had it in your possession Mr Vane, you can't tell me you weren't curious about it?"
He looked up at the Lieutenant, wondering if she was somehow reading his mind and he exhaled deeply again.
"Brooks and I were on our way back to the gantry when I noticed the marks on it, I was interested in it" he said softly, "I pressed one of the controls."
His fingers searched around the device for the one he had activated and he pointed to it, showing the small woman.
"There were three weird looking wires that came out from inside it and it did this."
He held up his finger, bearing the burn mark, where the tendrils from the inside of the coronet had touched him.
She took the crown from him and looked at the symbol he had indicated, standing up freely from the chair.
Kara was still convinced that there was more to the crown and she was determined to get to the bottom of it, but she still couldn't rule out Vane's involvement, too many things about his movements didn't add up.
She left the cell slowly and stood in the corridor beside the guard as her head swam in circles. With the crown in her grasp, she darted off towards the spiral as another thought came to her.

Time-Ryder: Powerstone Book One

Time-Ryder: Powerstone Book One

CHAPTER THIRTY NINE

The Doctor had secured the crystal in a metal framework, hemming it together as she trained a large magnifying glass over the surface. Henry was enamoured by the glass shell and had noticed the strange symbols all around the inside, much like the crown device that Trooper Vane had brought back with them. He had one of his many small notebooks in his hand, scribbling down a loose representation of each glyph in the hope that he might be able to decipher it eventually.

Elizabeth straightened back on her stool. As far as she could see there were no imperfections within the structure of the crystal and she pushed away the magnifier stand that hovered over the gem.

"I can't see any irregularities that might differentiate it from a regular crystal" exclaimed the Doctor. She widened her eyes and pulled off her glasses, tossing them onto the workbench and rubbing her eyes profusely.

"Are you sure that it originated from here?"

Henry scratched his beard and put the ball back down on the bench, he was sure that the spheres had come from here.

He loved puzzles, but there was a large, very vital piece missing from all of this; and he knew that with Jack's help, it was the only way of providing answers, even if it meant going back into the mine to discover them.

"I think it's safe to assume that it is from here Doctor!" he answered without giving too much away.

She looked at the red gem again, enamoured by the colour context and the way it shone.

"There is another test I'd like to try Henry if you'll agree to it?" she wasn't sure of his reaction.

"If it helps with anything Doctor, of course!" he smiled at her and she almost blushed.

Time-Ryder: Powerstone Book One

Elizabeth was a beautiful woman, and had always put her career before anything else, but she was at an age now where the prospect of finding male company was slipping farther away and she was enjoying the attention she was getting from the Professor, regardless of the age gap between them.

"Please call me Beth!" she whispered, her French accent slipping out again.

She was already ahead of him, bringing out the larger piece of equipment that she laid out carefully on the bench.

Pulling out a deep rectangular glass dish, she shuffled over to the far end of the Medi-bay to the sink and placed the vessel under the tap, waiting for it to fill.

Once she was satisfied, Elizabeth returned and removed the crystal from the framework, immersing the jewel in the water.

He was intrigued by what she was doing, yet sat perfectly still and watched as Elizabeth took a portable drill from within the box she had produced and changed the head.

After careful preparation, she handed him a pair of safety goggles and pulled her own down.

Elizabeth strapped the drill into a large metal stand and it hovered over the crystal, ready to descend the drill.

She pulled the handle down and the drill head began to touch upon the crystal and slowly it began to glow again.

Laying down his spectrometer, Denton heaved the oversized sacks away from the area that was giving off the vibrant sound.

Set into the floor was a large metal plate, a small black glass section illuminated in the centre.

"It looks very like an indented vault sir!" Denton scanned his eyes over the surface warily.

His palm hovered over the black panel, his webbed fingers almost touching it.

Time-Ryder: Powerstone Book One

"Can you get it open?"
Denton lifted the Spectrometer and panned the device over the surface of the metal plate.
"It has a tri-centric lock system. I think Murray may have designed some special locking mechanism for it!" said the Blue giant.
He looked across the surface, his eyes narrowing strangely.
"What is it Denton?" Jack saw the perplexed look.
Even on someone with such a solid demeanour as Denton had, Jack noticed that there was something wrong.
Denton laid his palm flat, his webbed fingers outstretched over the plate and he felt the slight heat coming from the plate below. There were a few strange noises coming from within the floor compartment and Jack looked closer as the plate sprung open slightly with a brief hiss.
Denton lifted a rag from one of the shelves close by and heaved the metal hatch open, staring into the depths. The red glow from inside stabbed at their eyes as it became brighter and Jack guarded his eyes with his hand.
"What is it sir?" Denton didn't need to look away, his unique eyes taking in all that the glare had to offer.
Jack looked through the gaps in his fingers and gave a frown.
"It's another one of those damned crystals!"

Much the same was happening in the Medibay. Elizabeth still loomed over the crystal, trying to retrieve a section via the drill, but the tip hadn't even scored the surface.
Her annoyed look showed the Professor that she had been relying on the test to provide some answers. He was more taken aback when Elizabeth almost vaulted backward as the drill started to emit a high pitched whine and began to smoke.

Time-Ryder: Powerstone Book One

Elizabeth quickly pulled the release lever and the drill shot upwards on the stand, far away from the glowing crystal that had started to dim.

Moving to inspect the drill, she pulled the stand away from the desk and looked through her safety goggles as it.

"That was a diamond point Quadro four drill bit!" she exclaimed with a hiss.

"There's nothing in the world that is stronger than that!"

Henry removed his goggles and took a closer look at it, seeing the tip of the drill glowing and faint whispers of smoke trailing from the end of it.

"Well now it seems that there is!"

Elizabeth looked at the crystal in awe, watching as the red glow it had formed from the heat was beginning to dwindle and die.

"So much for doing a particle matter test!" she exhaled deeply.

Henry scratched his beard again in a nervous reaction. He pulled his collar away from his neck, feeling the increasing heat and he dabbed the back of his neck with his handkerchief again.

"So what now?" asked the Professor.

Elizabeth slipped on a pair of gloves and took the crystal out of the container with a pair of elongated tongs, resting it upon the framework again.

She gave him a smile.

"I haven't given up yet. Ships stores should have what I need, coming?" she said eagerly and half-dragged him out of the door.

Henry was only too happy to comply, enjoying the Doctor's company. He returned a grin and ambled after her.

Tossing the silver coronet into the computer, Kara tried to get the mainframe to have another go at concluding what the device was capable of.

Time-Ryder: Powerstone Book One

Abandoning all hope of establishing a link with its data core, she used the internal infa-red cameras to try and decipher the strange lettering and symbols on the inside rim.

Without much luck, Kara rubbed her eyes and slumped down into the large black chair that dominated the lower section of the flight deck. Two technicians scampered about the deck doing minor repairs as she stemmed her eyes toward the screen.

"Enlarge Image!" she called out ahead.

The doors to the right of the lower flight deck opened and Jack wandered in; a puzzled look upon his face.

She wheeled quickly, looking from his face to his hands.

He came directly over to the ops table and laid out the red gem upon the glass finish.

"Where did you get that?"

He gave a wry smile.

"Your glorious Captain had it hidden in a locker in the food stores!" he rasped, "Kara there's a lot more going on here than meets the eye. I'm going to get kitted up, can you page the others to get ready in twenty minutes?"

"But the storm is still going to last for another hour!"

"It's only a short trip to the domes and the rover will be able to handle it now that it's been repaired!" he returned and then saw the image on the large view-screen.

He looked up to the screen where he could make out the strange glyphs on the monitor.

"What are you doing?" he narrowed his eyes, trying to find a familiar pattern in the symbols.

"It's that crown thing you gave me. I found a set of markings on the inside rim. I thought System might be able to translate them, it's not being very co-operative though!" sighed the Australian once again. Shaking his head to free himself of the imprint of the memory that the symbols had taken, Jack straightened up and looked down upon the Lieutenant.

"Computers never are!" he said openly, knowing the Lieutenant disliked the computer so much.
"You should ask young Nova, he is an archaeologist, it might take his mind off Henry coming back to the mines with me!"
"That Kid?" she shrieked.
"That kid has quite a bit of experience with ancient texts, so the Professor tells me. He might be able to help you deciphering this!" Jack said sternly and turned back to the exit.
"Tell Denton I'll meet him in ship's stores, I have a few things I need to check on first!"
With that, he raced off to the side doors, leaving Kara with the boring task of the crown. She sighed and slumped down onto the stool.
"System, begin the next rotation!" she said aloud and the small camera began to revolve around the crown on the ops table.

The drab, yet extensive vehicle bay was devoid of all life. The only sound audible was that of the overly large Rover vehicle that was firmly locked down by the huge metal clamps on the floor.
Its engines powered up noisily, preparing to take Jack and his small team to the domes on the far side of the mountain, once they'd kitted themselves out with all of the equipment they needed for the journey.
The Rover's massive tractor treads stretched almost three feet across, like giant feet that held the body of the vehicle aloft and dwarfed over the smaller green vessel at its side that looked not far different from a minibus, although a little more sophisticated. The Rover was a burnt orange colour and would no doubt stand out from the crisp whiteness of the snow outside.

Time-Ryder: Powerstone Book One

Black tinted windows spanned both sides and the cockpit bay windows was also blacked out, masking anyone that might have been inside.

It was heavily armour-plated, and almost looked battle ready; but was fully equipped for any means.

Trooper Hoffman emerged from inside the Rover; a short man with an unkempt appearance.

He had an impish face with wide eyes, a slightly elongated nose, but a winning smile, not that he smiled too often. He was a quiet shuffling soul; who kept his head down and did his work; never questioning his orders, but always completing his tasks with ease and perfection.

Hoffman moved around the vehicle, doing the final system checks before launch as the doors opened and his co-pilot Dervish bounded through, full of life and vigour. Dervish was taller, thinner and had a more bubbly personality, but his lack of ambition meant that at the age of thirty-two, he was still only a lowly ranking trooper.

"Did you do the pre-engine preps?" he asked the smaller trooper.

Hoffman held out the large oil smeared spanner in his hand, in an almost threatening nature, annoyed that he had been left to complete the pre-launch systems while Dervish was swanning around the ship, trying to chat up the few remaining females on board.

"Checks all complete," he drawled with a dismal expression upon his face, "Where were you?"

Dervish just gave him a devilish grin of smugness and disappeared inside the Rover without answering.

Hoffman gripped the spanner tight and moved inside the Rover after him.

Time-Ryder: Powerstone Book One

The group consisting of Denton, Jack and the Professor made their way from the Quartermaster stores on the way to the Vehicle bay as they bumped into Nova and Valana on the way up to G deck.

The Professor stopped as Nova looked on; a bemused look spreading over his already beaming face.

"Well, what do you think?" asked the old man; he spread his arms wide, quite happy with himself.

He was dressed in a navy blue thermo jacket, padded for comfort and security, matching the one that Denton adorned.

Denton didn't know why he bothered wearing one of the jackets himself. His unique metabolism gave him a lack of body temperature and no reaction to hot or cold conditions. It didn't apply to clothing, but he'd come to terms with clothes, as it would look odd if he was naked for the most part.

The old man zipped the heavy links together and patted his stomach neatly as he sucked it in, quite pleased with himself.

"You look like the Michelin man!" scoffed the young man.

"It's not designed for appearance!" objected Denton.

"Neither is your ship. It's like one of those Blue Peter botch ups, only they didn't get time to finish it earlier!" Nova shot back, criticising the ship again.

"Believe me Nova, he'll need it in the mines, you saw how cold it gets down there!" assured Jack, affirming the status by zipping up his heavy jacket.

"Will you be leaving soon?" asked Valana, looking over to Jack, he returned his gaze to the young woman.

"Just a few checks to go over and then we'll be ready!"

Jack held his wrist out, eying the digital display on the elongated watch that he bore.

The small pager unit on his belt sounded off and he retreated to the comm box in the corridor, thumbing it on.

"Go ahead!"

Time-Ryder: Powerstone Book One

"It's Kara. Hoffman has just reported that all preps to the Rover are complete!" said the small box with a garbled crackle that didn't sound like the Lieutenant at all.

"Understood. Adams out!" he said, still using his nom de plume for the benefit of the youngsters.

He gave a nod to Denton and they watched the tall Lieutenant move swiftly along the corridor and disappear up the large white spiral to perform some last checks on the flight deck.

The Professor smiled wryly as the two young people followed on behind him.

"Are you sure you couldn't squeeze another two onto the team?" spat Nova.

Jack gave a deep exhalation of breath, turned on heel and pulled the young man aside, away from the others.

"I need you to do me a favour kid," he whispered.

Nova, paranoid as ever looked around, only to see the Professor and Valana canoodling by the door to the locker room.

"Me do you a favour?" Nova raised his brow, "Do I look like I'm going to do something for you? Especially when you've basically sent me to my room," he scoffed.

"Ok Kid, you don't like me, get over it!" barked Jack.

And in that instant Nova had a change of heart and saw what the Commander was all about, someone trying to keep everyone safe. He took a deep breath and gave the Commander a smile.

"This is the only time I'll feel comfortable saying this," he smiled "because you don't have a gun in your hand. So Shoot!"

Jack gave the smallest of grins, smiling at his sense of humour.

"I need you here just in case one of those things tries to penetrate the ship, you two are the only ones who know what they look like!" he announced and drew Valana closer, the Professor joining them.

"Big, and green with fingers like switchblades. I think Kara will be able to interpret the description. Who do you think she's going

Time-Ryder: Powerstone Book One

to expect? Kermit the frog with a flick-knife!" snapped the young man sarcastically.

He gave a disappointing glare as he remembered that they weren't the only ones who saw the creatures.

"What about Brooks!" declared Valana, close by his side; still backing him up.

"You two aren't going to let it go, are you?" asked the Professor.

"Would you think any less of me if we did?" retorted Nova.

"It's alright Commander, you go on ahead, I'll catch you up!" intervened the old man, noting that he was eager to go.

But Nova left the Professor and Valana talking as he broke off and moved over to where the Jack stood, poised at the top of the white spiral.

"Commander, wait a minute" he said, holding a hand out to beckon him back.

Jack faltered and motioned to Denton to carry on and the blue giant disappeared down the staircase.

He raised his brow and looked at the young man curiously

"Look we might have got off on the wrong foot. I just don't take having a gun shoved in my face too well!"

Jack smiled, he was more like the young man than he realised, he wouldn't have like it to happen to him either.

"What are you trying to say kid?"

"When you go back to the mine, watch out for him. He's not all that well, but he'd never admit it to anyone!"

Jack gave him a smile of reassurance and slapped his shoulder.

"Don't you worry Kid, just keep a lookout here, he'll be fine with me!"

Nova curled his finger and beckoned him closer as the tall American stooped over and Nova whispered softly.

"See if one more person calls me kid..." he tailed off as Jack descended the spiral.

Time-Ryder: Powerstone Book One

Nova rejoined the others by the wall as the Professor put his arms around the two young people, drawing them closer as if they were in a rugby scrum.
"Now listen here, I want you two to stay on board," he said softly, casting a fleeting eye over his shoulder to the vacant corridor.
"There's something else going on here, I'm not sure what it is, and it's only a gut feeling" he breathed.
"And you want us to find out what it is?" asked Valana.
Carlson nodded.
"Discreetly. I just get the feeling that there's something not quite right on board this ship!"
"You want us to see if Gold Coast Barbie knows anything?" smiled Nova mischievously.
Carlson smiled through his beard.
"If she does know anything, it's unlikely she'll tell you anything, besides the crystal is here in the Medibay. If Mr Vane really is in league with the creatures then I assume he'll try to obtain it. That is what they are after!"
"See I knew he was the one being held in detention!" Nova's face lit up, "didn't we say that!" he said excitedly.
Valana nodded in agreement for a second, happy that his deductions made him feel superior.
"All I'm saying is that you keep an eye on him if he's as dangerous as they are making out!" warned the old man. The death count had risen and Vane was the only one to have survived the first fatal mission, proving that he could survive anything, including a second outing to the mines.
"But he's locked up in a detention cell!" shrieked Valana, "what harm can he do from there?"
The Professor straightened up and unbuttoned the tight jacket slightly.

Time-Ryder: Powerstone Book One

"Commander Adams says that young man has been on board for some time. It's highly probable that he knows ways and means of getting out of such a situation. Nevertheless, keep an eye on that crystal and trust nobody. Doctor Gennero has it in the Medibay, which is where you two should be going right now!" he pointed to his arm, indicating that they were due for their innoculations.

"Oh you're funny!" drawled Nova with a smile and he began to back off to the stairway again.

"Here, what about that scrawny looking guy, do you think he has anything to do with it?"

"Like I said, trust nobody" Carlson pursed his lips and turned to Valana.

"Look after him; he has a knack of getting into terrible trouble?" he whispered.

She simply smiled and nodded.

"He said exactly the same thing about you!"

The Professor watched them both go; maybe there was a small glimmer of truth in what she had said. One thing was sure; he was enjoying himself too much to sit this one out.

Time-Ryder: Powerstone Book One

CHAPTER FORTY

Kara stood on the flight deck with the camera on V deck showing the large Rover vehicle powering up and preparing to exit the ship.
The massive ramp extended, touching down onto the docking pad and crushing the three feet of snow that had accumulated during the night.
The rest of the snowfall was more apparent around the exterior of the ship, but the constant heat generated by the massive vessel kept the immediate area to a minimum.
The stocky orange vehicle began to move off, the tractor treads moving the bulk of the Rover down until it kissed the snow and gripped the white blanket, slowly pulling the rest of the vehicle down onto the ground.
It was an extensively long vehicle, almost twenty feet long, yet it had an umbilical section that was connected to another, adding a further twenty feet to the back.
Kara watched it go as it sped off into the distance, heading for the domed settlement that was dwarfed by the mountain.
She flipped a control on the upper section of the forward console and the massive view-screen retracted back into the ceiling, and she stepped forward, beyond where the screen had been and looked out over the yellow railings at the front of the flight deck; overlooking the exterior of the ship where she could see the tiny vehicle speeding away.
"Good luck Jack!" she whispered softly.
Behind her at the back of the flight deck in his usual skulking manner, Craven kept to the shadows, plotting something in wake of the Colonel's departure.
He grinned widely and stepped back under the balcony, hiding in the darkness.

Time-Ryder: Powerstone Book One

Heading back to G deck, Nova led Valana back to their quarters, and into the serene and relaxed environment, away from the sound of water rushing through the pipes in the corridors, the constant whooshing of piston powered doors and the infernal chatter of the technician crews in the hallways.

"Why did you bring me here?" Valana perked up her nose in a slightly haughty manner.

"I wanted another look at that thing, remember you said that there was something missing from the centre and the crystal might have fitted in the gap!"

She nodded.

"Well what about the crystal in the Medibay, ready for the taking!" he answered and set his hand under the pillow to retrieve the strange device.

Nova's eyes suddenly went wide and he stared up at the girl in panic.

Turning back to the pillow that was strangely charred and blackened, he pulled it from the bed, showing nothing underneath, but the charred imprint of where it had been.

"Val. That weird unit! It's gone!" he hissed and looked up at her again.

She returned the gaze with a perplexed look.

"So someone entered your quarters without you knowing, sounds familiar doesn't it?" she asked him.

Nova nodded.

"And if Vane's in a holding cell, who could it be?" Valana looked down on him with the same realisation, but he was thinking about something else.

"If someone's got the unit and worked out the same as us, they'll be looking for the crystal to fire it up!" he replied in a hiss and she looked up at him.

"Then we'd better get there before they do!" she sighed.

Time-Ryder: Powerstone Book One

Kara put her feet up on the ops table and lay back in the chair. She'd thought about what Vane had said and sent for the Doctor, hoping that a medical opinion on the device might shed some truth on what it really was.

The large doors on the right parted with their usual expulsion of strained pistons and Elizabeth strode through quickly, rising up to the technician's pit where Kara was stationed.

"Quite comfortable Lieutenant?" she asked with a whimsical smile.

Kara forgot herself and eased her boots down off the workstation. She returned the smile with a look of amusement.

"What did you want to see me about?" asked Elizabeth as she stepped around the ops table while Kara flipped on the 3d display, showing a representation of the coronet in a blue tinged graphic.

"What is it?" Elizabeth took a seat, her brows narrowing in confusion at the device, which she couldn't make head or tail of.

"It might be the answer to those marks on the dead Doctor!" answered Kara in a hiss of breath.

Elizabeth rose from her seat just as quickly as she had sat down. "This thing?" she shrieked.

The wonders of the device had been running through her head all night, the prospect of what applications it might be capable of were endless and she thought of all new capabilities that it might have, but here was the physical manifestation of what had been keeping her awake for hours on end.

"Where is it?" she laid her hands on the console, watching the spinning representation and squinting at it with concentration.

"I've put it in System's internal spectrograph, analysing every detail before I release it to you. I'm trying to decipher the symbols upon it," answered Kara in a gruff hiss.

Time-Ryder: Powerstone Book One

Elizabeth moved around beside her, looking at the notes Kara had been making on the small hand tablet, without much success.

"You should ask Nova, he might be able to help you!" said the Doctor.

A strained look of frustration came over the small officer's face and she looked sternly at the Doctor.

"Why does everyone think he might be able to do it better?" and she paused momentarily before the Doctor replied, "I know he's an archaeologist!" she hissed.

Elizabeth started to make her way towards the door again.

"You can always ask him, it's not like he has anything better to do!" she turned upon heel "Just let me know if you have any progress with it."

And quickly, she was gone; leaving Kara to her problem, but the Lieutenant wasn't for giving up so easily.

"System, can you enlarge the section in the bottom left hand corner?" she said, squinting to see the circular symbols that were repeated on one section. The image grew in size so that Kara could see the markings clearer

"Enlarge once again!"

"Negative, image is at maximum resolution. Suggest report to medical bay for ocular re-examination" clipped the Computer's droning tone.

Craven entered through the side doors with a devilish smile and a gleam in his eye.

"I think she means you need your eyes tested!" he laughed, "Anything I can help you with?"

Kara rammed her index finger to one of the keys on the control panel and the image on the screen faded, replaced by a dull black void.

"I doubt it," she snapped.

Time-Ryder: Powerstone Book One

Craven paced the floor slowly to her position and watched the tiny rows of screens that ran up the sides of the massive viewer were full of activity. He gave a smile with a sly look and leered over Kara's small yet very voluptuous figure.

"You don't like me, do you Lieutenant?"

She gave him a vain smile as he motioned closer and she could almost feel herself cringe as he came within touching distance of her.

"It's not part of the job requirement is it?" she said sarcastically. But he knew exactly what she meant; somehow it made it easier for him, he knew she would tell him the truth.

"Then why don't we indulge in some light conversation? Who knows, we might get to like one another!"

"I wouldn't bet on it!" she murmured.

Without looking up, Kara's fingers spanned the keyboard as she carried on with her work.

"I'm busy. I don't have time to talk to you Craven!"

Waving to the two technicians with a finger, she dismissed them from the flight deck and revolved to Craven as they disappeared through the side entrance.

"Why are you so interested anyway?" she continued to tap away at the keyboard, without looking to the tall scrawny man as he slid closer to the ops table.

"Nine of the survey team were killed Lieutenant, I would like to know why!" he hissed, "It's not as if poor Mr Vane has anything to do with it, he wasn't even on Penithe when the murders started!"

Kara stared at him, wondering what game he was playing. Craven was the only one that escaped from the mines with the skin of his teeth and the one who sent the SOS, but like his miraculous escape, Vane's was just as convenient. He was the sole survivor of the massacre, making it out of the mines with two wounded crewmembers, both of whom were now dead.

Time-Ryder: Powerstone Book One

But why would Craven choose to defend Vane? And why bring up his name in the first place? The identity of the suspect was always kept between her and Jack, but she supposed it wouldn't have taken a rocket scientist to work it out.

"All I'm saying is that I don't think he has anything to do with the murders Lieutenant!" Craven smiled at her.

Kara gave him a wry grin, humouring him for an instant and turned her back to check on the station behind the ops table; making a few adjustments.

"Oh and who do you think has?" she smiled smugly, then the sudden realisation of the truth dawned upon her and her eyes went wide.

"Me of course!" exclaimed Craven with a bright beaming smile.

He removed a hand pistol from behind his back and aimed it on the defenceless Lieutenant's back, firing a shot a point blank range.

The bullet ripped through Kara and exited through her chest, smashing into the rear station monitor and setting it aflame.

"I found this in the armoury," he advanced, bearing the weapon down upon the wounded Lieutenant.

"I have to thank the Commander for his choice in weaponry. Or is it Jack? Now I am really getting confused Lieutenant."

His smile became wider, almost maniacal as he lifted the weapon up and glared at it.

"Go fuck yourself!" she cursed, gritting her teeth; which were soaked in her own blood.

"You know it really is most effective weapon, and very messy!" Craven smiled like a maniac as the screen erupted and sent Kara soaring from the blast.

He recoiled, still grinning inanely and put the weapon away inside his tunic.

Craven thumped across the deck plates to where the third terminal access station of the operating computer was.

Time-Ryder: Powerstone Book One

Shaking on the floor, Kara clenched her fingers tightly as she readied herself to rise from the floor. The pain was excruciating, but the adrenaline seemed to spur her on; although the blood continued to pour from her shoulder.

Craven laid his hands out on the console ahead of him in a rather arrogant stance.

"System, disable all officer access codes, access intermediate 1473"

"Please confirm with an officer verification!" announced the voice of the onboard system computer.

Craven gritted his teeth.

"Vesh!" he said, stamping the floor like a child in a tantrum. Kara felt the strength in her arms and she pulled herself up behind the liaison officer, she clambered over and prepared to attack.

Mumbling and unsure of what to do, Craven braced himself upon the console.

"That file name is not on record!"

Kara moved forward and stumbled, her foot clumping noisily on the floor as Craven wheeled around and saw the advancing Lieutenant. He caught the wounded woman off guard and punched her full in the face, stunning her briefly as he made a grab for her.

Grabbing hold of her short blonde hair, he swung Kara over to the computer terminal, with a strong grip, almost tearing the hair from her scalp.

Blood continued to seep from the wound on her chest as he pounded her violently towards the console, forcing her forward.

"Don't think I'm helping you, you Bastard!" cursed the Australian, straining to push herself away from the controls.

A thin red smudge of blood appeared upon her lips as she winced in pain, but she still tried to fight him back with every ounce of strength that she had.

Time-Ryder: Powerstone Book One

Pressing one of the keys on the board, Craven held the Lieutenant's head in a vice-like grip while the transparent ocular framework started to rise from within the depths of the computer terminal.

"But you are helping me Kara!" he threw her a wicked grin as she tried to push back again.

Still with her hair in his grasp, he pulled her backward and forced her face into the console, knocking her senseless.

She was dazed and she shook her head trying to free the slight disorientation.

Summing up one last burst of energy, Kara Everett threw her elbow back, catching the man sharply in the stomach.

He doubled over, letting go of her head and the pistol fell from his tunic, clunking noisily on the floor.

Everett reached out to gain control of the gun as Craven threw a punch to her head, but he missed and struck the wound on her shoulder.

Squealing in agony, Kara flew back to the cold metallic floor; her head pounding onto its hard surface and dazing her even more so. Craven grinned and eased himself on top of her, sitting on top of her chest, sustaining his weight upon her arms and leaving them redundant. He held her shoulders still.

"I won't be coy in saying this'll hurt me more than it'll hurt you," he paused and smiled wider, putting further pressure upon her arms, "Because it won't"

He pressed his right thumb into her wound, making the Lieutenant's jaws gape and she contorted in pain. Her eyes screwed up, showing the agony that she was in, but she didn't give him the satisfaction of hearing her scream.

Craven's grin began to spread wider than before as he enjoyed torturing the helpless Lieutenant.

Time-Ryder: Powerstone Book One

Like a ravenous animal, he rose from his seated position on Kara's chest and forced the woman up once more, holding her palm on top of the green pad.
He began to splay her fingers wide until they touched the outer edges of the highlighted area of the security initiator.
"Palm print accepted, Lieutenant Kara Everett. Awaiting retina identification," droned the computer.
Craven held her chin close to the transparent ocular frame, forcing all of his weight behind her.
Knowing what was coming next Everett closed her eyes firmly as the tall dark man delivered a blow to her stomach.
Gripping her hair tightly, he brought a knife out of his thigh pocket, waving it in front of her face.
"I only need one eye Kara, connected or not, it'll do the same job, your choice" he spat.
Holding her chin tightly with one hand, he put the knife away as Kara gave in and prised her eyes open. Craven's fingers held her eyelid with the other hand and he gripped her chin, forcing her into the poly-metal framework.
"Retina print accepted Lieutenant Kara Everett" finished the voice.
"Thank you" smiled Craven and he bounced the Lieutenant's face off the console and he bowed graciously behind her.
Craven collected his pistol from the floor and trained it on the young woman as he prepared to back off.
He could see that the exhausted Lieutenant was incapable of retaliating further and smiled at her gracious surrender, but Kara was able to lift one leg and she smashed her heel firmly into his kneecap.
Craven let out an embellished cry and clutched his knee in a collected moment of pain.
His smile spread wildly in amusement, but it was all that the young woman needed to distract him. She kicked again, this time aiming for the other knee, forcing him to drop the weapon.

Time-Ryder: Powerstone Book One

"Bitch!" he wailed.

Scrambling over to the pistol, Kara seized the gun and gritted her teeth. Her hand shook as she aimed it on his chest as she breathed heavily and settled her aim.

"I told you Craven, I'm not bloody helping you!"

Kara released the trigger and a smile gleamed across her face as the metal projectile blasted into Craven's shoulder and he soared backward, but it was only enough to sway him momentarily.

He got up from the tech pit slowly and moved his pained frame closer towards her as she aimed again.

"Awaiting Intermediate Authorisation voice print" announced the voice of the onboard computer to which Kara managed to sustain a momentary smile.

She fired again and the bullet ripped through the air, but was slightly off target and coursed through one side of Craven's throat, emerging from the other side.

He gargled in agony as the red fountain of blood rapidly streamed from his windpipe. He held his hands tightly to his throat as the crimson liquid released and made his larynx gargle.

"Bitch!" he spat again, his voice unrecognisable.

The blood wretched man began to wither to his knees as the computer's dull tones stretched above their heads again.

With an ironic smile, Kara levelled the pistol at Craven's chest, hoping to hit the right spot this time.

She creased her eyes and aimed.

"Try issuing any voice commands now!" she said with contentment.

Squealing in torment, Craven lumbered towards her clumsily as she levelled the pistol once again. Kara pulled the trigger and the gun clicked.

She tapped the gun's barrel as the blood soaked man staggered, snatching the weapon away and throwing the back of his hand in contact with her face.

Everett shot back, momentarily stunned.

"You Bitch!" he gargled with a squeal.

Wiping a trickle of blood from her mouth Kara looked up to him with a smile.

Throwing his hand out, the pistol butt caught Kara's forehead and knocked her to the ground. Craven released the gun clip and replaced it as the blood flowed down his tunic. Aiming the gun at the Lieutenant, he fired again; leaving her in a pool of blood. Ripping apart his tunic, he loomed over the computer terminal again, tapping into the keypad wildly.

"Intermediate access code one two three one two" croaked Craven as he held the piece of tunic up to his throat.

"Access Denied. Voice recognition rejected. Authorisation of transfer must be completed within thirty seconds!" announced the warning voice.

"Vesh!" he thumped his hand upon the terminal and retreated to the exit under the balcony as the countdown began. He had a slim chance to achieve his goal, but first he had to get off the ship before anyone suspected him.

Holding his wound tightly as he shuffled through the decks, Craven held his hand out to the green panel of the first bulkhead. The thin wafer of bright green light descended from behind the palm reader.

The main access door to the rest of the ship rose and he fumbled through, leaving his bloodstained print upon the green reader. Without wasting any time, he reached the white spiral stairway and stumbled down into the bowels of the huge craft, before the shutters came down and the internal plating sealed off all decks.

System's voice continued to drone out over the dormant flight deck, dormant except for the blood soaked body of Lieutenant Everett.

"Five, four, three, two one. Transfer Authorisation incomplete. Ship-wide lockdown initiated!"

The large main screen dropped out of the ceiling slowly and was illuminated with a huge warning in bold red lettering.

'AUTHORISATION DISABLEMENT. SHIP-WIDE LOCKDOWN IN PROGRESS'

The computer automatically set the controls and sealed the flight deck. The massive metal-rimmed glass doors glided tightly shut as the security placements came into force and all of the major access points over the entire ship were being secured and sealed tight.

"Ship-wide lockdown has been achieved!"

Time-Ryder: Powerstone Book One

CHAPTER FORTY ONE

"Ouch!" whined Nova, "That was bloody sore!"
T he young scot rubbed his arm as Doctor Gennero removed the needle and rubbed his arm to collect any stray blood.
"Don't be such a baby!" retorted the Doctor.
She stood up to her full height and took the blood sample to the analyser. Laying the vial down, she crossed to the two guests and nodded toward the red crystal on the workstation.
"Interesting little crystal you have there!" she remarked, "The Professor told me how you came to be here, it really is quite unbelievable!"
"That's what that Commander of yours said when we first met him. Did the Professor mention how painful the journey was?" replied Nova.
"I'd rather go through that a hundred times than have another one of your jabs," he moaned, rubbing his arm.
Caught off guard, Nova felt the tiny scratch as Elizabeth inoculated him again.
"Oh thanks" he smiled sarcastically, "Do I get a lollipop for being good?"
Elizabeth smiled at him and his attempts to lighten the mood but Nova continued to rub his arm as a perturbed Trooper Brooks entered the room slowly; his face confused, and he barrelled over to the Doctor, completely bypassing the youngsters.
"Doctor, what's going on? System has loaded the lockdown program. The bulkhead doors and all decks are sealed!"
Elizabeth shot off her stool immediately and eased over to the wall panel. She flipped the wall-com, but there was no sign of life in the communication channel.
"It's dead!" she remarked and moved over to the medical console, trying to access the systems to the flight deck.

Time-Ryder: Powerstone Book One

"System, access Doctor Gennero, code Alpha three six" she called out to the small screen.
"All access to data and terminal systems has been put on lockdown. Access must be granted by terminal three on the flight deck," droned the computer voice.
Gritting her teeth, Elizabeth leaned forward.
"Why has lockdown been initiated? Do we have intruders on board?" she asked, thinking it may be the only reason why security may be compromised.
"What does all this mean?" asked Valana softly; she looked over to see Brooks' worried face and he scratched his head, waiting for the computer to respond.
"All access must be initiated from terminal three on the flight deck!" repeated the voice.
Gennero switched the monitor off and uttered a curse under her breath, and clearly in French, as she was so frustrated.
Nova stared at the crystal, mesmerised by the faint glimmer of light that emanated from within.
He shook his head and eyed the Doctor strangely.
"Has anyone put this crystal near a heat source?" he asked.
Doctor Gennero returned her vision to the young man.
"We used a quadro point drill on it, didn't exactly go to plan, it destroyed the drill head!" she coughed.
He narrowed his brow curiously.
"I'm just wondering why it's starting to glow again, you know like when the sphere first activated!" he looked directly at Valana who knew exactly what it meant.
He sighed as the red shimmer started to recede from the crystal's outer shell.
"Can we get back to more important things!" hissed Brooks annoyed, "How are we supposed to get around the ship?"
"Does that mean we're trapped down here?" asked Nova, stating the obvious.

Time-Ryder: Powerstone Book One

"For the moment!" exhaled Elizabeth, "At least the oxygen pumps are still working. No panic there" she heard the faint hiss of air coming from the rectangular vent that stretched across the Medibay ceiling.

"There isn't another way out is there?" Valana asked, staring at the pensive Trooper Brooks, "You don't have protocols for emergencies such as this?"

The thought suddenly occurred to the Doctor; who crossed to the far end of the white dominated room.

"There's always the Evac-exit" she pointed to the wall; where the sealed bulkhead door resembled the rest of the vacuum formed white wall panels.

"That'll only get us off ship; we need access to the flight deck and re-establish the protocols. That'll remove the lockdown program!" announced the weary trooper.

He paraded the floor, his mind clearly working overtime on the problem.

"It's just impossible!" exclaimed Elizabeth in frustration.

Nova's mouth curled into a smile.

"That's what my English teacher always said about me, no wait a minute, she said you're impossible!" and he smiled widely, "I thrive on the impossible Doctor!"

Nova's mind was beginning to see things that Brooks wasn't; he was looking at the problem from a different view and bit his lip in annoyance.

"What are you thinking?" asked Valana, trying to think of a solution herself.

"The ship's designers surely wouldn't confine the crew on board would they?" he narrowed.

"That's what the Evac exits are for!" reinforced Elizabeth.

Brooks shook his head and took position on one of the stools; his ankle was starting to throb, not that he'd felt it at the time.

The situation was taking his mind off it.

Time-Ryder: Powerstone Book One

"Surely there would be something in place to override the situation!" shrieked Valana.
"This ship is twenty years old, but the lockdown program is updated every two months and it's infallible. There must be a senior officer on the flight deck to remove the lockdown; otherwise the automated system would move the access point to the next in command, which would be you Doctor!"
Brooks looked at her in shock as a blood-soaked hand grasped the rim of the Medibay door.
Elizabeth shrieked and her jaw dropped as crimson stained fingers flexed around the edge of the door. Craven pulled himself over the threshold into the lab, and he gargled, blood weeping from the side of his mouth as he tried to communicate.
Grabbing him in an act of second nature, the Doctor helped him over to the large padded bed and he rested his pained frame against it.
"What the hell happened?" hissed Brooks, trying to help.
"The flight deck" gasped the horrific looking man; "Those things have got on board!" he lied.
"They killed Everett, but she started to lockdown the drive computer!" he wheezed.
The group eyed him with sympathy and concern.
Valana turned away in disgust. She could smell the potent odour of his wound, even though he tried desperately to conceal it.
"Kara's dead?" exclaimed Elizabeth.
Craven gave the briefest indication of a nod that was just as painful as it would have been to speak.
The sudden grim reality came forward to the Doctor as it had with so many other crewmembers that she had known and had grown fond of.
She gritted her teeth and pulled a small pen torch from her breast pocket, shining it directly into Craven's eyes.

Time-Ryder: Powerstone Book One

He retracted instantly, almost shoving her away and she moved the beam across his skin, training it upon the crimson liquid that wept from his throat.

"Brooks, get me a Medi-pack, I need to seal this wound. You're losing too much blood!" she narrowed upon the ailing man.

Craven stared at her, his beady eyes thinking only of his escape.

"It seems to have torn your vocal chords, only just, you're very lucky, a few more millimetres and it would have hit your corotted artery!"

"I don't feel lucky!" he gargled.

Brooks passed the small green Medi-pack to Valana; who helped the Doctor apply them to the wound.

Nova abruptly pulled Brooks aside to the edge of the door.

"If those things are up on the flight deck, then it'll be sealed tight from the rest of us, right?"

Brooks nodded.

"The lockdown would have quadrupled the mag-locks. If they're up there, then they aren't getting out anytime soon!"

"That's just as well, because I'm not moving from here!" Nova was quite resilient in his statement, "They're stronger than us remember!"

Brooks shook his head and stood firm.

"Quite the opposite Nova, we have to find some way of getting back up there!"

"And how're you going to do that?" said Nova smugly.

Then he narrowed his eyes and stared at the short trooper.

"Wait a minute, how did he get down here?" Nova turned on Craven; still being attended to, his wound less horrific as it had been. Craven gargled, pushing back the Doctor who was trying to mop his wound.

"I got out before the lockdown was secured," he wheezed.

Elizabeth started to apply the tissue regenerator to his throat, essentially sealing up the open wound tightly.

Time-Ryder: Powerstone Book One

"You just left Kara up there?" hissed Nova angrily.

"She was already dead!" Craven lied again, wondering how long he could keep up the pretence.

Valana had only met Kara during the mission briefing, yet it seemed that part of her was concerned that the supposedly dead Lieutenant might still be alive up there. She, like the others were a bit wary of trusting Craven's word.

"Surely there's an escape passage from the flight deck or..." she asked and paused, looking up to the ceiling and pointing to the white covering.

"Or an air vent. Not that I'll be going in mind you!" objected Nova.

Gennero narrowed her eyes, gazing at the wounded man closely. "What about the conduits, they access throughout every deck!" she offered.

"Why didn't I think of that?" Brooks was disappointed with himself; he knew the ship backwards, yet it had never occurred to him that this might be a possible route.

Craven saw that they were getting too close to the truth and felt that he had to act.

Brooks smiled as the Doctor looked over his shoulder.

"There's an access port in the corridor."

Edging forward to the wound on Craven's shoulder, Elizabeth narrowed her eyes and squinted at the blood all around the opening.

"That's strange?" she narrowed her eyes curiously "If I didn't know any better, I'd say that it was a projectile wound!" she raised her eyes to meet Craven's.

Without taking any more chances Craven grabbed the Doctor tightly and squeezed her throat.

His pain was intolerable and he winced, trying to keep his eyes open as he felt that he was on the verge of collapsing.

Time-Ryder: Powerstone Book One

He'd lost so much blood, but it was only his determination that was carrying him on.

Craven's right hand removed the pistol and he pressed the nib into the Doctor's temple.

She felt the cold chill of the gun like an icicle.

Grappling her hands frantically, Elizabeth tried to free herself but Craven's arm began to tighten and squeeze around her throat.

"What do you think you're doing you animal?" spat Valana.

She glared angrily at Craven as he backed off into the corner of the room. The bangle on Valana's wrist began to glow with ferocity and she held her arm behind her back.

Unable to do anything, Valana stood back, full of anger, as she looked to Nova and Brooks, both of them equally as useless as she was.

"Just like a rat, eh?" Nova sneered, "backing off into a corner," he said, trying to provoke him into releasing the stranglehold grip that he had on the Doctor.

"Shut up Nova. He's going to kill her!" warned Valana, fixing him with a lethal stare.

"Look if it's a hostage you want then take me!" offered Brooks, holding his hands up into the air and showing Craven that he wasn't armed.

"You'll know the dangers of cornering a rat then won't you?" Craven gargled arrogantly towards Nova.

Valana felt herself getting angrier as the glow on the bangle intensified.

"She's just helped you and dressed your wound and this is how you repay her?" spat the girl angrily.

"An action that she will no doubt regret for the remaining few minutes of life that she has left" threatened the man; holding the cold steel against the Doctor's temple.

He lashed out his weapon hand and struck Valana across the face, sending her reeling as he returned the weapon to the

Time-Ryder: Powerstone Book One

Doctor's head, pressing it harder and making Elizabeth wince with the pressure.

Valana sank to the ground, mopping her mouth that was streaming with blood and slowly Nova helped her back to her feet.

"Try that with me Knobhead!" cursed Nova; the best retort that he could think of at the moment.

He started to edge closer as did Brooks, but seeing that his anger could result in further deaths, Nova held his position.

"Any closer and the Doctor dies, just like Lieutenant Everett!" smiled Craven.

Nova gritted his teeth as brooks held him back.

"You're going to kill her anyway" spat the young archaeologist, trying to see a flaw in his logic.

"Nova stop trying to provoke him!" snapped Valana.

"Yes Nova, stop trying to provoke me. You can see I'm armed. One squeeze of the trigger and she's dead!" hissed Craven.

It was like a stand-off between two champions, each sizing the other up, even though it seemed that Craven held the trumph card at the moment.

But the Doctor's life wasn't something that Nova was intending to play around with.

"Come on then, tell us what you're really after? I'm betting you're that Bastard who set up poor Joe, aren't you?" sneered Nova again, "It didn't take us long to work that one out!"

"A simple pheromone canister with his DNA sample in it, sprayed all around the Lieutenant's quarters, and it worked really well!" he said smugly, "shifted the blame away from me and was exactly what I needed."

Craven took in a pained breath and swung the weapon around, firing at almost point blank range.

Time-Ryder: Powerstone Book One

Nova winced, prepared for the worst as he closed his eyes, but after the shot fired off he opened his eyes and patted his body down.

The bullet hadn't touched him, but instead it had penetrated the short trooper by his side. Brooks slid to the floor, a thumb sized bullet hole in the middle of his forehead.

Craven grinned and returned it to the Doctor's head, squeezing her throat once more.

"You know I really am getting attached to this gun!" he said, waving it around.

Nova leered towards him and Craven levelled the gun in his direction, stopping the young man in his tracks.

"Don't make me fire another shot!" he warned as he backed off to the Evac-exit and slammed his gun into the wall release mechanism.

Pinning her gaze to the nearby workstation, Gennero spotted the upright rack of syringes that she had been preparing to synthesise. She threw out her hand and grabbed the nearest one, full of green liquid and she stabbed it into Craven's hand, pressing the contents into his bloodstream with the singular jab. The green substance flowed into him and he recoiled, shrieking in despair and releasing the Doctor from his grip immediately. Nova saw his chance and darted forward, levelling a fist and bringing it right up under Craven's chin.

Dropping the pistol in the sudden flash of activity, Craven was propelled backward from the blow and he soared into the wall panel. His dizzy gaze saw that the Evac-exit was starting to ease open as their weight upon it had activated the opening mechanism. Craven spied the gleaming gem resting on the bench where the Doctor and the Professor had examined it and he snatched it up, looking directly at the Doctor with evil brewing in his eyes.

Time-Ryder: Powerstone Book One

"You're going to regret you did that you bitch!" he spat and scooped up the pistol before Nova could retrieve it.

He aimed the pistol at the Doctor's head once again and felt the sudden sharp pain as Valana threw the nearest container at him. Distracted for a few seconds was all that Nova needed.

He lunged forward quickly and pushed Craven back against the metal barrier and forced him out into the howling wind and the calamity of the brewing snow-storm.

The exterior of the craft had a large metal walkway that stretched down to each level like the fire escapes on many buildings he had seen.

Forced back against the metal barrier, Craven felt the twinge of agony as his back thundered into the metal railing and Nova pursued him, fighting over the pistol that fired off a few shots into the air.

"Gimme the crystal you thieving bastard!" screeched Nova above the noise of the howling gale. He struggled to hold his position, being rocked back and forth.

"You want the crystal, come and get it!" enticed Craven, urging the young man on. The two men fought in the storm as the wind ripped through their clothing.

Creasing up his features, Nova felt a hefty punch and slumped back against the railings, his arms flailing. Craven slowly began to overpower the archaeologist to such a point that he brought the gun up to Nova's head.

"Goodbye!" he said politely.

Valana crashed out onto the metal parapet and lunged at the sullen man with one of the medical crates, smashing the container near to Craven's head and he turned the gun towards her.

Bringing up his foot, Nova kicked Craven's hand, hoping to free the pistol from his grasp, but merely set him off balance as a shot fired off close to the wall where Valana stood.

Time-Ryder: Powerstone Book One

"Val, get inside the ship now!" bellowed the young scot fiercely. Nova scrambled to his feet and shoved her inside the bulkhead door and he raced after her; while Craven regained his stance and pursued them.

"He's off his head!" exclaimed Nova; almost tripping inside the doorway.

Scrambling at the control panel, Elizabeth snapped the door controls back into place and a large section of the hull began to contract.

Craven's presence in the door with his outstretched weapon-wielding hand filled them with fear, not caring who was going to die first.

"The door Nova" shrieked the Doctor, "pull the release bar quickly!" she motioned to the large rail that spanned the wall and had originally opened the bulkhead when he had forced Craven backward.

Nova pulled on the bar quickly as the pistons strained and squealed with the accelerated movement. The large exit began to move home faster until it trapped Craven's arm in the gap.

The Doctor grimaced.

"You can let go now, the hydraulics will do the rest" she listened to the hiss as the door crunched Craven's arm and lodged back into place, drowning out his wailing screams of pain.

Time-Ryder: Powerstone Book One

Time-Ryder: Powerstone Book One

CHAPTER FORTY TWO

The elongated and heavily armoured Rover vehicle sped through the blizzard, avoiding the sudden gusts of wind that normally blacked out the windscreen.
The Orange vehicle motioned forward with its large tractor treads weaving the indented pattern in the thickened white surface of snow.
Within the cosy confines of the Rover, Dervish was at the steering toggle with such concentration that he cradled the wheel like a prized possession. Trooper Hoffman sat to his left and navigated through the storm with a large radar-tracking device splayed out across the dashboard.
In the back of the vehicle, Professor Carlson, Denton and Jack hunched themselves over the operations plan that was still having fine tweaks added to it.
"I have to say that I'm not relishing the idea of going back in there!" exclaimed the old man.
Without looking up, Jack gave a gruff reply.
"You and me both Henry!"
Denton's perplexed looks made them both turn their attention to him.
"What I don't understand sir is why these things are looking for the crystals?" he asked loudly.
"That's something none of us understands yet Denton!" said Jack, busy cleaning a large shotgun.
"But there's obviously some purpose to it!"
Professor Carlson sat back in his chair, his brows narrowing slightly at something he had been thinking about for quite some time.
"There's more to this mountain than meets the eye Colonel, maybe it would be prudent to do a further scan once we get closer to the mine!"

Time-Ryder: Powerstone Book One

"You think there's something else out there?" Denton asked.
The gills on the back of his head started to flap profusely.
Jack agreed with him, but turned swiftly as Dervish noted that the Domes were coming into sight.
"According to Mr Vane, a full schematic of the mountain was not done on their first entry into the mine!" said the old man.
"Are you saying that there might be sectors of the mine that we know nothing about?" asked the blue Lieutenant.
The Professor leaned forward.
"These creatures have the tendency of crawling out of the smallest of places Lieutenant, and with all of the tremors opening new sectors; do you think we should take the chance?"
"It's a bit too late for that Henry" said the Colonel in a hiss,
"You'd better buckle up gentlemen, we're almost here!" said Jack, fastening his belt as the engines screeched and powered the vehicle forward.

Dangling loosely from the Evac-exit was the lower half of Craven's arm, with the pistol still firmly in his hand.
Once the door was re-aligned and the sounds of the howling gale had vanished once more, the Doctor crossed to Brooks` body and removed a blanket from the bench, draping it over his bleeding carcass.
"How many of us are left on board?" asked Valana, still slightly shaken.
Elizabeth shook her head and tried to think.
"I don't know exactly, a dozen or so maybe!" she said distractedly, "If Kara is dead..." she continued but was cut off by Nova.
"What makes you think she's isn't'?" he hissed.
Valana stepped forward.

410

Time-Ryder: Powerstone Book One

"If he lied about those creatures being on board then he might have lied about that too!"
The Doctor stared at the covered body and turned to the two guests.
"No wait, she's got a point!" said Nova softly wiggling his pointing finger in the air.
"Brooks said that in the event of the death of the senior officer, the control functions would revert to the next in command. You he said!" he pointed at the Doctor.
Valana nodded in agreement.
"If the controls aren't accessible from here then surely it would point to her being still alive up there!"
Flying her hands over the console, Elizabeth stood back.
"Controls are still frozen. You're right, she must still be alive!"
"And if she is, then she's unable to remove the lockdown program!" Valana looked concerned.
"Then that git was lying all along!" stuttered Nova, his face suddenly turned white as the impact of the realisation came to him.
"And if he's the one that's been selling you lot out, then we have to get Joe out of confinement, he'll be able to help us!" Elizabeth said softly and tapped away at the keyboard to determine how many of the systems were shut off and what they had available at hand.
"But first you have to get to the flight deck. If Kara is wounded up there, she'll need all the help she can get and you'll need to do that in order to get to the decks to the detention block unsealed!"
Valana overlooked the Doctor's shoulder as she brought up a schematic of the medical deck, encompassing the laboratory, the morgue and the main Medi-Bay.
Elizabeth nodded without turning away from her concentration on the screen.

Time-Ryder: Powerstone Book One

"You'll be able to access it through these conduits!" she fingered the small pathway upon the blue screen.

Nova straightened and he became concerned, his face suddenly flushed.

"Em, what do you mean by <u>You</u>?" he said as both women looked at him.

"You're the obvious candidate Mr Mitchell!" spat the Doctor, "You can't expect Valana to go in the conduits can you, and I'll have to direct you from here!"

"Just call me Nova; you're starting to sound like the Professor," he drawled, "Making me sound like I'm someone important!"

"At this very moment, you are Nova!" replied Elizabeth, "you're the most important person on this ship!"

He blushed and suddenly became embarrassed.

"Well when you put it like that!"

Distracting the Doctor briefly, Valana pulled closer to her.

"What was in that syringe you injected Craven with?" she scanned her eyes over the rack of samples and stooped to collect the shattered syringe from the floor.

"Hopefully someone's urine sample!" exclaimed Nova.

"A urine sample in a syringe?" the Doctor eyed him strangely.

"I dunno, I thought maybe you were doing tests on it!" Nova shrugged, "Taking the piss either way!"

Elizabeth appreciated his attempts to lighten the tone after Brooks had been killed so senselessly, but she shook her head.

"It was the reptilian DNA that Henry brought back from the mines, one of those samples he took!"

Nova shook his head, his worried face taking on a perplexing look.

"What'll happen to him? Craven I mean?"

Elizabeth Gennero looked disturbingly at the two of them, worried about the statement she was about to utter.

Time-Ryder: Powerstone Book One

She looked at the empty syringe on the floor and scooped to collect it and she closed her eyes over
"What is it Doctor? What's wrong?" Valana grabbed her arm for support, her eyes wide with panic.
She opened her eyes slowly and looked back to the young girl. Elizabeth shook her head and had to take her seat in a moment of shock, even more so that when Brooks had been shot.
"The solution that was injected was the full solution of the third strand of the triple helix. I successfully managed to remove the entire strand and was going to use it as a base to mass produce an Antigen by making it the strand that the antibodies would fight against!" she shook her head again and closed her eyes.
"What are you saying to us Doc?" Nova's brows narrowed.
"It all depends upon his system. The third DNA strand will begin to integrate and start to fight for dominance of the host. Slowly taking over his nervous system and possibly turning him into one of those things," she announced feverishly.
Nova sat down on one of the stools and slowly put his head in his hands, thinking that they had enough problems on their hands. He prised his hands open and looked at the Doctor; who wasn't to know that this was going to happen.
"Maybe you're beginning to wish it was a urine sample now, eh Doc?"

Craven thrashed about in the snowdrift, dazed as the blood loss began to affect his coordination. He plunged through the snow and forced his severed limb into the cold comforts of the freezing temperatures. Somehow he relished the cold, it soothed him; made his body feel content and he smiled as his arm was embedded deeply in the snow.

Time-Ryder: Powerstone Book One

The searing pain from his limb was beginning to recede as the cold temperatures of ice began to contain the wound and restrict the blood flow.

Smiling at the thought of reclaiming one of the crystals, he thought that the loss of his arm would be worth it, considering the objectives that would open up to him when he presented it to Kersey.

After a few moments, he removed the bloodied stump from the cold wastes and summed up all the strength and pressed on throughout the white blizzard.

Disappearing into the path that led to the mountain, he plodded on toward what was left of the small domed community, holding the red jewel tightly to his chest.

The body of trooper Brooks had been cleared away to one of the morgue chambers, until such time that Doctor Gennero could prepare the body for whatever means would lay the poor trooper to rest. Nova sat on the stool next to the operating computer as Elizabeth's hands sped over the keypad.

"System, who initiated the lockdown program?" began the Doctor.

The droning voice of the ships onboard computer answered back. "*I initiated the lockdown!*" she said blankly.

Nova leaned on his hand, with his elbow balancing on the edge of the worktop.

"Why?" he muttered as his brows met.

"*The thirty second access procedure had not been completed. Voice authorisation by an intermediate was required and not given. I had no choice but to initiate the lockdown procedure until Lieutenant Everett could restore her original command codes*" finished System.

"Sounds like a bloody computer" spat Nova, "Thinks like a bloody Jobs-worth!"

Time-Ryder: Powerstone Book One

Valana; who had been sitting quietly by the Doctor's side suddenly burst to life.

"Can't you explain it to her that Kara could be dying up there and we need access to the flight deck?" she asked.

"System, did you get all that?" asked the Doctor.

"*Confirmed!*" boomed the female voice, "*Parameters state that the originator of the procedure must be the one to revert it, unless the originator is deceased then it reverts to the next officer in the line of command!*"

Nova raised his brow.

"In other words if she's saying that we wait until Kara is dead before it reverts control to you, until then we're all up shit creek!"

"*Access can only be granted by the third Terminal on the flight deck!*" continued the computer.

"Christ, that's logic for you!" spat Nova, "Even my old computer had more intelligence than you! You're not still on windows 95 are you?"

He looked up to the ceiling, taking in the large vents that stretched over its entirety and he followed it along the wall.

"Why are you both looking at me?"

Elizabeth smiled wryly and looked at Valana who smiled back and they both looked back at him.

"Nova, we're defenceless and running blind unless you can get System back online, and you're the only one small enough to fit in there!"

"Oh let's do height jokes now eh? It's not my fault you've got massive hips!" he resigned himself to the fact that he was going to have to go back in if it meant getting control back and rescuing Kara; if she was still alive.

Elizabeth removed a small headset from the wall and passed it to him, which he reluctantly slid over his tangle of brown hair.

Time-Ryder: Powerstone Book One

"I don't know why I get myself talked into these things" he moaned, "It's just I've got a thing about confined spaces" he squirmed and shrunk back from the Doctor.
"Nice try!" she smirked and pulled him over to the vent, knowing full well he was lying.
"No, it's true. There was this one time when I was fifteen, I was in this cupboard and this Nurse came in!" he spluttered before the Doctor tuned the headset to a high frequency and it almost deafened him, but cut off the end of his tale.
"I thought your Comm System was completely shot to bits?" Nova asked, taking another look in the sheet metal conduit.
Gennero tapped the headset.
"This operates on a different system from the internal comms"
Nova frowned as she ushered him forward and he took a last look at Valana's beautiful face.
"Kiss for good luck?" he raised his brow with a smile.
Elizabeth pressed his shoulder and forced him forward.
"Will you get in there?"
Nova crawled inside the gloomy crawlspace as the white vent was put firmly back into place.

The Rover came to a sudden stop, just short of the domes. There were five interconnected structures over fifty feet tall and of such a great capacity that the Professor didn't even dare to contemplate how large they were inside each of them.
They were originally red in colour although the paint had faded over the years and the constant tempests of snow and lack of maintenance had stripped the colour from them, leaving only the few straggly remnants of redness in the joints where each honeycombed section was buckled to the next.

Time-Ryder: Powerstone Book One

Professor Carlson looked out of the side windows of the vehicle as the others prepared themselves and he zipped up the toggle of his padded blue jacket, confident that it would keep him warm. The blizzard swirled high, winds giving life to fierce torrents of snow as the side hatch of the vehicle fell outward, gently kissing the surface of the snow.

Jack Ryder stepped out into the blistering wind, pulling his heavy orange goggles down over his face and pulling his hood up over his head.

Dervish and Hoffman emerged from the small cabin behind him with a reluctant Professor Carlson following the tall blue skinned Lieutenant Denton into the open.

Henry's movements were slightly restrained with the heavy thermal jacket that he'd been given. It made him feel larger than he was and even more uncomfortable, but he was going to be thankful for it once they got back inside the mine. They strained their eyes through white void as they stepped down from the vehicle ramp and onto the untouched snow.

"Bearing?" roared Jack above the howling wind.

Dervish branded the spectrometer in the air and panned the area slowly, trying to get a reading.

"Fifty metres sir!"

Jack cocked his pistol and gazed through his goggles, filtering out the whiteness and making it far easier to see the landscape around him.

"The tracker's pointing us up this way sir" motioned Dervish with the swish of his hand. He brought it around to the left where the vein-like paths stretched upward to the top of the craggy mountain.

The trooper eyed the tracker again and looked at the tiny blip on the screen as the yellow dials.

Time-Ryder: Powerstone Book One

"Disregard the tracker until we're inside the mine, I want motion sensors switched on until we clear the service tunnel!" hissed the Colonel as he moved closer to the nearest structure.

"Denton, have you got the access codes for the doors that Lieutenant Everett gave you for the dome?" he asked as they trod closer to the massive tomb like doors that overshadowed them.

The tall blue-skinned man brought forward the large digital pad device that he had strapped to the sleeve of his padded jacket, but he raised his eyes to the area ahead.

"I don't think we're going to need it sir!" he said coldly and pointed forward.

The flap covering the display functions on the door was open and Jack looked to the ground where he could see that the door was slightly ajar.

With lightning reflexes, he reached inside his backpack and pulled out a long weapon that resembled a pump action shotgun, at least a weapon that the Professor was familiar with.

"What is that?" hissed the old man.

Jack cocked it and popped a cigar into his mouth, lighting it and stowing away the lighter.

"Henry, allow me to introduce Mr Smooth!" he grinned and almost caressed the shotgun as his boot lifted off the ground and kicked the door open. "Like my inter-cred card, I never leave home without it!"

Jack disappeared inside and the old man looked at Denton; whose blank face showed that he was equally as bewildered. Without another word, they followed the Colonel inside.

Huddled around the computer display in the Medibay, Elizabeth Gennero tapped the keyboard lightly and whispered into the small, extended microphone on the top of the small screen.

Time-Ryder: Powerstone Book One

Valana smiled and then grinned as she leaned over behind the Doctor, patiently waiting for the communication connection to be established. Elizabeth removed the headset and plugged it into the socket by the side of the screen so that Valana could hear the impending conversation.

Static filled their ears, making the blonde haired girl wince as the Doctor turned the volume down with a swift twist of her thumb.

"Are you comfortable now?" she asked.

Nova grimaced as he crawled on through the conduit. He pulled out his Zippo lighter to guide the way ahead and flipped the flame on, filling the enclosed space with light.

"Come out to the coast, we'll get together, have a few laughs!" he mumbled to himself in his best Bruce Willis impersonation.

"Of course I'm not comfy Doc," replied the young man in a hiss, "You try crawling through a laundry chute!"

"We don't have laundry chutes on board" rallied the Doctor's voice. Nova turned up his nose.

"Well that's not what it bloody smells like!" he retorted and elbowed his way forward.

He squeezed his eyes up to see the area ahead of him.

"I hope there aren't any spiders in here!" he widened his eyes.

Doctor Gennero rolled her eyes and capped her hand over the microphone.

"Does he always moan like this?" she said, turning to Valana. The blonde shrugged her shoulders and turned back to the map on the screen.

"I've only known him since yesterday, but he does give that impression, doesn't he?" she replied with a giggle.

Elizabeth leaned forward, withdrawing her hand from the mic.

Time-Ryder: Powerstone Book One

"You're scared of spiders?" she asked.
Valana smirked, amused at the thought of someone so afraid of many things.
She wished that her memory would return and she'd find out if she had any such affliction.

"Spiders! Don't get me started about them" called out Nova as he edged forward slowly.
"Rats, snakes. They all give me the jeebies!" he cringed at the thought and the very mention almost sent a ripple up his spine.

The two women in the Medibay giggled at his expense, Elizabeth straightened her face and turned back to the screen, following the path on the display with her finger.
"If you go straight on there's a turning to the left, watch for the signs marked reptile house!" she hissed and burst out laughing, Valana erupting in a belly laugh. Elizabeth capped the microphone again to mask their amusement.

In the conduit, Nova's eyes went wide at the mention of reptiles, but heard the muffled cries of giggles on his headset and knew she was making fun of him.
"Oh very droll!" he hissed, "I've got your number Frenchie, just you wait!" he smirked, saw the funny side and elbowed his way to the junction. Still holding the lighter for guidance, he manoeuvred himself around the bend to the left and carried on.
"I can't believe you're afraid of spiders," exclaimed the Doctor's voice, slightly elevated, but still amused.
Nova grinned.

Time-Ryder: Powerstone Book One

"When you've been on as many archaeological sites as I have you'd be surprised what you see" he remarked, "Big strapping guys reduced to blubbing like a girl at the sight of insects or even worms. I'm just a bit dubious of anything that's got more legs than me, especially after seeing that massive one in the mines!" he shuddered.

Nova had Doctor Gennero shivering from the description. No one gave the slightest idea what she was going through while doing a post mortem and the complexities involved. It was bad enough with such a task, but it was emotionally draining when the subject was someone close.
Valana pointed to the monitor again, where they could see Nova's position registered by a small white blip, moving slowly across the junction.
"You're almost there!" hissed Valana.

Gasping for breath, the young archaeologist pulled himself up to the end of the enclosure and fumbled with the covering, almost burning himself with the lighter.
"This place really could do with a clean!" he babbled as he struggled with the heavy wall plate. His fingers tightened around the hatch and he creased up his eyes, straining to move it.

"I'll be sure and pass your recommendation on to the cleaning staff when you get out!" smiled the Doctor.
Valana smiled back at her and saw his position was stationary.
"Something's wrong!"

Time-Ryder: Powerstone Book One

Straining with the hatch, Nova threw his weight into it and shot forward into the small junction.
"It's stuck!" he gritted his teeth again.
Nova bounded forward again and toppled inside as the hatch finally gave way and he lay across the floor of the darkened access junction.
"Now you'll find another hatch just above you, remove the magnetic straps and it'll release the environmental clamps, once they're free you can open the hatch!"

The deserted flight deck gave way to a shrill cry from Kara Everett. She pulled her bloodstained body to the centre of the console, her vision distorted and blurry.
She'd suffered severe blood loss and was straining to stay awake. Her once pristine duty uniform was soaked in her blood, it had wept so much that she couldn't see the extent of either wound. Removing her shirt with great discomfort, Kara tossed it aside, revealing her white vest top underneath, although not so much white anymore.
The crimson stain was so apparent that any passing onlooker would think it amazing that she was still alive.
She fumbled under the desk, grasping hold of a smooth, rounded field pistol, hidden for unforeseen circumstances such as this.
Slipping back the safety catch, she turned back to the area of the flight deck where the clicking noises were coming from.
Her hand shook as the gun bore down on the metal floor plate as it opened with a creak and slowly started to rise.

Time-Ryder: Powerstone Book One

CHAPTER FORTY THREE

In the gloom at the back of the central control room, Blackthorne was still hunched on the floor; his posture bore the pain of his discomfort, yet it was self-imposed, so he had no one to blame but himself.

He had many an opportunity to escape from the room, noting that Kersey and Gage were slower than all of the other creatures and would be no match for him if he did make the attempt, but he was gathering information for whatever diabolical scheme they were plotting and trying to determine an equal plan that would bring them down.

His arm restraints had been loosened for some time and he slipped them off with ease, yet opting to remain as he was, his only annoyance was listening to the arrogant nature of Kersey, who seemed to be controlling everything, but not quite everything as he'd noticed.

Gage had been concealing things from him and Blackthorne wondered if he was as focussed on this restoration as Kersey was.

It would only be a matter of time before he found out.

His attention was swayed as the heavy doorway swung inward and the wounded reptilian creature hobbled into the chamber, its posture almost broken and weakened.

As the cloaked creature swept into the room, it collapsed on the floor, crawling effortlessly into the centre, one bloodied appendage reaching out with the gleaming sphere in its grasp.

Kersey shot over to the creature so quickly, forgetting the pain that the movement was causing him and he took the sphere from the creature's grasp, glaring down into its face.

"You've been injured!" he grated and tipped the creature's chin back with his clawed fingertips, noting the blood and ooze over its clothing.

Time-Ryder: Powerstone Book One

Kersey tossed the ball to Gage, who put it into a capture device, strapped into a framework as two small claws emerged from the side and penetrated the ball from above, separating the shell and opening it wide.

"Well? What are you waiting for?" Kersey roared impatiently, his neck snapping around in the direction of the smaller creature.

"It.... Its empty!" stuttered Gage, "the shell is empty!"

Kersey flew into a tirade of frustrated squeals and inaudible curses as he turned back to the wounded reptilian.

"You let them harm you and now this!" roared Kersey, his clawed finger wavered under the creature's chin and with a quick slash, his claws parted open the creature's throat, letting the rivers of ooze flow over the floor and the beast fell.

"It's just not your day is it?" sniggered Blackthorne with a smile to which Kersey strode over to the workstation and removed the empty shell from the clutches of the claws.

With his pain responses at breaking point, he pushed past them and launched the half open shell to the Captain where it landed just inches away.

Blackthorne looked down at the open ball and narrowed his eyes, peering inside, where he could see the miniscule tracking device and he smiled that all was not lost after all.

The blizzard was getting so severe that it forced Craven's exhausted body to slump uncontrollably into the deep snow.

He collapsed facedown, heat escaping from his body rapidly in the freezing temperatures, and he lay still while snow filtered down onto his unmoving frame.

Using the last of the strength he had, he propped himself up onto his remaining arm and steadied his form, before standing fully.

Time-Ryder: Powerstone Book One

He found it difficult to stay upright in the blistering torrent of snow that bounded all around him and shook his head from the dizziness that the snow was causing.

Craven's face was matted with frozen icicles, etched into his dark beard. He peered through slit-like eyes, cracking the very thin coat of ice that adorned his face, and grimacing in the coldness of the blizzards path while looking upward to the trail ahead.

He located the desired target, way off in the distance between the ragged peaks of the mountain and he straightened up, swaying in the gale that ensued.

With his mind focussed; he pressed onward at a snail's pace, lurching toward the top of the path, still holding onto the crystal, for all the good that it would bring him.

It took him some time, but he reached the open area that Jack's team had escaped from.

Christened with a newborn layer of snow was the metal hatch, thrown free from the site of Trooper Vane's handy work and totally masking the one entry point that he knew about.

With all the strength he could muster, he cleared the rocks away violently and gritted his teeth in pain but he finally gave in with an exasperated hiss of frustration. He would need to find an alternative route inside; hopefully there would be another access point further around the mountain.

Craven squeezed his eyes tight in agony before lowering himself down into the slopes below, scouring the area for a gap, crack or even a small pathway that would lead him to another entrance.

There was a path just in sight and he almost crawled through the snow, the cold beginning to affect him, but he carried on; only his determination pushing him forward.

Time-Ryder: Powerstone Book One

The light blue hatch set into the flight-deck floor flew open, clanking noisily onto the surface of the technician's pit.
Kara's eyes squinted, holding the field pistol in the line of the hatch covering, hoping to get a round off before Craven returned to finish her off, but in her current state of health, she was no clear match for him.
Catching him off guard was the best, safest alternative, assuming that it was Craven.
A splutter of coughs echoed from inside the tiny hatch as a slim hand emerged and gripped the ridged edge of the decking plates.
Kara gently started to squeeze the trigger; her hand shaking, trying her best to maintain her focus on the target.
She pulled the trigger and a flash of blue energy tore over the top of the hatch, narrowly missing the new arrival.
"Jesus!" yelped Nova's voice from the floor, "hold your horses" he called out and pushed the hatch over fully, "I'm no dangerous!"
The muscles on the Lieutenant's face eased as she relaxed her grip on the trigger of the weapon.
She dropped it into her lap and exhaled deeply.
"That's the last time I go in one of those bloody vents!" coughed Nova to himself as he popped his head into existence on the flight deck, "now I know how sardines feel!"
Sinking back into the chair, Kara grimaced and clutched her shoulder while Nova pulled his small frame out of the enclosed space and up onto the cold metal floor of the tech pit.
He ruffled his hair and dusted his clothes down; dancing around like his backside was on fire as he shook the dust and any other foreign bodies that he assumed had clung to him while he climbed through the conduit.
"Are you alright?" wheezed the Lieutenant.
Nova clutched his chest and snapped his head around, not expecting any company at least not from her.

Time-Ryder: Powerstone Book One

"You about gave me a heart attack shooting like that, who did you think it was?" he panted.

The small Lieutenant winced.

"I thought it might be Craven coming back!"

Nova narrowed his eyes and looked to the floor.

"What? Through the floor?" he rolled his eyes, "Don't you think he'd use the door?"

She winced again.

"Why didn't you?"

"It's that grumpy-arsed computer of yours, making us do things the hard way" he relaxed himself and propped his weight upon the deck, "She locked down the decks and wasn't going to give us access until you bit the big one!"

Kara squinted, trying to remember his name.

"It's Nova? Right?" she made an effort to point at him, affirming his identity.

She was exhausted and the blood loss was increasing, making her woozy.

"Are you alright?"

"Never mind about me!" he spat, spying the pool of blood by her side, "aren't you supposed to be dead?"

He still looked around, trying to see if there were any visitors that may have attached themselves during his journey through the cramped passage.

"Dead?" asked Kara.

She gave the smallest hint of a smile, slightly amused, even though she felt quite close to it.

Nova withdrew the headset and pulled out his glasses as he approached her, trying to have a closer look at her injuries.

"That's what the Pratt with the pantomime beard said!"

"You've lost me!" Kara winced; she felt the blood from the wound as he looked to the extent of the opening.

Time-Ryder: Powerstone Book One

"Craven told us you were dead, said he killed you and all!" Nova replaced the shirt to her shoulder and pressed it tightly.
There was that slight tickle of static charge again and he withdrew his hand.
"Try to keep pressure on it!"
"Craven?" she stammered, "Where is he?" she gritted her teeth again, aggravated by the pain.
With his free hand, Nova pulled the headset back from his face and spoke into the microphone, annoyed that it decided now was the time to stop working.
"He's off the ship, minus one hand!" replied the young man, "Oh wait a minute, I'd better tell them I'm here!"
"Val, can you hear me?" he tried the headset again.
His earpiece was filled with static and he dropped it to the floor. He stuck his finger in his ear and
wiggled it, feeling the discomfort of the high-pitched whine.
"You won't be able to get through, there's a communication suppressant system in place on the flight deck, it blocks any unauthorised transmissions" gargled the Lieutenant.
She could taste the saltiness of her own blood and it began to worry her. Kara slowly lapsed into unconsciousness and dropped to the floor as Nova bounded forward and tried to rouse her.
He'd thought about slapping her face for a second, but held back and put his fingers to her throat, feeling her pulse.
Nova looked up to the main screen that was blank.
"Oi computer, can you hear me?" he spoke aloud to the screen.
"My ship registry designation is System. It would be appropriate if you addressed me as so" chimed the computer.
"Don't get uppity with me, you glorified toaster!" he retorted gruffly. "I need to get in contact with the Doc, can you do that?"
He looked from Kara's downed form to the screen that became alive with the large red lockdown lettering again.

Time-Ryder: Powerstone Book One

"Unable to comply!" replied System, *"The access to the main ship's functions including communication, have been withheld. The Oregon is in Ship-wide lockdown!"*
Nova rolled his eyes.
"Typical frustrated woman!" he sniped, "I'd get more sense out of a bloody Atari!" he snapped, annoyed by the computer's stolid nature.
"All systems can be re-accessed by the ranking duty officer!" announced System, her female voice sounded almost sarcastic in the reply and almost sounded like his aunt Hester when the cat peed on her cooker hob. He smiled wryly.
"Does Kara, I mean Lieutenant ever-ready have that access?" he asked and then sided the question, "What am I saying, of course she has!" he stated firmly, flapping his hands and realising that he was getting ahead of himself.
"System, please access authorisation with Kara!" he said politely, even though he wanted to thrash the innards of wherever her mainframe was with a baseball bat.
"Retina print and palm scan needed, please use terminal three!" confirmed the computer.
Looking around, Nova saw the shattered remains of one of the monitors that were flickering with a tiny flame in the heart of its circuits. Over to his left, he noticed the desk that was required. He wheeled the Lieutenant over on the castor driven chair and propped her against the desk.
"Hey Kara, wake up. I need you right now, can you hear me?" He shook her gently but she failed to reply.
"Sod it!" he cursed.
Nova slapped her face gently, trying to revive her, but she was still unconscious.
He propped her upright, prising open her eye with his fingers while trying to steady her with his other hand. Nova put her chin

Time-Ryder: Powerstone Book One

into the rest and the green scanner slowly glazed over her eye, the fine beam of light verifying her identity.

"Retina print accepted, awaiting palm scan!" announced the computer.

Spreading her fingers out on the glowing pad, Nova saw the strip of light begin to map her pattern until the illuminated pad went dark once again.

The intricate markings were displayed upon the large ops table alongside the verified retina print and Kara's personnel profile and mug shot. System pinpointed the familiar characteristics of her registered palm print and overlaid the image with the new one, making them a perfect match.

"Palm scan accepted and verified, re-establishing ship-wide defaults. What is your next command?" asked the computer.

Racking his head, Nova scratched his temple.

"Return everything back to normal. Em, de-activate ship-wide lockdown" he babbled, "Just make it so the doors will open eh?"

The dim red hue all over the flight deck vanished immediately and the deck was flooded with bright illumination.

The glass silver rimmed doors at the top of the stairs parted with a whoosh and the communication channels were open.

"System put me in touch with the Medibay!" he gasped, his face enlightened but still concerned for Kara.

"Doc, can you hear me? I've done it. She's alive, well barely!" he gasped again, breathing a sigh of relief.

The crackle of static panned over the flight deck speaker system.
"Understood. Stay there, I'll be with you in a few minutes!"

Nova shook his head, looking at the fallen Lieutenant.

"There's no time for that Doc, she's bleeding out. I'll come to you!"

Without time to lose, Nova heaved up the limp and lifeless body of Kara Everett and carried her off to the side doors, swiftly moving out of the flight deck.

Time-Ryder: Powerstone Book One

The inside of the main dome was dark and the nervous pair of troopers followed Denton and the Professor as they moved slowly into the main entrance just behind Jack Ryder; who waved Mr Smooth in the air as he made sure there were no mysterious visitors like they had come across in the mine.

It was only the infrequent glow of Jack's cigar that provided any light, but Denton had disappeared in the gloom to locate the main generator, if it was at all possible that it would be working after all these years.

He'd read the Colonel's report of the gantry incident and the elevator cage and deduced that the technology would probably be viable even after decades of neglect, especially if the dome had been sealed unlike the mine, which was open to the elements.

He flipped the massive switch and the slow vibrating hum of power began to creep annoyingly into their audible range and the lights sprang to life, dominating the extensive entrance area.

"All this has been sealed for thirty years?" asked the old man.

Denton nodded and looked all around, trying to find a navigation map.

"This is the main reception dome, others are split into accommodation and the ore processing centre!" he answered, but the old man still looked around the scope of the dome in awe.

"It's almost as large as St Paul's!" he remarked, a smile creeping across his face.

Jack puffed on his cigar and turned back to them.

"We're looking for the tunnel entrance point. Denton, see if you can get up a schematic on the database and contact the ship, tell them we've arrived!"

Without objection, the tall blue-skinned giant withdrew to the wooden reception desk and stooped over the controls.

Hoffman gripped his rifle tightly, his eyes wandering over the complexity of the structure, noting every detail of the architecture and the construction, whereas Dervish let the cannon

Time-Ryder: Powerstone Book One

flail on the shoulder strap and he utilised his toothpick for another task and began to clean the wax from his ears.

The old man came alongside Hoffman, both of them the same height and he looked up around the carved intricacies on the dome ceiling.

"It really is quite fascinating isn't it?" said the old man softly.

Hoffman agreed with him with a discreet nod and he cleared this throat nervously.

"I never thought I'd take architecture so seriously sir!" he whispered, "but working with engines so much, you start to appreciate how things are built!"

The Professor was taken aback by the trooper's approach and he nodded.

"I always found archaeology a chance to take a breath and think through the eyes of the people that held the objects I uncovered, the beauty of buildings such as this fills me with the same feeling!"

Hoffman made an effort to smile, that almost curled into a laugh and the Professor smiled back at him.

"What's so funny?"

The small trooper had no choice but to open up, he was enjoying conversing with the old man instead of being forgotten about and left at the back as he had been under the Captain's command.

"I always felt at home in dusty old buildings, places that have collected centuries of memories. I guess that's why I enjoy working with engines; I just love getting my hands dirty"

The Professor gave him a wide grin.

"Its part of the fun getting your hands dirty isn't it?"

Hoffman smiled.

"You're not the only one into excavation sir!" he whispered and nudged the old man to see Dervish almost undertaking an exploratory mission of his own and poking his toothpick further into his ear.

The Professor stifled a laugh as Denton interrupted them.

"The Comm-sat isn't responding sir, it might be the weather. Do you want me to return to the Rover and signal the ship from there?" he asked as Jack sparked up his lighter and chomped down on another cigar.

"No, it shouldn't matter Lieutenant, here are the signs for Ore processing!" he pointed to the dull, lime green placard that pointed them the way forward. Denton moved around from the console and proceeded to follow the Colonel into the bleak corridor ahead as the others moved slowly behind, yet Dervish didn't hear them.

Hoffman fetched a smile and looked past the Professor to the other trooper.

"Hey Dervish, you're not going to find anything else in there, are you coming?"

Slightly embarrassed, Dervish discarded the toothpick and stumbled after the group, heaving his heavy cannon in front of him. As they left the reception, two distinct shadows shifted in the background and their presence took root behind the control console.

They were clad in heavy padded suits; much like the Colonel's yet with a slightly different design and were black in colour.

Their heavy boots were clipped up to their knees, almost as if it was a one-piece outfit.

Taking off the black gloves and tinted visor that masked the eyes, the first newcomer set the glasses down upon the desk and began to unfurl the long scarf that was wrapped around the head.

The unblemished face of a dark skinned young woman lay underneath as her muscular companion tore off his scarf and showed his face, also dark skinned.

Time-Ryder: Powerstone Book One

He was almost bald, his head shaven so close, yet a peculiar pattern etched into what hair he did have left, almost like a brand, but his face was unshaven, showing that he had no access to items to groom his appearance for a few days or more.
They both looked at each other, their faces stern and full of concentration as the voices of the Colonel's group became more distant.
"You didn't expect that did you?" hissed the girl, slapping his arm hard and turning to the controls as she ruffled her long brown hair and started to pull it out of her hood.
"We never expected anyone to come here!" he drawled roughly, his voice deeper and full of contempt.
"But what are they doing here? That's what I want to know!" she hissed and started rifling through the systems to see what ones had been activated.
"They've done a search into the internal systems!" she said softly and leaned forward, pulling a stool so she could see the screen more clearly.
"They're looking for access to the mine!" she turned and looked at her companion, "If that's what they want, that's what we'll give them!" she said with a smile, but her stone-face companion said nothing and stared on at the screen, still wondering why they were here.

Lockdown had been de-stabilised and the Oregon had returned to normality, or the closest approximation regarding that there was a skeleton crew on board and one of the crew was still being held in the detention block.
Nova had summed up every vestige of strength and had heaved Kara down through the decks to the Medibay.

Time-Ryder: Powerstone Book One

Regardless that she was of a small disposition, he heaved her down the last step of the white spiral stairway and headed around the last corridor to the Medi-bay.

He was beginning to feel that he was out of shape, too many quiet nights in the pub with a cold beer for company, whiling away his sorrows and recent bad memories.

Nova propped the Lieutenant up onto the white leather gurney as Elizabeth shot straight to work and began peeling back Kara's blood-soaked white vest.

"You really need someone to program some manners into that computer of yours" he wheezed and stepped back as Valana stood by the Doctor's side, ready to offer any assistance if needed.

"She has the equivalent of how can I say this? A bug up her arse!" he blurted out.

But no one was listening to him as Elizabeth ran the Medical spectrometer over her body and concentrated on the readings as the tiny wings at the front of the device went wild.

"She has two substantial wounds," Elizabeth said softly, her eyes creasing in concentration.

"The first bullet has passed right through her shoulder, but the second is still in there, it's embedded in her chest cavity" she looked over at Valana.

"Your skills as a Nurse may be required!" smiled the Doctor as she felt around Kara's body, touching the wound ever so gently.

"That's a cue for me to make myself scarce!" smiled Nova and he took one last look to the fallen Lieutenant, crossing and putting his hand on her bare shoulder.

He retracted quickly feeling the spark and the jolt of blue energy that he'd felt before.

"What was that?" Valana narrowed.

Nova shook his hand and started to withdraw from the room, his brows narrowed in confusion. Why did it keep happening?

Time-Ryder: Powerstone Book One

"It's nothing, just like Kara said it's an old ship!" replied the young scot and he backed off to the door, vanishing out into the corridor beyond.

The power had been restored to minimal sections of the bio-dome, Denton having maintained most of the energy for life-support through the main dome to the sections that they were travelling through.
Jack waved his long barrelled torch around the huge crescent-shaped passage ahead, massive burgundy metal doors stretching twenty feet across the divide and a huge set of bolts pinning the outer edges into the frame.
"Is this the entrance to the tunnel?" asked the Professor, his open face peering at Denton; who was concentrating upon his hand device frantically jabbing the controls.
"Yes. I've re-routed the main system functions to my spectrometer sir, in case there are any system malfunctions!" he answered softly.
Jack gave him a nod and moved forward to the doors, his hand fumbling with the digital display screen that was identical to the one on the exterior of the dome.
Denton motioned forward with his Orange device in front of him, remotely activating the screen and waiting for the sound of the locks releasing themselves from the framework above them.
After a pregnant pause, the clunk of bolts snapping out of their housings could be heard, and the door opened with a cough of stale air from within, giving life to the passage again for the first time in decades.
Jack parted the door and took a look inside the gloom, tipping his torch and pointing it into the gap.
"It looks clear, let's move on!" he said and stretched the door wide as his entourage followed him into the dark.

Time-Ryder: Powerstone Book One

Denton cocked his head aside and his steely blue eyes shot to the side as his unique hearing thought he'd heard something. Dismissing the sound, he unbuckled his torch and pushed the beam into the passage, following it in.

Jack led the way through the darkness, his torch barely making out anything in the gloom, for all they knew it could be a dead end by the time they got to the end of the passage.

It was barely fifty feet since they had entered the tunnel from the dome when Denton came to a stop and the Professor careered right into the back of him.

"Excuse me Lieutenant!" apologised the old man and then he noticed that the blue skinned officer was looking all around, yet his torch-beam was pointed directly at the floor.

"What is it?" Jack turned around in concern and tried to follow the Lieutenant's eyes, as it appeared he was looking for something, "Lieutenant?"

"Can't you hear it sir?" said Denton softly, his steely eyes still looking warily around him, but his hearing wasn't as fine tuned as Denton's was and he gave him a blank look.

"The pumps have stopped!" he confirmed his supposition and already had his spectrometer in hand.

"Sir, the controls have been overridden, we'd better get back to the dome!" his eyes went wide and he began to run towards the large bay doors, just as they closed over and he could hear the sharp click of the door bolts snapping into place and closing the air tight pressure seals.

Jack slammed upon the metal doors and turned back to the others with a raised brow.

"I didn't see this one coming!"

Time-Ryder: Powerstone Book One

After much deliberation, Nova had returned to the Medi-bay, dressed warmly in what he could find in his quarters, carrying a heavy satchel that he had began filling with allsorts.

It peaked the Doctor's curiosity and she came over, her brows meeting, Valana trailed close behind her.

"What on earth are you doing, you look like you're getting ready for war?"

In a way he was. He'd overcome his fear of confined spaces due to his time in the conduits and now he was endeavouring to overcome some of his others, and hopefully find a few answers along the way.

He stiffened his gaze and looked up as he laced up the backpack.

"War, Doctor?" he spat with a slight laugh, "You haven't seen anything when I get started!"

He turned to face her and his head looked up, for the first time since he'd arrived he was totally focussed on what lay ahead.

Valana creased her brow and as just as confused as Elizabeth was and she peered over her shoulder.

"What are you planning?"

Nova pursed his lips, took in a small breath and eyed both of the curious women forlornly.

"With that nut-job Craven out there, we can't take any chances. The Professor and every one of them might be in more danger than they ever were before!"

Elizabeth was horrified by what she knew was coming, but it didn't stop her from trying to intervene.

"What do you think you're going to be able to do? You're just a kid!" she spat.

"I've been hearing that a lot lately!" Nova smirked.

He'd been hearing that all his life and was never taken seriously about anything.

Nova stiffened his posture and leaned forward to both women as his usual comical attitude became a more stern and forceful one.

He took a breath and looked them both in the eye as an unexpected statement passed by his lips.

"I'm not the cleverest guy you're ever going to meet, but that old man means everything to me, and I'm going to do my damnedest to make sure he's safe."

He stood straight and eyeballed both women very sternly.

"I don't care how long it takes, but as soon as I get someone to guide us and gather some supplies, I'm going back to that mine and I'm bringing them all home...!"